WIDE
OPEN

WIDE OPEN

Larry Bjornson

BERKLEY BOOKS, NEW YORK

THE BERKLEY PUBLISHING GROUP
Published by the Penguin Group
Penguin Group (USA) Inc.
375 Hudson Street, New York, New York 10014, USA

Penguin Group (Canada), 90 Eglinton Avenue East, Suite 700, Toronto, Ontario M4P 2Y3, Canada
(a division of Pearson Penguin Canada Inc.) • Penguin Books Ltd., 80 Strand, London WC2R 0RL,
England • Penguin Group Ireland, 25 St. Stephen's Green, Dublin 2, Ireland (a division of Penguin
Books Ltd.) • Penguin Group (Australia), 250 Camberwell Road, Camberwell, Victoria 3124, Australia
(a division of Pearson Australia Group Pty. Ltd.) • Penguin Books India Pvt. Ltd., 11 Community
Centre, Panchsheel Park, New Delhi—110 017, India • Penguin Group (NZ), 67 Apollo Drive,
Rosedale, Auckland 0632, New Zealand (a division of Pearson New Zealand Ltd.) • Penguin Books
(South Africa) (Pty.) Ltd., 24 Sturdee Avenue, Rosebank, Johannesburg 2196, South Africa

Penguin Books Ltd., Registered Offices: 80 Strand, London WC2R 0RL, England

This book is an original publication of The Berkley Publishing Group.

PUBLISHING HISTORY
Berkley trade paperback edition / June 2012

Bjornson, Larry.
Wide open / Larry Bjornson.
p.   cm.
ISBN 978-0-425-24748-8 (pbk.)
1. Hickok, Wild Bill, 1837–1876—Fiction.   2. Abilene (Kan.)—Fiction.   I. Title.
PS3602.J68W53 2012
813'.6—dc23
2011046324

PRINTED IN THE UNITED STATES OF AMERICA

10   9   8   7   6   5   4   3   2   1

WIDE OPEN

PROLOGUE

All our lives changed in the moment my cousin Albert tripped me. None of us knew it at the time, not me, or Mother, or Father, and certainly not my little sister Jenny, then only three months old. As I fell to the floor beside Uncle's supper table, scattering my serving bowl of string beans over Aunt Phidelia's beloved Turkish rug, fate turned our four lives and pointed us toward a destination we could not have imagined.

On this day the shadow of a summer rainstorm had cast the interior of the dining room into murkiness. And there, seated around the table in the gloom, sat the three of them—Uncle Pleas at the far end, Aunt Phidelia nearest the kitchen, and Cousin Albert at the side—each in their own manner waiting impatiently.

I always placed serving bowls at Uncle's end of the table. He served himself first; then Phidelia and Albert were free to fill their plates.

As I brought the steaming bowl from the kitchen, where

Mother was cooking supper, I made the mistake of choosing to squeeze through the space between the wall and Albert's chair. As I approached, he smirked and tilted back just far enough so that I couldn't pass.

"Albert, dear," said Aunt Phidelia, "you're blocking Will. Lord knows he's slow enough as it is."

Albert allowed his chair to drop with a thud but left his farthest foot trailing behind. Too angry to notice, I lunged forward as soon as the opening was wide enough and, just as Albert had hoped, caught my foot on his and went down, flinging beans in an arc across the floor.

"My rug!" cried Aunt Phidelia.

"Damnation!" yelled Uncle. "Can't a boy ten years old walk into a room without fallin' on his face?"

"He's a clumsy one, ain't he, Papa?" said Albert, sneering down at me. He was a couple years older than me, and for two and a half years, ever since Father had gone off to war and left us in his brother's tender care, he had not once missed a chance to torment me.

"I'm nine and a half," I muttered as I got to my feet.

"You're whatever age I say, you little fool!" Uncle shouted back. "Now pick up them beans."

"My rug," Aunt Phidelia repeated.

"Shut up, Philly," said Uncle. "He's pickin' 'em up."

Down on my hands and knees, burning with shame, I gathered the beans one by one.

"But, Pleas," Phidelia persisted, "they're all buttery. They'll just ruin my wonderful carpet."

Uncle Pleas, short for Pleasant, groaned in put-upon annoyance.

"You know," said Albert, "I s'pose I could walk through this room a thousand times and not fall on my face even once."

Beneath the table, he put a foot on my shoulder and gave me a sharp shove, banging my head into a table leg. The table jumped with the impact, and cups and dishes above clattered.

"Will!" shouted Uncle. "I ain't gonna stand for no more foolishness."

I clenched my teeth hard and said nothing.

"Eleanor," Uncle called out, "get in here!"

After a moment, I heard my mother's approaching footsteps on the floorboards. I straightened up on my knees so she could see me. Mother paused in the doorway, her face flushed from the heat of the oven. She glanced at me inquiringly before brushing back a sweaty string of auburn hair. "Yes, Pleas."

"Your cross-footed son dropped your beans—"

"Onto my fine Turkish rug," said Phidelia.

"Yeah, yeah," said Uncle. "Anyway, get us up another batch. And be quick about it. I'm not sittin' here all day."

"Will, are you all right?" said Mother.

"Yes."

"And when we're done," said Uncle, "I want you to get any butter or whatnot left by them beans out of this rug. Scrub it good, understand?"

"No slapdash cleaning, Elly," added Phidelia. "Any butter left behind is sure to pick up dirt."

Mother nodded.

"Do it before you and Will eat," Uncle added.

Mother and I usually ate in the kitchen after the family had finished. Uncle liked having us available to wait on them during their meals.

Mother wasn't a weak person, but she took this foul treatment without complaint, as she always did. Father had twice come home on leave from his regiment, and she had never so much as hinted to him what our life was like when he was absent.

She feared that worrying about us might distract him, and in some instant of inattention, a leaden ball hot from the flame of a Rebel gun would find him and strike him down, and she would never, never, see him again.

She continued in this practice even though by now the war was over; General Lee and the Confederacy had surrendered 111 days ago. That seemed a long time, but still Father had not returned. Now, with each day that passed, our dread grew.

"I'll do the best I can, Pleas," said Mother.

Uncle dismissed her with a disgusted wave of his hand as if her best wasn't near good enough.

Mother turned to go, but a cry from Jenny, who had been napping, rang out from upstairs. She stopped, raising her head toward the insistent sound.

"Oh, that baby!" Aunt Phidelia exclaimed. "I say, if that isn't the cryin'est child on God's green earth."

"Wah, wah, wah," said Albert, leaning close to my face.

Still looking upward, Mother took a few steps toward the stairs that lay in a little alcove between the dining room and the kitchen. "I better check on her."

"Now, hold on," said Uncle quickly. "Runnin' to that kid every time she yaps 'tisn't good upbringin'. Let her sing. Besides, I want my supper."

Mother paused at the foot of the stairs.

"Eleanor, am I not makin' myself heard?"

A few moments went by, and hearing no more of Jenny's cries, Mother turned and disappeared into the kitchen.

"How much am I supposed to put up with?" Uncle asked. "I give 'em a home, as a favor to my improvident brother, and what do I get? Trial and tribulation. You'd think people would be more grateful for good deeds done 'em."

He said all this as if I weren't in the room.

Sometimes I was angry with Father for leaving us in this friendless place, not that I believed he knew how it would be.

Aside from being my father, J. T. Merritt was a fearless speculator. Before the war he'd been doing well, but then he'd gotten involved in a land deal that soured. Father rarely spoke of it, referring only occasionally to his "setback," but I could feel the damage, and I knew much of our happiness had vanished.

In time, I came to suspect that Father had joined the 12th New York Cavalry and gone off to fight as much to escape his problems as for patriotism. By the time he departed, though, we had so little money that depositing us with Uncle seemed the only option.

Here in this house, Mother and I had few friends and no feeling of belonging. We were unwelcome visitors under a hostile roof. The arrival of Jenny, nine months after Father's last visit home from his regiment, seemed only to make matters worse with Uncle and Phidelia.

I hated being alone.

Snatching up the remaining beans, I retreated to the kitchen. Mother stood at the counter, staring fixedly out the window. She said nothing, and I knew she was struggling inside with her own fear and anger.

"We should leave here," I said petulantly.

Mother sighed. "We've no place to go, and no money."

"Doesn't Father send us money?"

"Yes, but it comes to your uncle, and he keeps it."

"He steals it!" I almost yelled.

"Shhhh, Will!"

"I wish they were dead."

I expected Mother to tell me not to say such things, but she was silent, and that terrified me. For the first time, I believed Father might not come home. What had become of him?

"Will, would you get me some split stove wood?"

"You wish they were dead too."

"Try to keep it dry."

After grabbing an oilcloth, I went out onto the raised veranda that wrapped one side of the house from the front entrance to the rear. A light rain pelted my face, cooling the glowing heat of my anger. I stood there, looking across the weed-choked field at the rear of the property to the muddy local road just beyond. A path cut diagonally across the field, the consequence of Uncle driving his buggy to and from his business, the Merritt Linen Thread Company.

Uncle was a reasonably prosperous businessman—it was said that Pleasant G. Merritt held costs and cockroaches in the same low regard—and everyone assumed that Father would work for him when he returned from the war.

If Father returned—I couldn't escape that unthinkable thought. I bit down hard on the inside of my cheek, then harder yet, letting the pain overwhelm my aching thoughts. I put a hand across my eyes, breathing in sharp bursts, and again tightened the vise of my teeth on the fold of skin. Suddenly I felt the flesh give. I released my grip, tasting blood, and leaned forward to spit red onto the green-painted floorboards. The rain at once began to dilute and wash away the color. I spat again and straightened up, trying to hold myself together.

Glancing down the tree-lined road toward town, I saw no one. The rain was keeping folks home. Rousing myself, I went down the veranda steps and over to a small lean-to woodshed attached to the rear of the kitchen. After collecting my stove wood and wrapping it in the oilcloth, I headed back to the veranda.

At the stairs, I glanced again, out of habit, toward the road. It still appeared untraveled, but as I was about to look away, a rider emerged from behind one of the homes fronting on it, perhaps an eighth of a mile down. I stopped at once and stared, but the rider disappeared behind other homes.

"I hope you don't have far to go, mister," I said aloud as I trudged back up the steps to the kitchen.

"You were gone awhile," said Mother when I reappeared with dripping hair and water-darkened shoulders.

"Sorry . . . nice to be out of the house." I unfolded the oil-cloth and stacked the split wood beside the stove.

"I understand." She smiled. "Look in on our benefactors. Let's try to keep your uncle quiet."

Mother was right, but I couldn't, not just yet.

"Sure, um . . . I'll be right back. I think I left the woodshed door open."

I swung about and hastily banged through the kitchen door. There was no need to return to the woodshed. I hadn't left its door open. I went straight to the veranda railing and looked again to the road. The rider, dressed in blue, was approaching our property. My heart began to pound. He was looking at me, but with his broad-brimmed hat and the collar of his greatcoat turned up against the rain, I couldn't make out his face.

But then my doubts vanished. The rider threw his hand up and, spurring his horse, wheeled into our field and rushed toward me at a gallop.

There was no time for the stairs. I vaulted over the railing, landed hard on my feet in the sodden gravel walkway, and sprinted toward him.

Father was home.

"You're so big!" Father called as he swung down from his horse. "I thought you were Albert."

"No, I'm me."

He strode forward and threw his arms around me. My face

disappeared into the damp folds of his heavy cavalry greatcoat and shoulder cape. He smelled of wet wool, and a bit of wet horse. I held on as hard as I could, hard enough that if he were somehow snatched away again, I would be carried with him.

"Is everyone fine?" he asked.

"Yes, everyone. You have a daughter, Jenny."

Father gave me a quick squeeze and then pushed me back, holding me by the shoulders and inspecting me.

"You're not a little boy anymore."

I grinned stupidly and looked away.

Father released me. "Well, I want to see my wife. And my new baby?"

I hesitated, thinking.

"What horse is this?" I said, looking to the sturdy black horse standing peacefully behind Father.

Father smiled. "This is General." He stepped back and patted the horse fondly on the neck. "My constant companion for over a year. When we were mustered out, I bought him from the Cavalry Bureau for fifty dollars. He and I came in on the train an hour ago."

I came forward and stroked the bridge of General's nose. "It's supper time. Everyone will be in the dining room. Why don't we surprise them all at once?"

Father's eyes immediately showed interest.

"If you sneak in the front," I went on, "and wait in the hall, you could walk in right when everyone is together and—"

"Yes, we'll catch 'em napping, won't we? Yes!"

Father was a showman, and I used this, knowing he'd never pass up the added drama of a well-timed appearance. I didn't feel right about it, but I was still brimming with anger, and now our protector was home. I wanted him to see our lives.

Father laughed, clearly enjoying the prospect of what he assumed was our plan. Turning to General, he unhooked his saber and scabbard from the saddle. Pushing back his coat, he clipped the scabbard onto the leather sword straps that hung from his belt.

"Have to look my military best," he said cheerfully.

I returned to the kitchen, but at the veranda stairs, I looked back to Father. He was carefully spreading his greatcoat over General's back. Once in the house, I sprinted through the kitchen, escaping before Mother could question me about my absence. In my hurry, I emerged noisily into the dining room, a staccato of hard shoes on a hard floor.

"I'm supposed to see if you need anything," I announced breathlessly.

I was dripping from my time outside, and briefly, they stared at me, bemused. In that moment of quiet, I could just hear the front door clicking open out in the entry hall.

"Yes, you little fool," Uncle bellowed abruptly, "we need something. We need our damn supper!"

"You've got muddy shoes!" declared Phidelia, her voice rising to its highest pitch. "How can you serve our supper? I won't have you on my rug. Pleas, he has muddy shoes!"

"Do we need anything!" Uncle continued. "Is that a joke, Will? You think that's funny?"

"No, sir."

"Where's our food?"

"Maybe we'll eat you," said Albert, picking up his knife. "Not much meat, but we're starved."

"What's your mother doin' in there?" said Uncle.

"Can't say. Maybe she's tending the baby."

"Tending the—! Damnation, didn't you all hear what I said

about that? She can tend that girl once I've eaten. Didn't I say that?"

I took a step forward. "You wouldn't talk like this if my father was here."

Uncle came up from his chair. "Watch your mouth, you little guttersnipe! I'll have the lot of you sleepin' with the horses, you see if I don't."

Mother came up behind me from the kitchen. "What is going on?" she asked a bit indignantly.

I turned to her. "I told them they wouldn't treat us like they do if Father was here."

"That's the kind of child you're raisin'!" yelled Uncle. "That's it in a nutshell, right there."

"He's a fine boy, Pleas," said Mother.

"So that's your idea of fine, is it? 'Tain't my idea, no ma'am, not a'tall."

"And why's he all muddy?" Phidelia added.

"Your father," said Uncle, speaking to me now, ignoring Phidelia, "will take what I dish out. He's lucky I had the generosity of spirit to take you all in after he failed. His poor judgment will always bring him down. So if he expects a job at my factory, he won't be telling me what to do. It'll be t'other way around, yes sir, t'other way around."

"We'll see," I said, not backing down.

Now Albert was on his feet. "Who says he's comin' home anyway? I say he ain't. If he was, he'd a been here by now."

Mother gasped at this, and almost in the same instant, Jenny once more cried out upstairs. Mother whirled to go to her, but my hand shot out and grabbed her by the wrist.

Father stood framed in the dark opening of the hall doorway.

When Mother saw him, she burst into tears. Father stepped past me, dropping his faded blue cavalry hat to the floor before throwing his arms around her. She was now sobbing almost uncontrollably.

"I've longed for this moment," Father said softly. Mother nodded rapidly against his shoulder, her emotions sweeping away her ability to speak.

"I hear we have a daughter," said Father. Mother nodded again, and this time laughed a bit through her tears. She took a deep breath and finally calmed herself enough to whisper, "Genevieve."

"Well, this is certainly a wonderful surprise," said Uncle unconvincingly. Father ignored him, but I turned and took them in—Uncle, Phidelia, and Albert—all the very picture of people who wished to be elsewhere.

They had reason to be anxious. Even as he tenderly held Mother, I realized that Father had returned from a journey that had transformed him. I first saw it when he had appeared at the doorway, his face grim. He was no longer someone to challenge. And suddenly, my uncle, a man who had loomed so large among us, seemed very small indeed.

Father took a step back from Mother and, as he had with me, held her at arm's length by the shoulders, just looking at her. Mother reached out and put the palm of her hand on his unshaven cheek. After a long moment, he took her hand in his and came around to face Uncle.

With his free hand, Father took hold of the lower edge of his waist-length dark blue cavalry jacket and gave it a quick downward tug, pulling it taut and smooth. The jacket had a single row of gold buttons down the front and gold-framed rectangular captain's bars on each shoulder. On his right hip he carried a Colt revolver in a flap holster, and on his left, the long cavalry saber in its steel scabbard. In his knee-high black horse-soldier boots, he was nearly six feet tall.

"Hello, Pleasant," Father said, unsmiling.

"Yes, yes, great to have you home, J.T.," said Uncle with as much bravado as he could marshal.

Father released Mother's hand and moved past Phidelia to the side of the table opposite Albert. "Evening, Phidelia," he said, gazing down on her.

"Good to see you home, John," she answered stiffly.

Father looked across the table. "You've grown some, Albert."

Albert smiled weakly but couldn't seem to come up with anything to say. He began chewing a fingernail.

Then, for what seemed a very long time, Father said nothing, letting the silence exercise its unnerving effect. Unable to bear it further, Uncle began to speak. "So, J.T., now that you're home, we'll have to . . ."

His voice trailed off. Father had unhooked the leather strap from the lower ring on his saber scabbard. He then unhooked the top ring and laid the weapon on the table. We stared at it, riveted, wondering.

"Pleas," said Father, "let's step outside and catch up some, just two brothers." His words were friendly, but his tone was not.

"Well," said Uncle, "we were about to eat, and—"

Father looked him in the eye, and again there was silence.

"Yes," said Uncle after a few agonizing seconds, "let's talk." He looked across the table at me, perplexed, and suddenly his eyes widened and his lips parted as the truth of what I'd done came over him.

Uncle pushed his chair back slowly and then moved past Father with a weary tread, heading for the entry hall as if it were the gallows. Father followed him out, grabbing his hat from the floor as he passed. Mother touched his arm, a caution.

As soon as they were gone, I went to the table and stood before the saber. Then, the hair on my arms rising, I picked it up. The steel scabbard had a few dents, and it was dull, not polished as it had once been. The saber's grip was leather wrapped with wire. Three brass branches curved upward from the hilt and then down to join again at the pommel, forming a guard for the hand. Wrapping my fingers around the grip, I looked up at Albert, who was watching me intently, his mouth slightly open. I began to slide the saber from its scabbard. It sang with a metallic voice as it came.

"Elly," said Phidelia, alarmed.

"Will," said Mother.

The saber emerged fully from the scabbard, the steel blade clean, shining. Etched in the metal was an inscription in flowing script: *Bright and Beautiful*. I raised the blade upward before me.

"Will," said Mother again.

I locked eyes with Albert. He was utterly motionless. He was afraid. That was what I'd wanted to see.

I turned and walked quickly from the room, taking the saber with me into the hall. Father and Uncle were not there, but the front door was open.

I found them out on the gravel drive. Father had his hat on against the rain, but Uncle's shirt was soaked, his thinning hair hanging wet on his forehead. Father was talking, and suddenly Uncle reacted angrily, raising his hand and pointing a finger. At once Father slapped him hard across the face, and Uncle fell back two steps, his hand flying to his cheek.

Several hours later in drizzling darkness, we left Uncle's house, our few belongings piled in his buggy. We stayed that night and into the following week in one of Mechanicville's small hotels.

At last, I thought, the hard times were over, but I was wrong. We would become wanderers, drifting from place to place, following Father as he chased his fortune. I understood that we had no money, but as I grew older, I realized that we had no roots either. For us, home was nothing more than an oft-broken promise.

But with each stop, with each new town, we drifted farther and farther west until finally we arrived at the edge of the wilderness, and there my life truly began.

ONE

I'm sorry, but I simply don't understand why this town would hire . . . a killer," Mother declared.

"Now, Mother, they're doing the best they can," Father replied. "Stop fretting."

Crouching outside in our sparse flower bed, I was eavesdropping on my parents' conversation through an open parlor window.

"Mayor McCoy and that city council bunch must be mad," Mother went on, "bringing such a man here. And why should you be involved?"

"I'm only meeting him at the depot."

"Well, if you ask me, Joe McCoy is sending you because he's too scared to meet the train himself. I think—" Something had interrupted her thoughts. "Where is Will?" she said.

Uh-oh, there it was. I'd hoped Mother would forget about me. Her footsteps came toward my window, and I pulled my legs in and pressed my back against the house. Looking upward,

I saw the underside of her jaw poke out the window. I held my breath.

"Will! Will Merritt, if you're out there, you get in the house this minute." She paused, listening, then made the *pfttt* sound that was as close as she ever came to cursing. Her head disappeared back into the house. I exhaled. Today might be one of the best days of my fifteen-year life—but only if I could dodge my mother.

"I better go," said Father. "The Express is due at eleven."

"Oh, John, can't someone else do this?"

"Mother, he's not going to step off the train shooting."

"But I've heard such terrible things."

"I'll tell him that if he shoots me, he'll have you to deal with."

Mother didn't laugh. "Come home as soon as you're finished."

"I will."

As Father stepped out the front door, I slipped around to the side and sprinted westward. Worried that I might be seen, I glanced over my shoulder at our home, a white two-story clapboard house with a small red barn a hundred feet or so to the rear. The whole property, about two acres, was surrounded by a white four-board fence that kept our horses, General and Rambler, from wandering off.

When we'd moved in a few years ago, our house had been one of only a handful of homes. Now, though, we had lots of neighbors. And with the arrival of spring, the sound of hammers and saws again filled the air as more homes sprang up around us.

I n the years after the war, Father's nomadic pursuit of success was as determined as it was fruitless. We arrived in each new town with high hopes, buoyed by Father's relentless optimism. Soon, though, I would sense disappointment behind my parents' forced smiles. Then, usually at the supper table, there would be an announcement that we were leaving.

I'd never really experienced the feeling of home. We'd had houses, lots of them, but never a home. The world seemed full of people who knew what it was to have the life of a place flowing in their veins. For me, though, this simple thing seemed forever elusive.

Just before coming here to Abilene, we'd been living in Springfield, Illinois, Mother's hometown. Before marrying Father, she had never lived anywhere else. There she had family, friends, and history. Her sense of belonging was quickly picked up by me, and I began to think our long search for roots was over.

Then Father received a letter from his friend Joe McCoy advising him to come west and get rich. Shortly after, only days before Christmas 1867, Father boarded a train, alone, and was gone. It was frightening to see him leave us, but not long after, his letters began arriving, each one bursting with enthusiasm for Kansas.

In February, he wrote that we were to join him, Mother, Jenny, and me. And so, filled with sadness, we locked up our small rented house in Springfield and left. Once more we were off to yet another doubtful paradise, a raw and remote town called Abilene. Five days later, we arrived in a place so isolated, so sparse of trees, and so different from the luxurious civilization of the East that Mother seemed almost to lose her breath.

Of all the places we'd lived in, this one seemed the least promising. But it was here that we did at last find a real home. And, just as Joe McCoy had promised, Father did get rich.

I angled across a few grassy vacant lots and then headed south to Abilene's business district. A few streets eastward, Father would be riding General down to his office, where he would leave the horse before walking to the train depot. I would catch him on his way—and hope he wouldn't send me home.

I was dawdling now, giving Father time to get to his office. To my left, I could see the distant roofline of the huge Drover's Cottage Hotel. The Cottage was the symbol of our town's control of the hugely profitable Texas cattle trade.

Each spring, the rambling, three-story Cottage filled with cattle buyers from Chicago, ranchers from Montana, stockyard reps from Kansas City, salesmen from St. Louis, and even bureaucrats from the Indian agencies. They all came to do business with the lordly Texas drovers, men who brought vast herds— two to three thousand head each—up the long trail from Texas. The first herds of "the season" would arrive soon, and Abilene was buzzing with preparations.

When the Texans were in town, there was no more exciting place on the face of the earth.

It hadn't always been like this. Around the time we were living with Uncle in New York, Abilene had been little more than a sparsely settled mud hole. It was the arrival of the Texans that had made us who we were—a fabulously prosperous shipping center for Texas cattle. And so, although Abilene is a Kansas town, our story really began in south Texas just after the Civil War.

The soldiers of Texas returned from war defeated and penniless. Their most valuable resource was the millions of longhorn cattle running wild in the mesquite thickets. But cash was scarce in Texas, and a cow was worth only about three dollars.

To make real money, cattlemen needed to get their longhorns to the wealthy cattle markets outside of Texas, distant places like Kansas City and Chicago. But how? At this time, Texas had no railroads linking it to the rest of the country.

Then, in 1867, word spread of a solution. The Union Pacific Railroad was laying track westward across the wilderness prairie. Shortly after the UP tracks arrived at the collection of huts known as Abilene, my father's friend, Joseph McCoy, stepped off a train and started looking around. He soon purchased 250 acres upon which he would build feed barns, an immense stockyard alongside the rails, and the Drover's Cottage. To the scattered residents of Abilene, it seemed that the good Lord had dispatched a squandering madman to lighten their godforsaken destinies.

But Joe McCoy's madness was the answer to the prayers of Texas cattlemen. To reach Abilene they would have to drive their herds north across nine hundred miles of unsettled lands. But if they could make it, they would find buyers who would pay forty dollars for a longhorn steer, more than ten times the price in Texas.

Outside of Texas, however, a different story was being told about Abilene and Kansas. The U.S. government was urging settlers to go west and build new lives. From Illinois to New York, and as far as Europe and Russia, families were hearing that the government would give them, *free*, a quarter square mile of Kansas prairie. All they had to do was live on it and farm it, and the land would be theirs.

And so, as the Texans began driving their herds toward Abilene from the south, settlers were heading for the little town from the north and east. When they arrived, both groups would want the same land, one to graze cattle, and the other to plant crops.

My family and I would be caught between them.

———

Coming down Broadway, I made my way around dozens of wagons parked at all angles along the storefronts, each piled high with the goods our merchants would be selling to the Texans. Brooms were sweeping clouds of dust out open doorways. Windows were being cleaned. Some business owners were giving their stores fresh coats of white paint, at least on the fronts. I waved to a clerk at the Huff House who was busy nailing down loose boards on the restaurant's sidewalk.

Half a block farther south, I came to the broad open area, maybe three hundred feet across, that held the railroad tracks. The railroad ran east and west, slicing Abilene in two. It was an important boundary.

Most of Abilene's permanent residents lived and worked north of the tracks. These were solid, settled, businesslike folks who tried hard to be uninteresting.

But south of the tracks, Abilene became Texastown, a rowdy hodgepodge of saloons, dance halls, hotels, and, most fascinating of all, brothels. It was a place of cowboys, guns, gambling, liquor, and other mysterious wickedness.

Even from a distance you knew Texastown was different from the rest of Abilene. The place itself was disorderly—its buildings lined up unevenly, its streets crooked, its people slouching and loose jointed. One might have believed that each ingredient of its creation had been decided by the throw of dice.

Yes, the devil was wallowing in velvet south of the tracks. And naturally, north-side children were told never to go there, and naturally, few of us ever missed a chance to take a big, cheek-bulging bite from the forbidden Texastown apple.

But regardless of whether it was north or south, nearly every structure in town had been built during the last four years. Nothing in Abilene was old. It was as if a prairie lightning bolt had struck the grassland, and our town had appeared fully formed from the flash.

But what we lacked in history, we made up in enthusiasm. There was a feeling that the future was wide open. A feeling that nothing was decided—not for individuals, or families, or even the land itself.

Opposite me on the Texastown side of the tracks was one of Abilene's "older" buildings—our tiny, one-room train depot. Not long ago, we'd been proud to have a depot, any depot, but now the town had outgrown it, and its humbleness was a source of shame.

I threw a quick westward glance down the tracks but saw no sign of the Express. With that, I wheeled about and ran east, hoping to find Father. His office was about two blocks up on the north side of the tracks, just past our glorious new train depot, now under construction.

From here, I could see the new depot's still windowless brick walls and the wood framework of its sharply pitched gabled roof. I got so wrapped up watching the carpenters working in the rafters that I almost ran smack into Father.

"Whoa there!" Father called out, catching me by the shoulders. He wore his usual dark gray coat and trousers, befitting his prominence in the community. The solemn effect was softened somewhat by a light tan, medium-brim hat, chosen, as he would say, to avoid looking too much like an undertaker. He was smiling cheerfully, which was his natural state.

"You must've heard your mother calling, and now you're hurrying home, right?"

"Oh, did Mother want me?" I said, looking down.

Father laughed. "Yes, she did, as you well know." His smile

faded a bit. He smoothed his neatly trimmed mustache with the edge of his thumb. "But, for now, you can keep me company."

I could have hugged him right there in front of the whole town. As calmly as I could, though, I said, "Sure, are we going someplace?"

Father's smile returned. "We're meeting a train, as you also know." Reaching inside his coat, he pulled a heavy gold pocket watch from his vest and checked it. "Will, when we meet him, I want you to be seen and not heard. Understand?"

"Yes, sir!"

I turned and looked up the tracks again. Far off on the western horizon, beyond the Mud Creek Bridge, I could just see the smoke curling off the stack of the Express and drifting southward on the prairie wind.

TWO

You can see a long way on the plains. From the moment I first saw smoke, it was ten minutes before the Express arrived.

As the engine drew near, the depot platform hummed beneath my feet and then trembled. I felt the steady huffing pulse of the big smokestack in my chest. "Aaaa-bilene! This is Aaaa-bilene!" the brakeman called out. Bell clanging, the train rolled slower and slower, and then with a lurch and a heavy slamming of the iron couplings, the Express was motionless, breathing evenly.

"How will we recognize him?" I asked.

"Oh, I don't think that's going to be a problem."

A good-size crowd, and a few dogs, had gathered. The twice-daily arrival of passenger trains was always something of an event. You never knew who or what you might see.

I preferred trains from the west, like this one. Trains from the east often brought settlers, and that always made me sore as a boil.

It might seem that Father and I were settlers, but we didn't see ourselves that way. A settler was a farmer. Town folks such as us were too well bathed and high toned to be settlers. To me, a settler was someone who grubbed around in the dirt.

And it was that grubbing in the dirt that angered me. To my way of thinking, this was cattle country, and every new settler plowing up the prairie meant less room for the Texas herds. After all, it was the Texans, not the settlers, who had made Father a success.

Our family had arrived in Abilene just as the cattle trade was getting started. Even before Mother, Jenny, and I joined him, Father had opened a small real estate office, which had thrived from the first day. A few months later, he took all our meager savings and every cent he could borrow, and he bought twenty-five town lots in what would become Abilene's business district. At that time the lots were cheap. Sensible people might have called them worthless, but sensible people didn't come to Abilene.

As the cattle and cattle money began pouring in, Abilene boomed, and the value of our land climbed higher and higher. Before long, we were one of the town's leading families.

As for me, well, Abilene was a strange place, different in a thousand ways from other towns, but it was truly home. Mostly that was because I had real friends here, people that liked and accepted me. I felt safe here. Far from the lonely torment of my uncle's house, far from the rootless wandering of our years after the war, I was now part of a place. My blood had mixed with the life of Abilene, and I was certain I would never be an outsider again.

Still, despite all the advantages Abilene had brought to us, its own progress had not been trouble free, and that was why today was so important.

Most of the passengers who were getting off had done so, and the crowd at the depot was already beginning to thin.

"Where is he?" I asked. Father only shook his head.

At the rear of the train, several shiny new plows were being noisily unloaded from a boxcar. I scowled and murmured, "Damn farmers."

Glancing at Father to make sure he hadn't heard, I saw that something else had his attention. I whirled to look where he was looking.

A tall figure stood motionless on the back platform of the nearest car.

"Mr. Hickok," Father called out.

The man nodded, and as he stepped down from the platform, sunlight glinted off two chrome pearl-handled revolvers stuffed into a red Mexican waist sash. Few men wore such guns. This was Abilene's new marshal, Wild Bill Hickok—Civil War spy, army scout, former sheriff of Ellis County, Kansas, and general all-around merchant of death. For a fact, he was the most famous and feared gunman in the West. Even the President of the United States and the Queen of England knew who Wild Bill was.

All us boys had read the dime novels about the great gunman. We all knew he'd killed at least seventy-five hardcase men, not counting Confederates. And right now, he was looking square at me. I was sure that when he spoke, flames would shoot from his mouth.

At first glance he looked like a true enough badman. Along with those awesome guns, he wore a buckskin coat with Indian beadwork on the shoulders and fringes hanging from the arms. A full reddish brown mustache curled around his mouth.

Unlike our close-cropped town men, Hickok wore his hair long, past his shoulders in the style of the plainsmen. His broad-brimmed hat was like the ones worn by cowboys. For certain, he was no dry-goods counter hopper.

"Mr. Hickok, I'm J. T. Merritt. I've been asked by Mayor McCoy to welcome you and get you situated."

My father held out his hand. Until now, Wild Bill had rested his hands on his hips, keeping his coat back from his guns. But he took Father's hand without hesitation and shook firmly. "Mr. Merritt, thank you, sir." He towered above Father, who was not a short man.

"This is my son, Will," Father continued, putting a hand on my shoulder.

Once I got a closer look, there was something disappointing about Wild Bill—he didn't seem very wild. I'd seen some real, untamed pistoleros around Abilene. They were loud, dirty, swaggering sorts, and I'd imagined Wild Bill would be the loudest, dirtiest swaggerer of them all. A man who would raise hell and put a prop under it, as the cowboys liked to say.

But he wasn't like that. He was neat, spotless, almost elegant. I thought he'd pass even my mother's finicky standards of cleanliness.

But when I looked into his eyes, my doubts fell away. I knew then that all the stories about him were true, or ought to be. He came toward me, and I couldn't help it—I stepped back. I would've given anything not to have done such a cowardly thing, but I had.

The way Hickok reacted was something I never would've expected. He drew himself back just a little, then crouched down on one knee and made a show of adjusting his pant leg over his boot top. "I appreciate you meeting me here, Will. It makes a person feel kind of low to get off a train and have nobody there." Looking up, he extended his hand, and I came forward at once and shook it. I never was afraid of him again.

Hickok rose up and said, "Mr. Merritt, tell me about your town."

This brought Father fully to life. Abilene was his favorite subject.

"Well, sir, over three hundred thousand Texas cattle came up the trail last year, and we expect twice that this season. Twice! I don't suppose I'm cutting it too fat when I say Abilene is set to be the next great metropolis of the plains. Look around, look how many of our buildings are built of brick. Folks wouldn't use brick if they didn't expect to be successful."

Hickok nodded.

Father rushed on. "Our city council recently approved twenty thousand dollars for construction of a new school building. Think of it, twenty thousand dollars! Try to find another town that can afford such liberality. You won't find a one."

Suddenly, Father's face became solemn.

"You know, Mr. Hickok, this is a special place. For folks with gumption and good sense, it's pure opportunity. There's nothing to hold anyone back."

Hickok nodded again.

Father smiled a little shyly at his own passion. "Oh, yes, here's something that'll interest you. We've just built a new jail, out of stone."

Wild Bill didn't look very interested. I wasn't either. I'd heard all this a thousand times.

Father directed the station agent to deliver Hickok's trunk to the Drover's Cottage, where a room had been reserved. We then set off for the hotel, strolling eastward alongside the tracks. As we walked, Father boomed the town, pointing out the county courthouse, the Novelty Theatre, which was under construction, the new Universalist Chapel, and other points of interest.

Hickok listened quietly, but I could tell he was getting impatient. Abruptly, he interrupted. "Why has the town waited until such a late hour to hire a marshal?"

"Our last marshal got his head cut off by a crazy settler," I blurted.

"Will!" Father almost shouted.

"Sorry," I said meekly. I could've sworn I saw Hickok smile.

Father tried to patch up the damage. "It was a freak incident. Marshal Smith was . . . caught unawares . . . with an ax, while making an arrest."

Father paused to see if our new marshal had any comment. When Hickok said nothing, he quickly changed the subject. "So, over there to your left is Mr. Gaylord's Twin Livery Stables, probably the largest stables in all the West. Fine place to hire a buggy or purchase a horse."

As Father rambled on, I wondered what Hickok thought of the town he would be policing.

In many ways, Abilene was like any other small prairie town. Despite Father's talk of brick, most of our businesses were wood with square false fronts that hid the simple gabled roofs behind. Excepting the Red Front grocery, painted buildings were usually grimy white or dreary gray.

We had no streetlamps or concrete sidewalks. The roads were unpaved, with prairie grass sprouting in the less trafficked areas. A few homeowners had planted spindly immature trees, but in the business district, there wasn't a tree or bush to be seen. Hogs ran at large in search of edible garbage, which wasn't hard to find.

Looking up any street, you saw that the frantic human energy at the center weakened rapidly as you moved outward.

Within five or six blocks, the houses dwindled to vacant lots and then the roadways ran off into the grassland and faded away. Beyond that loomed the wilderness, the vast vacancy of the Great Plains, fanning out to a far distant encircling horizon.

But, no one could walk our streets for long without realizing that Abilene was different.

Although we had only about eight hundred year-round residents, the south side was crowded with substantial hotels.

Livery stables were normally unimpressive, but Abilene's Twin Livery had two mammoth barnlike structures that ran a full block from Second Street to Third Street.

East of the Cottage, the recently enlarged Great Western Stockyards spread across seven acres in a stunningly complex array of chutes, lanes, pens, and other enclosures.

West of the Cottage was central Texastown, where it appeared as if a flock of migrating saloons had set down on Texas Street and decided to stay. Surely we had more saloons than any small town on earth.

And strangest of all, every one of these outsize wonders was eerily empty and lifeless. They were all waiting, but not for long.

When we arrived at the Cottage, Hickok sat right down in one of the veranda chairs and offhandedly asked if we could get some lemonade. As soon as Father had gone to order our drinks, Hickok began questioning me.

"Will, to hear your father, Abilene is so well-off it hardly needs a marshal. What do you think?"

I knew Father wouldn't want me being free with a lot of loose talk, but Lord, this was Wild Bill himself asking my opinion!

"Well, they aren't hiring you to be marshal of Abilene. They're hiring you to be marshal of Texastown. I guess Texastown is officially part of Abilene, but it's a whole different place."

"How's that?" said Hickok, leaning forward.

"Folks north of the tracks are here to settle down and make money. South of the tracks, it's just Texans looking to have a big time and go home. And they do get kinda crazy. That busthead whiskey Texastown saloons sell would make rabbits fight a wolf pack, so it's not all their fault."

"You like them."

"Oh, yeah, I like 'em fine. I wish I was a cowboy. Nobody has more adventures than them. And they're real good to us kids." I stopped there, knowing I shouldn't say more.

"But?" said Hickok, staring at me, unblinking.

I couldn't resist. I kept talking.

"Well, we're sort of fighting the Civil War all over again here. We're Northerners. The cowboys are Southerners. They know they're only tolerated 'cause of the money they spend. It grates on them. Father worries that someday something will set them off, and they'll burn us out. By June, there'll be four thousand Texans here, a lot of them armed and drunk. They'll outnumber us five to one."

"How did last season go?"

"Not so good. Father told you we've got a new stone jail. That's because an angry mob of Texans burned down the old wood one."

"Ahhh," said Hickok with a grin.

"And that's not all." I was getting carried away now. "The settlers hate the cowboys because the cattle trample their fool crops. Everyone worries that some stupid farmer is going to start a war because a longhorn takes a nap in his corn patch."

Suddenly my loose talk made me feel guilty.

"Don't blame Father for not telling you all this. He wants you to stay. It frets him to have his family in a place like this."

Father reappeared down the veranda, holding a tray loaded with drinks and sandwiches.

My curiosity was killing me. I was dying to ask Wild Bill if he really had killed seventy-five hardcase men, like the dime novels said.

"If you don't mind me asking," I said, lowering my voice, "is it true that you—"

"No."

THREE

Word of the famous gunman's arrival was spreading fast, and more and more gawkers were gathering near the Cottage. Hickok lounged in his veranda chair, one thumb hooked in his sash, and never once took notice of the stir he was causing.

Before long, I spotted the bright red hair of my best friend, Jasper Hardeman, moving among the folks across the street. I pretended not to see him. I had Wild Bill to myself, almost, and I wasn't going to share.

Sometime around noon, Hickok said he had to go see Mayor McCoy. As we were parting, Father made one last comment.

"Mr. Hickok, would you join us for supper this evening, around five? My wife is a wonderful cook."

"Thank you, Mr. Merritt. I'll look forward to it."

"We're about five blocks directly north. Anyone you see can point the way."

Mother wasn't going to like this. I sure didn't want to be around when Father broke the news to her.

"Will," said Father, "run home and tell your mother to set an extra place."

"Wha . . . ?" I croaked. "Me? Aren't you going home?"

"No, I've got some business outside of town. Tell your mother not to worry if I'm a tad late."

"Can I get Rambler and come with you?" This would at least get me out of the house after I delivered my message.

"No," said Father, his tone telling me to drop it.

Beneath my alarm over Mother, I wondered why he didn't want me along. I often joined him when he rode out to inspect some piece of land. But recently he'd been saying no and wouldn't explain why.

When I got home, I told Mother straightaway about Wild Bill coming to supper. "Put Jenny down for a nap around three thirty," was all she said. Then she went into the kitchen and closed the door. The kitchen was awful hot when cooking was being done. She would never shut the door unless she wanted to be alone.

I was glad Wild Bill was coming. It was exciting. But Mother felt something else. Something here in Kansas made her afraid. To her, our home was a tiny, leaky life raft bobbing about on an ocean of peril. And now, evil had found a way into her house. A killer would sit at her table and eat her good, wholesome food.

Why had Father done this?

The hours crept by but eventually it was almost five, and Father still had not returned. Mother became increasingly anxious, going repeatedly to the windows to look for him.

"Where is your father?" she asked, her voice almost desperate.

I had no answer. My enthusiasm for Wild Bill's visit had dwindled. Watching my mother's growing dread was too hard.

At exactly five, there was a knock on the front door. Mother's hand went to her cheek, and she stood perfectly still.

"I can answer it," I said quietly.

"No, no, I will go."

When Mother opened the door, Wild Bill was huge, filling the opening. Before him, Mother appeared small and fragile. A shiver of concern ran up my spine.

"Ma'am, I'm Mr. Hickok. I hope I'm expected."

He was holding his hat before him with both hands. He wore a white shirt and a black, neatly pressed broadcloth coat. I wondered if his revolvers were beneath the coat.

"Yes, you are expected," said Mother. An uncomfortable moment of silence followed. It occurred to me that she might tell him to leave, but her good manners got the best of her. She stood back from the door. "Won't you come in?"

"Thank you, ma'am."

He wiped his feet on the doormat before stepping into our narrow foyer. Mother asked to take his hat. When he handed it to her, his coat opened up, and I was relieved to see he wasn't wearing his guns.

Hickok winked at me. "Hello there, Will."

I grinned, glad to be noticed. "Hi, um . . . Marshal."

"My husband should be here any moment," Mother said as she hung the big hat on the wall rack.

"We all had a fine talk this morning," said Hickok. "Will here was a great help to me."

"Is that so?" said Mother coolly, unable to hide her disapproval. There was another uncomfortable silence, and then Mother said, "As I mentioned, my husband should be here presently."

"Mr. Merritt says you grew up in Springfield. I'm from Illinois myself. Born in LaSalle County."

At the thought of home, Mother smiled in spite of herself.

"I have a brother who lives in LaSalle," she said. "He has a farm on the Vermilion River. It's quite beautiful."

"Yes, I know it well."

Mother didn't reply, and after a moment Hickok continued. "My father brought our family to Illinois around the time of the Black Hawk War. My mother still lives there. I went home for a visit about two years back. Seems like yesterday. Do you know the feeling?"

"Yes, I do." Mother smiled again.

The conversation paused, and Hickok began to look around. From our foyer, a hallway ran back to a tiny room Father used as an office. On the right, a stairway climbed the wall to the upper floor, and on the left, a doorway led off the hallway into a long open room that served as a parlor up front and a dining area at the rear. A lean-to kitchen, entered from the dining area, was tacked on to the back of the house.

Peering through the parlor door, Wild Bill spotted Mother's upright piano and smiled.

"Did you bring your piano from Springfield?"

"Yes," said Mother. "I couldn't leave it behind."

Wild Bill went into the parlor and ran his hand lightly over the piano's dark polished wood.

"The music helps, doesn't it?"

"Helps?" said Mother.

"I once visited a settler's home only fifty miles east of here. It was the roughest kind of sod house, a floor of packed earth, buffalo robe for a door. The family used old barrels for chairs and straw ticks for beds. The wife usually went barefoot to avoid wearing out her only pair of shoes."

Mother sat down slowly on the piano seat as Wild Bill spoke. Her face had softened, her fear and anger ebbing away.

"But against one wall was a piano, much like yours. It was

all the woman had left of her previous life. She told me that without her music, she believed she would have gone mad."

"It's so different out here," said Mother, almost whispering. "I miss so many things I once took for granted, like the forests. It never occurred to me there were places without forests. Men seem to love this empty land, but it makes me feel small."

Hickok laughed. "Ma'am, a person who brings a piano past the edge of civilization cannot be small. It's folks like you that grab a wilderness by the throat and make it behave."

Mother blushed at this, but she also looked very pleased. "Thank you, Mr. Hickok."

I knew she truly was thankful. Somehow Wild Bill, of all people, had eased her fears.

Hickok patted a sheet-music booklet propped up above the keyboard. "Would you play something for us, Mrs. Merritt?"

"Certainly, Mr. Hickok. And please take a seat."

As Mother began playing, Wild Bill slipped into one of the horsehair armchairs we'd also brought from Springfield.

Jenny, just turned six, had not awakened from her nap until the sounds of the piano began to carry through the house. After a few minutes, she appeared at the hallway door, rubbing her eyes and yawning. When Wild Bill saw her, he smiled and waved her over. To my great surprise, Jenny went to him and crawled into his lap without a word.

And that's how Father found us when he returned home twenty minutes later.

FOUR

Mother had not adjusted easily to Abilene, and yet Father was completely at home here. He was seen as a man who was creating order and wealth where none had existed. That was progress to Westerners. Father was admired, and so were we, his family. But behind our success, Mother saw a terrible flaw—Texastown.

Texastown slept during the winter. But with the arrival of the first herds of the season, it jerked bolt upright with a Rebel Yell, arms wide for trouble. Soon, sounds of drunken laughter, angry quarrels, gunfire, and rough honky-tonk music would come to us on the nighttime winds.

During the season, our town profited greatly from the cattle trade—but no one felt safe. Intoxicated cowboys often fired their guns wildly into the air as they rode to and from Texastown. One morning, Mother discovered a bullet hole in her kitchen wall. The slug had slammed through the boards and pierced one side of the stovepipe before it was stopped. After that, she believed the sins of Texastown threatened us all.

I've always felt that Father had a purpose when he invited Hickok to supper. Somehow, he had seen something in him that could help Mother, and against all odds, the infamous gunman had not only charmed her but also given her courage.

Mother still understood that Hickok was a gunman, but she overlooked that now. If nothing else, he was our gunman, our protector. In time, she would even claim that the men he had killed must have provoked him mightily.

I, however, was annoyed with Father for putting us through such an ordeal, and I carried my resentment into supper.

As we were sitting down to eat. Jenny caught me off guard and slipped into the seat next to our guest. "Hey," I yelped, "I'm sitting next to Wild Bill!" Mother's reaction was instant.

"Will! I won't have you addressing Mr. Hickok in that manner. He is Mr. Hickok or Marshal Hickok to you. Now, take a seat on the other side of the table."

Jenny gave me a triumphant smirk. I was humiliated, but to tell the truth, "Wild Bill" didn't seem fitting anymore. "Mr. Hickok" sounded more like the man I saw before me.

"We have fresh cranberries tonight," Mother said cheerily, trying to move past my social stumble. "Just arrived at the Red Front yesterday."

There was a lot more than cranberries. Mother's meals were lavish. Tonight we were having roast quail with giblet sauce, fried sweet potatoes, green peas, johnnycake, and buttermilk biscuits.

Hickok was clearly a happy man. I was sure he didn't eat like this often. "Mrs. Merritt," he said, "your husband told me your cooking was a marvel, and I see he wasn't exaggerating."

Mother beamed. If Father had been in the doghouse, he was

out now. Mother did, however, give him one little mischievous needling.

"By the way, John, what kept you so late? I thought you were coming right home after meeting the train."

I glanced at Father just in time to catch him giving her a warning look. I had expected him to be quick with apologies, but instead he was almost curt.

"I visited that little piece of land we've been talking about. We can discuss it later."

Oddly, Mother dropped the subject instantly. I was surprised she'd let him off so easily.

I wouldn't though. "You got us worried," I said with more edge in my voice than I intended.

Now Father gave me a warning look, but Mother intervened before he could speak.

"Mr. Hickok, are you pleased with your accommodations at the Cottage?"

"Yes, ma'am. Quite a hotel."

"Where did you reside before coming to our town?"

"West of here. I was scouting for the army out of Fort Harker. I also hunted deserters, particularly if they departed on a government horse."

"Oh dear. Was that dangerous work, Mr. Hickok?"

"Yes, ma'am, a number of deserters were injured."

Father and I burst into laughter at this, and after a moment of hesitation, Mother allowed herself a polite giggle.

"The army is winding down operations at Harker, and I was inclined to a job that didn't require so much saddle time. So here I am."

"Yes," said Father, switching to his heartiest salesman voice, "and we're expecting another banner season. The Texas drive is predicted to be the biggest yet."

"Is that a fact," Hickok said absently, his attention captured by Mother's good food.

"Yes, indeed," Father barreled on. "Of course, it does bring problems. There has to be a limit to the shenanigans of these Texans."

"You know, Mr. Hickok," said Mother, "I hear most of these Texans are just common criminals who've fled west from the more civilized states."

"Shame," said Hickok, glancing up from his quail.

"I'm sure there's good men amongst them," said Father, trying to sound fair-minded, "but there's also those that would shoot a man just to see which way he falls. And frankly, some of our citizens are tired of walking on eggshells."

"Understandable," said Hickok. "Jenny, dear, would you please pass me those cranberries?"

"Cowboys are bad," Jenny announced as she reached for the cranberries.

"They all seem given to drink," said Mother, who had never met a cowboy in her life.

"Now, a man can have a drink and not be a villain," said Father, "but it's their lazy shiftlessness that gets my back up. Why, to them, a dollar is just a thing to throw away."

This kind of talk gave me fits. In my family, only one person had spent time with cowboys, and that was me, only I couldn't say so.

Hickok was smiling wickedly. He pointed at me with a little quail drumstick. "Will, what do you think of these Texans?"

"Like many of our youngsters," said Father, "Will here thinks they're heroic."

"Let's hear what the boy has to say," said Hickok.

"Well," I began, "cowboys can do things with a horse and a rope that hardly seem possible. Drunks couldn't do such things.

And folks say they're half-civilized, but I've never yet heard of them being rude to our womenfolk. And our men say they're honest in their dealings."

"Agree, Mr. Merritt?" Hickok asked.

"There's something to that."

Feeling encouraged, I went on. "And I don't see how they're lazy. They bring huge herds a thousand miles to get here. Seems like hard work to me."

Father was looking at me with some pride, but Mother would have none of it.

"Nonsense," she said. "We cannot settle our future in the hands of a violent, soulless people. I hope to see the day when this prairie is divided into neat, orderly farms."

I couldn't contain myself. "This is cattle country! Farmers can't make a go here. Everyone knows that."

"Will, you're too full of pepper for my taste," said Father. He turned to Hickok. "For now, the cattlemen rule the roost, but that might change. It all depends."

"Depends on what?" I demanded.

"Will, watch your tongue," Father snapped.

"This is exactly what worries me," said Mother. "Our children pick up all sorts of bad habits living amongst these Texans."

"No dessert for Will!" Jenny piped gaily.

Hickok stepped in to restore order. "Will, why can't farmers prosper here? They're doing well farther east in Kansas."

"It's different here, drier and hotter than eastern Kansas."

"As you know, we get scorching winds from the south in late summer," said Father. "Some years the winds kill crops utterly. Other years the damage may be less, but the belief is that over time, farmers will suffer too much loss. Eventually they'll all fail."

Hickok turned to me. "What do you say, Will?"

"I say they're just moochers that couldn't make it on better land back East. Most of them don't work anyways. They just sit around bellyaching."

"You must know quite a few of these farmers."

"Um, no," I said, feeling uncomfortable. "I just know what everybody knows."

"Farmers are bad," added Jenny.

"Jenny, hush up," said Mother. "Will, you're being unkind."

"Yes, ma'am. Sorry."

"Mr. Hickok," said Mother, "many around here agree with Will. But I believe God made this prairie for farms. Such soil! Rich and dark. And the land, so level and open. It invites the plow. I'm certain a way will be found to make it produce."

I expected Father to challenge this, but he didn't. I assumed he didn't want to argue in front of a guest, but even still, it was odd. Father had always doubted the farmers' chances here.

There was a knock at the front door. Father went to answer it, and after a moment returned with Mayor McCoy.

Joe McCoy, like Father, was in his midthirties. He had unruly brown hair, a bit longer than most of our men's, and if you happened to catch him at rest, his face was a bit plain. But the mayor was rarely at rest, and as soon as he spoke, the plainness was swept away in the rush of his energy.

"Sorry to interrupt, folks, but I have news. A runner from a surveying party working down around Holland Creek says the first Texas herd of the season has arrived—Columbus Carrol with twenty-five hundred head. As we speak, Carrol is camped below the Smoky Hill River about six miles south of town. Tomorrow they intend to make a big push and cross the river."

"Well, well," said Father, "another season begins."

"That's not all," the mayor rushed on. "I've received a wire stating that herds totaling over a hundred thousand have already passed Red River Station and moved north into the Indian Territories."

"Lord help us," gasped Mother.

"What a season this will be!" exclaimed the mayor.

I let out a cheer that made Mother grimace.

As he was about to leave, the mayor turned to Hickok. "Odd thing, but Carrol's men already knew we'd hired you as our marshal. Apparently, word has gone down the trail like wildfire."

Hickok nodded grimly.

Mother began to ask Mr. McCoy to stay for dessert but broke off in midsentence and looked upward. There was an unmistakable plinking sound on our tin roof.

"Rain," said Jenny.

FIVE

It's definitely drier and hotter around Abilene than to the east, especially in late summer, but in the spring, we can match our rain against anyone's. And this particular storm was like nothing I'd ever seen.

It rained three days straight, except when it was hailing. Lightning bursts slashed down from the sky into the prairie land, and the downpour sometimes came in such torrents that there hardly seemed room for the air itself.

Around noon on the third day, I sat in my creaking oak chair, leaning forward to the glass of my upstairs bedroom window, entranced by the panoramic drama of the storm.

Abilene lay on the north slope of a valley that held the Smoky Hill River. But it wasn't much of a slope, and it wasn't much of a valley. To the eye, there was the impression of flatness, enough so that newcomers often raised an eyebrow when told they were in a valley. Our house was two miles north of the river, but it was only about thirty feet higher than the river bottom.

But with that thirty feet and the added height of an upstairs window, I could see far up and down the valley and south to the Smoky Hill. This was not an orderly river. It curved and looped about crazily as it headed more or less eastward. From a distance, the river was so thoroughly hidden by the trees and bushes growing along its banks that it appeared as an endless leafy snake crawling over the featureless bottomlands.

The farthest rims of our feeble valley were capped with low, dull yellow limestone bluffs, and behind that, on both sides of the river, lay the uplands. Again, I would say that anyone seeing the uplands for the first time would think it too strong a word for such modest geography. But they would be wrong. For the uplands were the shallow rolling stair steps to the endless prairies. A wilderness of grass rivaled only by the sky in immensity.

Safe and dry in our home, I loved the excitement of a wild prairie storm. But what of the Texans and their cattle? How could they stand in the open and survive such violence?

In time, the rains ended and the skies cleared. Several days passed but nothing was seen of the Texas herd. Even if they were alive, they were cut off from us by the flooding Smoky Hill River, now a churning brutish monster ten times its usual width.

Despite our concerns, we still had to go to school. For me, sitting in class while this mystery developed was difficult, but for my best friend, Jasper, it was purified torture. He loved the cowboys even more than I did, if that were possible.

Wednesday morning, Miss Campbell had Jasper standing before the class reciting a poem from his McGuffey Reader. Jasper was no scholar, and he was making a bad job of it.

"The plez . . . ant rain. The plez-ant rain. By fits it sp . . . spl . . . splash-ing . . . falls."

Jasper's freckled cheeks glowed with embarrassment. I lay on my desk, head in my arms, trying to muffle my laughter.

"It comes. It comes. The plez-ant rain."

Jasper paused, glaring at me. I buried my face deeper in my arms, but a chuckling snort escaped. Still, I kept one eye on him. You never knew with Jasper. Even though I was his best friend, he might suddenly dive at me with fists flying.

"Continue, Jasper," Miss Campbell said as sternly as she could. She was only about five years older than me, dark hair, slim, very pretty. We all liked her, but this was her first year teaching, and she was still working on her confidence, especially when dealing with us older boys.

Jasper jabbed a hand savagely through his orangey red hair. "I drink its cooler . . . breeth, uh, breath. It is . . . rich . . . with sighs . . . of . . . faint-ing flowers."

Another snorting laugh got away, but this time not from me. Jasper lowered his reader and eyed Johnny Hodge.

Johnny led a small group of boys we regarded as our blood enemies. All had fathers whose businesses catered to settlers, and to us, that made them infidels.

"Hey, Johnny," Jasper said in a low, menacing voice. When Johnny looked up, Jasper drew a finger across his own throat in a slicing motion. Johnny let out a jeering hoot, but I knew he was intimidated. I could see it.

"Jasper," said Miss Campbell, her voice tinged with uneasiness, "let's continue, please."

Jasper was scary. Even I knew it. Not because he was big or powerful; he wasn't. Jasper was scary because he brimmed with an anger that could make him crazy. You had no faith that he would stop where normal people would stop. Johnny Hodge was a tall, sturdily built blond kid, a year older than Jasper and me, and no coward, but he wasn't stupid.

As Jasper looked for his place in the reader, the door at the rear of the schoolhouse opened and closed. After a moment, Reverend Christopher emerged from the coatroom and strode up the center aisle.

Miss Campbell looked puzzled. "Reverend Christopher, what a surprise."

"I apologize, Miss Campbell, for disturbing your lessons," the reverend said. "I have news of grave importance."

"Oh dear," said Miss Campbell, "has someone been injured?"

"To the contrary, Miss Campbell, it is my mission to prevent an injury. The good Lord has seen fit to impose another mournful trial upon the joyful spirits of these innocent children." He paused as if he'd said all anyone needed to hear.

"I'm not sure I understand, Reverend."

"I have come to admonish each of you to turn your back on evil. The Texan curse will again dwell in our midst."

Jasper's eyes widened. "How's that, Parson?" he asked, his impatience showing.

Reverend Christopher sighed. "A Texas rider scouting the Smoky Hill has signaled that they will attempt to bring their herd across. The fools."

Carrol and his men were alive! I was filled with happiness. They had survived a mighty storm and now they were going to challenge the flooding Smoky Hill. Oh, this was a wonderful day!

Then panic swept over me. A dozen Texans were about to swim 2,500 longhorns across a wild river—and I was stuck in school! I looked at Jasper and saw the same panic on his face. His eyes started flitting about wildly, from me, to the windows, to the rear door, and back to me. Then his feet began inching forward.

Reverend Christopher held out his arms. "I believe we might have a quick prayer to—"

"Damn!" Jasper yelped. "I got to get down to that river!"

Jasper's reader fell from his hands, and he ran like a deer past the good reverend. Instantly, I was out of my chair and hot on his heels. In a flash, every kid in class, even Johnny Hodge, even the teacher's pets, was rushing for the door. Mouth agape, the good reverend spun like a top as the mob flew past him.

Jasper and I led the charge toward the center of town. When we arrived, it seemed the whole population was heading for the river. Store owners were hanging CLOSED signs. Riders galloped by on agitated horses. Ladies were being helped onto wagons and buggies. Other folks were striking out on foot.

I called to one of the Red Front clerks who was pulling away in a delivery wagon. "Jimmy, goin' to the river?"

Jimmy nodded and waved us aboard. "Looks like school's out," he said with a grin.

SIX

All the traffic down to the river had churned the road into a muddy mess. Our horse began to huff with the strain of pulling the wagon through the sucking quagmire. We were all headed for Texas Crossing, normally a safe, shallow place for herds to ford.

But as we came closer to the river, we gasped. It was huge, well out of its banks and spreading far over the bottomlands. Tawny water swirled high around the trunks of trees that grew along its usual edge.

"Look at that!" Jasper exclaimed. "Carrol must need to sell his cattle awful bad."

It was true. To sell his herd and get his money, Carrol needed to reach Abilene's cattle buyers—and they were on our side of the river.

But crossing the Smoky now, just when it was on a big rise, was risky. A river like this could kill. If things went badly, hundreds of cattle might drown. And if that wasn't enough of a caution, there were four cowboy grave markers just up the road from Texas Crossing. Of course, two of those graves didn't actually have anyone in them. Sometimes the river swallowed people up and never gave them back.

So why was Carrol in such a hurry? The water would likely fall in a few days. Why not wait it out?

About a hundred yards from the waterline, Jimmy pulled the wagon off to the side, and I stood up in the bed and looked around. Most folks had left their horses, wagons, and buggies scattered nearby and had walked the rest of the way down to the river. Among them, surrounded by a clump of other dark-suited men, my father was talking with Mayor McCoy.

Jumping from the wagon, Jasper and I called out a thanks to Jimmy and headed toward the water.

Some years back, a broad swath of riverside on both banks of the crossing area had been cleared of trees to make it easy for cattle to enter and exit.

Looking south over the chaotic water, I could see more than a mile to the opposite rim of the shallow river valley. The Carrol herd was out there, somewhere, beyond the rim.

"Jasper," I said, "where are they? Do you think they're crossing someplace else?"

Jasper was my best source of information about Texans and cattle. His parents were dead, and he lived above his uncle's Texastown saloon. No one I knew spent more time talking to cowboys and learning from them.

"Naw," Jasper replied, "they're comin'. There ain't no crossin' better'n this one."

As we joined the waiting townspeople, I suddenly wondered if Marshal Hickok was here. Searching the crowd, I had turned almost all the way around before I found him. He was off by himself, arms crossed, staring out over the river, his two Colt revolvers occasionally glinting in the sunlight that came and went through scattered clouds.

I wondered what he was thinking now that the first of thousands of wild Texans was coming. Was he afraid?

Behind me, a familiar laugh broke into my thoughts.

"Hey, Will, why don't you swim across and prod them Texans? Tell 'em we're gettin' impatient."

I turned to find three of my other close pals behind me. It was Billy Mayfield along with Gordon McInerney and Booth Kelsy.

"Billy," I said, "if I did, those longhorns would take one look at me, all wet and muddy, and stampede clean back to Texas."

"No need to get all worked up," declared Gordon. "They'll be comin'. Ain't that so, Jasper?"

"Uh-huh."

"See there," said Gordon, "Jasper and me aren't worried."

I sighed. Gordon and I got along fine when Jasper wasn't around, but Gordon seemed to resent that Jasper had chosen me to be his best friend.

"Me and Billy were just joking, Gordon," I said. "Nobody's worried."

"They look worried, don't they, Jasper?"

"Shut up, Gordon."

"Sure, Jasper. All I was sayin' was—"

Billy laughed. "Well, I'm worried, and impatient, and don't care who knows it. I may swim over myself if they don't come soon."

"We wouldn't be seein' nuthin' if Jasper hadn't got us out of class," said Gordon.

"Somebody had to," said Jasper.

I felt a tug at my sleeve and knew it was Booth trying to get my attention. A childhood case of scarlet fever had left him deaf in his left ear and mostly deaf in his right. Although he could speak, he usually chose to say very little.

When I turned to him, Booth smiled and made a quick pointing gesture toward my left with his thumb.

Off by themselves was a bedraggled cluster of two or three settler families.

Their clothes were either too big or too small, and many garments appeared to have been made from something else, old tablecloths or curtains or perhaps the tent they'd lived in when they first arrived.

The men wore those cheap wool hats with the brims that sagged down after they got wet a few times. One settler leaned forward slightly and spit a long stream of brown tobacco juice, not all of which cleared his already stained bushy beard. Another was smoking an old-fashioned long-stem clay pipe. No townsman with an ounce of dignity would ever be seen in public with one of those in his mouth.

The womenfolk looked weary and self-conscious next to the better-dressed town ladies. I couldn't help feeling sorry for them. For a moment, I imagined my mother wearing one of their drab, shapeless dresses, frayed and dirty at the bottom, some tied at the waist with a cord or a limp old ribbon. The thought made me shiver.

The children's clothes were laughably ill-fitting, worse by far than the adults'. The boys all had different colored patches on their trousers and overalls. Half of them were barefoot. One boy had shoes, but he'd apparently outgrown them because the fronts had been cut away to make room for his protruding, well-tanned toes. Some of the kids seemed to have the itch, and they scratched and rubbed pretty much nonstop.

They seemed undeniably primitive, awkward, and ignorant.

Their graceless appearance alone confirmed our cruelest beliefs. We harbored no doubts, felt no duty to look deeper, allowed ourselves no sympathy; these were people destined for failure, and they deserved it.

"What a sorry bunch," sneered Gordon. "I guess they don't care a lick what they look like."

"What're they doin' here at the crossin'?" said Billy. "Hey, maybe they're tired of growin' dead crops. Maybe they're headin' down the trail to become cattle barons." Billy chuckled at his joke.

"Fools!" Jasper said hotly. "I hope it's 150 degrees all summer and burns out every last one of 'em. Let 'em starve and be damned."

Billy, Gordon, Booth, and I sort of enjoyed feeling superior to the settlers, but Jasper was different. Jasper hated the settlers, so much that sometimes he scared me. I was never sure where his hatred might lead him, or me.

Jasper caught one of the settler boys looking at us and yelled out, "Hey, clodhop, what're you gawkin' at?" The boy didn't answer, but he didn't seem afraid either. Jasper pointed at him and then spit on the ground with as much insult as he could. The rest of us laughed and jeered heartily.

"That's it, Jasper! That's it!" Gordon cried. "Let 'em know they ain't wanted."

Down closer to the river, I spotted Johnny Hodge with a couple of his pro-settler friends. Unlike the settler kids, Johnny and his buddies were town boys like us. But because Abilene was so dependent on cattle, there weren't as many of them as there were of us, so they stuck together pretty close. In fact, if our two groups hadn't been at such a public gathering, there would likely have been a fight. Jasper would've seen to that.

My friends and I all had fathers whose businesses depended on the cattle trade. Billy's father worked at the stockyard.

Booth's father was building a hotel in Texastown. Gordon's family owned a shop that made boots with a red Texas Lone Star stitched on each one. And, of course, Jasper's uncle sold booze to thirsty cowboys.

Booth suddenly took a step toward the river. "There," he said calmly.

We all whirled to look. Two riders had appeared on the far side at the highest point of the gentle upslope from the river. Booth usually saw things before others, and it was a few moments before the rest of the crowd took notice and began to stir.

The riders were pretty far off, and one of them was inspecting the river with field glasses. After a few minutes, the other rider broke off and headed down toward the water.

When he reached the river bottom, the rider entered the water some ways upstream from us. His horse felt its way along until the water was up to its belly, and then stopped. The rider urged his mount on, and suddenly the horse leaped forward, almost flying out of the water. When they came down, horse and rider disappeared into deep current.

We all held our breath in alarm, but then the horse bobbed up twenty feet downriver, with the rider still in the saddle, and a roaring cheer went up from our shore.

The cowboy's horse was swimming strongly now, his head lunging rhythmically forward with each stroke of his submerged legs. Water blew from his nostrils with a regular snort that made me think of a steamboat. The rider angled him toward our outlet with gentle slaps on the neck.

Everyone began moving closer to the river, and my friends and I ran zigzagging through the crowd until we were up front.

"Jasper," I said, "it sure strikes me as peculiar that they want to cross in such big water."

"It strikes me you're peculiar," said Gordon quickly. He laughed and then glanced at Jasper for approval but got none.

Soon, the cowboy brought his horse into wading water at the outlet. He was barefoot and hatless and carried no gear that would weigh him down if he were swept from the saddle.

As his horse stepped from the water, the cowboy combed back his long, dripping brown hair with his fingers and gave the people gathering around a big grin through a three-month beard. He was a young fellow, no more than twenty.

"Well, if I'd known the whole town was gonna turn out, I would've put on a better shirt." That brought a laugh from all of us. Surprisingly, he didn't have a Texas accent.

The cowboy dismounted and began untying the saddle cinches that gripped the flanks of his hard-breathing horse. I noticed he was missing a pinky finger on his left hand.

"My name's Mike Williams," he announced as the cinch straps dropped free beneath his horse's belly. "I'm with the Columbus Carrol outfit, and I'm to ask for Mr. Joe McCoy." With obvious fondness, he stroked his horse's neck a few times before turning to face the gathering townspeople.

"I'm McCoy," the mayor said, making his way through the crowd. "What can I do for you?"

"Pleased to meet you, sir." Williams extended a damp hand, and he and the mayor shook. "Mr. Carrol wants to cross and take his herd straight to market. I've scouted the river and will advise him that it can be done if he chooses."

"Excellent," said the mayor, "but if you don't mind my asking, what's the rush?"

"Can't say. My business is to push the cattle where Mr. Carrol says. The why of it is his business."

McCoy smiled. "I understand."

"Mr. Carrol asked me to inquire if we are the first herd to arrive."

"Yes, sir."

"Are there buyers in town ready for business?"

"Yes again."

"Good. Well, I've got to get back to the herd."

Almost everyone reacted to this with amazement.

"Son," said Mayor McCoy, "are you sure you need to do that? This river's awful wild. You've already crossed once; I don't think Mr. Carrol would hold it against you if you stayed put."

Williams waved this off. "Don't matter to me what Carrol thinks. I didn't come all the way from Texas to miss this last crossing." He turned to his horse, adjusted the saddle, and then began re-tying the cinches. "Besides, they ain't made the river that can drown me."

Mayor McCoy glanced at the roiling river and smiled faintly. "I wish I was as certain as you."

"Aw, don't you worry, this is the fun part. Besides, I've got a natural talent for this sort of thing."

A moment later, Williams was up in the saddle. He wheeled his horse, rode upstream a ways, and then with a laughing whoop, splashed back into the river. Before we knew it, he was on the far side, riding south at a gallop.

SEVEN

There they are!" someone cried.

All eyes turned to look across the river. A mile off, two point riders and a wedge of longhorns had emerged from the southern uplands. Soon a seemingly endless column of longhorns was snaking down into the valley. Cowboys rode along both sides of the herd, guiding it and keeping it together.

A short time later, the mayor held up his arms and asked everyone to leave the crossing area. No one needed to be told twice. This was a cattle town; we all knew that the sight of a crowd of humans on foot would upset those cranky longhorns. Either they'd refuse to come ashore, or they'd come ashore and take out after us.

Every few moments as we retreated, I peeked over my shoulder. The herd was now more than a quarter-mile long, and the whole of it still not in sight. I could just hear the sharp yells and whistles of the dozen or so cowboys maneuvering the huge serpent toward our crossing. Before long, we were all gathered well back and to the sides of the crossing area, waiting and watching.

The lead longhorns and point riders were now nearing the water. The rest of the cattle stretched out behind them all the way to the valley crest and beyond.

The herd would enter the water a good distance upstream. The river would then sweep them downstream as they swam for our shore. If their progress was too slow or the current too swift, the river would carry them past our cleared outlet. That would be a disaster. Cattle that missed the outlet would be trapped in the water by tangled debris, partially submerged trees, and cutbanks that lined the shore farther down. Many would drown.

And there was something else to worry about. Cattle aren't too smart, but they have enough sense to know that swimming a flooding river is something to avoid. If the cowboys didn't plan everything just right, the skittish longhorns might refuse to cross.

The two point riders brought the herd's leaders up to the water slowly. The riders then let their horses wade out ahead of the cattle into the shallows and take a drink. The lead longhorns hesitated but then followed. When they were knee-deep, they too dipped their muzzles into the water and drank. The longhorns didn't know it yet, but they were about to be tricked into swimming the Smoky.

The long column of cattle behind the leaders continued feeding into the water. The lead longhorns were just settling in for a drink when newly arriving cattle began jostling them from behind, nudging them farther out. As more and more longhorns entered the river, they pushed the leaders into deeper and deeper water.

Suddenly, the quiet scene became a bedlam. In the crush of bodies, nervous cattle began to bawl and snort. Their huge horns clacked loudly against one another. Experience told the cowboys that this was the moment to shove the herd into the river.

The men erupted in a storm of yelling, cussing, whistling, and arm waving. They rode their horses wheeling, charging, and splashing back and forth along the edge of the bewildered mass of longhorns, always driving them outward.

And then, the cattle farthest out, the leaders who had arrived first, fell into swimming water. Immediately, one rider and then another leaped his horse into the current just downstream of the swimmers. When the dunked longhorns surfaced and tried to veer back to the shallows, the cowboys blocked their way. Hollering and waving their arms, splashing water in the longhorn's faces, even shoving them with their feet, the cowboys turned the leaders out into the Smoky Hill.

The jam of longhorns in the shallows was pushing ever more cattle into deep water. Now the longhorns' herd instinct took over. Cattle like to stick together and stay with their leaders. When this next bunch of cattle fell into swimming water, they saw the leaders striking out for the far shore, and they followed. Soon, the whole herd was taking to the water, streaming through the shallows without a pause.

More cowboys came up now to help with the crossing, among them Mike Williams.

The Texans were making it all look easy. Soon the lead cattle were trotting out of the water on our side. The herd now spanned the river in an unbroken line, swimming like smugglers.

But no crossing is a success until it's over. Now one of those things happened that makes river crossings so dangerous. Unnoticed, a small log, seemingly only a yard long, came down the middle of the river, drifting toward the line of swimming cattle. As it neared the herd, it stopped, an odd thing for a log floating in the current of a river.

On the far side of the cattle line, Mike saw what was happening. He began yelling frantically at a cowboy closest to the mysterious log. But with all the other yelling, the cowboy didn't notice the warning, and as he moved past the log, it came to life.

With a groan, a huge skeletal hand rose high out of the river and plunged down onto the unsuspecting cowboy and his horse. Both disappeared beneath the murky water. The giant leafless tree limb followed them under, until once more only a small portion of its trunk could be seen.

As the water carried the limb downstream, its long branches reached down to the river bottom and scraped along in the sticky mud. Soon, the branches again jammed deep into thick mire and stuck fast, and as before, the section of the trunk at the surface stopped dead, moving water swirling impatiently around it.

In moments, the limb pulled free of the muddy bottom, and like before, the powerful current rolled it around and then upward into the air, raining water as it climbed. This time it swung over and fell upon the orderly line of swimming cattle. Instantly, three longhorns vanished. Others panicked, thrashing about, trying to escape, and the current grabbed them, rolling them over and over before pulling them under.

Mike had guided his horse toward the break in the line searching for the cowboy that had vanished. Suddenly, the man popped to the surface, wild-eyed, choking and gasping for air, splashing crazily with his arms. I could see that he didn't know how to swim.

The cowboy was only yards from Mike, but in the powerful flow of the river, it was too far. Mike urged his swimming horse toward him, leaning out from his saddle with his hand extended.

It didn't work. The cowboy slid past, missing his outstretched hand by inches. "Grab the tail!" Mike screamed.

"Grab hold of the tail!" That did work. The cowboy brushed past the hindquarters of Mike's horse and caught its floating tail.

For the second time, a deafening cheer arose from the watching townspeople. Mike pointed his horse toward our shore, towing the bedraggled cowboy behind. When they reached shallow water, Mike gave his comrade an arm up onto the horse's back. Soon, they were on solid ground and riding up to us. A few moments later, the horse that had gone under with the cowboy came in and followed. Out on the river, the big tree branch that had caused the trouble was continuing downstream, and the disrupted line of swimming cattle was re-forming.

I rushed forward and threw myself into the throng of people, hoping for a chance to shake hands with the two heroes.

Pushing and elbowing until I was in close to Mike, I again noticed that he didn't sound like most Texans. Suddenly, I felt a hand on my shoulder. I looked up and saw that it was Hickok. "Mr. Williams," he said, "what part of Texas are you from?"

Mike smiled. "Kansas City, Missouri. Born and raised."

EIGHT

Deep in the night, moonlit ashes wafted through my open bedroom window. For a time I was so taken with their lazy, weightless movements that I failed to wonder what they were. Or why I was so suddenly awake.

A piercing wail cut into the peace of the darkness, fell away, and then rose again. Far away, a second fainter howl sounded. Now I understood. The big stock trains were coming for the Carrol herd. It was their shrieking whistles that had awakened me. And as the first train pulled off onto the long siding that ran past the stockyards, the cinders belching from its stack cooled to ash and drifted over the town.

That morning, after wolfing down breakfast, I was out the door at a run. Behind me, Mother's voice called out, "Will, you stay on our side of the tracks! Do you hear me?" I heard, but I was in too much of a hurry to answer. It was Saturday, and I was off to find Jasper, Booth, Billy, and Gordon.

In less than a week, Abilene had been transformed. The great Texas herds were now arriving almost hourly, and cowboys filled our streets. On the prairie around town, campfires, bed-rolls, tents, and rough, temporary shanties were sprouting like mushrooms. Once again, the rowdy sounds of laughter, rough music, and occasional gunfire were heard coming from the saloons and dance halls of Texastown.

At first daylight, clouds of dust and the odor of longhorn rose from the Great Western Stockyards. This was the real beginning of the season. The bawling of cattle being loaded, the yelling and whooping of working cowboys, the heavy clanking of railcars—it would all continue from now until fall. The Carrol herd, 2,500 strong, had been sold, and today it would be railed to Chicago.

And, having sold his cattle to a Chicago meat packer, Carrol was now happy to explain why he'd been in such a hurry to cross the Smoky Hill.

"Here's the true facts," he'd begun. "Back in Texas, I seen how big this year's drive was tallyin' up. Maybe twice last year's. I'm figurin' there's more herds than Yankees to buy 'em. So while other outfits was nappin', I put my herd together right quick and struck out, aimin' to get to market before them sons of Lincoln realized how much was comin'.

"Course, it weren't like I was God's select. There's other folks saw what was shapin' up and set out not too long after me. So, when the rains held me at the Smoky, I thought, if this ain't nearly hell. A dozen herds on my heels, and soon they'll be pilin' up all around me. If I sit here water-bound too long, word's sure to get around that every cow in Texas is comin' to Kansas. Prices was bound to drop like a cannonball tossed off the Ala-mo's parapet. So I stepped lively, big water be damned, and made the crossin'. Now, as you can see, I'm rollin' in fat.

"But, mark me, drovers who was tardy in getting away is

gonna pay for their lack of hurry up. Prices are fallin' already, and I 'spect my price to be the best we'll see all season."

Mr. Carrol had a right to his opinion, but so far every cattle season in Abilene had been bigger than the last, so getting worked up about a big drive struck most folks as silly. It was true cattle prices had dropped recently, but in the longer run, they'd always favored moving higher.

Busy with my thoughts, I almost stepped in front of a wagon that was making its way along the north side of the tracks. The driver pulled up his horses sharply, and I jumped back in surprise. A closer look at the wagon brought a frown to my face— settlers. Saturday was the day settlers from all around flocked into town to trade and do their marketing.

The creaking wagon was being dragged along by a team of heavy, weary-looking plow horses, so different from the quick, wiry mounts of the cowboys. At the reins, a bearded settler regarded me with dark eyes. Beside him sat a rail-thin woman with wispy yellow hair. Her fair skin, not meant for the punishing prairie wind and sun, looked raw.

There were a number of kids in the wagon box. A girl about my age stood behind her parents, gripping the wooden seat back. She had light brown hair parted in the middle and cut off straight just above her shoulders. Unlike her mother's, her face was tanned rather than burned red. There was something saucy about her. She was giving me a look with sharp gray eyes, a look that said I was a foolish, spoiled town boy who'd be lucky to make it through the day without getting himself killed. She made me mad.

I was about to wave them by when a distant, growing rumble grabbed our attention. Turning, I looked down the tracks toward Buckeye, the next cross street. Something big was coming fast, barreling up Buckeye out of Texastown. The sleepy plow horses awakened, snorting and clomping their hooves fretfully in the dirt. The low rumble became a roar, and we all held our breath.

From the Buckeye opening, a tight mass of riderless horses, a hundred or more, poured out at a dead run. At the edges, four cowboys shouting and whistling wheeled the bunch eastward, toward us but on the lower side of the tracks. The ground began to tremble, and all around us fine dust began to rise from the surface of the street like wispy smoke. Terrified, the settlers' plow horses whinnied urgently and began shoving the wagon back and away from the wild onrushing horde. Panic-stricken, one reared in its harness as the bearded settler yelled, "Whoa, whoa!"

Laughing as they came, the cowboys galloped headlong beside the flying herd. To me they seemed born to the saddle, balanced with every rhythm and motion of their mounts. As they flashed by us, one cowboy, a black man, swept his hat before him and called out to me, "Hello, Kansas!" He socked in the spurs and his horse leaped, soaring over a pile of rail ties lying by the tracks. With a yell I jumped high, throwing an arm skyward, waving like a crazy person.

And then they were gone, swallowed up by the dust of their own crashing hooves. After a moment, the settlers' frightened team quieted, sinking back into weariness. The girl with light brown hair put a hand gently on her mother's shoulder and leaned down, saying something I couldn't hear. The woman was crying.

As the wagon rolled past, the girl glared at me. I looked away. She made me feel guilty, and that made me mad all over again. What had I done except cheer some fun-loving cowboys in my own town?

When the wagon had passed and the dust had cleared, I saw that Jasper was just across the tracks, grinning at me. That brought the joy back to my soul. Jasper always made me feel that every day had great promise.

"Ain't those Texas punchers a caution?" he yelled.

"If they ain't, I don't know who is," I called back. I made my way across the street and, ignoring my mother's orders, stepped over the tracks.

"I 'spect Carrol's gonna sell those horses to some Northern rancher needin' saddle stock," Jasper said. He glanced darkly toward the retreating settler wagon. "What's their problem?"

I didn't want to get him started so I changed the subject. "I don't know. What do you want to do?"

Jasper's face brightened. "Come on," he said, "we're all meetin' up over to the Cottage."

"Hold on, Jasper. What happened to your face?"

Jasper turned fully toward me and smiled oddly. His cheek was red and he had the beginnings of a shiner. "My uncle's what happened."

"Oh . . . was he drunk?"

"Nope, just irritable."

Jasper's troubles with his uncle were well known. Joe Hardeman owned the Elkhorn Saloon in Texastown. He was a rich man by Abilene standards. There were rumors that during the season his fleabag saloon took in astonishing sums, as much as four thousand dollars on a good night. To the world, he was a talkative, good-natured fellow, unless you rubbed him the wrong way—and Jasper rubbed him the wrong way a lot.

Jasper never talked about how he came to live with his uncle or what had happened to his parents, but I knew. One afternoon the previous summer, I arrived home and heard voices coming from the parlor window. Mrs. Mayfield and Mrs. Crayton were paying a call on Mother. Hoping to avoid being put on display for the ladies, I circled to the rear of the house and snuck in the kitchen door.

I was about to tiptoe down the hallway and up those squeaky

stairs to my room when I heard Jasper's name mentioned. That wasn't surprising since Jasper had just the previous week burned down the Hodges' carriage house. A joke that went bad, Jasper had claimed, even though gunpowder had been involved. Anyway, I stopped, curious to hear what the ladies thought of my friend.

"I saw young Jasper Hardeman today," said Mrs. Crayton. "He looked a little ragged. I daresay that dreadful uncle of his came down pretty hard on him for the Hodge fire."

My mother spoke next. "I hear Joe Hardeman gave Mr. Hodge one thousand dollars cash money to settle the matter. I suppose a man of his lights can afford it, but still, it had to give him fits."

"You know, Elly," said Mrs. Mayfield, "I see your Will with that boy from time to time. I do hope they aren't friends."

Now, knowing my mother, I would've thought she'd disapprove of me being friends with a saloon boy, but she'd surprised me. Every day, she told me to stay away from Texastown, but she'd never once told me to stay away from Jasper. I'd always wondered why.

"I don't discourage their friendship," Mother said with a touch of curtness. "Naturally, Will is forbidden from Texastown, but if Jasper comes up to see him, it's fine with me. That boy's had a difficult life, and I don't intend to add to his troubles. I know he's full of devilment, but perhaps Will can be a good influence on him."

"Well, you beat all, Elly!" Mrs. Crayton exclaimed. "Jasper might just as well be a bad influence on Will!"

"And besides," Mrs. Mayfield added, "what kind of difficulties could excuse that boy's cussedness?"

"I'm not excusing anything," Mother replied, her voice hardening. "But, I believe I know more about this matter than some folks."

"Joe Hardeman is one of Satan's own sons," said Mrs.

Crayton, "and Jasper Hardeman hasn't fallen far from the family tree."

"There's not a thing wrong with Jasper's family tree!" Mother declared. "My husband has had occasion to speak with Joe Hardeman about the events that brought that boy to our town."

"Is that a fact?" said Mrs. Mayfield.

"It most certainly is," Mother went on. "Jasper comes from respectable, industrious parents. According to his uncle, they farmed a nice piece of land over in eastern Nebraska. But when Jasper was seven, the good Lord took his mother in childbirth. They were a long ways out, and the poor woman had passed on by the time the doctor arrived."

"Well, even still," Mrs. Crayton began, "that doesn't account for—"

"Hattie, let me finish. The following year, Jasper's father cut his hand while plowing. The injury didn't seem bad, but soon it was obvious that something was wrong. The man tried to keep working, but his muscles ached and he was terribly tired. Before long, he was forced to take to his bed. The next morning, he felt a stiffness around his jaw and mouth—it was lockjaw."

At this, Mother's friends gasped with genuine horror. We all feared lockjaw. It could come with any cut or scrape, and it was a fearful disease. Fearful not only for the person it struck, but also for anyone who had to watch what it did to the human body.

Mother went on to say that Jasper and his younger brothers and sisters had been trapped in their isolated cabin as their father died horribly. No one knew if Jasper had tried to get help. He was only eight then, and the nearest neighbor was miles away.

In time, someone happened by and found them, three small children, a baby, and a dead man. Afterward, the children were separated, scattered among various relatives. Jasper ended up with his uncle Joe and hadn't seen his brothers and sisters since.

When Mother finished her story, I tiptoed upstairs as silently as I could. In my room, I lay on my bed thinking about what I'd heard. I'd often wondered where Jasper's hatred of settlers came from. As far as I knew, he'd never spoken of his terrible experience to anyone, not even me.

And who would want to speak of such a thing? Lockjaw was unspeakable. Jasper had seen the disease turn his last surviving parent into a monster.

What would it do to a little boy to watch his father suffer such a deadly ordeal? To watch his face and then all the muscles of his body unmercifully tighten and tighten until they froze. To sit by his bed, surrounded by frightened, crying brothers and sisters, as the poor man's face slowly contorted into a permanent ghastly grin and his body twisted and bent itself into inhuman positions.

What unnatural contortions had this horror left inside Jasper? To beg your father to tell you what to do and realize that he could not answer. To beg him to eat or take a drink and discover that he could not swallow, no matter how he tried. And at the end, to pray that he would take a breath, a simple breath, and see that he could not.

Now, at least, I thought I knew why Jasper was different. Oddly, his hatred of settlers had begun in his own isolated settler cabin. A cabin in which both his parents were taken from him.

Billy, Gordon, Booth, Jasper, and I stood high atop the majestic Drover's Cottage.

Standing along the rear edge of the Cottage's flat, black-tar roof, we looked eastward up the wide bottomlands through which the Smoky Hill meandered aimlessly. Almost hidden in the grass, a few of the shallow burbling creeks that veined the surrounding prairie could be seen winding down from the north and up from the south before ultimately pouring themselves into the Smoky Hill.

Three stories up, we were just high enough to peek over the valley rim and into the vastness of the prairie, a lush green cloth interrupted by dozens of immense dark Texas herds and by the occasional geometric squares of small fresh-planted farm parcels.

Stretching out just below us, the Great Western Stockyards sprawled against the south side of the tracks. Lined up on the siding that veered off the main line to the yard sat two long stock trains, one being loaded and the other waiting its turn. Each had about thirty cattle cars, heavy enough to require two locomotives apiece.

Spreading over many acres, the yards boiled with noise, swirling dust, and organized commotion. To the rear, cowboys on fast cutting horses were rapidly separating groups of twenty longhorns from the main herd. Other riders then ran these groups down fenced lanes to loading chutes. Standing on planks above the chutes, shouting and cursing cowboys with long poles prodded the balky cattle up ramps into the cars. When one set of cars was filled, the trains would all pull forward, bringing up more empty cars.

Below us, the engineer of the second train was leaning out of the polished walnut cab of his locomotive, talking to a cowboy on horseback. I called out a hello, and when the men found us high above, they both waved. On the count of three, we all yelled, "Hooray for Texas!"

Jasper draped his arm around my shoulder, completely happy. We were at the center of the universe.

NINE

Jasper brushed his red hair back from his freckled face and glanced up at a Cooper's hawk swooping low over the street. He and I stood in the sunlight just beyond the long morning shadow cast by the Drover's Cottage.

The other guys had gone swimming down at the Smoky Hill. Jasper couldn't swim and didn't want to go, so I stayed with him. Once we were alone, Jasper reached into his pocket and drew out a few pennies and a nickel. "Let's go to the Red Front and get some candy," he said, grinning.

It was my reward for sticking with him. Jasper always had more money than any kid I knew. Most of it came from rushing the can. For a dime and a penny tip, he'd deliver a big lard can full of beer to anyone in town who was thirsty. Once, my mother had seen Jasper trotting down the street with his can and asked me what he was doing. I told her he was delivering paint.

To get to the Red Front, we crossed the tracks, back to respectable Abilene. By now, the open area along the rails was busy with settlers arriving from outlying farms and cowboys riding in from their camps.

I happened to look down the tracks to the east and among all the folks flowing into town, I noticed one rider heading out. When I looked closer, I realized I knew who it was—my father.

There he was leaving town again, and at a strange time too. What was he doing? He was by himself, so he wasn't showing land buyers around.

Several times, I'd asked him where he went on these solitary expeditions, but he'd never given me a straight answer. Something about the whole thing made me uneasy, but I couldn't have said why. Maybe it was the uncomfortable look that came over him, and Mother, whenever I brought up the subject.

A yell from Jasper interrupted my thoughts.

"Hey, ya dumb sodbuster, that's a fool place to park your wagon."

About forty feet ahead, a farm wagon with two settlers aboard was sitting on the rails. The driver had tried to cross, but with only a single gaunt-looking horse pulling the heavily loaded wagon, he'd gotten stuck trying to get the rear wheels over the second rail.

The driver, a thin fellow with a deeply tanned face, urged his horse forward, but it seemed to give up easily.

Jasper laughed gleefully. "Hey, if you ever fed that swayback some oats, he might be good for somethin' besides sleepin'."

Eyes blazing, the driver called back, "You shut up or I'll come teach you a lesson right quick."

"Yeah, sure, and while you're chasin' me, the Express'll come barrelin' in and scatter your wagon through six counties."

"That's right," I chimed in, "the Express is due right now."

Actually, it wasn't due for an hour, but I figured these settlers didn't know that.

"And it don't stop for fools," Jasper added. "Hell, it don't even slow down."

That was the last straw. The driver swung around in the wagon seat preparing to jump down, but that was as far as he got.

Four mounted Texans appeared and put their horses between the settlers and us. One of the cowboys, a man who looked a little older than his companions, moved his horse forward. He untied a long rawhide cow whip from his saddle and let it uncoil to the ground.

"You, dirt man, d'ya see how edgy you're makin' our horses?"

"What?"

"Our horses, they're gettin' jumpy. That's 'cause they ain't used to seein' a human bein' park his wagon on a railroad track. Makes 'em fretful."

"Now listen," said the driver, "them two smart-mouthed us and deserve a lesson in manners."

"These two? Why they's some of the politest boys in town. You're lucky it weren't some of the others come along."

Jasper and I laughed as loud as possible.

"Let me introduce myself," said the cowboy. "My name is Jake Waring from Williamson County, Texas, and where I come from, we don't ride around dirt men." Waring's voice lost its humor and went cold. "Move that wagon out of our way!"

"This ain't none of your business," said the driver. "We just—"

"Move!" Waring roared. Several of his partners moved their hands to their revolvers.

"Ho, boy, this is gonna be somethin'!" Jasper whispered gleefully. "These are Print Olive's men, and they're a gun outfit."

For me, suddenly, the fun was gone.

The wagon driver, his face red with anger, whipped the reins, and his horse made another effort. The wagon wheels started to rise up on the rail, but then the horse just quit, and the wagon settled back with a weighty thump.

"Good God, man," said Waring, "that horse is as worthless as you are. Maybe the lot of you need a touch of the whip to get thinkin' straight." As he spoke, he swirled his cow whip in easy looping circles off to the side of his horse.

"Watch this!" Jasper said excitedly. "He'll skin 'em for sure."

I was pretty certain I was about to witness something I didn't want to see. I was so absorbed with the tragedy playing out before me that I didn't become aware of Hickok until he was in front of Waring's horse.

"Coil up that whip and move on," said Hickok, looking up at the mounted horsemen. "All of you."

Waring was quiet for about half a moment. I don't think he'd seen Hickok coming either. But if the cowboy was taken aback, he regained his nerve quickly.

"Ya know, Marshal, I don't s'pose the four of us feel like takin' orders from the one of you. Maybe it's you that should move on."

As he spoke, he turned almost sideways in the saddle toward Hickok, pulling his far leg up and wrapping it around the saddle horn and then removing the other from the stirrup and allowing it to dangle. He rested his right hand casually on his holstered pistol butt and gave Hickok a taunting smile.

Everyone was quiet for a time, measuring their odds, deciding how far they wanted to take this.

"Well, then," said Hickok, breaking the silence, "nobody wants any trouble." He took a slow peaceable step toward Waring, as if he just wanted to come closer so they could talk things out.

"Oh, I don't know," said Waring, "I'm fine with trouble. So are my boys."

"Yes," said Hickok, sounding almost fatherly as he took another casual step closer, "you Olive boys do have a reputation."

"That's right, we do," said Waring. Certain now that he'd won the test of wills, Waring twisted a little further around in his saddle to grin smugly at his three companions. And that's when his eyes left Hickok.

The marshal moved so fast that even though I was a good distance away, my body reacted with a surprised jerk. He closed the remaining distance to Waring as if shot from a cannon. As he came, he yanked his pistol from its holster and then brought the barrel down hard on the upper shin of Waring's dangling leg.

The cowboy howled in pain, instinctively bending down, reaching for his shin. In the same instant, Hickok gave the Texan's horse a sharp slap on the rump. The horse fell apart at once, leaping straight up and then bolting. Bent over and sideways in the saddle, Waring was in no position to save himself. The first buck sent him soaring into the air, and he came down like a sack of potatoes thrown from a passing train.

Now Hickok had his revolver trained on the remaining cowboys. Still stunned by what they'd seen, none had found the presence of mind to react.

"All right," Hickok said to them, "the three of you take off while I remove the one of him to jail. Don't let me see any of you again." As he spoke, he leaned over and removed the pistol from Waring's holster and stuffed it into his belt. He then picked up the cow whip from the dirt and tossed it to the nearest mounted cowboy.

"Thanks, Marshal," one of the farmers called out.

Hickok frowned. "You two get that wagon off the tracks. I don't care how you do it as long as you're gone in the next two minutes."

As quick as that, the farmers jumped down from the wagon.

One pushed against the wagon box from behind while the other urged the reluctant horse on. With a lurch and a jolting thud, the wagon was over the rail and free. "Thanks again," the driver called.

The whole episode had left me awestruck. Two minutes ago, I wouldn't have given the marshal very good odds in a fracas with four armed cowboys from the notorious Olive outfit. Now it seemed like those poor fellows never stood a chance.

"Jasper," I said breathlessly, "have you ever seen anything like that?"

"Nope," he replied blandly.

I'd expected him to be as keyed up as I was, but when I heard his tone, I understood. Hickok's skills must have impressed him, but in his mind those skills had been used against the wrong side. I wanted to talk about what we'd seen, but I decided to drop it.

And there was something else. Much as I disliked settlers, I was glad to see these two men get away unharmed. They hadn't done anything wrong. Sure, they'd gotten themselves into a fool's fix, but that was no cause to be whipped or shot. The odd thing, the thing that confused me, was that while I despised these settlers as a group, I found it hard to wish real harm to them when they stood in front of me. Jasper had no such confusion; he hated them as a group, and he hated them as individuals.

"Jasper, let's go get that candy."

"You bet." He started to follow me but then drew up. "Uh-oh, hold on, Will. This show ain't over yet!"

A tall man with jet-black hair and chilling pale gray eyes was walking toward Hickok and Waring.

"That's Phil Coe," said Jasper, his voice brightening, "one of the owners of the Bull's Head, the only real Texan saloon in town. I hear Coe and Hickok are at war."

"What's he want?"

"Probably wants to take up for a fellow Texan," Jasper said, pointing to Waring, who by now was sitting up but apparently still didn't feel like standing.

"Gosh, Jasper, Coe's even bigger than Mr. Hickok."

"Yeah, I bet he's the only man in town that looks down on Wild Bill."

As Coe approached, Hickok changed his position, moving behind the sitting Texan so that he could keep Coe and the mounted Texans in front of him.

"Mr. Coe, we don't need any help from you."

Coe ignored the warning and kept coming. "Maybe not, but I ain't gonna stand by while a son of Texas lies in the dirt of a Kansas street."

"Kansas didn't put him in the dirt, Mr. Coe. That was his own doing."

Coe strode up to Waring and held out his hand. "Come on, son, shake out them cobwebs and get to your feet." Waring took his hand, and Coe helped him up.

"You all right, son?"

"I'll live. Thanks."

"You come on over to the Bull's Head when you get a chance. You and your friends here. I'll stand treat for the lot of you. Everything on the house. Understand?"

"Yes, sir, thank you."

"Texans have to stick together, don't we?"

"Yes, sir."

Hickok's limited patience was running out. "That's enough, Coe. Move on."

"Marshal, I'm just waitin' for the day you try treatin' me like you treated this young fellow. I'm waitin', ya hear?"

"I hear, and I've heard it before. Every town on the prairie's got a grandstander like you."

Coe turned again to Waring. "Son, if you need any bail money, you just send word and I'll cover you."

"Yes, sir. Can't thank you enough."

"No need. None a'tall. Only way to get a fair shake in this Yankee town."

And then to my astonishment, Coe swung around and pointed at Jasper.

"Y'all see that youngster with the carrot hair? His uncle runs the Elkhorn, one of those Yankee joints set up to skin Texas boys. Y'all can guess how much help ol' Hardeman would give a Texan beat to the ground. In fact, y'all could wait all season before a single citizen of this town offered up a sideways glance."

Jasper squirmed, and his face reddened, but uncharacteristically he didn't respond.

"Well, Mr. Coe," said Hickok, smiling now, "that was a speech to remember. I suppose when word of your generosity gets around, it'll be awful good for business over at your own skin joint."

"See, the truth ain't welcome here," said Coe. "But remember, Wild Bill, I'm waitin'." With that he shook Waring's hand, went over and shook with the other cowboys, and then walked away.

Pointing after the departing Coe, Hickok addressed the three mounted cowboys. "Follow his example and get out of my sight. Your friend here will be safe in the calaboose until police court meets at eleven tomorrow morning."

Hickok looked our way then, and winked. I gave him a little wave in return.

"Come on, Jasper," I said, "let's get that candy."

"Sure," said Jasper, sounding a bit low.

"You all right? Coe didn't have cause to talk to you that way."

"Aw, it's okay. He don't like my uncle much, but then I don't like my uncle much either." He smiled thinly.

"Maybe, but he didn't need to pick on you."

"Yeah, and I know Mr. Coe ain't no hero, but it's just that . . . well, he's foursquare for Texans and cattle, so I s'pose that's good enough for me."

We glanced over at Hickok just in time to see him urge Waring forward with a solid kick to the butt. Jasper flinched as if he'd received the kick himself.

TEN

The Red Front was never busier than on Saturdays. From every corner of the county, settlers streamed into town to shop and trade. Most settlers had little cash, so they traded the things they did have for the things they didn't. They would bring in eggs, homemade butter, lard, beeswax, and live prairie chickens and swap for dishes, pans, blankets, flour, coffee, a new sunbonnet, and maybe even a window or stove.

The store sat at the center of a solid line of north-side businesses that faced south, looking across the tracks toward Texastown. They seemed a wall of wholesome Kansas commerce standing firm against the festering evils gathered on the lower side of town.

Today more than a dozen farm wagons were crowded haphazardly along the Red Front boardwalk. Settlers were busy carrying the baskets, tubs, pails, and crocks of farm goods from their wagons into the store.

As we passed between the wagons, Jasper tapped the shoulder of a young boy struggling to lift some hefty slabs of bacon. "Dang, son, ain't nobody told you? The Red Front ain't buyin' dog meat no more."

"This ain't dog!" the boy declared, looking shocked. "This here's bacon."

"Is that a fact?" I said. "Well, you stubble jumpers sure are raisin' scrawnier and scrawnier pigs these days." I laughed noisily and pushed past the boy toward the store.

True to its name, the Red Front's broad front wall was painted a dull red. A weathered, unpainted wood awning hung out over its board sidewalk. In one window a large sign read, FURS AND HIDES TAKEN AT HIGHEST CASH PRICES. And just beneath, BUFFALO HIDES—5¢/LB. WOLF HIDES—75¢/LB.

The sidewalk was jammed with all manner of goods. It always seemed there was more for sale outside the store than in. Today there were racks of brooms and shovels, crates of potatoes and onions, tubs of eggs, stacks of earthenware dishes and tin buckets, and boxes of candles. At the far end, there was a six-foot-square chicken coop filled with multicolored clucking chickens.

When I hopped up onto the sidewalk, I noticed a handbill for Johnny Hodge's family business tacked to one of the awning poles. In bold letters it declared:

JOHN DEERE
PLOWS
NOW AT
J. M. HODGE
THE GREAT
PLOW OF THE AGE

I'd hardly finished reading before Jasper's hand shot out and tore it from the pole. He wadded it up and tossed it behind the rack of brooms. Just then, Jimmy the clerk appeared chasing a yellow dog out the store's front door. "Git!" he yelled. The dog scurried away with its tail between its legs.

"Hey, Jimmy," said Jasper, "why d'ya let Hodge post them plow flyers on the store?"

Jimmy shrugged. "Johnny Hodge comes by and sticks them up for his father. A lot of settlers come in here. I guess it's a good place to catch their eye."

"Yeah, but why do you let him?" Jasper demanded, looking exasperated.

Jimmy shrugged again. "I just work here. It don't mean nuthin' to me."

Scowling, Jasper leaned to me and whispered, "He ain't much smarter than that dog."

Jimmy went back into the store and we followed. Even on the brightest days, the interior was pretty dark. Little sunlight made it past the awning and all the signs and goods that covered the store's two smallish front windows. What light did get in arrived as we had: through the open front door.

Coming in from the sunny street, my eyes struggled to adjust to the sudden dimness. I always used this moment of blindness to inhale deeply through my nose. I loved the smell of this place. The odors of molasses, ground coffee, leather goods, cut tobacco, dried apples, cinnamon, kerosene, and a hundred other ordinary things were blended into a single exotic and delicious atmosphere. If the Red Front had charged for the aroma it held, I would gladly have paid.

As my vision returned, a scene of frenzied activity opened up before me. In the narrow aisles jammed with barrels, sacks, shelves, and crates, clerks rushed this way and that, waiting on customers. Townspeople and settlers milled about, noisily gossiping among themselves and haggling with clerks.

At the right rear corner of the store, I could see the town's new post office. It had a small counter and a bank of lockboxes in the front. Behind the counter, the back wall was covered with mail-sorting cubbyholes. I suppose it wasn't much, but it seemed very citylike to us, and we were proud of it.

Jasper and I made our way to the main counter at the left, our footfalls clunking on the board flooring. The candy was kept in four tall gleaming glass jars lined up on the edge of the counter. The nearest clerk was busy hacking heavy triangles from a huge circular orange cheese, so Jasper and I settled in by the candy jars. With all these adult customers, it would be a while before anyone got to us.

Jasper spotted a crock of honey sitting nearby on the counter. He gave me an evil grin and sidled over to it. After glancing about to see if anyone was looking, he lifted the crock's lid and reached inside with an outstretched finger.

"Jasper!" Jimmy's voice rang out from behind one of the shelves. "You stick your finger in that honey, and I'll throw you out of here headfirst."

Jasper sighed and gently lowered the crock's lid.

"Nice try." I snickered.

I started idly looking around, passing the time. Above us, hanging from the rafters by cords, were bulky hams, dried codfish from back East, and an assortment of cooking pots. On the floor at my feet was a box with a sign that read, BABBITT'S BEST SOAP—CERTAIN DEATH TO LICE AND OTHER VARMINTS.

Nearby, a traveling salesman with a red bow tie and a light gray derby was slouching against the front wall, one foot resting on his sample case. He looked bored.

The salesman was going to have a long wait. Ever since we'd arrived, Mr. Crutchfield, the owner, had been arguing with a burly, bearded settler, and the settler looked like he was just getting warmed up. Jasper had noticed the dispute too. "Lookit," he said, "another lazy farmer tryin' to get somethin' for nuthin'."

And that's when I saw the girl with light brown hair again. She was standing just behind the bearded settler. It was the same family whose wagon had almost run me down earlier this morning. The girl saw me staring at her. I was about to give her a nod, maybe even a smile, when she stuck her tongue out at me.

ELEVEN

I couldn't have told you why that girl made me so mad. It certainly wasn't the first time a girl had stuck her tongue out at me. Didn't I know the world was full of silly, cheeky girls? Sure I did.

Of course, I was too much of a gentleman to return the insult. And, to be honest, I was so surprised I didn't know what to do. At least Jasper hadn't seen what happened. He would've thrown a walleyed fit.

The best thing was just to ignore her. I'd show her that as far as I was concerned, she wasn't even alive. Trouble was, the more I tried to ignore her, the more curious I got. What was she doing? I was sure she was staring at me, waiting to insult me again. After a while, I couldn't stand it, I had to look.

I braced for another dirty look. What could you expect from settler people? But when I peeked her way, she wasn't paying me any mind at all. She and her mother were inspecting a bolt of gingham cloth rolled out on the counter. I began glancing at her more and more, but she seemed to have forgotten about me.

So, good riddance! The whole bunch of them were a pain anyway. Why, even now, the father had really gotten his hooks into poor Mr. Crutchfield. Even with all the noise in the Red Front, I could hear them arguing clean across the room.

Mr. Crutchfield had offered the settler, whose name was Dunham, fourteen cents a pound for butter he'd brought in. But Dunham howled that it was robbery to offer any less than seventeen cents for butter as good as his wife's.

Then they tangled over Mr. Crutchfield charging fifty cents a yard for gingham. Dunham said that where he came from they'd never paid more than thirty-five cents for gingham. To which Mr. Crutchfield answered that this particular gingham wasn't where Dunham came from. No sir, he said, it was here in Abilene, in the middle of nowhere, and it was darn expensive to get it here.

All this quarreling gave me a pain. I turned to Jasper and said, "These people would rather cheat us for a dollar than earn one."

"There ain't no bigger cheapskate in the world than a hay barber," Jasper agreed.

I rested my hand on the side of one of the glass candy jars, one finger pointing to some long red-and-white-striped candy sticks. "If anyone ever gets to us," I said irritably, "that's the one I'm getting right there."

Dunham's face had filled with indignation as Mr. Crutchfield ranted. He had drawn himself up for a counterattack when suddenly the room quieted. I'd been giving the settler girl another stealthy glance, and to my surprise, she seemed to be staring at me. But there was an odd look to her eyes, and pretty quick I realized she was actually looking past me.

I turned and saw the dark figure of a tall, lanky cowboy standing in the front doorway. Like me earlier, he had paused to let his eyes adjust. He was only a silhouette in the brilliant backlight of the entry, but no one had any trouble making out the big revolver holstered on his side.

Half-asleep near the door, the traveling salesman with the red bow tie was still leaning against the front wall with his foot propped on his case. But when the cowboy stepped fully into the room next to him, the salesman stood up straight with a startled jerk. Then, real slow, his foot came down from his case to the floor, as if he didn't want to make a noise that'd draw attention. After that, his eyes never left the Texan.

And small wonder. This particular Lone Star hombre looked like he'd eat you up without salt. He apparently hadn't been to the barber since coming off the trail; his dark hair was long and stringy, his beard and flowing mustache sunburned. Around his broad-brimmed hat was a rattlesnake-skin band with a sweat stain rising upward from it. A dirty red bandana swung loose and low around his neck. In one hand, he held a quirt, a short rawhide whip, which he cracked sharply against his boot top as I watched.

I cringed a little. Having just gone through the ordeal with the Olive boys, I wasn't yet in the mood for another overbearing cowboy. Jasper, of course, grinned from ear to ear, no doubt hoping this fellow would liven up the morning by shooting a settler or two.

After getting his bearings, the cowboy headed straight toward Jasper and me. The big, spiked, silver rowels of his Mexican spurs clinked and rang on the floorboards as he came. Settling in beside us, he leaned up against the counter on one hip and again popped his quirt impatiently against his boot top.

I found myself staring at his holstered Colt revolver. Its oiled, blue-black metal looked like Death waiting to be let out. A chill ran through me. Looking away, my eyes settled on his left hand, which rested on the countertop. His pinky finger was missing, cut clean off at the first knuckle. A roping accident, I supposed.

Then I remembered that Mike Williams was missing that same finger. I'd been avoiding looking him in the face. Much as I admired them, the Texans were a little menacing, especially at the beginning of the season when we weren't used to seeing them. But now, curious, I chanced a look, and sure enough it was Williams. He looked a little different dry, but it was him.

Williams gave his boot another smack with the quirt. He looked all about, and then his gaze fell on me. He took me in silently and then said, "What's a man gotta do to get some service from one of these counter hoppers?"

"Saturdays are pretty busy," I said quickly. "Um, if you don't mind me asking, aren't you that Missouri fellow, Mike Williams?"

"The hero of the Carrol crossing," Jasper added, without a trace of insincerity.

I thought this was laying it on a little thick, but the cowboy smiled. The hand with the missing finger came up and twisted the end of his mustache. "The very same."

"How's that fellow you rescued doing?" I asked.

"Still spittin' up Smoky Hill water," Williams said. Jasper and I laughed like this was the funniest thing anyone in the entire history of humanity had ever said.

"We heard Mr. Carrol sold his herd."

"Yep, loaded 'em out this morning."

With that, Williams seemed to lose interest in us. Looking about, he spotted Mr. Crutchfield, who was still arguing with Dunham. "Say, Colonel," he called out loud enough to rattle windows, "how's about a little service!"

When Mr. Crutchfield saw who was hollering at him, he cut

Dunham off in midsentence and rushed over. "Yes, sir, what can I do ya for?"

That was too much for the girl with light brown hair. Her mouth fell open in disbelief, and she said something heated to her father. When he didn't answer, she stalked off, storming past us and out the front door.

Williams began leading Mr. Crutchfield around the store ordering all kinds of things. He asked for plug chewing tobacco, a box of cigars, four cans of peaches in syrup, a bottle of liniment, and three bars of the soap that killed "varmints." Mr. Crutchfield put everything in a box and said, "That comes to two dollars and fifty-five cents, sir."

Without a word of argument, Williams tossed down three shiny silver dollars.

Mr. Crutchfield started to thank him, but Williams cut him off.

"Don't rush me, Colonel. I ain't done yet. My main purpose here is to pick up the Carrol outfit's mail."

"Oh, yes, sir. The post office is to your right at the far corner of the store."

Williams picked up his box and turned away, not even bothering to wait for his change. But as he came around, he took another look at Jasper and me, then at the candy jars beside us.

"Colonel," he said, turning back to Mr. Crutchfield, "I got some change comin'. You give it to these two gents in candy."

Mr. Crutchfield's smile wavered a bit, but he held up pretty well. "Certainly, and thank you again for your custom, sir."

A few minutes later, our pockets bulged with every kind of candy imaginable. We were rich. Jasper was sucking on a peppermint ball that made his cheek stick out an inch. I had two striped candy sticks hanging out of the corners of my mouth. What luxury! We burst out onto the sidewalk chattering and laughing with the joy of our good luck.

We almost ran over the settler girl. She still looked angry, and Jasper started right in on her.

"Hey, sodbuster, you left too soon. That cowboy bought us piles of candy. I don't s'pose your daddy is gonna spring for any candy, huh?"

"Who cares!" the girl shot back.

"You do, ya dumb farmer. I'll bet there ain't a one of ya that's had any candy since you dragged your sorry selves into Kansas."

"Have too!" said the girl.

"Ha!" I said. "Your whole family couldn't get two plug nickels together." My twin candy sticks danced up and down as I spoke.

"Yeah," said Jasper, "your father's probably one of those fools tryin' to farm the uplands. You're gonna be poor forever, soddy."

That did it. The girl lunged forward and slammed Jasper full in the chest with both fists. Jasper toppled over backward, smacking his head on an awning pole. When he hit, I heard a *crack* that sounded like someone snapping a thick piece of chalk. I was sure Jasper's skull had broke, but that wasn't what I'd heard.

Jasper sat dazed for a moment before leaning over and spitting out two halves of the peppermint ball—and also a piece of a tooth. Woozily, he stared at the bloody fragment lying on the boardwalk. "I busted my tooth . . ." he said absently. He spit some blood and then explored the deep interior of his mouth with his tongue. "Busted on that . . . hard candy." Suddenly his mind seemed to clear, and he looked up at the girl, eyes flaming. "No," he screamed, "*you* busted my tooth!"

"You had it coming," the girl answered. She was standing her ground but her voice was shaky now.

Jasper came to his feet in one jump. I knew I would have to stop him. He was too angry to think straight. Spitting the candy sticks from my mouth, I leaped between them and called over my shoulder, "Girl, you better go back inside!"

But before she could react, a new voice spoke up behind me. "She doesn't have to go anywhere."

I swung around, and froze. It was our sworn enemy, Johnny Hodge, and three of his pals.

Almost immediately, Jasper's wild rage seemed to disappear. It hadn't though. Jasper was only setting it aside while he considered our new situation. "This ain't none of your business, Johnny," he said in his smoothest, most threatening voice. "She busted my tooth."

Johnny Hodge took a step forward. "Jasper, you and Will leg it out of here." As he spoke, I saw one of his pals grab a shovel from the store's wall rack.

I knew we were up against it. It was a dead immortal cinch that Jasper wasn't going to back down. And for once Johnny and his pals outnumbered us, a situation that didn't happen too often. Oddly, though, none of this seemed to bother Jasper.

"Now, Johnny," said Jasper, smiling wickedly, "I thought we were friends. Why d'ya wanna crowd us like this?" Jasper was starting to move around, and I realized he was looking for a chance to take a shot at somebody. I wondered what it was going to feel like when I got hit with that shovel.

"You thought wrong, Hardeman," said Johnny. "Get going, or we're gonna take the snap out of you and Will right now."

The girl had been standing behind us, watching the pressure build. "Look," she said to Jasper, "I shouldn't have said you had it coming. I'm sorry you got hurt." She glanced at the boy holding the shovel. "I don't want anyone fighting about this."

Jasper was coming unstrung again. "Keep your sorries! You people wreck everything you touch."

"Will," said Johnny, "why do you hang around with this wolf? You ain't a bad guy. I don't get it."

"Listen, Hodge, if Jasper says he's staying, I'm staying too. I don't care if there's ten of you."

I looked over at Jasper, and he had the most grateful expression I'd ever seen. I thought seeing that look was pretty fair payment for the thrashing that was coming. But then Jasper surprised me.

"Come on, Will. It ain't worth it. Let's go."

Jasper was a strange person. If I hadn't been there, he might have punched that girl. If I hadn't been there, he would have taken on Johnny Hodge and his pals single-handed. Never mind that he'd get killed fair and proper. But now he was going to swallow his pride and walk away to save me from going down with him.

"I'll get you, Hodge," was all Jasper said as we left. Johnny never said a word, but his pals bullyragged us pretty good as we walked off.

I glanced over my shoulder. The girl was looking at me, and this time she didn't stick out her tongue.

For thirty minutes or so, Jasper and I ran around town, getting into as much trouble as we could, but around noon I had to go home to do some chores.

Jasper offered to come help, but I made excuses and turned him down. I wasn't sure why. "Well," Jasper said, "if you see that settler girl, give her a piece of my mind." I laughed, but the comment made me feel squirmy inside.

As I set off for home, I had no intention of seeing the girl again. After all, she'd caused me nothing but trouble. Just the same, I found myself going out of my way, veering toward the Red Front as if it were a big red magnet.

When the Red Front came into view, my heart sank. There

she was, still out front. Only now her younger sister and two small brothers were with her. I turned sharply and headed for an alley so as to avoid her. But within a few steps my feet rotated under me and carried me on toward the Red Front. I had the feeling of being rushed toward a cliff.

I stared straight ahead as I approached the girl, and as I passed by, I resisted even a sideways glance. But again, my feet slowed and brought me around, and they didn't release me until I was right in front of her.

The girl and the kids were all staring at me, waiting, but for the life of me I couldn't think of a word to say. Not one. The silence grew and grew, and I just couldn't find a way out of it. To tell the truth, I was scared to death. I'd never experienced anything like it.

Suddenly, my hand reached into my pocket and pulled out a hard candy. I held it out to the girl, and after hesitating, she smiled and took it from me. The other kids all watched intently, their eyes never leaving the candy.

Embarrassed, I whirled about and walked off. Once more, though, my feet took control and marched me back. This time, I dug deep into my pockets and then went around giving candies to every one of those wide-eyed kids. I was so nervous that I couldn't bring myself to look at the girl again.

As soon as I'd given away my last piece, I took off, almost at a run. And this time, my feet let me go. Behind me, I heard the girl call out, "Thank you, Will."

Good Lord, I thought, what would Jasper have said if he'd seen me do that?

TWELVE

Tonight we were going to Texastown.

A very unsettling week had gone by since I'd met the girl with light brown hair. She had stayed in my head. I found myself endlessly reviewing everything that had happened, everything that had been said, from the time I met her to the time I ran from her. It was like a quirky tune you can't stop whistling, a tune that worms its way into you until it becomes a torment. And with every note, I found myself lacking. I'd been foolish, awkward, even cruel, and worst of all, it bothered me.

But tonight, I would put it all aside. This was Friday, but not just any Friday. This was the last day of school, and to celebrate our freedom, my friends and I had planned a late-night expedition to Texastown.

Just before midnight, a small rock struck the outside of my upstairs bedroom wall with a sharp rap. It was Jasper's signal, but he needn't have bothered. I was already up and waiting when the dark figures of my friends slipped over our corral fence and stole across the open area to the front of the house.

I climbed out my window onto the slanted porch awning and then dropped to the ground among them—Jasper, Billy, Gordon, and Booth. Grinning broadly, Jasper gave me a friendly cuff on the arm. "Let's go!"

It might seem that any kid who visited Texastown at night would be reported, but it wasn't like that. Few upstanding citizens ever went down there. Anyone who did risked losing his reputation, and maybe his job. And even if a north sider did see a kid in Texastown, he didn't dare mention it because then he'd have to explain why he was there in the first place. So, over the last few seasons, I had made half a dozen late-night escapes to Texastown with my friends.

Even still, I was tense. There was always a chance of getting caught sneaking out. My parents' bedroom only had windows at the rear of the house, but I still worried. Father wasn't shy about getting out of bed to look around if he heard something peculiar.

Over in the barn, General let out a shrill whinny. We all froze. I looked back to the house, praying that Father wouldn't poke his head out of the front door, but the house remained still, and we pressed on.

This would be a poor time for me to get caught doing something bad. Father and I hadn't been getting along too well. It all started when I asked him to buy me a hat like the Texans wore. One with a wide brim. Maybe even a snakeskin hatband. Father laughed and told me to forget it. I should've dropped it, but his laughter got my back up, and I told him he wasn't being fair.

That was a mistake. Father's face colored red, and he threw down his newspaper and came out of his chair so fast it almost fell over backward. Jabbing a finger at me, he said he would not spend good money to make his son look like a Texas desperado.

The odd thing was how angry he got. And not just with me; he seemed angry with the Texans too. As far as I knew, he hadn't had any run-ins, but he was put out with them just the same.

By nature, Father was a cheerful person. Lately, though, something was grating on him. I still hadn't figured out what he was doing on all those secret trips out of town, but I couldn't help thinking they had something to do with his prickly mood.

One thing I did know: Father was taking a great interest in the local farmers. At the supper table, he'd tell Mother which farmers had finished their planting, who was late, and who was running a good operation.

To me it was silly to worry so much about crops that were likely to die when the scorching late-summer winds swept up from the south and gave them a good frying. Father knew this, but for some reason, it didn't lessen his interest.

Tonight, though, my pals and I were on a first-rate adventure, and that was all I cared about.

Walking as quickly as we dared in the feeble light of a quarter moon, we crossed the rest of my yard without further trouble, and once over the fence, we all relaxed some.

But I never relaxed completely when I went to Texastown. It was a strange place, particularly at night. A place where anything could happen. For me, the thrill of going there was always mixed with a dollop of fear. Maybe that was part of its attraction, the growing tingle in my spine as I headed toward it.

Cutting over a few blocks to the west, we turned south on Buckeye, now aimed straight for the heart of Texastown. Our side of town was fast asleep. Every home was still, every window black, the thin moonlight just sufficient to color the buildings a dim ghostly blue. The town seemed deserted. In the silent gloom, it was easy to imagine that everyone who lived here had just ridden away and disappeared into the endless prairie.

Continuing down Buckeye, I began to see an orange glow above the southern rooftops, and the silence around us began to give way to a low growl. Now, with each step we took, the brightness and sounds of Texastown grew and grew. Soon I could make out laughter, rough voices, and music. And then— *bang*—a gunshot. For a few seconds the growl fell away, then quickly surged back, as if nothing had happened. Jasper gave me a grin that I couldn't find the confidence to return.

Booth looked at me quizzically and said, "Gunshot?" He had a hard time identifying sounds when there was background noise.

"Yes," I said in a loud voice. "We're okay."

Booth nodded that he understood.

"Wild Bill hasn't taken the buck out of them Texas boys yet," said Jasper happily.

"No, but he ain't shot none either," said Gordon.

"My father says he'll have to shoot somebody so's they'll respect him," said Billy.

"I respect him already," I said.

"Well then, I guess he won't need to shoot you," said Gordon sarcastically.

"Ya know," said Billy, "he might shoot somebody tonight, right while we're there. That'd be somethin'."

"I don't want no Texas boys shot," Jasper said sharply. That shut everyone up.

But, truth was, midnight to 3 A.M. was Texastown's busiest and wildest time. We were walking into the heart of the storm.

As we neared the tracks, the boiling life of Texastown had become a roar. The air above it blazed with torchlight. Except for Jasper, we were all pretty subdued now. Only Jasper, who lived in a room over his uncle's saloon, was truly comfortable down here, especially at night. At the rails, everyone halted, each of us asking himself whether he really wanted to cross over.

I looked up into the night sky. The Milky Way swept across the blackness in a hazy white band. A billion stars hung over our heads, and not one of them knew or cared about Texas-town. "Come on," I said, "what are we waiting for?"

I took a deep breath and stepped over the rails. Jasper let out a whoop and made a show of jumping over both rails in a big leap. "See," he cried, "I ain't struck dead!"

"Shut up, Jasper," said Billy as he and Gordon stepped across. "Nobody's afraid." For good-natured Billy to speak harshly like this was a mark of the tension we all felt.

Jasper laughed. "Good, 'cause for a minute there, I wasn't sure you hotspurs had the nerve. I'd hate to see the sights by myself."

I gave Jasper a look that said he was going too far.

From the tracks, we gazed at the dark, rear outlines of the buildings that faced onto Texas Street. Light from the street beyond poured through gaps between the buildings, reaching out to us but falling short. Within it, distorted shadows lurched and danced. This close, the sounds of boisterous humanity, numerous stage bands, and the general movement of men and horses blended into a steady din so loud that we had to raise our voices to be heard.

As we moved forward again, I realized Booth wasn't with us. Still below the tracks, he stood hunched over, examining some-thing he held in his hands. "Booth, come on!" I called impa-tiently. He didn't seem to hear. He held up something round and dimly luminous in the near darkness. "Saddle concho," he called out, grinning. "Silver."

I waved sharply for him to follow us. "Booth, it's not real silver!" Booth shrugged, and, still studying his prize, he started toward the rails.

Again the sharp crack of a gunshot broke through the general commotion. To my horror, Booth went down hard onto the tracks. I wheeled to go to him, but Booth quickly raised a hand, and called out, "Tripped." He stood up, but having apparently dropped his concho, he began to search in the gravel around the rails.

"Booth, forget it!" I yelled. I took a few quick steps toward him, annoyed by his dawdling. As I approached, I thought I heard something new mixed in with the raucous noise of Texastown, something deep and resonant. I paid it no mind, but a second later, my irritation at Booth vanished into a swirling panic.

"Train!" Jasper screamed. "Train! Booth, get off the tracks, get off!"

My head jerked down the tracks, and there I made out the massive looming black shape of an engine rolling quickly toward us, already astonishingly close.

Like many stock trains, this one's big coal-oil headlamp had been extinguished before entering town. Engineers had learned that the bright circle of light was a choice target for the pistols of drunken cowboys. The practice saved headlamps, but it meant that night trains were hard to see as they coasted toward the stockyard. And on a night like this, the roar of Texastown overwhelmed even the rumble of the engine.

I leaped the remaining distance to Booth, who was still absorbed in the search for his concho. Grabbing his arm, I screamed, "Train! Train!" Suddenly Booth understood. His head swung toward the oncoming engine as a growing tremor built beneath our feet. "Go! Go! Go!" I yelled, pulling him sharply toward me.

The train's whistle abruptly cut through the air. In his scrambling panic, Booth again caught his foot on a rail and went down. The front of the locomotive towered above us now, its whistle shrieking a relentless violent note. I still had Booth by the arm, but there was no time to get him to his feet. I dug my heels into the gravel and used all my strength to drag him with me.

Groaning and hissing, the massive bluish black shape of the locomotive passed just behind. Oily fumes, steam, and the heat of the engine washed over us. The engineer leaned from the cab yelling and shaking a gloved fist.

As the train rolled on down the tracks toward the stockyard siding, we all gathered in a little circle, catching our breath and exchanging stunned glances. Even Jasper looked frayed. Booth pulled a handkerchief from his pocket and dabbed at a bloody scrape on his arm with a shaking hand.

Jasper broke the silence, leaning close to Booth's ear. "I guess you gave that engineer a good scare, huh?"

Booth nodded. "Whew," he added in his usual minimal manner. We all smiled nervously.

"All right, nobody's hurt. Let's go," said Jasper.

"Booth, you okay?" I asked.

"Uh-huh." He reached out and patted me on the shoulder. His thank-you.

"You would've been nuthin' but a pile of steaks exceptin' for Will," said Billy.

I didn't say anything. It was all sort of embarrassing. Jasper, impatient as usual, came to my rescue.

"Okay, okay, Will's a big hero. Now, can we go?"

"Yeah, let's go," echoed Gordon. "But if you ask me, Jasper was the hero. He's the one saw the train."

"Who cares?" said Billy.

"I'm just sayin' it ain't all Will," Gordon grumbled.

Jasper threw up his hands in exasperation. "All right, Gordon, we hear you. Can we go?"

Picking our steps carefully, we let Jasper lead us toward a gap in the crooked line of buildings that crowded Texas Street. At the rear of a saloon, we passed a corral overflowing with horses. Some of them nickered and snorted fretfully when we came near.

As we made our way through a narrow space between the buildings, a side door suddenly swung open, and a bartender wearing a dirty apron tossed out a couple of empty boxes. From the brightly lit barroom behind him came wild laughter, singing, clinking glassware, and a jangling piano tune. The bartender eyed us and then slammed the door. A boozy, sweaty saloon smell wafted out into the passageway.

A few more yards, and then, at last, we stepped out onto Texas Street. Now my doubts about coming here vanished. There was no place like this in all the world.

North of the tracks, our town was neatly arranged in straight lines, but Texas Street wasn't orderly. As if to show that it obeyed no law, it zigzagged drunkenly off to the west. Its buildings, mostly saloons, dance halls, and hotels, sat all over the place. Some jutted forward, some dropped back, some sat at angles.

And filling this jagged place, as far as I could see, was an ocean of humanity. Once, on a night like this, a visiting newspaperman had counted four thousand people.

Tonight, though, there might have been even more. Just as Mr. Carrol had predicted, cattle prices had started to fall as soon as the immense size of this year's drive became fully known. Rather than sell their herds on arrival, many owners were holding them out on the prairie, hoping for better prices. That meant there were more cowboys here than ever. Instead of being sent home, they were staying on to watch all those unsold herds.

But now they were pouring into town, released for a time from the tedium of camp life and itching for excitement. In groups of ten, twenty, and fifty, horsemen thundered in at a gallop, racing down the middle of Texas Street, skimming past the crowds that spilled off the boardwalks.

At any opening, the riders would veer in, swinging down from their saddles as their horses slid to a halt in a storm of dust. Whooping and laughing, these new arrivals would quickly mix into the rowdy throngs that topped Texastown to the brim.

Horses were as much a part of this scene as cowboys. There were thousands of them. They lined Texas Street, they jammed the corrals behind, and they filled the gigantic Twin Livery Stables. Many stood at the hitching posts still dripping with water from crossing the Smoky Hill or Mud Creek.

We didn't worry too much about the cowboys, but you had to watch the horses. These were real horses, not the tame pets our townfolk kept. Get near a Texas cow horse in a mean mood, and he'd kick you clean across the street. Or maybe bite a hunk out of you as big as the heel of your shoe. Get really unlucky, and he might get you down and kill you with his hooves.

Not everyone on two legs could be trusted either. Texastown was thick with gamblers, peddlers, beggars, street swindlers, saloon girls, dance hall girls, and, of course, the owners of the saloons and dance halls. These folks had one thing in common—a desire to take the cowboys' money without getting shot doing it.

"Well," said Jasper happily, "what do you boys want to do now?"

"How about we go to the Bull's Head?" Gordon piped up.

Jasper's face drooped. The thought of seeing Bull's Head

owner Phil Coe again wasn't attractive. Neither Jasper nor I had told anyone what Coe had said to him during the incident with Waring and Hickok.

"No, the Alamo!" I said, eager to rescue Jasper. "Let's go to the Alamo."

THIRTEEN

The most famous saloons in the West were on Texas Street, places like the Arcade, the Pearl, Flynn's, and, of course, the Elkhorn, which was owned by Jasper's uncle. Some saloons had better reputations than others. But the working cowboy's favorite had to be the Bull's Head, a fairly ordinary saloon, but the only one in town owned by Texans—Phil Coe and his partner, Ben Thompson. Until recently, Thompson had been known mostly for his skill in shooting people.

Despite Thompson's violent reputation, it was Coe who was causing a stir. There were rumors that he and Hickok were feuding. Some said over a woman. Others swore it was because the marshal had said publicly that the Bull's Head gaming tables weren't honest. Then there were those who said the two men had locked horns just because they were both filled up with natural, God-given contrariness. No one really knew, but everyone on both sides of the tracks was waiting to see how it would play out.

To the cowboys, Coe and Thompson were heroes, and Hickok was a killer hired by money-grubbing Northern townsmen. The two saloonkeepers were rich and dangerous, but most of all they were Texans. They were the men who stood between the cowboys and Hickok.

But tonight we all assumed we were going to bypass the Bull's Head and instead haunt Texastown's other star attraction, the Alamo, a saloon like no other.

Getting there wasn't easy though. Squeezing our way through the dense, jostling crowds was slow going. Also, there were a lot of sights we had to stop and see. Texas Street was as much carnival as street.

The air here was a thick soup of sounds and smells. The roaring music of saloon brass bands mixed with the cries of sidewalk peddlers and the babble of street shows. At every doorway, a fast-talking roper-in kept up a constant jabber. "Right this way, folks! Come on in. Everybody happy. Everybody welcome." From open windows came the click of poker chips and the calls of "Bets!" and "Get your money down, gents." And always, everywhere, there was the boisterous din of thousands of people moving, talking, and laughing.

Odors rose and fell as we moved along—horse manure, sour cigars, cooking food, French perfume, kerosene lamp fumes, washed and unwashed cowboys, and a hundred other smells.

All around us, big, brightly painted signs screamed the names of saloons and dance halls down to the restless throngs. At business entrances and on every street corner, tall flaming torches cast wavering light and shadow that made everything jump and vibrate.

"Look there!" said Jasper, pointing. "That's somethin' you don't see every day."

We all looked toward a brightly lit display window of the

Arcade Saloon. In a little fenced pen behind the glass there was a young pig.

Billy laughed. "Sorry, Jasper, but I see pigs every day."

"Not like this one," said Jasper. "Look closer."

The pig was standing with its side to us, and as we drew nearer, it slowly turned and looked straight at us—it had two heads. The second head was a little smaller, and its eyes were closed, but it was a sure-enough head.

"Gawd!" exclaimed Billy. "What is that? Is that a real head?"

"Sure it's real," said Jasper. "If you watch long enough, it'll open its left eye."

"No kiddin'," said Billy in wonderment. "How do you s'pose Mr. Pig decides which way to walk or which head gets to eat first?"

"I've studied on it," said Jasper thoughtfully. "The bigger head is the boss."

"Oh," said Billy.

"I've heard about stuff like this," said Gordon. "I read once about a chicken that—"

"This ain't no chicken," Jasper interrupted. "A chicken ain't nuthin' compared to a real pig."

"Oh, sure, Jasper, you're right, it's just that—"

"But what's it doin' here?" I asked. "Why's it at the Arcade?"

"What's it doin'?" said Gordon, puffing himself up. "That's plain enough. It's an attraction. It attracts folks, just like it attracted us. The Arcade knows it'll slow people down and bring 'em inside where they'll spend a pile of money. This is maybe the most valuable pig in the whole world. Ain't that so, Jasper?"

"Yeah," said Jasper unenthusiastically. He glanced at me and rolled his eyes. He didn't appreciate know-it-all Gordon jumping in and stealing his pig story.

The pig's bigger head snorted, and just as Jasper had told us, the smaller head winked its left eye.

"There ya go!" hollered Jasper.

"Woke the little guy from his nap," suggested Billy.

I put my hand on Booth's shoulder to get his attention. "Some pig, isn't it, Booth?"

Booth smiled faintly the way he did when he couldn't understand you.

I raised my voice almost to a yell. "Some pig, huh?"

Booth nodded. "Two heads ain't better'n one, I bet."

I chuckled. "Nope, I wouldn't think so."

"He'll still end up bacon," growled Gordon.

A sudden commotion farther down the street on the opposite side distracted us from the pig. Ducking through the crush of people, we found an open spot at the edge of the boardwalk.

"Hey, there's a man up there!" said Billy.

High atop the Pearl Saloon, a man was walking back and forth on a narrow platform. Torches had been placed at each end so that folks below could watch him.

Booth laughed gleefully. "Lunatic!"

"No," said Jasper, "he's worse than a lunatic. He's a fool settler."

"What's he doin' up there?" asked Gordon. "He come all the way to Kansas to break his neck?"

"Naw," said Jasper, "he's been hired by the Pearl as an attraction."

The man wobbled and almost lost his balance. Thinking he might fall, the crowd roared excitedly.

"He doesn't look too steady," I said.

"I guess he ain't!" said Jasper. "He's been up there since yesterday, and he ain't had nuthin' to eat or drink since."

"What!" I said. "Why would anyone do something as dumb as that?"

"I told ya. He's a fool settler. The Pearl is takin' advantage of his foolishness to fight the two-headed pig."

We all looked bewildered. Jasper sighed impatiently, but he was clearly pleased to have a new story to tell.

"It's like this. The Pearl was upset 'cause the Arcade's two-headed pig was ropin' in too many customers."

"Yeah, so?" I said.

"So, the Pearl got its own attraction. They found this settler that needed money and offered him twenty-five dollars if he could stay up on that platform for seventy-two hours. There's a catch though. He can't have no food or water, and he can't sit down. The longer he stays up there the closer he gets to his twenty-five dollars. But meanwhile, he's gettin' hungrier, and thirstier, and weaker."

Jasper glanced up at the settler. "Naturally people gather 'round. No one wants to miss it if he falls and breaks his neck. And after a while, they get thirsty and drift into the Pearl for a drink and a little gamblin'. But the Arcade's fixin' to fight back. It's hired a fellow that busts things with his head. Things like doors and fence posts and such."

"I'd like to see that," said Billy.

"But what happens if this settler falls?" I asked.

Jasper shrugged. "Can't say. Maybe they'll replace him with a three-headed pig."

Picturing that made us laugh, even if it did involve a bad end for the settler. Still, it struck me as odd that a settler would take such risks. Of course, I knew one reason. He was broke. Simple as that.

But was it? This man couldn't eat or drink, or even visit the outhouse. He had to be suffering terribly. It didn't make sense. To my mind, settlers were lazy quitters. They sat on their land, doing just enough to get by and hoping some other fool would come along and buy them out. Anything to avoid honest work.

And yet, here was a settler who was chancing his life for a bit of money. Why didn't he quit? Why didn't he pack up and go back to wherever he came from? That's what I would've expected.

My father was a man who believed in hard work and determination. As far as I was concerned, he was the very opposite of these shiftless settlers. But would he do such a thing if we had no money?

"Let's go," I said. I didn't want to think about this anymore.

"Ah, come on," whined Billy. "I wanna see if somethin's gonna happen."

"Yeah," said Gordon, "let's see if he breaks his neck."

"Let's go," I repeated sternly.

We went. And soon, Texas Street's many curiosities made me forget the settler.

In the gaps between buildings and on all the street corners, there were men selling candy, cigars, postcards, and especially, quack medicines. The cries of peddlers could be heard everywhere.

One fellow calling himself Professor Xerxes was holding up a brown bottle of something he called Ancient Egyptian Worm Destroyer. It was, he declared, made with "undiluted, triple-refined rattlesnake oil." None of the cowboys gathered around seemed to doubt there were rattlesnakes in Egypt.

In a glass jug at his feet, the professor displayed a coiled, forty-foot-long tapeworm—"recently driven from the body of the Sultan of Cairo by a single dose of this age-old elixir." We were impressed until Jasper whispered that the "tapeworm" was actually a long noodle.

Farther along, we came upon a gambler running a three-card monte game on the sidewalk. At first glance, he seemed ordinary enough. He'd show you three cards, a queen and two number cards. Then he'd turn them facedown and mix them around real fast on his little table. When he was done, you pointed to the card you thought was the queen.

Such games were common in Texastown, but this gambler had a gimmick—he had six fingers on each hand. He swore loud and often that his extra digits made him clumsy, but no one found the queen while we were watching.

Eventually, we came to the corner of Cedar and Texas. From here, the biggest, gaudiest, most talked-about saloon in the uncivilized world came into view—the Alamo.

FOURTEEN

No Texas cowboy came to Abilene without visiting the Alamo.

South Texas was a primitive place, and most cowboys were really just simple country boys. Many were still teenagers. For those coming up the trail, Abilene was a delicious taste of a larger world. Here they saw their first trains, maybe even their first painted houses. They were introduced to white sugar and white wheat bread. They bought their first toothbrush. Many had never seen paper money larger than a one-dollar bill.

To be sure, these things and others were marvels. But none compared with the experience of strolling through one of the Alamo's three big, polished, beveled-glass double doors. On summer nights, the doors were thrown open, and light from the saloon's dazzling interior fell onto the street in long glowing rectangles that tempted everyone who passed to enter.

The Alamo had another attraction—it was the "headquarters"

of Wild Bill Hickok. The cowboys didn't like Hickok. Some
said they hated him. Some even daydreamed of challenging
him. Still, they were curious about him, and awed, though few
would have admitted it. Hickok was a genuinely famous man,
probably the only famous man they would ever see.

As we neared the big saloon, I sprinted away, dodging
through the crowd. My friends were right on my heels. Laughing and yelling, we bounded up onto the Alamo's veranda and
rushed wildly through the center double doors. Once inside,
though, we all slid to a stop and just stared.

The Alamo was a palace. Most saloons were cramped, drab
places, but not the Alamo. At its broad entrance, the floor was
covered with thousands of tiny black-and-white tiles set in a
pattern that formed a huge longhorn head. The sweeping horns
spread across the full width of the room. Beyond the entry, the
floor was polished marble, an astonishing sight.

The huge room was crowded with poker tables, roulette
wheels, faro layouts, chuck-a-luck cages, and a tall rotating
wheel of fortune. On a raised stand far to the rear, an orchestra
played gentler music than the tunes heard in less refined bar-
rooms.

Everywhere you looked, there were towering potted plants.
From the ceiling, great gas-fired chandeliers with hundreds of
crystal prisms lit the room like sparkling daylight. Ornate gold-
framed mirrors shone against walls covered with rose-brocade
wallpaper.

Between the mirrors hung paintings of practically life-size
naked women, mostly plump, sleepy-looking ladies who seemed
to have gotten tangled up in their bedsheets. I felt sort of
immoral looking at them, but being as how I hadn't ever seen
an actual naked lady, I just couldn't make myself not look.

Jasper must've read my mind. He declared that the paintings

were "masterpieces" painted by French fellows. "You know," he said solemnly, "real art is perfectly all right to look at. They say it'll even improve your mind." I didn't think my mother would agree, but just the same, I improved my mind as much as I could.

The Alamo had real live women too. They weren't naked, but they wore disturbingly short dresses, and you could actually see their legs. Respectable women kept even their ankles hidden under long dresses. If it hadn't been for Texastown, I wouldn't have known what a woman's leg looked like.

These Alamo girls would sit in the cowboys' laps, laughing often and loudly, running their hands through the men's hair, and sometimes whispering in their ears. Not once had I seen Mother sit in Father's lap, or laugh like these girls, or just be so free.

After the paintings of women and the real women, it was the Alamo's bar that grabbed attention. The bar was a massive, black-walnut structure that ran the whole length of the saloon's south side. Behind it, a fifty-foot diamond-dust mirror reflected the bustling bartenders and the rows of gleaming glassware and liquor bottles.

In front of the bar, shoulder-to-shoulder Texans rested their feet on a polished brass foot rail and propped their elbows on the white marble counter. And if a man needed to wipe some beer from his mustache, a clean fluffy white towel hung from a ring just below the counter. For any cowboy who had just survived three months of trail dust, standing here seemed like heaven.

It wasn't heaven though. People said that the elegant bar was lined with bulletproof iron plating that the bartenders could dive behind if a gunfight broke out.

I started looking around for Hickok, wondering what would happen when he saw me and my friends. He might send us home, though I didn't think so. The marshal tended to leave folks alone until they stepped over the line. He didn't make much effort to prevent trouble, but when trouble started, people said he seemed to appear out of nowhere.

It wasn't long before I spotted him. He was on the far side of the room, his chair tilted back against the wall, studying his cards.

At the very instant I found him, his eyes snapped up from his cards and met mine. He found me clear across the crowded floor, looking right past all the other people and distractions. It was as if I had called out to him in an empty room. He stared at me, unblinking. I smiled nervously, but he didn't smile back.

I turned to Jasper, but I never got a chance to speak. Over his shoulder, I saw a horse and rider leap up from the street onto the Alamo's veranda. With a crash of hooves, the horse skidded to the open doorway only yards from where we stood. A young laughing cowboy was trying to spur the snorting beast into the saloon.

When my friends and I saw that wild-eyed, thrashing bronc, we scattered like rabbits. The cowboy, whooping and waving his hat, continued spurring his resisting mount. Suddenly, the horse jumped forward, but when its front hooves hit the smooth tile floor, they slipped from under him. Falling sideways into the doorframe, the horse dropped to its front knees. Even with this, the cowboy was still in the saddle.

By now everyone in the Alamo was on his feet. To my right, Hickok was coming fast through the tables. In a few seconds, the rowdy cowboy would have more trouble than he could imagine.

But as the horse was struggling back to its feet, a young man in a brilliant blue vest came forward and approached the cowboy. A few tables away, Hickok had paused, apparently curious to see what would happen.

"Whoa there, cowboy," the man called out cheerfully. "Glad to see you havin' a good time. You deserve it. It's a long way up from Texas, isn't it?"

The cowboy was surprised at first. "Uh, yeah, that's a fact, sir." Then he puffed himself back up. "And I'm aimin' to have the best damn time anybody ever had in this town!"

"Sure you are," the man went on. "I've tipped a few whiskeys myself tonight. Got me this blue flower-bed vest just today. How do I look?"

"Looks real fine."

"I came up the trail from Nueces. Where d'you hail from?"

"Matagorda," the cowboy said grinning proudly. "We come clean from the coast. Can't come no farther unless you start from the middle of the ocean."

"I knew it! You've got the look of an experienced hand. But I'm guessin' you're new in town, right? Just arrived?"

"Uh . . . yeah. Yesterday."

"That explains it then."

After a short silence, the cowboy frowned. "Explains what?"

"Oh, nuthin' much. It's just that this is the Alamo. It's a class place. Folks just don't ride horses into a place like this." The man lowered his voice. "It makes you look a little green."

"Oh," said the cowboy, embarrassed now.

"But," the man continued, "I'm sure if you go on down the way and ride your horse into Flynn's or the Old Fruit, they'll be glad to have you."

"Oh . . . all right. Maybe I'll do that."

"Sure, sure," said the man. "Of course, if you catch 'em in a bad mood, they might send you on your way with a load of buckshot, but most of the time they're real friendly."

"Well," said the cowboy, "I guess I'll be movin' along. Thanks."

"Anytime, anytime. And, say, that's a fine saddle horse you

got there. Admired him as soon as he came flyin' through the door."

The cowboy smiled, then turned the horse away and hopped him down from the veranda.

Hickok came up, looking pleased. "You did quite a job of letting the gas out of that Texas puppy."

The man responded with a grin and a dismissive little upward wave of his left hand, as if to say it had all been so easily done as to be unworthy of comment. But as his hand came up, I spotted a missing pinky finger.

I knew that voice had sounded familiar. But I could forgive myself for once again not recognizing Mike Williams. He looked like a different person now. Fresh from the barber and bathhouse, the trail dust gone, clean-shaven with neatly trimmed hair visible beneath a brand-new, cream-colored Stetson hat. And then there was that blinding blue vest. In fact, everything he was wearing from the boots up was new.

"He wasn't a bad kid," Williams declared, even though he himself was only a few years older than the "kid."

"Maybe so," said Hickok, "but he's lucky you got to him before I did. You still with Carrol?"

"Naw, Carrol's on his way back to Texas. I just signed on with the Olive outfit."

Hickok had been smiling until this. "Olive, huh."

"Yeah, they're holdin' a few herds hereabouts, and I thought I'd just stick around for a while. See what this town's all about."

"I'm not a big admirer of the Olives." There was a hint of a warning in Hickok's voice.

"I know, I know, some of 'em are mean as badgers. I'm just watchin' their cattle until I decide to move on. Nuthin' more."

Hickok nodded and then glanced at us boys. Exasperation crept into his face. For a moment, his eyes rested on me. "Mike," he said, "do me a favor. See these five gentlemen here? Feed 'em and send 'em home. Tell the bartender I said so." With no further comment, he turned on his heel and strode back to his poker game.

Mike looked us over for a moment, and then he noticed Jasper and me. His face brightened. "Well, lookit here! It's the candy kids. You two don't know who I am, do you? I'm all barbered up nice and pretty."

All of a sudden I realized Mike was more than a little drunk.

"I know who you are," I declared.

Jasper laughed gleefully. "Why, you don't even look like the same person!"

Mike threw back his head and howled with laughter. The quick motion caused him to lose his balance, and he almost fell over backward. Catching himself, he lurched back toward us. "By God," he almost shouted, "my own sweet mother wouldn't have known me t'other day." He ran a hand proudly over his shiny blue vest. "I am cuttin' quite a swell, ain't I?"

"I'll say," said Jasper. We all nodded rapidly.

"Yep, I'm fit to meet the governor. Plant yourselves right there, gents." He pointed to a nearby table just vacated by a group of cowboys.

As we were taking our seats, Mike stepped back to his own table, said a few words to his pals, and then poured himself another shot of amber liquor. He tossed the drink down in one swallow and then returned to us.

"Boys," he said, pausing to wipe a trickle of booze from his chin with a shirtsleeve, "the lunch counter"—he waved a little wildly in the general direction of the bar—"is at your service. How'd y'all like to sample some chow that's all the rage with the Texans?"

We all nodded eagerly. Oh, yes, we definitely wanted what

the cowboys liked. No one paid much notice to the curious twinkle in Mike's eye.

The Alamo's free lunch counter was at the front end of the bar and, despite being called *lunch*, was open morning, noon, and night. The idea was that giving away food, usually salty food, brought in customers and made them thirsty.

Mike ordered for us, and then returned again to his own table for another shot of liquor. He said something to his friends in a low voice, and they all burst out laughing.

A few minutes later, the attendant tossed some plates down in front of us. The smell almost knocked us out of our chairs.

"Phew, what is this stuff?" Jasper cried. "And what is makin' that nasty smell?"

"This looks awful," I added.

"My uncle don't *ever* serve nuthin' like this stuff," said Jasper.

Mike reappeared, smiling wickedly. "Well, boys, this is it, eat up."

"Yeah, but what is it?" asked Billy.

"Just eat," said Mike.

He reached over my shoulder, snatched a slimy gray thing off my plate and popped it into his mouth.

"Mmm-mmm, *that* is good eatin'!" His eyes seemed kind of unfocused now. "You rascals are eatin' like kings and complainin' about it." He pointed to his mouth. "This here's a oyster from Long Island, New York. Didja know that?" He snatched a grayish oyster off Billy's plate and slurped it into his mouth. "Brought here by train, packed in ice. A pure wonderment. Used to be we only got 'em in airtight cans. Now, though, it's as if they're fresh from the Yankee ocean."

He wiped his mouth on his sleeve again, burped, and continued. "That stuff you think smells so bad is Limburger cheese. It is a tad powerful, but that's the price you pay for its deee-lishush taste. That other article, the fat reddish one, is buffalo tongue. Good and chewy. Y'all best have some; buf is gettin' scarcer and scarcer these days."

We stared at him, then at our plates. No one made a move. I noticed that Mike was swaying slightly as he stood watching us.

As we hesitated, a frown formed on his face. He brought out a big Monogram "seegar," bit off the tip, and jammed it in his mouth. After a few false starts, he lit it with a weaving hand. Taking a puff, he pointed it at Jasper and then me. "Y'all eat! Go on, fly at it."

The foul smell continued to drift up from our disgusting plates. Even Mike's forceful prodding wasn't getting anyone to take a bite.

"I can't eat this," Jasper announced after a long pause. "I've . . . um . . . I've got a bad tooth."

"'Zat so?" Mike said. "What's wrong with it?"

"Broken" was all Jasper would say. I knew he didn't want to explain that a mere slip of a settler girl had busted it on Mike's gift peppermint ball.

"Lemme see," Mike said.

Jasper opened his mouth wide, and Mike bent real close and peered in. He put a hand on top of Jasper's skull and twisted it around until he got the light just right. Cigar smoke and whiskey breath mixed with the Limburger fumes curled around Jasper's face. Jasper started to look a little woozy.

"Hmm," Mike said, "looks like you cracked a chunk off'n one of the big ones in back." He poked at it with a finger, and Jasper winced. "Loose too."

He jerked up straight and again staggered back a step. "Whoa!" he called out to himself and then swayed back to Jasper. "Kid, you're in luck! A man in my outfit had a bad tooth, and a dentist just acrost the way fixed him up proper. Cheap too. Let's go see him."

"Who?" asked Jasper. "Your friend?"

"Naaaww! The dentist."

"Now?"

"Yessir, right now! That tooth ain't gonna fix itself. Besides, I got a idea, somethin' that'll make you famous. Somethin' that'll have 'em talkin' about you from here to the Lone Star State."

Jasper's eyes widened. Now he was interested.

FIFTEEN

We had apparently become Mike's pet project. He rounded up some of his friends, and we all marched out of the Alamo. Hickok eyed us as we departed, probably assuming we were being escorted home.

We plunged back into the mass of humanity jamming the sidewalk and started working our way north toward Texas Street. After we'd gone a little ways, Mike said a strange thing to one of his friends. "Quince, get my horse and bring it along to the dentist." I noticed he didn't want all their horses, just his. The man veered into an alley and disappeared.

I whispered to Jasper. "Are you sure about this? Why don't you wait and see the town dentist?"

"Can't," said Jasper, staring straight ahead.

"How come?"

"My uncle will get plenty sore if he has to spend any more money on me. Besides, maybe Mike really will make me famous."

I didn't think so. This whole thing was giving me a bad feeling. I kept my thoughts to myself though. Jasper was set on this, and arguing would be pointless.

As it turned out, the dentist was a small Chinese gentleman occupying a torch-lit space between the Planter's Hotel and the Bull's Head, a location that only added to my unease.

He was dressed in a thin, loose-fitting, dark outfit topped off by a shiny round cap. On his feet, he wore what looked like house slippers. And, amazingly, a long pigtail, like a girl's, dangled down his back. He was an odd sight in this sea of Texans.

As we approached, the dentist was standing quite motionless with one hand resting on an ordinary desk chair. The words PAINLES DENTIST were painted in crooked white letters on the seat back. At his side, a box of dental tools rested on a folding stand. Behind him, many long strings of beads hung down from a cord tied across the narrow walkway between the hotel and the Bull's Head. When we got closer, I saw that the beads were actually the teeth of previous customers.

The dentist sprang into action when he realized we might be customers. Bowing and smiling, he said, "Welcome, welcome," in a strange accent.

Jasper was hanging back, and so Mike helped him along with a little push. "Broke tooth," said Mike to the dentist. He thumped Jasper on the shoulder to indicate who needed attention.

"Ahhh," said the dentist. He motioned Jasper to the chair. "Sit, sit."

It was soon plain that the dentist spoke very little English, and since we spoke no Chinese, my bad feeling ticked up another notch.

Within minutes, a crowd began to gather. Soon there were about thirty people watching us and more coming. Jasper's already famous, I thought, and we haven't even gotten to his tooth yet.

After some coaxing from the dentist, Jasper opened his mouth wide. Mike stayed right there. He hovered next to the dentist, the two of them ear to ear studying poor Jasper. Every moment or so, Mike would stick a pointing finger into Jasper's mouth. The dentist kept trying to look for himself, but Mike was always ahead of him.

I could tell the dentist was getting annoyed, but he couldn't seem to chase Mike away. Finally, he asked Mike to hold up a lamp in a certain spot about four feet behind him. It didn't put much light in Jasper's mouth, but it got Mike out of the way.

Now the dentist studied Jasper in earnest. He poked and pondered as if Jasper's tooth were a true medical oddity. He um-ed and ah-ed. He made Jasper turn his head this way and that. Every so often, he would pause and think for a bit, and then he would begin prodding the tooth all over again. I began to wonder if Jasper's situation was more serious than I'd thought.

Everyone waited breathlessly for the dentist to announce his opinion. We waited quite a while. In due course, though, the dentist turned and faced us. He studied us with as much care as he had studied Jasper's tooth. His expression was thoughtful, slightly troubled. At last, he spoke.

"One dollar."

"Done!" yelled Mike. He set down his lamp and pulled a fat roll of cash from his pocket. Peeling off a bill, he slapped it into the dentist's waiting hand.

Just then the crowd parted and Mike's friend Quince appeared leading a glowering black horse. The bronc didn't like the big crowd close around it and looked skittish and bad-tempered. Mike didn't seem to notice. When he saw his snuffy horse, he grinned as if he'd been reunited with a long-lost brother.

Word was spreading that something interesting was about to happen. More and more cowboys were arriving all the time. Quite a few were coming out of the Bull's Head. Billy, Gordon, Booth, and I just stood there exchanging nervous glances.

Mike, it seemed, was a man known for his ideas. People just naturally came running when they heard he was up to something. I hoped this was a good thing, but my hopes were dashed as I listened to the cowboys around me. "Ho, boy," said a man to my left, "here we go again." Someone behind me said, "You s'pose there'll be a fire like last time?" Another suggested that maybe "we shouldn't be standin' so close."

Now I understood. People weren't gathering around because Mike's ideas were good. They were gathering because his ideas usually went bad—in a big way.

The dentist was at last ready to set to work. He motioned for Mike to come over and hold Jasper down, but Jasper waved Mike off. "I ain't doin' this unless Will here hangs on to me!" Somebody shoved me forward, saying, "Don't let him buck you off, kid."

After that, everything went okay until the dentist brought out his tooth-pulling pliers. Of course, Jasper went white as a sheet, but it was Mike that made a fuss.

"Whoa, now, perfessor," he cried, jumping forward. "You don't need them pliers. That tooth is loose, ya hear, loose! Just tie some strings around it, and we'll yank 'er out. Comprende?"

The dentist didn't "comprende." For a moment, he stared at Mike with a confused expression. Then, he burst into a torrent of angry, rapid-fire Chinese and wild arm waving.

Jasper was looking kind of low. "Ah, geez, I don't know about this."

"Jasper," I said, "we can still call it off."

Somehow, through all the yelling, Mike overheard this.

"Now, Jasper, don't you worry," he called out, "everything's under control. Just let me settle the perfessor down."

The dentist was still madder than a hornet. Mike rapidly pulled another dollar from his pocket and handed it to him. It had an instant calming effect.

"You said I'd be famous!" exclaimed Jasper.

"I did. I did. And you will!"

"How?"

"Son, that tooth's gotta come out. Right?"

"Yes, but—"

"Well, then, you don't want it pulled with a dang pliers. Why, that's how shopkeeps and stubble jumpers get their teeth yanked. Ain't that so? Well, ain't it?"

"I guess."

"Sure, sure it is. You ain't no farmer. You want your tooth pulled with some style, now ain't that so?"

"What kind of style?" I asked.

"Yeah," said Jasper, "what're you talkin' about?"

"I'm talkin' about pullin' that tooth in a way that's goin' to set people to marvelin' and talkin' for a month of Sundays."

"How?" Jasper yelled.

"With a horse."

"With a horse!" I said, stunned.

"That's right," said Mike, ignoring me and looking Jasper square in the eye, "with a horse." He turned and gestured grandly toward his grumpy black steed. "Not just any horse though. A gen-yoo-ine Texas cow horse. A mustang that was runnin' wild just one year ago. That horse there! The best damn cow horse in all the world!"

Jasper's eyes brightened. "But how?"

"Wait a minute," I said to Mike, "didn't Marshal Hickok tell you to send us home after we'd eaten?"

Mike gave me an indulgent smile, humoring my pathetic lack of understanding. "Well, sure, but, son, you know well as me that was before we were awake to this young gent havin' a terrible ailment needin' perfessional attention. Now, that's a fact, ain't it?"

"Yes, but—"

"Why, I'm sure to a certainty the marshal would lay into me somethin' awful if he was to find out I'd shirked my duty to you younguns."

Word of Mike's plan was now spreading like a prairie fire in a high wind. By now maybe three hundred folks were packed in a big semicircle around us, all craning their necks for a better look at Jasper.

One way and another, Mike showed the dentist that he wanted the tooth pulled with string. The dentist didn't like it, but he did what Mike asked. Reaching into his box of dental tools, he came out with some heavy silk thread, which he began wrapping around Jasper's tooth. It was a good-size rear jaw tooth, and the dentist decided it would need more than one thread to pull successfully. Jasper soon had four strands hanging down his chin.

And that was when Mike stepped up and swiftly fastened the threads to a knot at the end of a rope. The dentist watched, puzzled, perhaps thinking this was some odd local custom.

The dentist's confusion only increased when Mike's horse was brought up alongside Jasper's chair. Mike fed out some of the rope and began to step up into the saddle. Suddenly, the truth dawned on the dentist. "No, no, no!" he cried out. "I pull tooth! I pull tooth!"

Mike ignored him, slid into the saddle, and gave the rope a turn around the saddle horn. "Boys," he yelled to the crowd, "here we go!"

Now the dentist jumped forward waving his arms. "No, no! No horse! No horse!" In his haste, he bumped his box of dental tools off its stand. The box crashed to the ground, flinging shiny, tools beneath the nervous horse's feet.

Mike's horse just blew up. With a bawling scream, the maddened animal arched its back like a bow about to fire an arrow. Its head shot downward, deep between its front legs. Then it exploded upward. Straight up it flew, as if there were no such thing as gravity. Its eyes rolled up in their sockets until all I could see was the white. Another enraged grating scream split through the air like flying glass.

Jasper's tooth came shooting out, but no one even noticed, not even Jasper. Mike and his rampaging horse were the show now. The cowboys scrambled out of the way, falling over themselves, yelling, cheering, and whistling.

"Stay with him!"

"Ride 'em slick!"

"Look at that horse go!"

In midair, the horse's flank muscles pulled hard, and its body spun clean around, front to back. Mike was still deep in the saddle, one arm flying for balance, his face calm, matching his horse move for move.

Flying hooves whistled past Jasper and me. I flung myself back and sat down hard in the dirt, then scrambled away crablike as fast as I could. The dentist tackled Jasper and threw him, chair and all, into the opening between the buildings. Their falling bodies ripped loose the cord holding the curtain of old teeth, scattering them everywhere.

When the horse came crashing back to the ground, it hit like a pile driver, all four legs straight as fence posts. Dust shot out from under its hooves, and the heavy saddle leathers slapped like a gunshot. The shock of the impact blasted through Mike's body. His head jerked down, chin slamming into his chest, and his backbone wrenched until I thought it would surely snap.

But Mike wasn't broken. He was laughing. The horse reared and pitched with increasing power, determined to shake the human from its back. It tried every trick it knew, but Mike stayed on.

Then—and I'll always swear it did it on purpose—the horse bounded from open ground onto the covered sidewalk along the front of the Bull's Head. When it hit, sections of the wooden sidewalk split and collapsed, but the horse never slowed. With a snort, it again launched itself upward. Mike's head became a battering ram, smashing through the boards of the awning. The horse plunged down, its violent force splintering more of the sidewalk.

Up it went again, kicking out its hind legs. Hooves shattered a front window and sent customers inside diving for cover. Once more, Mike's head was slammed up into the awning, and boards flew off into the street. Mike wasn't laughing anymore, but somehow he was still in the saddle.

Suddenly it was all over. The horse jumped back out onto the street. Halfheartedly, it bucked a few more times. Then it just stood there, pawing the ground and throwing its head from side to side, as if to show it still had some fight left.

Mike slid down from the saddle a little painfully. His hat was crushed, but he seemed okay. After slapping some dust off his shiny blue vest, he took off his hat and studied it disgustedly. "I ain't even wore this hat one full day," he said. Then a big grin spread over his face, and he turned to the crowd of cowboys. "Say, ain't this horse a top! Put me right through that awnin'. Can't nobody say he ain't one smart horse!"

The cowboys cheered wildly.

"If this horse ever decides to run for Congress, I want y'all to vote for him."

The crowd cheered again. The horse snorted. I found myself wondering how Mike could ride like that while full of Alamo whiskey.

The Bull's Head was almost empty now. Everyone wanted to see what was happening outside. Among the mob, one man towered above all the others. His face flushed red with anger, he roughly shoved his way into the clearing where my friends and I were standing.

"By God," he roared, "what's goin' on here?"

Phil Coe looked as big as a house, an angry house. His pale eyes seemed lit by their own light within the darkness of his sharply angled face. Everything about him said power and menace. Mike's horse lowered its ears flat, and for the first time, even Mike looked uncertain. The previously rowdy crowd was now as quiet as mourners around a casket.

Astonishingly, I heard Jasper's voice.

"Mr. Coe, we was just pullin' my tooth." Jasper held up one end of Mike's rope. His tooth swung from the threads attached to the end of it. He leaned over and spit some blood into the dirt. "Things got a little out of hand."

Coe stared at Jasper like he was a polar bear painted up with red stripes. "What the . . . ?" was all he managed to say. He couldn't make heads or tails of what he was seeing. His angry shoulders slumped. He studied Jasper. Then he turned and looked at his splintered sidewalk and broken window. He took in the wrecked awning.

Suddenly it all seemed to make sense to him. His shoulders came back up, his chest inflated, and his eyes glowed again.

"Your uncle put you up to this!" he bellowed.

Jasper cringed. "Wha—*No!* No, you don't under—"

He never finished. Coe was on him. Coe's huge hand grabbed a wad of shirt at Jasper's neck and nearly lifted him from the ground. "Your uncle must think this is terrible funny. That jackleg's pigsty can't compete with my place, so he sends a runt like you to cause me trouble." Coe's fury was building. He tightened his grip, and Jasper's feet swung free in the air. "You wreck my place. You steal my customers. You make me look a fool. Now I'm goin' to—"

Mike stepped forward. "Mr. Coe, that boy ain't done nuthin'. Let's just talk this over, and—"

"Talk!" Coe erupted. He pointed at Mike with his free hand. "You got a part in this too. We'll see how you talk after I've pulled your head off, you damn Missouri rooster." Mike's eyes widened, and for the first time tonight, he was fresh out of words.

I couldn't watch this any longer. I had to do something. Coe was going to kill Jasper. I ran up and took hold of Coe's arm, the one holding poor Jasper.

"Let him go!" I screamed. "It's like the cowboy says. It's all an accident."

I caught a glimpse of Mike starting toward us, his face strained with fear. Then Coe's massive free hand seized my head like a ball and shoved me hard to the ground. When I opened my eyes, I heard a familiar voice.

"Coe, put the boy down." It was a calm voice, but not one a person would ignore, not even Phil Coe.

Still holding Jasper at the neck, Coe turned, stepping to one side. When he did, Hickok came into my view.

"Marshal, this ain't none of your business," said Coe. "Why don't you just toddle on back to your poker game?" The cowboys in the crowd laughed at this.

Hickok took a step closer. "Put the boy down."

"I ain't surprised you're a part of this," Coe said loud enough for the gathered cowboys to hear. "You always take the side of the Northern businessmen against us Southerners. I reckon you and Joe Hardeman are in this together."

Hickok moved closer yet.

"I ain't gonna stand for it," said Coe. "Us Southerners are gonna stick together on this. Ain't we, boys?"

The Texans cheered. They hadn't really liked the treatment Coe was giving Jasper, but they weren't going to side with Hickok under any circumstances.

"I've said all I'm gonna say, Marshal. Now you git. If you don't, maybe me and these boys will just take you apart." The Texans rumbled agreement. Meanwhile, Jasper dangled like a rag doll in Coe's grip, his face beet red.

Hickok had heard enough. As I'd seen him do before, he closed the remaining distance to Coe with startling speed. His chrome revolver flashed through the air and the barrel clubbed Coe just above his ear with a heavy *thunk*. Coe's eyes went blank. He took a wobbly half step and dropped face-first into the dirt. Jasper landed lightly on his feet, looking stunned.

For a moment, all you could hear was Mike's horse pawing the ground. The Texans just stared. I thought this must have been how the Philistines felt when they saw their champion Goliath go down.

Hickok took Jasper by the arm and hustled him over to me and the boys. "Go!" he said.

None of us moved. I don't know how I could have helped, but Hickok was alone facing a mob, and I couldn't walk away. My friends didn't move either. They were waiting on me. Hickok saw it. He leaned close and said, "Will, take your friends out of here." There was a note of pleading in his voice. Suddenly,

I understood how dangerous the situation was. Hickok had put me in charge of getting my friends to safety.

I turned away, and Jasper, Billy, Gordon, and Booth followed without a word. Walking slowly, I looked back every few steps. Hickok had drawn his other gun and turned to face the crowd. The cowboys were no longer silent. They were becoming an angry, surging mob, inching forward, tightening their grip around the marshal even as more and more cowboys were rushing to the scene from every direction. I could see certain men yelling and threatening, but the mob had its own sound, a deep murmuring growl. Phil Coe still lay at Hickok's feet, a sight that fed the Texans' anger.

The next time I turned to look, Hickok had disappeared. The crowd was all around him now, blocking my view. At any moment, I expected to hear a roar and erupting gunfire. I kept moving, filled with fear and misery, leading my friends away.

Then, I heard a welcome voice sing out over the din of the mob. Mike Williams was visible above them, probably standing on the dentist's chair, talking to the cowboys and grinning from ear to ear.

"Now, boys, this ain't nuthin' to get all het up about. The marshal couldn't let Phil here break that kid's neck. Y'all know that."

The mob quieted a bit.

"Listen here, Phil can get irritable and start thinkin' a little crooked. Now, ain't that so? Why, if he'd killed that kid, he would've felt just awful about it tomorrow mornin'."

A number of cowboys laughed, others nodded.

Mike pointed at some men in the front of the crowd. "Why don't you boys pick up Phil and take him inside. The rest of you go on in with 'em and order yourselves a drink. That'll warm Phil's heart considerable when he wakes from his nap."

That was the end of it. It was as if Mike had pulled a plug, and the Texans' anger had drained right out. In little more than a minute, the fearsome mob changed back into fun-loving cowboys, and the street began to clear.

My relief was hard to describe. Something bad, something terrible, could so easily have happened. And if it had, I knew it would have weighed on me for the rest of my life. A guilt from which I would never have been free.

We should have gone straight home, but we didn't. You can't just go home after a night like ours. First, you have to talk about it among yourselves. You have to share it, and explore it. Then you can go home.

For quite a while, we sat on the Mud Creek Bridge at the far western end of Texas Street. There, in the darkness, each of us told his version of what had happened. We laughed some, but everyone knew how close we'd come to disaster.

Sometime around four in the morning, we broke up. Jasper went south to his uncle's place. Billy, Gordon, and Booth all went north to their homes above the tracks. For some reason, I chose to walk back down Texas Street, like a criminal returning to the scene of his crime.

Texastown was a different place at this hour. There were still cowboys around, but most had ridden back to their camps. Many businesses were closed. Only a few of the lamps and torches continued to burn. It was almost peaceful.

Soon, I was back at the Arcade Saloon. This end of Texas Street was deserted. I stepped up onto the Arcade's sidewalk and went to the window where the two-headed pig had been. The window was dark now. I cupped my hands around my eyes and pressed against the glass. The pig was gone.

I turned away and continued down the sidewalk. At the

corner, I would cut north and head home. But my footsteps slowed. I felt I'd forgotten something. And then I was ashamed because I knew what it was.

Stepping out from under the Arcade's awning, I looked down the street, toward the Pearl. Despite the dimness, I could see him, a black outline against the gloom of the night sky. The settler stood at the far left of his high platform. The torches that had burned earlier were out now, and the settler was gripping one of them for balance. I couldn't make out his face, but I was sure he was watching me. I waved, but he didn't move. I waited a few moments, and just as I was about to turn away, his hand came up.

SIXTEEN

When I crept back through my bedroom window, I was grateful to be home. Our boring old house seemed a wonderfully safe and good place to be. In the darkness, I found my bed and sat wearily on its edge, letting out a deep sigh.

I heard a familiar creaking sound, followed by a low voice.

"Where've you been, Will?"

I jumped so high I flew off the bed and landed on the floor with a *thud*.

In the darkest corner of the room, Father sat in my loose-jointed old chair, waiting. At some point after I'd snuck out, he'd leaned in to check on me, as he sometimes did, and discovered I was gone.

I ended up telling him the truth—but not the whole truth. I decided to skip the part about starting a riot and nearly getting Marshal Hickok killed.

Even the whitewashed truth was bad enough to get me

restricted to the house and yard. I'd expected a whipping, but it never happened.

The following week, things were gloomy around our house. Mother feared for the health of my immortal soul, and I could only guess what Father thought because he hardly spoke a word.

Something was weighing on Father, and he was lost in his own thoughts. At meals, he only picked at his food. Twice Mother caught him going to work without his tie and shirt collar. Sometimes I would speak to him and he wouldn't hear a word.

Mother was especially patient and tender with him. Whatever the problem was, she appeared to understand.

Besides Father's strange mood, something else puzzled me. Every day that week, Mother was gone from the house all afternoon. And just as Father refused to explain his mysterious trips out of town, Mother refused to explain what she was doing. It was all very curious. Housework wasn't being done, meals were skimpy, and Father never uttered a word of complaint.

Life outside our house continued without me. Hickok's confrontation with Phil Coe and the cowboys caused the city council to pass an ordinance forbidding the carrying of firearms, even in Texastown.

By the time Wednesday came around, I was feeling pretty low. Spending half a week of summer stuck in the house was hard. At supper that evening, though, I got a piece of good news. Father announced that he'd gotten me a summer job—at the Drover's Cottage. Starting next month, when the season was in full swing, I'd be working in the hotel stables, putting up the guests' horses. I couldn't believe my luck. Sure, I'd have to muck out the stalls, but I'd be hanging around all the cattlemen. Mother didn't like this one bit, but Father said it was better than having me sneak off to Texastown in the middle of the night.

Thursday I got out of the house for a while. Mother sent me

to pick up some items at the Red Front. On the way, I passed the barbershop, and there was Hickok, tilted back in the chair getting a shave. His eyes were open and watching even as the barber worked on him, and he held a shotgun in his lap for all to see. I waved hesitantly. Hickok stared back, but then a hint of a smile appeared. It was enough. Life suddenly seemed a lot better.

But I was wrong. In fact, my life was getting ready to fall off a cliff.

The next morning, well before sunup, Father was shaking me awake.

"Will, after breakfast, saddle up General and Rambler. You're coming with me today."

"Where are we going?"

"You'll find out soon enough. Get moving."

About forty minutes later, Father and I were riding south on Buckeye toward the railroad tracks. I was still half asleep, and neither of us said much as our horses clip-clopped along.

When we reached the tracks, Father turned General east. I trailed along behind, feeling glum. Within a block, the big white Drover's Cottage loomed up. At this hour it was quiet, not yet crowded with bustling cattle people.

Just beyond, the Great Western Stockyards were strangely motionless. A few yardmen were standing around, but there were no stock trains and few cattle in the pens. Despite all the alcohol-oiled dealing that went on at the Cottage, not many cattle were being sold and shipped these days.

Several blocks farther on, we approached the large lot occupied by J. M. Hodge & Company. Row upon row of new farm machinery filled the lot around the Hodges' office and repair shop. The bare steel and fresh paint of plows, harrows, mowers, and reapers gleamed in the morning sun. Marvels of modern farming. Bah! I snorted in disgust.

I was pained to see Johnny Hodge standing with his father at the front of their store. When Mr. Hodge noticed us, he waved and called out, "Mornin', J.T.!" Johnny followed with a halfhearted wave of his own. He and I locked eyes for an instant, but Johnny never smiled, and I didn't wave back.

Father, though, wasted no time returning their greeting. "Good morning to you!" he called, plainly delighted by this commonplace ritual. Father liked people and liked being liked.

We followed the rails out of town. The vastness of the prairie opened up before us as the town's buildings thinned and fell behind. It was agreeably cool, and General and Rambler were feeling frisky, setting a quick pace without urging.

After traveling awhile, I could look back and take in all of Abilene in a single glance. As we moved farther out into the grasslands, the town shrank and shrank, swallowed up like a low sandbar in rising water. In time, only the top of the Drover's Cottage was visible on the horizon, and then it too sank beneath the waves of grass.

On our right, a winding band of trees marked the un-inhibited course of the Smoky Hill River. In a land this flat, nothing forces a river to go straight, and so the Smoky looped and curved this way and that like a bee exploring a flower bed. Over and over as we moved along, the river and its wrapper of trees would push toward us and then veer away.

Tucked in the bends of the river we could see crop fields and farmhouses, but almost no Texas herds. Most herds were held farther out, along the small creeks that meandered over the land before draining into the Smoky.

Until recently, this custom—farms on the Smoky, herds out on the creeks—had kept the peace by keeping the two sides

apart. But as farm sites along the Smoky filled up, newly arriving settlers had to claim land out on the creeks. Now the herds
and farms were mixing together, and that meant trouble.

About four miles out of town, Father turned north, into the
sparsely settled uplands. Soon both the herds and farms began
to thin out.

I was awake now and getting curious about where we were
going. Then, as if I'd been whacked with a fence slat, I realized
what was happening. Father was going to show me what he'd
been doing on his long, solitary rides. He was going to reveal his
secret.

As if he had read my mind, Father began to talk.

"Will, what you see today is to be kept secret. You may discuss it with your mother, but no one else. Understood?"

"Yes, sir."

"Will, I've often heard you call our settlers shiftless losers. I
know you believe what you say, but the fact is, you don't really
know any settlers, do you?"

"I see them in town. Anybody can see what they're like."

"Maybe you see what you want to see. Look, I'll grant you,
a few years back when the cattle first started coming and the
value of land shot up, we did get a lot of loafers looking for an
easy buck. Those people had no interest in building a life here.
They just wanted to grab a chunk of prairie and sit on it until
they could sell it for a profit."

I nodded, unsure what to say. Suddenly Father pulled up his
horse.

"Will, the settlers coming here now aren't like that. These
new people want a new life. They're builders. And if they fail,
Will, if they lose everything, if they're driven out, it will be a
terrible thing. No one will come after them."

"Then this would be a ranching area."

Father sighed. "I suppose. I hope not."

I almost gasped when Father said this. I knew he had some sympathy for the settlers, but I'd always assumed it was only because he felt sorry for them. It never occurred to me that he might actually support them. After all, one way or another, everything we had came from Texas cattle.

"But why? What's wrong with ranching?"

"This land is better than that."

"Mayor McCoy says this is natural cattle country."

"I know he does." Father hesitated, staring at me. I could see frustration in his face. "Well," he said finally, "the mayor doesn't know what I know."

"What do you know?"

Father smiled. "Let's get moving."

As we neared a little farm that seemed to be the farthest edge of settlement, Father raised his arm, pointing. "Look at these fields, Will. This farmer isn't lazy. He's worked hard and done a good, careful job of preparing and planting his land."

The fields, about twenty acres of wheat and corn, were a bright, healthy green against the rich brown of the soil. Not a weed or a wilted stalk could be seen. Every plant was strong and glowing, trembling gently with each breath of prairie breeze.

The farmer with a team of oxen was plowing a new field on the far side of his crops. After watching us for a moment, he gave a big wave. Father waved back, also swinging his arm in a wide arc. I realized that the farmer had seen him pass by many times before.

"This wheat and corn looks fine," said Father as we moved on, "but you know what's likely to happen to it?"

"Yes, sir."

I couldn't help but feel a little sad. This farmer's fields, like all the fields we'd seen, had been planted in the spring, only a couple of months back. The wheat was barely knee-high and the corn only a little further along. These were still young plants. It would be months before they were ready to harvest, months before the emerald wheat turned golden and the corn was heavy with ripe yellow ears, and by then . . .

"The hot winds will come and destroy them."

"Yes, probably so."

"But why does this farmer try? Why do any of them try?"

"Ahh, well, they hope for the best. Farmers live on hope. But out here, they'll need more than that to survive."

Father became quiet again, involved in his own thoughts, and soon we'd left the lonely little farm far behind.

We were riding into open prairie now. From this point on, there would be no Texas herds, no farms, no buildings, no railroad tracks—nothing. Back home, on the busy streets of Abilene, it was easy to forget how big and empty the prairie was. But not here. In this place the power of the wilderness was awesome. An endless world of grass and sky and silence.

The unbroken line of the horizon encircled us, impossibly distant. Twisting in my saddle, I let my eyes run along the border where land met sky, following it all the way around. I shouldn't have done it. The sheer size was too much, and fear rushed over me, a feeling of being small and helpless. From then on, I kept my gaze down, staring at Rambler's steadily rising and falling neck. Even so, I couldn't escape the sense that with each step of the horses, Father and I were being swallowed up.

The spell of the land was upon me now, and my mind filled with disturbing thoughts. Maybe we were lost and Father was hiding it from me. What if we were riding in circles, going nowhere? Who could tell? Every direction looked the same. Perhaps we'd never find our way home.

And then Father began to whistle, an odd, cheery little tune, something I'd never heard before. When I thought about it, I couldn't recall ever hearing Father whistle. It wasn't something he did. He seemed so happy. But why? To me, everything seemed empty and pointless.

Suddenly, a terrifying thought wormed its way into my head. What could possibly be out here for us to see? Was Father going mad? What else could explain his actions? This was a wasteland. Why would he come out here over and over and over?

I'd heard stories about people who were driven mad by the plains. It was said that some people's minds just couldn't cope with the unchanging flatness, the never-ending winds, the pure loneliness. But those were tales about poor, isolated settlers, not a successful man who lived and worked in town. I'd never once heard of a town person going crazy. But that didn't mean it couldn't happen.

Where was he taking me?

We continued north, maybe half an hour, maybe an hour, I couldn't say. My mind was so busy that time became blurry. And then, abruptly, I'd had enough. I pulled up Rambler and was about to demand to know where we were going when, apparently, we arrived.

"Ah-ha! There we are," said Father.

I looked up, and then around, but saw nothing except the eternal grass and sky.

"What?" I said.

"Oh, sorry," said Father, as if he'd forgotten I was with him, "the fellow we're meeting is just up ahead."

Just up ahead? I didn't see anything. My fears about Father's mind blossomed again.

"Where?"

Father pointed. "There."

I followed his arm, squinting. And sure enough, very far off, just below the horizon, I could make out a tiny dark dot.

We headed straight for that dot as if it were the world's smallest bull's-eye. We rode on and on, but it seemed like we never got any closer. Distance is mysterious on the plains. It stretches and wavers, and it's almost always greater than you think.

In time, the dot did begin to grow, and finally I could tell that it was a wagon. As we drew nearer, I made out a man standing beside it. A bit nearer yet, and I saw the man give us another of those big sweeping waves that are so common out here. Big spaces require big waves.

When at last we rode up to the wagon, a stocky, bearded man came forward and called out, "Hello, Mr. Merritt. Who's that you got with you?"

"Hello there, Caleb. This is my son, Will."

The man studied me for a moment. "Oh, yes, we've sort of met already."

As he spoke, a second person stepped from behind the wagon, a girl. She had a book in her hand, and I guessed she'd been reading on the shady side of the wagon. I knew her at once, just as I knew her father. It was the girl with light brown hair.

"Hello, Will," she said, smiling.

I felt embarrassed, although I couldn't tell you why. I held her gaze only for a fraction of a second before looking away. I knew I was grinning like a fool.

Father looked at me and shook his head in amazement. "You know Anna too?" He laughed to himself as he swung down from the saddle.

So, her name was Anna.

After we'd tied our horses to the back of the wagon, Father turned to Mr. Dunham.

"How's it looking, Caleb?"

"A fine sight. Some of the prettiest I've seen. Does Will know what's here?"

Father put a hand on my shoulder. "No, not yet." He sounded apologetic. "Will, why don't you and Anna go on up to the top of that rise and take a look."

I turned toward the rise but didn't move. From where we stood, the ground rose gently upward for about a hundred yards, hiding whatever lay beyond. Anna must have decided I needed a push. Taking me by the hand, she said, "Come on," and side by side we started up the grassy slope. My heart began to pound in my chest. Somehow I felt that whatever was up there was going to change my life.

"You really don't know what this place is?" Anna asked.

"I really don't."

As we moved closer and closer to the crest, my curiosity became almost unbearable. I wanted to run the rest of the way but couldn't bring myself to do that in front of Anna, or Father. I gritted my teeth and trudged along, eyes fixed on the uppermost point. Again, Anna sensed my thoughts. She laughed and sprinted away. Despite myself, I chased after her.

In a few moments, we were at the top. I slid to a halt and stared.

"There it is!" Anna cried breathlessly.

Yes, there it was, but what was it? I'm not sure what I'd expected, but this wasn't it. Before us was just another field of wheat whispering in the breeze. It was a small field, maybe only five acres, but nothing about it struck me as being worthy of a great secret.

And yet, there did seem to be something different, something . . .

"Isn't it beautiful?" exclaimed Anna.

It was beautiful. The field's tall, waving golden stalks set it off from the shorter carpet of green prairie grass surrounding it.

"Papa says it'll be ready soon," said Anna.

That was it! I felt as if I'd been struck by a bolt of lightning. This wheat was golden. It wasn't green. It wasn't young. This field was nearly ready to harvest. Ready now, long before the hot winds would come. It didn't seem possible.

"But how? How can it be so far along? There hasn't been time for it to ripen like this. It's only June."

Anna laughed and threw her arms out toward the field. "It's winter wheat, Will, winter wheat!"

"I don't understand. All the wheat I saw today was green. It was months from harvest. What is this?"

Anna looked at me as if I were a four-year-old. "That was spring wheat. It's all spring wheat—except right here, in this field. This is Minnesota winter wheat."

"Yes, but . . ."

"You aren't much of a farmer, are you, Will? All that other wheat was planted two months ago, in the spring, but this field was planted last September."

"September?"

"Uh-huh, nine months ago."

"But that can't be. What happens to it when winter comes, and it snows?"

"Nothing happens. That's why it's called winter wheat. Plant it in September, and by the time the snows come, it's already sprouted. Then during the winter it just sort of sleeps. The cold doesn't kill it. When the snow melts in spring, the roots find plenty of water, and the plants start growing again."

"A head start," I said.

"Yes," said Anna softly, "a head start. Winter wheat has

already had at least two months of growing time when spring wheat is planted in April."

I stared at the billowing wheat in the little square field. For the very first time, I wondered if maybe the settlers could make it here after all.

"Anna," I said, still looking out over the golden field, "why aren't all the farmers planting winter wheat? How come only your father has figured this out?"

"Oh, Will," said Anna, sounding startled, "my father didn't bring this wheat here. Your father did."

SEVENTEEN

After saying our good-byes, Anna and her father climbed onto their wagon and rolled eastward across the prairie. Father and I headed south. We'd gone only a short ways when I turned in my saddle and looked off to the Dunham wagon. When I did, I saw Anna looking back at me. I was already wondering when I would see her again.

Father and I rode a few miles, mostly in silence, before he began to talk.

"I suppose you've got questions about all this."

I did have questions, but I wouldn't ask them. Asking Father for his story would seem like approval, and I didn't want to approve of what I'd seen. Father, it seemed, wanted to help the farmers. And, in a way, with his small field, he'd become a farmer himself.

So I kept my mouth shut. After an uncomfortable moment, he sighed and began without me.

"Over a year ago, I happened upon a Chicago newspaper in

the lobby of the Drover's Cottage. In it I found an article about farmers who had come to America from northern Europe and settled in Minnesota. It said they were growing something called winter wheat and having great success.

"That got me thinking. Minnesota winters are colder than ours. If winter wheat could survive up there, surely it could survive here too."

Father paused and gave me a look. When I said nothing, he went on.

"In secret, I had some winter wheat seed shipped to me. Then I began looking around for a farmer to plant and tend it for me. About that time, Caleb Dunham came into my office. He and his family had just stepped off the train, and he was looking for advice on where to settle. He seemed like a good man, someone I could trust. So I told him about my plan."

"Why'd you keep it a secret?" I asked sullenly, my curiosity getting the best of me.

"I didn't want to get people stirred up until I knew winter wheat could make it here. So I hid the field far from town, far even from settler areas. If insects or disease or the cold of winter killed my wheat, I would've dropped the whole idea. No one the wiser."

"Father, why'd you do it? The Texans have been good for Abilene, and for us. Why change things?"

Father looked away, and after a moment he said, "Maybe I was bored."

Suddenly, he laughed, as if an unexpected truth had popped from his mouth, surprising even him. I didn't laugh with him, and when Father saw my frowning confusion, his hilarity vanished.

"Machines," he said.

"What?"

"Machines. That's the answer to your question. Have you ever thought about how farmers plant and harvest their crops?"

"No."

"By hand. They plant wheat by scattering seeds from a bag. They plant corn by chopping a hole in the ground with an ax and dropping in a few kernels. Many harvest their crops with a butcher knife, handful by handful. It's killing hard work, and slow. So slow that few farmers ever work more than twenty or thirty acres.

"But now there's something new—machines that do the work for them. You've seen them at Hodge's. They do the planting and harvesting automatically. Harrows that prepare the soil, drills that plant the seed, and harvesters that cut the grain. The farmer sits up high on a seat and rides over the land. The horses or oxen do most of the labor.

"And, these machines work particularly well on our flat, smooth prairie. Drive them in a straight line for a quarter mile before turning. With these machines, a settler can work five hundred, even a thousand, acres. If . . . if he can find a crop that will survive out here. A crop that will pay."

"Winter wheat," I said.

"Yes. Bring winter wheat together with these new machines, and we'll produce more food here than the world has ever seen. And this is what Mayor McCoy doesn't account for when he says this is cattle country."

"But even if that's so, Abilene is just fine with cattle. Why change? Why stir up trouble?"

"Will, I came to Kansas to make things happen. We're at a turning point. The future is open. Someone had to choose, and I decided that person would be me."

Father stared at me, measuring my reaction. The dark look on my face answered him.

"Settlers like Caleb Dunham came here to build and to make something of themselves. I understand these people.

I want them to succeed. And I believe that if they succeed, I will too."

"But, Father, the cowboys and cattlemen, they aren't bad people. They work hard. They have dreams."

"Oh, I'm sure that's true, Will. But I can't put my faith in those folks. A few years ago, during the war, they were shooting at me. Not easy to forget. Even so, that's not the reason for my decision.

"The cowboys don't want to make a life in Abilene, or even in Kansas. They want to sell their cattle and go home to Texas. But before they go, they get drunk, fire their guns in the streets, throw away their money, and give our town a bad name.

"I'm a down-to-earth person, Will. In time, I think you'll find that you are too. In the end, folks like us put our faith in the solid types, people like Caleb Dunham."

Father reached across to me and put a hand gently on my shoulder.

"This is a bittersweet thing for me. I'm excited that my wheat has thrived, but I'm burdened by what I'm about to unleash. If winter wheat takes hold here, it'll mean the end of the cattle trade. Many of my friends, particularly Joe McCoy, own businesses that depend on cattle money; they'll be ruined, and they'll know I was responsible."

Father sighed, and his hand tightened a bit on my shoulder.

"I also know that you'll be hurt by this, and that you will blame me if I can't convince you that I've made the right decision. That's something that weighs on me more than you might guess. But, Will, please, don't hold any of this against your mother. I have many reasons for what I do, but she has only one. She wants Abilene to be a safe place for you and your sister. That's all she cares about."

I didn't answer. I knew if I spoke, I would cry.

EIGHTEEN

There it was, sitting at the end of the long bar. And just as Jasper had said, it looked like the biggest glass jar in the world. I moved closer, slowing cautiously as I came within a few feet of it.

"Whew, Jasper, you weren't kidding. I've never seen one that big."

Jasper grinned. "Told ya."

It was around nine in the morning, and we were alone in the barroom of Jasper's uncle Joe's Elkhorn Saloon. Strangely enough, despite Father's winter wheat revelation, I was happy as a lark. A week had gone by and nothing more had happened. Life went on as usual, and it was easy for me to dismiss Father's peculiar little wheat field as just another game he played to keep himself entertained. He was, after all, a man with a restless mind.

Still, Father needn't have bothered swearing me to secrecy

about his wheat. Just the thought of Jasper catching wind of it gave me the chills.

"Uncle and one of the bartenders stretched it out on the floor yesterday," said Jasper. "Measured almost six feet long. It ain't a two-headed pig, but it's the closest the Elkhorn's got to an attraction. So go ahead, stick your hand out."

Unlike the Alamo, the Elkhorn was a murky, sour-smelling box, twenty-five feet by eighty feet, made out of rough-cut boards covered on the inside with dirty canvas. Uncle Joe didn't bother to lay down sawdust, so the bare plank floor was stained everywhere with tobacco juice. Behind the battered old bar, a rack of fifty-gallon whiskey barrels, each with its own spigot, lined the right wall. A ratty old elk's head was mounted above the barrels, spiderwebs draping the horns of the once-magnificent beast.

The Elkhorn was a fly-buzzing dump, even by Texastown standards. There wasn't a single thing in the place that was clean or refined or handsome. But Jasper and I weren't here for the atmosphere; we were here to settle a bet.

I moved closer to the big glass jar. Its bottom was filled with several inches of sand from the Smoky Hill. Lying coiled upon the sand, eyeing me as I approached, was a huge greenish gray rattlesnake marked with a repeating pattern of brown blotches.

"Where'd you get it?"

"Some fool sodbuster brought it in and wanted five bucks. Uncle gave him two. Hah! I guess snakes is the best-payin' sodbuster crop hereabouts."

I took another step, and abruptly the snake's body coiled tighter and its head lifted, curving up into a scaly question mark. The ominous sharp, papery sound of the rattle issued from the burlap-covered opening at the top of the jar.

"Go on," said Jasper, "stick your hand on it."

I extended my hand.

"No closin' your eyes. You close your eyes, you lose."

I nodded and continued inching my hand toward the big jar. The snake's head drew back, tightening the question mark. The instant my fingers touched the glass, the snake struck. Of course, it could only bang against the inside of the jar. I knew that. I knew there was no danger. But I couldn't help it; I jerked my hand away.

And lost the bet.

Jasper howled with glee. "I knew you couldn't do it!"

"I was sure I could. I was so sure," I said, shaking my head.

"All right," said Jasper, "pay up."

Reluctantly, I turned sideways to him, hunching slightly with my arm muscles tensed. Grinning wickedly, Jasper made a fist and drew it back. I closed my eyes, grimacing, but when the blow came, it was only a light tap on my upper arm.

"Why'd you go easy?" I asked.

"Ah, the bet was kind of a trick, so I can't really pound you."

"Why was it a trick?"

"Well, it seems like an easy thing to do, since you know the snake can't get you—"

Jasper paused to chew a sardine from a platter his uncle had set out. Then he grabbed a couple crackers from another platter. "Want some?"

"Naw. So why was it a trick?"

"Come on, this is regular food. None of that stinkin' Limburger or slimy oysters."

"Why's it a trick?"

"Oh, well, I've been watchin' men try to hold their hand to the glass without flinchin' for a week. Except for one person, no one's been able to do it. So I knew you couldn't either."

"Who did do it?"

Jasper laughed. "Wild Bill."

"Ah."

"Yeah, and oh boy, you shoulda seen it! The marshal come in to collect the city liquor license fee. Uncle kind of smirks and says, sure, he'd love to pay, but he don't have the money right now. A big fat lie. So the marshal smiles and steps over to the snake jar, looks into it real casual, and then lays his hand on the glass."

Jasper popped a sardine and cracker sandwich whole into his mouth.

"Jasper!"

"Sure you don't want some?" Jasper said, spraying cracker crumbs as he spoke.

"No! What happened?"

"Okay, okay, so a'course, as soon as Bill's hand touches the glass, that monster strikes out like lightning, and Bill don't even twitch. Don't even blink. Then he turns to Uncle, starin' him in the eye hard, hand still on the glass. Not sayin' a word. After about three seconds, Uncle caves in like a sodbuster's new-dug well, sayin' maybe he does have some cash layin' about after all. Couple minutes later, Bill's out the door with Uncle's money in his hand. Funniest thing I ever saw."

Jasper reached for another sardine, but his hand never got there.

"Hey, get yer grubby hands out of there!"

Uncle Joe had appeared suddenly from the back room. Before Jasper had time to pull his hand back, Uncle Joe flung a sopping bar towel that caught Jasper on the side of the head with a watery *splat* that almost knocked him off his feet. Jasper gathered himself and sprinted for the door with me on his heels. Outside, Uncle Joe's curses blew past us from behind, but he didn't pursue us.

Half a block away, Jasper slowed and wiped his damp neck and hair with his shirtsleeve.

"Ugh, whatever he was usin' that towel on sure stunk."

"You okay?"

Jasper grinned. "Yeah, I just wish I'd gotten a couple more sardines."

I grinned back, feeling a surge of admiration. Jasper was a tough kid. Life with his uncle was hard, and yet he usually managed to laugh at his troubles and keep his head up.

Mixed in with my admiration, though, was an uncomfortable sense of responsibility. I knew something that maybe even Jasper didn't know: I was a source of his strength. Our friendship was what held him together and kept him from flying apart. Something about that frightened me. What would happen if I couldn't be there for him?

We strolled eastward on Texas Street. In the morning, Texastown was a different place than it was at night. After carousing deep into the early hours, most cowboys left town and rode back to their camps. Only those too drunk to sit a horse, or those who had town business, remained as the sun came up.

In the morning hours, Texastown looked somewhat like respectable Abilene. Just a busy commercial place getting ready for a new day's business.

Wagons big and small rolled up and down Texas Street bringing supplies to the saloons, outfitting houses, and hotels. Men with cups of coffee stood in doorways watching the world go by. Others swept up with brooms, put away newly delivered goods, or sat at sunlit window tables doing paperwork.

At the next corner, Mr. Edwards pulled his ice wagon up to the Alamo. The cowboys in recent times had decided they liked their beer cold rather than room temperature. So now the railroad regularly delivered carloads of ice cut during winter from the frozen Republican River up in Nebraska and then stored. Each morning, Mr. Edwards made the rounds, delivering heavy foot-square ice blocks for six cents a pound.

Other wagons, piled high with barrels of whiskey, gin, and other hard liquors, trundled along from saloon to saloon.

Wagons also crowded around Jake Karatofsky's Great Western Store. Jake was a Russian Jew who had somehow ended up in Kansas selling supplies to cattle outfits. At the rear of his store, hulking freight wagons were delivering tons of goods from the railroad warehouse. Out front, bleary-eyed, hungover Texans were loading up supplies, stacking them high in their smaller camp wagons.

"Ho, watch out there, boys," a man called as he tossed a big bucket-load of watery kitchen scraps out the front door of the Old Fruit Saloon. Jasper and I skipped ahead hastily to avoid the flying glop.

It was a close call, but we weren't offended. Front doors, back doors, side doors, and windows were seen by all as open invitations to get rid of anything unwanted. Trash lay scattered or in heaps outside nearly every opening in every building. The town would have buried itself if it hadn't been for the troops of hogs that roamed the streets and alleyways devouring much of the mess.

Still, there were many things even the hogs wouldn't eat. Ashes discarded from stoves and fireplaces during the winter lay in dirty gray piles behind most buildings.

Adding to the ashes was grimy sawdust. Unlike the Elkhorn, most saloons spread a layer of sawdust on their floors to soak up the tobacco juice, spilled drinks, and sometimes blood that landed there. Each day the sawdust was swept out and replaced. Over time, so much sawdust collected behind these places that you might've thought they ran sawmills rather than gin mills.

Boxes, barrels, crates, and empty booze bottles lay everywhere. And amid the clutter, there were always a few snoozing cowboys left over from the night before, sleeping where they fell after one drink too many.

Strangely, Texas Street was also strewn with playing cards. To reduce the risk of cheats using marked cards, gamblers opened fresh decks several times a night. The used cards were often thrown out a window. Now, as Jasper and I walked along, each gust of wind swept up the forsaken cards and sent them swirling about like autumn leaves. The wind also fortified the atmosphere with powdery horse manure, ashes, sawdust, and the ever-present Kansas grit. To keep our eyes clear, we pretty much squinted constantly.

"Hey, Jasper, look there. It's the Wonder."

In the window of the Lone Star Restaurant, the Armless Wonder was eating breakfast.

"Yep, sure enough," said Jasper, "and we get to see him for free."

The Armless Wonder was a gentleman who had apparently been born without arms. He had a sizable tent down at the southern edge of Texastown, where he charged the cowboys a dollar apiece to view him performing a variety of tasks with his wonderfully agile feet. The high point of every show came when the Wonder grabbed a rope between his toes and sent a whirling loop across the tent and around the neck of a stuffed longhorn. The cowboys cheered until they were hoarse.

We waved at the Wonder. He nodded to us and then slipped a forkful of scrambled eggs into his mouth with a bare foot.

"You know, Jasper, I'm still thinking about Marshal Hickok scaring that fee money out of your uncle. What do you think would've happened if your uncle hadn't given in?"

"I don't care a damn. Course, I guess I don't really want to be a orphan again."

"Aw, come on, the marshal wouldn't of shot him."

"I don't know. He's got hangman's eyes when his back is up."

"He's real good to me, but I've read he's killed dozens and dozens of men."

"I'll betcha he's killed more'n that."

"How many d'ya think?" I asked.

"I don't know. Hundreds, maybe."

"Go on! Hundreds?"

"Sure, 'specially if you throw in Confederates."

"Naw, you can't count Confederates."

"Why not?"

"That was war. Everybody kills folks in a war."

"Well, I still think Confederates should count."

"I saw a magazine that said he took a Cheyenne war lance right in the leg a few years back."

Jasper nodded. "Stuck clean into the bone, that's what they say."

We both cringed at the thought.

"But you never know for sure," I said. "Folks are always gassing about stuff they don't know nuthin' about."

"You wanna ask him how many he's potted?" said Jasper.

"Do you?"

"Sure. He won't shoot us."

I smiled. "Good, 'cause he's right there." I pointed up the street. "I dare ya."

"I will. Don't think I won't."

NINETEEN

At first glance, it seemed Hickok was just standing in the middle of the street. After a moment, though, I saw him gesture to a cowboy over by the sidewalk and call out, "Hey, Texas, you aren't done there. Dig it out deeper."

The cowboy was working in the gutter with a shovel, which was peculiar enough, but the truly odd thing was that he had a heavy chain leading from his ankle to something that looked like a big black cannonball. And it might well have been a cannonball, because it took a big effort to drag it along whenever the cowboy took a step forward. And he wasn't the only one. Three other cowboys were close by, and each of them was also attached to a shovel and a ball and chain.

"Jasper," I said, "look at that."

Jasper frowned but said nothing. I knew he didn't like to see cowboys working like farmhands.

Hickok had his back to us as we came up. With one hand

resting casually on the top of a gun butt and the other holding a cigar to his lips, he seemed relaxed and confident.

But then Jasper scuffed a foot, and instantly Hickok spun toward us. I saw that his free hand had slipped down over the revolver. He hadn't drawn the gun, but Jasper and I froze in our tracks anyway.

When he saw who we were, Hickok was clearly annoyed and embarrassed.

"I can stand a good deal, but I won't stand sneaks," he declared roughly.

"We weren't trying to sneak up on you," I said. "We were just—no, Jasper was just going to ask you a question."

Hickok flipped his cigar into the street. Still annoyed, he turned to Jasper. "All right, ask."

Jasper gulped. "We only wanted to know what you're doin' out here with these Texans." He gave me a shamefaced glance.

"These gentlemen are wards of the city," said Hickok. "We feed 'em, put a roof over their heads, and in return we ask only that they do a little something for their keep."

"So . . . they're prisoners?" Jasper said.

"Exactly."

Hickok pulled a fresh cigar from his pocket and pointed it at one of the shoveling cowboys. "Hey, Texas, tell the boys here why you're working the gutter."

The cowboy sneered and called back, "'Cause Texans don't get no more show than a dog in this shit-box Yankee town."

Hickok got a dark look in his eyes, and I thought he might go over and give the cowboy a thrashing. Instead, he sighed heavily, and said, "What our saucy Texas friend means to say is that he rode his horse, at a gallop, down a busy sidewalk, knocking a fellow clean through a window. The other three did things just as thickheaded."

A dark look came over him again. "You know, if these mouth-fighters knew the wholesome dislike I have for rascals, they'd step careful around me."

Hickok sighed again. "I guess I'm touchy this morning. I'm on duty till four in the morning, and usually I sleep till noon. But today I'm up early to take care of my street commissioner duties. Puts me off my feed. Did you know I'm now street commissioner as well as marshal?"

Jasper and I shook our heads.

"Well, I am. City council voted me that honor just a week ago." Hickok bit off the tip of his cigar, spit it out a little too forcefully, and lit up. "Anyway, our four guests are improving the flow of the municipal gutters."

"'Tain't right to make 'em dig," Jasper muttered, looking down at his feet.

"What's that, son? Speak up."

Jasper straightened. "'Tain't right to make 'em dig," he said in a low intense voice. "They ain't farmers."

"Son, on this day, these fools belong to me. If I want 'em to be farmers, they'll be farmers."

"Can't you find somethin' they can do on a horse?"

Hickok laughed. "On a horse! Like what? Ride out of town and disappear?"

Jasper's passion wilted. He turned toward the laboring cowboys. "I don't know, just . . . somethin'."

"Doesn't seem right for the council to give you extra duties," I said quickly. "Not without asking anyway."

Hickok nodded, still studying Jasper suspiciously.

"Anyway," I said, "we came over to talk because we were wondering, you know, because we read all the books and magazines about you, and—"

"Six thousand," Hickok interrupted.

"Huh?"

"Six thousand."

"Six thousand what?"

"You were about to ask how many men I've killed. The answer is six thousand, or thereabouts."

"Is that on the square?" said Jasper. "Or are you pullin' our legs?"

"You aren't calling me a liar, are you, son?"

"Oh, no sir, it's just that—"

"I'll tell you, confidentially," Hickok went on, lowering his voice almost to a whisper, "and I don't think I'm cutting it too thick here, six thousand might be on the low side, but I'll not have it said that I'm a braggart."

"Does that six thousand include Confederates?" I asked.

"Confederates! Absolutely not. War killing doesn't count. I only count genuine civilians."

I gave Jasper a victorious smirk before turning back to Hickok.

"But you've been here all summer," I said, "and you haven't killed anyone, not even one."

"Well, that's right, I admit it."

"But—"

"Now hold on, I know you cubs think this killing thing is all fun and glory, but it's also a lot of hard work. I was shooting, oh, a dozen men a day, month after month—all black-hearted scoundrels who deserved their fate, mind you—anyhow, I had killing down to a fineness."

Jasper and I nodded in awed wonderment.

"This went on for years, and finally all that killing just sort of lost its novelty. Truth is, I was ready for a breather around four thousand, but I kept at it, not wanting to be thought a quitter. But can you guess what finally made me call a halt?"

"Fear of eternal damnation?" I suggested.

"Well, there was that, naturally, but the thing that really tipped the scales was the expense. Wearing out all those guns, buying carload lots of ball and powder. I just couldn't bear the cost."

"How come the magazines and books never mention six thousand?" I asked.

Hickok gave me a sly smile. "Because they know no one would believe such an outlandish tale."

When I saw Hickok's smile, I knew we'd been had. "And neither should we?" I said.

"Exactly. Neither should you."

I looked at Jasper and we both laughed at our own gullibility.

"Well, then," said Jasper, "I read in *Prince of the Plains* that you took a Cheyenne war lance in your leg?"

"Yes."

"Did it go right into the bone?" I asked.

"Yes."

"But if you didn't kill six thousand," said Jasper, "then how many did—"

"It's not a question one man ought to ask another."

And now Jasper and I had another realization. This man wasn't Wild Bill Hickok, the ten-foot-tall, indestructible hero of the dime novels. He was a real man, and we were asking him questions we would never have asked anyone else. Suddenly we both felt ashamed.

"Oh . . . sorry," said Jasper.

"Yeah," I added sheepishly, "we didn't mean to—"

"I know you didn't," said Hickok. He clapped me on the back.

Abruptly, as if something had just occurred to him, Hickok looked all about the street, up, down, left, and right. I recalled how edgy he'd been when we first came up.

"Hey, Wild Bill," one of the prisoner cowboys called out, "you look a little cat-eyed. You aren't expectin' anyone, are you?"

"Scairt of his shadow," said another with a cruel laugh. "Hell, I'd be fish-belly white all the day long if I had as many folks lookin' to kill me as is lookin' to kill him."

"Is someone threatening you, Marshal?" I asked.

"The whole state of Texas is threatenin' him, kid," said the cowboy nearest to us. "Someday someone is goin' to shoot ol' Wild Bill so full of holes he won't hold hay."

Hickok took another puff of his cigar and tipped the ash into the street. "Time will tell who gets filled with holes. Meanwhile, you monkeys stay at them gutters."

Now another voice was heard.

"Say, Bill, I hear someone put a pistol ball right next to your ear last night."

It was Phil Coe. He was leaning against an awning post with a fat quid of Navy plug chewing tobacco in his cheek and a troublemaking grin on his face.

"Big ol' lead ball makes a nasty sound when it slaps that close, don't it? You can just imagine how it'd scramble your brains." Coe leaned and spit a stream of tobacco juice in our general direction.

"Coe, I've still got some shovels left," said Hickok. "I can have you digging gutters right quick."

"Only askin' after your health, Wild Bill. No need to get het up."

"Ask after someone else."

"Fair enough. Young Mr. Hardeman, how're you recoverin' from your recent tooth pullin'? Our last conversation was cut short."

Jasper glared. "None of your business."

"Ya know, I sent your cheapsneak uncle a bill for my broken

window, et cetera. He told me to go to the devil. I'm not one to low rate a man, but he wasn't very polite."

"He's polite as he needs to be," said Jasper.

"Yes, and the same can be said of you, young Mr. Hardeman." Coe's gaze shifted back to Hickok. "I'm not one to forget a wrong done me."

"You're walking right on the line with me, Coe," said Hickok. "Go about your business."

"Well, mistreatment of fellow Texans is my business, Wild Bill."

The prisoners had stopped working. They smirked and snickered and generally offered Coe whatever support they could.

"Say, boys," Coe called out, "let me tell you somethin'. If it weren't for Texas cattle and the money you Southern boys spend, this town wouldn't be more'n a buffalo wallow. Ain't that so?"

The cowboys all nodded, and one of them called out, "That's the truth." Another threw down his shovel, and immediately the others did the same.

Hickok began moving toward Coe. "Get going, Coe."

Coe only smiled. "Uh-oh, hold on there, Wild Bill. You think I'm trouble. Here comes real trouble." He raised his hand and pointed up the street.

We all looked and saw Mayor McCoy coming toward us with a quick step and a determined look.

"You need to be more careful, Wild William," Coe said. "The mayor almost caught you nappin'. If he'd been of a mind, he could've come up behind and blowed your guts out."

I knew Hickok wanted to beat Coe to fragments, but the appearance of the mayor made that impossible. Frustrated and annoyed, he whirled on the rebellious chain gang cowboys.

"Pick up them shovels damn quick!"

The cowboys heard the tone of his voice and snatched up their shovels like they were long-lost friends.

"Ah, Marshal," boomed Mayor McCoy, "excellent. Do you have time for a word?"

Hickok scowled. "No."

The mayor smiled grandly. "Just a quick word, Marshal, just a quick word."

Hickok flipped his second cigar into the dirt, and folded his arms across his chest.

McCoy looked at me, and his exuberance faded. "What are you doin' down here, Will?"

"Nuthin'," I said, picking at something on my shirtsleeve.

"Well, you shouldn't be—"

"Mr. Mayor," said Hickok, "what is it you need?"

McCoy let his disapproving gaze linger on me briefly before turning to the marshal.

"Marshal, it's good to—"

"Mr. Mayor," Coe called from the sidewalk, "Texastown welcomes you. What thievery brings you below the tracks?"

The chain gang cowboys guffawed loudly. With some effort, the mayor maintained his cumbersome smile. Making a show of ignoring Coe and the cowboys, he moved closer to the marshal. As he came in, the marshal drew back slightly.

"Ah, well," the mayor began in a low voice, "I see you have the heathens hard at work for the public good."

Hickok only nodded.

"Where are the rest?" the mayor asked, glancing about.

Hickok frowned. "This is all of them."

Now McCoy frowned. "This is it! Marshal, please, Texastown is a modern-day Sodom and Gomorrah. How can there be only four prisoners after a busy weekend? There should be dozens."

Hickok didn't bother to respond. Among Abilene's solid citizens, he was earning a reputation as a man who was difficult to control. Our previous marshal, Tom Smith, had had good relations with the town fathers, but Hickok was hard to get to know and cared little for rules and regulations.

Of course, Marshal Smith was dead—murdered—so it was tricky for folks to tell Hickok to be more like him. Still, there were many who thought Wild Bill was too wild. He drank, played poker every night, kept company with a variety of women, and refused to stir himself unless the Texans were causing serious trouble.

Given this attitude, one might've thought the Texans would've loved him, but they didn't. When a situation did require action, the marshal usually preferred his own harsh justice to a formal arrest. Disorderly cowboys were run out of town amid a hail of insults or simply knocked unconscious with the barrel of his revolver. To the proud Texans, such humiliating treatment was worse than being shot.

So, the Texans hated Hickok, and the town fathers distrusted him. And yet, everyone agreed, he had kept the peace.

McCoy glanced at Coe and then stepped a little closer yet to Hickok. He was about to speak when he again took notice of Jasper and me.

"You boys run along," he said. "I've got town matters to discuss."

McCoy's voice was naturally loud, and Coe must have overheard. "Yeah, boys," he yelled, "y'all run along. The mayor and Wild Bill want to cook up some mean piece of business in private."

We started to leave, but Hickok caught me by the arm. "Mayor, just consider these two special deputies, unpaid of course. Besides, I bet whatever you're about to say will give 'em an education." Jasper and I beamed.

"Oh, for cryin' out loud," exclaimed the now-exasperated mayor. He then lowered his voice again. "Listen here, Marshal, you don't seem to understand the situation I'm in."

"What situation is that?"

"Well, crime is, of course, repugnant, but from a city revenue standpoint, it isn't entirely a bad thing. Properly handled, arresting and fining Texans helps keep taxes low on our law-abiding citizens."

Hickok looked scornful.

"Now, Marshal, your salary is expensive, so naturally we expect you to pay your way. These Texans always squander their money and go home broke, so where's the wrong in taking a modest slice for the good of the town?"

Hickok rolled his eyes. "Ah, the good of the town."

"The good of the town!" echoed Coe. "Ho, watch out, boys, a Yankee hand is gettin' ready to grab some Texas money." The chain gang cowboys hooted and began pounding their shovels on the ground.

McCoy fumed. "Yes, the good of the town. You know I'm all for the cattle trade. I'm the one that brought it here. But some of these Texans are a nuisance, and it's fitting for them to pay for the disturbance they bring upon us."

I could tell that when the mayor said *us*, he wasn't including the marshal.

"And besides," McCoy continued, returning to a near whisper, "I've got that everlastingly pious Reverend Christopher on my back. I can hear him now—Abilene is a byword for everything vile, we reek of brimstone, and all that. It never ends. I need arrests, lots of them, something I can throw in his face when he comes whining about how Abilene is the devil's playground."

I couldn't stay quiet any longer.

"Mayor," I said, "Mr. Coe thinks the marshal is too hard on the cowboys. You think he isn't hard enough. What's he supposed to do?"

The mayor didn't even look at me. "The marshal isn't here to please Mr. Coe," he declared in a voice that suggested I was the worst kind of imbecile. "Tell me, Will, what would your parents say if they knew you were down here?"

That shut me up.

But it annoyed Hickok.

"Mr. Mayor," he said, now keeping his own voice low, "last night someone took a shot at me in the dark. Two nights before someone put three shots through the walls of my cabin. Not a day goes by that I don't get a death threat in the mail, and most all of them have a Texas postmark."

"I understand, Marshal, but—"

"No, you don't! My job is to keep the peace, and so far I have. We haven't had a single death this season. If you want to do my job, if you want to stand in the street with a big bull's-eye on your chest, you go right ahead. But if you ever again come around talking city finances or preacher troubles, I'll kick your sorry butt from one side of this town to the other. You understand?"

McCoy looked stunned, but he recovered quickly.

"Oh, Marshal, we've clearly had a serious misunderstanding. We all know you're doing a difficult, dangerous job, and we honor you for it."

Hickok nodded.

"I can't hear a word," Coe called out, "but y'all's conversation sure looks interestin'. Say, Mr. Mayor, why is it an upstandin' citizen such as myself can't be let in on the town's dirty laundry?"

The mayor had been ignoring Coe, but now he spoke back. "Mr. Coe, you are not a citizen, and you wouldn't be upstanding if you were."

Coe had been enjoying himself, but now his smile vanished. "Mr. Mayor, I bet you wouldn't talk like that if your hired killer wasn't standin' next to you. We'll see how you talk if I ever run into you alone."

"Coe," said Hickok, "take yourself to some other quarter, now, or you'll wish you had."

Coe leaned and spit a big brown wad of tobacco into the street. Straightening, he gave the marshal a baleful look, waved to the chain gang cowboys, and sauntered off. But he hadn't gone fifty feet before he paused and leaned up against another awning post, staring our way.

"Well, I have to get going," said the mayor, his voice rising to its normal lofty volume. "Lots to do. And, Marshal, my sincerest apologies."

Hickok didn't even bother to nod.

"Good day, Will, Jasper," said the mayor. He walked away briskly, but after a few steps, he turned and came back.

"One more thing, Marshal. And I am reluctant to bring this up, but, well, the town feels it's important." He paused here, more cautious than before, waiting for Hickok's approval.

"What?" said Hickok.

"Well, it's these dogs, Marshal. They're a threat to the public. They roam the streets in packs. Chase the children. Bark all night. Threaten us with hydrophobia. Our ladies complain the curs relieve themselves on the vegetable boxes on the grocery sidewalk. Of course, the groceryman is partly to blame for that, putting them so low, but—"

"Mr. Mayor!" said Hickok. "What do you want?"

"Too many loose dogs, Marshal. Too many! I think most come up the trail with the Texans. Worthless curs. Anyway, the council has authorized the city treasurer to pay you fifty cents for every dog you shoot, or otherwise eliminate."

Hickok's shoulders sagged slightly. "You want me to shoot dogs?"

"Yes, but only the ones *without* city-issued dog tags. City tags are round with a big *R* on them, *R* for *registered*."

The mayor grinned, apparently quite unaware that the world's most famous gunman might consider the assignment demeaning.

Hickok stared at the mayor and then closed his eyes and rubbed his forehead. "Good Lord" was all he said.

"I knew you'd be pleased," said the mayor. "Extra money for you. Easy money at that." He turned again to leave, but again something else occurred to him.

"Speaking of money, the treasurer tells me that you're one day late with your month-end accounts. Remember, your statement and collected fees need to be turned in on the first Monday of every month. Just a friendly reminder. Well, good day to you all."

With a tip of his hat, McCoy strode off in the direction of the Cottage. Hickok watched him for a moment and then drew his revolver, pointed it in the mayor's direction, and fired. Instantly, a plume of smoke flew out before us, hiding the mayor from view.

I am sure that my heart actually stopped beating. The shock of what I'd seen was so great I almost fell to the ground. A moment later, though, the smoke drifted away on the Kansas wind, and there was the mayor. He was on his feet, staring bug-eyed at us, mouth agape, hands held out before him, and, as far as I could see, uninjured. A few playing cards fluttered past his feet in the breeze.

Hickok calmly gestured up the street, past the mayor, with his revolver. We all looked, even the mayor, although he was clearly reluctant to take his eyes off the marshal. About forty feet beyond the mayor, a brown and black mongrel dog lay dead in the roadway.

"You owe me fifty cents, Mr. Mayor," Hickok called out.

TWENTY

Two weeks had passed since Father had taken me to the winter wheat field. By now, I'd convinced myself that he was not going to turn Abilene on its ear after all. Father was always coming up with ideas, and most were false starts. Winter wheat was just one more half-baked scheme thrown into the dustbin.

It's easy to believe what you want to believe.

About five o'clock Saturday afternoon, Mother came to my room and told me to put on my best suit. Excepting little Jenny, we were all going to a meeting at the courthouse. I noticed that she had a folded square of midnight blue velvet cloth held under her arm.

Meetings at the courthouse were common, but until now, no one had ever asked me to go. It was peculiar. And, when I thought about it, Mother had never gone either. Most people, men and women, believed it wasn't proper for ladies to involve themselves in public affairs. Women were to concern themselves with matters of the home and leave the larger issues to the worldly wisdom of men.

Still, I was pretty sure I knew what the meeting was about— it was about our angry settlers.

The problem began with the low price of a cow. Cattle buyers weren't buying because they were waiting for prices to go lower. And herd owners weren't selling because they were waiting for prices to go higher. As a result, Texas herds were piling up all around Abilene, and that was trouble for the settlers. Crops were being trampled, vegetable gardens eaten up, fences knocked down. Naturally, the settlers were sore at the Texans, but they also blamed Abilene for doing little to solve the problem.

Too bad for them, I thought as I slipped on my suit coat. The longhorns are here to stay, and those whining sodbusters better get used to it or leave.

When I came downstairs, Mother and Father were back in the kitchen talking in low tones. I approached quietly, hoping I might hear something not intended for my ears, but I couldn't make out anything they were saying.

Coming into the kitchen, I found Father at the table wrapping something in brown paper. Seeing me, he hurriedly closed up the last flap of paper, but I was able to catch a glimpse of the midnight blue velvet that Mother had held under her arm earlier. The package, which he tied up with a length of string, was about three feet long and half a foot across.

"What's that?" I asked.

"A surprise," Father replied. He turned slightly toward me, not quite looking me in the eye, and smiled, a bit nervously I thought.

"Are you taking it to the meeting?" I said, trying to chisel out a little more information.

"Yes," said Mother. "Now stop asking questions."

"But why do I have to—"

Father cut me off, but he spoke without sharpness. "Will, anything we tell you will only bring up a dozen more questions. Have patience. You'll understand soon enough."

So I shut up, but now I was feeling nervous myself. What was going on?

Mother took Jenny over to a neighbor, and then she, Father, and I set out for the courthouse on foot. Ordinarily, we would have taken our carriage, but Father seemed restless, and I figured he wanted the exercise. He held his package in front of him rather than tucking it under his arm, treating it gingerly, as if it were something fragile.

The county courthouse was an imposing redbrick structure with pale yellow limestone trim. It sat just north of the tracks at the center of town. When we arrived, Father told us to go on inside and find some seats. He then put on a big smile and plunged into the throng of local businessmen gathered in the street near the entrance.

From the top of the steps, I looked back, watching him work the crowd, calling out hellos and first names, shaking hands, laughing, thanking people for coming, and inquiring about wives and kids. Men flocked around him, hoping for a word or a favor or a bit of his time. He was the center of attention. I admired him.

And, of course, everyone was curious about the package and asked him what it was, but Father told them no more than he'd told me. "All in good time, all in good time," he would say, giving each of them that big, winning smile that came so naturally to him. I smiled too. What a showman.

And yet, despite Father's hearty performance, something about him was off-key. He smiled too relentlessly, laughed a little too loudly, shook people's hands a tad too vigorously.

"Will, come along!" Mother snapped sharply.

If Father's nerves were frayed, Mother's were coming apart at the seams. Just by standing on the courthouse steps, she was violating an exclusively male world, and she knew it. In all her life, she had likely never been so close to a courthouse. Even I, a boy of fifteen, had more right to be here than she did. She knew that too.

Then there were the settlers. They were here too, several dozen of them, crowded around their wagons farther down the way, keeping to themselves.

We were about to enter the building when Jasper's uncle, Joe Hardeman, came slouching up the steps. He recognized me and said, "Hello, kid," in a bored voice. When he saw my mother, though, his eyes widened and he snatched off his hat. "Evenin', ma'am." Mother only nodded, unable to fully hide her disapproval.

We all began gathering in the main courtroom, the biggest meeting place in town. The townsmen seated themselves in the rows of benches while the settlers collected at the back of the room, standing against the wall.

Among the settlers, I spotted Mr. Dunham. My heart quickened as I searched the crowd for Anna, but I didn't see her anywhere.

Mother selected seats near the front, telling me to save room for Father on the aisle. The men of the town soon filled in around us, and their frowning, furtive glances at Mother made it clear that her presence wasn't welcome.

Mayor McCoy, a number of councilmen, and Marshal Hickok had just entered when Father appeared beside me. He stood for a moment, smoothing his mustache distractedly, and then sat down, still holding his bundle. One of Father's friends passed by and said hello, but Father didn't seem to notice him.

Suddenly, I felt uneasy. Father was right beside me, but he barely knew I was there. What had taken hold of him?

I turned to Mother for reassurance and got another shock. Her face was drained of color. She held a sheaf of papers I hadn't seen until now, and the papers quivered in her grasp. She was trembling.

The noisy room suddenly quieted. All around us, townsmen began turning in their seats, looking to the rear. Astonishingly, around thirty ladies, many of them my mother's friends, were silently filing in. Among them, I spotted my friend Billy's mother arm in arm with Johnny Hodge's mother.

Some of the townsmen stood to offer their seats, but the women declined. Instead, colorful and elegant in their Sunday best, they spread out along the back wall among the rough settlers. The noise level in the room rose again as the men began discussing this exceedingly curious development.

Conversing in low voices among themselves, the mayor and councilmen sat facing the room from behind a long table. Hickok, I noticed, had taken up a position in the far right corner. Perfectly still and almost in the shadows, he was still a presence everyone was aware of.

Satisfied that the room had filled, Mayor McCoy stood and raised his hands for quiet. This brought Father out of his thoughts, and he took a deep breath and then seemed to force a smile onto his face.

"All right, let's get started," the mayor began in his most formal voice. "Welcome to you all. Especially to our ladyfolk visitors. It is . . . good to see the fairest among us taking such an interest in our town's practical matters. Gentlemen, we will have to be on our best behavior."

Many of the men chuckled.

"We meet here today because some of our settlers claim they

have been harmed by the cattle trade. I do not speak now of the shiftless loafers among them. Nor of those habitual croakers for whom grumbling comes as easily as breathing. No, I speak of good people with good intentions.

"They complain of crops trampled by the Texas herds. Of disease passed to their cows and oxen by those same longhorns. And of cowboys who are ornery. They charge that our town ignores these matters because the Texans enrich us.

"To them I say that this is cattle country, not crop country. God decided that, not Abilene. Ten years ago, this land was covered with untold numbers of buffalo growing fat on its rich grasses. Now the buffalo are nearly gone, hunted to a fragment of what they were—but this land remains a natural paradise for grazing animals. That is our true destiny!"

"Nonsense!" cried Mr. Dunham from the back. "True enough, the buffalo eat our prairie grasses. But I say if that grass thrives here, so can crops. And so can farmers, if we're given half a chance!" The men behind him all nodded and murmured agreement.

Mayor McCoy took a deep breath and his voice rose to full volume.

"Many, such as this gentleman, do not understand the true purpose of this land. Our leaders in Washington do not understand. They're mostly uppity Easterners who've never been west of their bedposts, yet they think they know what's best for us. With a misguided promise of free land, they tempt trusting farmers to come to a place that will ruin them.

"Why? Because too often the burning winds of late summer wither and kill crops before they can be harvested. Our native grasses have learned to endure in this harsh land, but weakling crop plants brought from gentler eastern climes cannot.

"Many so-called settlers actually know this. These people

come here not to build, but to swindle. They sit on their free government land, growing nothing and taking up space. Their only goal is to make a nuisance of themselves until the town's businessmen offer them money to get out of the way. It is a crime."

"A crime!" bellowed Dunham. "I'll tell you what's a crime! It's a crime that townspeople grow rich from cattle that do us great harm. And it's a crime that you call us fools, criminals, and loafers when we object."

The settlers behind him cheered and called out, "Yes!" and, "That's the truth!"

"I'll tell you something else," Dunham continued. "Farmers do more real work in a day than you townsmen do in a month!" The settlers let loose another hearty cheer.

The mayor tried to restore order. "You'll have your turn, sir. Let me speak. I admit that while some come to swindle, others come with good intentions." McCoy paused and swept his arm before him, pointing to the line of settlers.

"Perhaps we should expect you to be angry. When people make a mistake, it is only human to blame others. In truth, though, the fault is in your own belief that this is farm country. The quicker you see your error, the quicker this land can fulfill its true purpose—cattle raising. Soon, like the buffalo before them, beef cattle will cover our prairies as far as the sharpest eye can see, and . . ."

The flow of the mayor's words dried up. My mother was standing. Jaws dropped in astonishment. No woman had ever attempted to speak in a public meeting. The room hung in silent expectation.

Mayor McCoy looked at her in confusion. "Mrs. Merritt? Are you unwell?"

I felt the iron grip of fear coiling around my chest. This was it. Whatever had been coming was here. And I knew, I just knew, that nothing would ever be the same afterward.

Mother's handful of papers fluttered slightly in her trembling hands. She started to speak, but her throat had gone dry and the words failed to come. She swallowed and tried again.

"I am quite well, Mayor McCoy, but I am troubled. Like our farmers, I also rise to declare an injury done to us by the cattle trade. Our town is being built on crime, and drunkenness, and immorality. It is said that we must accept these evils or the Texans will stop coming and our town will die.

"I say that you give up too easily on our farmers. This is a new land. Here we can create any kind of civilization we choose. The future is wide open, and what we build will show our children and our children's children what kind of people we were.

"Mayor, I know you believe the evils of Texastown can be kept south of the tracks. But there is no Texastown. Not truly. Texastown is just south Abilene. It's a part of us, and what goes on there cannot be kept from our sons"—Mother glanced down at me—"and daughters, our homes, and our lives."

She then held up her papers defiantly. "I have a petition here signed by over one hundred of this town's decent women. It demands that you, Mr. Mayor, and the council, bring an end to Texastown. Let the cattlemen accept this or go elsewhere. And if they choose to go, our town will not die."

Mother made her way past Father and me, and then up to the long table where the mayor and councilmen were seated. Standing before Mayor McCoy, she held out the petition. Her hands no longer trembled.

I understood now what Mother had been doing all those afternoons away from home. She'd been out talking with the local ladies about Texastown and gathering the signatures on this petition. And somehow, working quietly within the separate world of women, she'd found the support she wanted.

The mayor hesitated. He looked to my father but got no help. Mother's hand remained outstretched. Reluctantly, the mayor took the papers from her.

As the farmers roared their approval, Mother returned to her seat. Grinning and laughing, the town ladies clapped their hands, more passionately than was usual. Johnny Hodge's father, the farm equipment dealer, jumped up cheering and shaking hands with the small number of other pro-farmer businessmen.

The pro-cattle townsmen sat in sullen silence. Many glared at Father, and me, as if the Merritt men were at fault for not controlling Mother.

As soon as Mother returned to her seat, Father stood and raised his hands to speak. "Mr. Mayor!" he called out in the turmoil.

The room became quiet again. After Mother's surprise statements, everyone wondered what her husband would say. Father, after all, was a man who had prospered from the cattle trade.

"Go ahead, J.T.," said Mayor McCoy hopefully.

"Thank you, Mayor," Father began. "Ladies and gentlemen of Abilene, beef cattle created this town."

A good number of townsmen applauded. Everything was going to be okay. J. T. Merritt would put his impudent wife in her place.

"The trade has allowed this town to outdo all its competitors. It has raised us up and made us a city to be reckoned with."

More nods of approval and clapping from the pro-cattle crowd.

"However . . . it has taken us as far as it can, and now it damages our reputation, puts us in physical danger, and scares away new businesses and residents."

"What?" exclaimed a townsman. "Why, that's nonsense! This town's doing real fine."

"Perhaps," Father answered, "but we'll never do better than this. And don't think we can build our future on local ranching. Big ranching means few people will ever occupy our vast prairie, and those that do will be unattached cowboys owning little beyond a horse and saddle. Wild, irresponsible men who'll make a hash of our town's good name.

"But farming will mean a different future. Many more people will live on the land around us—fathers, mothers, children, people tied to their land, real citizens who'll call this place home."

"Now hold on, J.T.," Mayor McCoy interrupted. "Even if that were true—and I say it isn't—you still can't get around the fact, *the fact*, that the weather here will kill too much of the farmers' crops for them to survive."

Father paused, looking around, taking in the faces of his friends and neighbors, and then he went on.

"Right now most of you believe the mayor, but I tell you that our farmers can thrive. And Abilene will prosper with them because everything they need, from plows and stoves to crop seed and cook pots, will flow through us."

Father paused again. He turned to Mother, grabbing just a moment of eye contact. He looked like a man who was about to bet the grocery money on the turn of a card. Then he swung back to the restless crowd, took a deep breath, and in a loud firm voice he said what he had come to say.

"Gentlemen, ladies, reluctantly, I say it is time for the Texans and their herds to go!"

The room simply exploded. If the roof hadn't been nailed on, it would've blown clean off and landed somewhere in Nebraska. Most of the pro-cattle businessmen leaped to their feet, yelling, swinging their arms, and generally having a nail-spitting fit. A few among them, however, remained still, seemingly lost in thought. I wondered whether they had been persuaded by Father's sermon or were merely plotting our murder.

Father ignored the uproar. He picked up the package from his seat, winking at me as he did, and then strode confidently up to the mayor's long table. Laying his package in front of McCoy, he untied the string that secured it and then calmly began to fold back the brown-paper wrapper, flap by flap. The big courtroom was still a bedlam of raucous humanity, but as Father slowly revealed more and more of the midnight blue velvet, people began to pay attention, and the room became quieter and quieter.

With a flourish, Father swept the brown paper away from the roll of blue velvet. As the paper drifted down to the floor, the crowd was now almost silent. Certain that he had captured their attention, Father rested his hand on the velvet object and began to speak.

"I say that the evils of the cattle trade must go because, from this day forward, Abilene can thrive without them."

Then, with a quick sweep, he rolled the velvet out flat over the table, revealing a thick bundle of wheat, beautiful wheat. Bearded heads heavy with plump, ripe grain kernels nodding atop long slender stalks. Against the dark blue background of the velvet, the tawny wheat looked almost golden. It looked as if it were glowing with its own light.

But most of all, it looked like wealth.

What a showman.

Now the room buzzed with murmuring whispers. People craned their necks to see past their neighbors. Many of the settlers moved up the aisles for a closer look, their mouths agape in unspoken exclamation.

"Minnesota winter wheat!" Father fired out the words. He leaned over and spread the golden wheat across the velvet. "Grown right here in Dickinson County, in our own uplands. Planted last fall, and cut from the soil—yesterday."

"Liar!" yelled someone.

Father only smiled at the accusation. "I have five acres where this came from. Doubters and cynics are free to examine the crop at their pleasure."

He paused, letting the silence linger, daring them to question his honor again. No one spoke out.

"It's a month or more," Father continued, "before the heat of the southern winds arrive, but this winter wheat is ready to harvest and sell now. This is the crop our farmers have prayed for. Winter wheat is our destiny, ladies and gentlemen, not cattle."

Father said other things that night, but I wasn't listening. I was too busy brooding over the wreck of my happy life.

TWENTY-ONE

W hat in the world's got into you, J.T.?" cried Mayor
McCoy on the courthouse steps.

That's right, I thought, what in the world? Father and
Mother had pulled the rug right out from under this town.
With her plea for morality, Mother seemed to have many of
the women behind her. Father, though, had made an enemy of
almost every man in town who depended on cattle money, and
that was most of them. Of course, there were a few who supported him—men like Mr. Hodge, who sold farm implements,
and maybe the Red Front's Mr. Crutchfield, who did a lot of
business with settlers—but there weren't many.

Still, even I realized that Father's winter wheat looked pretty
good, but to tell the truth, I didn't really care about the wisdom
or foolishness of Father's vision. What I cared about was me.
What were my friends going to say when they heard my parents

wanted to run the Texans out of town? Lord, what was Jasper going to say?

Would I have even one friend left?

Would I again be alone, an outcast, as I had been at Uncle's house in New York? Would I again be left standing outside, witnessing but not part of the life around me? Standing there between Mother and Father, I believed I could feel Abilene pulling away, releasing me from its embrace. I believed I could feel the loneliness I'd been so certain I would never have to endure again.

My mind spun as I tried to find a way to save myself. I'd tell Jasper and the boys that I was the same person I'd always been. I'd tell them I had nothing to do with my parents' nutty ideas. Yes, that's what I'd do. My friends would understand, and they would . . . hate me!

If I had to, I could make friends with Johnny Hodge and his bunch . . . the enemy. I didn't want that . . . but I didn't want to be alone either. I'd have to force myself to be friends with them. But wait—why would they want to be friends with me? They didn't like me before; they wouldn't like me now.

I missed Jasper already.

Father was about to answer Mayor McCoy when Joe Hardeman interrupted.

"Merritt, that was a mean piece of business you pulled in there. I don't know what you're up to, but I ain't gonna stand for it."

"I said what I think is best for the town," Father replied calmly.

Joe Hardeman stepped up close to Father. "You did what's best for J. T. Merritt! I don't know how or why, but I got a feelin' you're gonna come out of this mess smellin' pretty sweet. Aren't you?"

"That's right," said Mayor McCoy, my father's former friend, "I don't like the smell of this myself."

"I've said all I'm going to say," said Father.

"Is that so?" shouted Joe Hardeman. "Well, I'll tell you this: If you hurt me and mine, I'll return the favor double and triple. You get my drift, Mr. High and Mighty J. T. Merritt?"

Before Father could answer, we all became aware that Hickok was standing among us. I hadn't seen him approach, but here he was.

"Evening, Mrs. Merritt, J.T., Will," said the marshal. "If you're heading home, I wonder if I might walk along with you."

Despite Hickok's polite words, we all knew he was offering to protect us. I began looking around, and what I saw ran a shiver up my spine. Unfriendly faces surrounded us on all sides, the faces of people who had been our friends only an hour before. I realized then that this situation was more than just my problem. The Merritts, all of us, even Jenny, were going to be outcasts. It was hard to believe we needed Hickok beside us just to walk safely home, but perhaps we did.

"Thank you, Marshal," said Father, "but I don't think we require assistance."

"Of course not," said Hickok, giving Joe Hardeman a dead hard look, "but it's a pleasant evening. I'd enjoy the walk."

Mother spoke up quickly, perhaps fearing Father would refuse the marshal's offer again. "Thank you, Mr. Hickok. We'd be pleased to have your company."

And so Wild Bill escorted us home. He never mentioned the meeting and gave no hint of his opinions on the matter. He made only small talk and soon had us laughing with some of his outlandish stories. At one point, he told me that he'd gotten Mike Williams a job as a special deputy at the new Novelty

Theatre. The Novelty had been under construction since spring and would open soon.

"Who's Mike Williams?" Father asked, unable to place the name.

"You remember Mike," I said. "He's the cowboy that swam the Smoky ahead of the Carrol herd back at the beginning of the season."

"Oh, yes," said Father. "Good man?"

"Yes," said Hickok, "he's a talker, but the Texans listen to him."

This was getting a little too close to my Texastown adventure for comfort.

"That's wonderful, Mr. Hickok," said Mother. "I do worry about you and pray for you."

"Thank you, Mrs. Merritt." Hickok glanced my way. "I believe some of your prayers were of use to me recently."

I found a fingernail to pick at.

A few days later, Abilene's newspaper, *The Chronicle*, reported that more than 125,000 unsold Texas cattle were now being held near the Kansas rail line. Cattle prices continued to fall, and buyers were scarce. Despite this, more herds were arriving every day.

In the minds of most townsmen, Father had betrayed Abilene. Many of their businesses—hotels, saloons, boot makers, supply stores, clothing stores, the stockyard, and many others—depended directly on Texas money and wouldn't survive if the cattle trade disappeared.

Other people felt they profited indirectly from cattle money. When the Great Western Store sold supplies to the Texans, the owner, Jake Karatofsky, turned around and spent the money he'd made at other Abilene businesses.

Still others simply feared the unknown. For them it was a matter of not wanting to rock the boat.

Some of these people would never be persuaded that farming was the future. But Father was a great salesman, and I knew he had carefully calculated his odds of ultimately bringing enough of our citizens over to his side.

Of course, Father was more than a salesman; he was also a gambler, and this time he had gambled big. He had challenged the town's bedrock belief that the prairie was useless for farming. He'd rejected the judgment that the settlers were lazy fools and freeloaders. He'd staked our whole life in Abilene on his faith that he knew what the town's future should be. It was a frightening risk, and I understood now why he'd been so withdrawn and distracted in recent months.

The night after the courthouse meeting, someone threw a rock with a threatening note through our parlor window. Fearing that someone might try to burn us out, Father sat up the rest of the dark hours with a Winchester in his lap.

On Monday, Father released me from my Texastown-adventure jail sentence, but I still felt like a prisoner. None of my friends had come by, and I was too nervous to seek them out. I was scared. I admit it. Abilene was a tiny, lonely speck of humans on a never-ending prairie, and now I was alone within Abilene. Yes, I was scared, but I was also angry.

At breakfast on Tuesday morning, Father came to the table and sat down wearily. For a moment, he stared at his hotcakes and bacon and said nothing. Then he looked up at me.

"Will, I'm sorry to have to tell you this. Mr. Gore at the

Drover's Cottage sent word yesterday. He won't be . . . needing you to work in the stables after all."

"Horse poop," said Jenny, wrinkling her nose.

"Jenny, hush up," said Mother quickly.

"Well, there is!" said Jenny indignantly.

I closed my eyes and tried to ignore my sister's foolishness. So, Mr. Gore didn't like Father's politics, and he was taking it out on me. What could I expect? The Drover's Cottage would go out of business if Father chased the Texans away. I wondered if Jasper or one of my other friends would get my job.

Jenny studied me and then piped up once more. "Mama, was Will bad again?"

I threw Jenny a dirty look but said nothing. Glancing at Mother, I found her staring at me as if I were a puppy whose bone had been taken away. For some reason, being pitied lit my fuse.

"Why did you change your mind about the settlers?" I burst out, almost screaming. Tears spilled down my cheeks. "I don't understand. It's stupid!" I turned on Father. "We were happy!"

"Mama," said Jenny urgently, "Will *is* being bad!"

"Shut up, Jenny!" I bellowed.

Mother's eyes were wide. "Will! I won't have you talking like that."

"I don't care! You don't make sense. You turned the whole town against us. For what? For a bunch of stupid farmers. Or because a Texan you'll never know or talk to has a good time below the tracks. You don't make sense, neither of you!"

Mother started to object again, but Father held out his hand. Surprisingly, he wasn't angry.

TWENTY-TWO

I spotted him about half a block ahead as I emerged from Broadway and turned to walk along the row of stores facing the railroad tracks. Lit by the late afternoon sun, Jasper's red hair glowed like an ember against the dusty street. His back was to me, and for a moment, I considered ducking down an alley to avoid him.

Scuffing along in the dirt, he was carrying a quart-size tin can by its wire handle. The weather was getting hotter now, and I knew he was delivering beer to some thirsty workman or shopkeeper.

Jasper may have been "rushing the can," but he wasn't rushing; he was dawdling. Every few steps he'd swing the can in a big looping circle at arm's length—up, around, and down—never spilling a drop. He might have seemed cheerful to most folks, but I knew better.

I hadn't seen Jasper or any of my friends in the two weeks

since the big courthouse meeting. No one had come to my house. No one.

That didn't surprise me. My parents' house was enemy territory now. What did surprise me was the way I'd acted. I'd made no effort to see my friends, staying close to home, hiding and unhappy.

Sitting alone in my room, I often wondered if our midnight trip to Texastown was the last time my pals and I would be together. Texastown seemed now as if it had happened in someone else's life.

Jasper was still tramping ahead, unaware that I was behind him. I bit my lip, wondering what I should do. I missed all my pals, but most of all I missed Jasper. He had always been my best friend, and I wanted to call out to him. Only a month ago, that would've been the easiest thing in the world; now it was the hardest. What would I do if he turned me away?

Much had happened since the big meeting at the courthouse, and none of it was likely to put Jasper in a forgiving mood.

After Father revealed his success with winter wheat, he had flown into action, tirelessly selling his new ideas. All day, every day, he bent the ear of anyone who would listen.

Father began by spreading the gospel of winter wheat among the settlers. At shabby, hardscrabble farms all over the prairie, Father told them that this new land required new ways. He told them that spring wheat was fine back East, but here in the West it would rarely survive the heat of late summer without heartbreaking damage or complete destruction. He told them that in time even the strongest among them would give up and crawl away from their land like whipped dogs.

But after he'd thrown cold truth in their faces, he would give them hope. He told them the story of his secret winter wheat field. He told them that winter wheat was made for Kansas. More than that, it was made for a new kind of farming. He told them that with winter wheat and the new farm machines, they would cast off their old dreams to make room for bigger, taller dreams.

And then, one after another, Father would lean closer and tell each settler something astonishing. He told him that someday the harvest of his farm alone would fill an entire train. Not a train car, but an entire train. He told him that his farm would produce like nothing the world had ever seen. He told him that he would feed the world. He told all this to a man who, at that moment, could barely feed his family.

At first, Father spoke to settlers one at a time, standing in a field beside a plow and steaming oxen or sitting in the darkness of a sod hut. But as word of his ideas spread, more and more people gathered wherever he spoke. Now, when he arrived at a home, ten, fifteen, or twenty farmers would be waiting to hear him.

Of course, Father was not content to sing the praises of winter wheat only to settlers. Here in town, he stopped people on the street. He barged into their offices. He waylaid them before church. He persuaded. He argued. He reasoned. No one could escape him, or discourage him.

Mother and her friends were working for the cause too. They were more discreet but just as relentless. At dinner tables, in parlors, and in bedrooms all over Abilene, women argued against the cattle trade.

Most townsmen turned away from these new ideas, but here and there a few began to listen. Still, it was far from clear whether my parents would win or lose their dangerous gamble.

And what did I think of all this? I thought that if Father and Mother had their way, everything that made Abilene special would disappear. Texastown, the cowboys, the Drover's Cottage, the huge longhorn herds, the noise and excitement, even Marshal Hickok—all would go away.

But beyond these things, I was lonely, desperately lonely. And every day that passed, every day that I sat in my house, I grew more and more angry.

I couldn't stop my anger. Everything around me fed it and made it stronger. Maybe Father and Mother were right about the future of Abilene—part of me believed they were—but that didn't seem to matter.

No, in the end, the big things didn't matter. What mattered were the little things. What mattered was that Jasper, my best friend, was just ahead of me, and I couldn't bring myself to call to him. That was what mattered. That was what made me angry. It was an anger that burned right over all of my father's grand ideas and my mother's good intentions.

Jasper continued down the open area between the tracks and the storefronts, and I followed some distance behind. Jasper's feet dragged and his shoulders slumped. I wondered if his uncle was being hard on him again.

I half hoped Jasper would catch sight of me, but I also feared it. I was walking just a little faster than he was, getting closer all the time. But at every alley and doorway, I fought the urge to turn away. My mouth had gone dry, my palms sweaty.

We were almost to the Red Front when a squealing pig burst out of the store's doorway. Jimmy the clerk was right behind it, swinging a broom, yelling, "Out! Out!"

As soon as Jimmy disappeared back into the store, Jasper came to life. He ran toward the pig, waving his arms and blocking its path. Beer sloshed all about from his can. I knew right away what he was doing, and I couldn't help but smile. He hadn't changed.

When the pig saw Jasper coming, it veered sharply, trying to go around, but Jasper stayed with it, waving his arms, spilling more beer. The pig whirled and ran back toward the Red Front, then spun about and made another dodge around Jasper.

Jasper lunged to block it, but the pig was faster, squeaking past his flailing arm. Now it was coming straight for me. Before I knew it, I was hollering and charging the poor pig. I heard Jasper laugh.

Together, we drove the panicked pig back toward the Red Front. Running as fast as it could, the panicked pig raced for the safety of the store's open doorway. Seconds later we heard a crash inside, and then pig squeals and Jimmy's curses filled the air.

As soon as the pig disappeared into the Red Front, Jasper and I were fleeing the scene, laughing all the time. At Mulberry Street, we skidded around the corner and pulled up.

Breathing hard, Jasper turned to me, grinning happily. His mouth opened to speak, but then, abruptly, he seemed to remember what had come between us. His smile faded, his body slumped, and he looked away.

He was too late though. I'd seen through him. In fact, I marveled that it hadn't occurred to me before. Small wonder something about him hadn't seemed right—Jasper had lost his best friend too.

"So," he began, after a moment, "I s'pose you're a farmer now."

"In a pig's eye! I'm no kind of farmer."

"Well, maybe you just like 'em. Maybe you just think a farmer is a dandy sort of fellow."

"Yeah, maybe. And maybe water's gonna run uphill."

Jasper smiled slightly.

"Who got my job at the Drover's Cottage?" I asked.

"Gordon."

"Gordon! Why not you?"

"Ahh, I coulda got it, but Uncle says I got work enough at his place."

I pointed to his can. "You lost all your beer chasing that pig."

Jasper peered into his empty can. "Yep, I 'spect so." Then his head snapped up and he grinned. "But it was worth it. Even if my uncle gives me a whippin'!"

Another silence settled upon us. It was hard to talk like friends. Neither of us was certain that we were. Then, to my relief, Jasper spoke up.

"Did you hear what's happenin' between Hickok and Phil Coe?"

"What's that?"

"They're still feudin', and when Phil gets a few drinks in him he noises it around that he wants to kill the marshal. If you ask me, the day's comin' when Wild Bill is gonna get his fill."

"Yeah, I think so too."

"Bill sure liked the way Mike Williams handled hisself that night in Texastown. He got Mike a good-payin' job as a special deputy at that new Novelty Theatre."

"Marshal Hickok told me that himself," I said proudly. "But what exactly is a special deputy?"

"That's a fellow what keeps the cowboys from tearin' up the place if they don't like the show. And the cowboys are pretty cranky these days. Bein' here so long, they've drunk their wage money down to nuthin'."

"That must make it sort of hard on Mike."

"Well, he ain't actually started yet. The Novelty don't open for a few weeks. Mike's still out on the prairie with the Olive outfit. A while back, one of Print's men got kicked in the teeth by a horse, and Mike talked his way into the fellow's job."

"How's your uncle?"

"Fit to be tied. The Elkhorn ain't makin' the money it used to."

"Is he takin' it out on you?"

"Some, but he's mad as holy heck at Wild Bill right now."

"The marshal! Why?"

"The city council ordered Bill to close up the dance halls and run the gamblers out of town. Uncle Joe thinks Bill is takin' his work too seriously." Jasper paused and an odd look came into his eye. "But me, I think the trouble started with your mother's sorry petition."

"My mother's petition—"

"Uncle says the council's all a bunch of cowards, lettin' a woman lead them around by the nose. He says it ain't fittin' for a woman to be doin' such public things. Interferin' in matters best left to men. A lot of folks are talkin'."

"Who's talking?"

"I told you," snapped Jasper, "lots of folks,"

I should've stopped him right there. I should've told him that if he said another word about my mother I'd flatten him. But when I opened my mouth something else came out, something low and cowardly.

"Jasper, all this stuff that's happened, it's my father and mother's doing. I'm no different than I ever was."

Jasper nodded. "They're also talkin' about this fool winter wheat your father's pushin'."

"Yeah."

"Sounds stupid to me." Jasper eyed me, watching for my reaction.

"Me too," I said hastily.

"People say your father is just lookin' to ruin Abilene so he can grab the land cheap. They say it's a big steal, and he don't care a whit about his friends and neighbors."

I didn't say anything—but I nodded. I nodded as if I agreed. I nodded even though I knew it was a lie.

I saw now that, like me, Jasper was brimming with anger. He was a person with many good qualities, but anger brought out his cruel side, and now he was turning that side toward me, rubbing my face in my parents' crimes.

And I took it. I took it without a word of complaint. I passed up every chance to defend Mother and Father. Fact was, I was willing to swallow any abuse to get my friends back.

And Jasper knew it. He was testing me. Daring me to kick about his insults. He would take me back, but only if I jumped through every hoop he held up. I gritted my teeth, but I jumped, and jumped, and jumped.

Afterward, I knew what I'd done was wrong. I felt the wrongness in my bones. I was learning that I would do almost any low thing, even betray my family, to keep my friends and escape becoming an outcast. My worst fears, born in my uncle's house and during our years of wandering, were echoing down from the past and making me into something contemptible.

When I got home, I went up to my room without a word to Mother. I couldn't face her. I just closed my door and lay on my bed, staring at the ceiling.

Around five o'clock Father peeked in.

"You asleep, Will?"

"No . . . just resting."

He came into my room and strolled over to the window. Bending slightly, he peered out.

"Everything all right?" he said offhandedly, still looking out the window.

"Uh-huh."

Father turned to me. "Your mother says you're a bit quiet. She thought you might be coming down with something."

"I'm fine."

He kept staring at me, frowning slightly, so I said it again. "Really, I'm fine."

Having Father so close, so concerned, speaking of Mother's worries, made me feel even lower. Why had I let Jasper walk all over me? Why hadn't I found the strength to stand up to him?

"Good," said Father. He turned back to the window and looked out again, clasping his hands casually behind his back. "Because I have a job for you."

TWENTY-THREE

"Will, if you have any kind of trouble, you turn right around and come home," said Mother.

"Yes, ma'am."

She tied a good-size sack to General's saddle. I grinned when I saw it.

"I'm only gone till this afternoon. That's food enough for a week."

Mother reached over and gave me a hug. "Hush up. There's no harm in having a little extra."

Father came down the walk from the house. Mother's smile disappeared. He was carrying his Winchester.

"Will," he said, "you leave this rifle alone unless you've got one heck of a problem. You hear me?"

"Yes, sir."

Father slid the Winchester into the saddle scabbard. "Get back here before dark."

"I will."

"Have you got my note for Mr. Dunham?"

"Uh-huh," I said, patting my pants pocket.

"One more time, in case you lose it, what does it say?"

I made a face. "I'm not going to lose it. But it says you're going to speak at Kirby Schoolhouse, Saturday at six, and you'd like Mr. Dunham to come and say a few words to the farm folk about winter wheat."

"Good. Now get moving. I'll have your hide if you aren't back by sundown." He reached out and shook my hand.

I gave Mother a hug, which she held overly long, and mounted up.

"Bye."

"Be careful, Will," said Mother.

I nodded and turned General away. As I reached our gate, though, I heard a high-pitched voice. "Good-bye, Will, good-bye." I twisted in the saddle to look back. Jenny was standing on our front steps, still in her nightclothes, her hair wild from sleeping. She waved solemnly but broke into giggles when I waved back.

Father had his arm around Mother, and she was resting her cheek on his shoulder. They waved too. For some reason, the sight of my family sapped my courage. Suddenly I felt like quitting the whole trip, and I might have if it hadn't been Anna's home I was headed for.

It was just a little before seven in the morning, and the town's streets were quiet. The rhythmic beat of General's hooves rang out clearly in the calm. At the railroad tracks, I turned left and headed east out of town. Above me, the telegraph wires that ran alongside the tracks thrummed atop their tall poles.

Following Father's directions, I kept an eye on the course of the Smoky Hill off to my right. After a half hour or so, the meandering river curved sharply toward me, coming right up to the tracks. It was here, according to Father, that I would find Lone Tree Creek, which flowed down from the north. Sure enough, just ahead the tracks crossed over a creek on a small trestle bridge.

I breathed easier. Getting lost was always possible. There were many creeks out here and no signs to identify anything. Of course, there were farms nearby, so I could stop to ask directions. But I was shy about that. I was obviously a town kid. Who could tell how they'd react? After all, my friends and I had never been very good to them. Better that I find the Dunham place on my own. I turned General north, leaving the tracks behind, following the drowsy, burbling stream that I hoped was Lone Tree.

After a couple miles, I turned in the saddle, looking back the way I'd come, and that's when I spotted them. Far off to the east on the sweeping plain, a huge Texas herd, well over two thousand head, was angling northwest toward me. A haze of dust rose like steam from the moving cattle. It was an impressive sight, but I didn't give it much thought. Cattle were often moved about in search of better grass and water, or to get away from settlers.

Even this early, it was starting to get warm. The weather had changed recently. Two days before it had topped eighty-seven degrees. The green prairie grasses were beginning to brown up, and the springtime flowers were long gone.

From here, I guessed, the Dunham farm should be pretty close. In the growing heat, sweat trickled from under my hat and rolled down my cheeks. I had now traveled far enough north that the farms had thinned out quite a bit.

Just ahead there was a small sod farmhouse, but it didn't fit Father's description of the Dunham soddy.

It was hard to imagine living in a sod house, which was mostly just dirt. I shook my head. Dirt-poor people living in dirt houses.

Looking all around, I couldn't see a single tree. At one time, Lone Tree Creek must've had a lone tree, but it was gone now, probably used by a settler for fuel or roof poles. Now there was only dirt, grass, and sky. And that was the problem. Houses couldn't be made out of sky, so that left dirt and grass.

Poor settlers like the Dunhams couldn't afford lumber. So, using shovels and axes, they cut hundreds of grassy squares from the ground and then piled them up like bricks to make the walls of their homes.

Life was different out here, and people who accepted such a life were different too. I felt as if I were riding into a foreign country.

I looked back once more at the advancing Texas herd. From here, the land sloped gently downward to the Smoky, and the vast scene shimmered through curtains of heat rising from the prairie floor. Even in a land as big as this, the herd looked tremendous.

I figured this bunch had been held to the east on a creek near the Smoky, an area that had likely gotten filled up as more and more herds arrived. Now it was being moved into the uplands to find some elbow room.

But that was none of my concern. My job was to find the Dunham place and deliver my message. At this, my face broadened into a smile. "And spend time with Anna," I said out loud.

Approaching the small soddy, I saw that it was deserted and beginning to melt and crumble back into the earth. Just another failed farm that had sucked all the hope from its owner. I snorted in disgust. Another fool had gotten what he deserved.

A bit farther on I passed another soddy. This one was inhabited, but again, it didn't fit Father's description of the Dunham place.

I began to look for a crossing. Another mile up and the creek bed broadened, shallow water rippling over a gravel bottom. General waded across easily and hopped up a low bank to the other side.

Uneasiness was slowly growing inside me. What if I wasn't

where I thought I was? Everything looked the same out here. Even with the last soddy and the Texas herd in sight, the size of the land made me feel very small and alone.

And then, to my right, I spotted something curious, something out of place. I turned General to it, and as I got closer, I saw that it was a short wall, about forty feet long. Oddly, though, it was made of yellow stone, not sod.

A little closer and I realized it wasn't just a wall; it was one side of an unfinished building. No roof yet, just a stone box with openings for windows and doors. And it was big, bigger than any house. No one was around, but there were signs it was being worked on.

What was a big, lonesome stone structure doing out here? Then I recalled Father saying something about the Dunham place being near a half-built church.

My eyes scanned past the building. Not too far away, I saw a sod house that seemed to lean up against a grassy wrinkle in the otherwise level landscape. I felt myself relax. Father had said to look for a soddy dug right into a slope. This was the Dunham place.

My relief was quickly pushed aside by disgust. Good Lord, was this oversize rabbit hole where Anna lived? I didn't want to go there. I didn't want to see anything more of how Anna lived.

Nearby, a man was working a plow behind a team of oxen. His straw hat hid his face, but I recognized the powerful, stocky body and bushy, dark beard of Caleb Dunham.

Unwilling to move forward, I looked back once more to the Texas herd. It was closer now. Moving slowly, the massive column stretched for maybe a mile. It was a grand spectacle, and again I wished I were with them.

And then, the terrible truth struck me. The lead cattle had reached Lone Tree Creek. There the cowboys allowed them a quick drink but then continued pushing them north. Like an army on the march, the great herd was heading for the tiny Dunham farm.

TWENTY-FOUR

I urged General into a trot, skirting the edge of the Dunhams' cornfield. Intent on his plow and oxen, Mr. Dunham still hadn't noticed either the approaching Texas herd or me. Plowing kept a man's head down. Slightly hunched over his plow handles, Mr. Dunham was fully absorbed with the insistent effort of keeping the steel plowshare slicing evenly through the unwilling sod, each new furrow running close against the last.

I glanced southward, measuring the relentless advance of the Texas cattle.

Like most homestead farms, the Dunham farm was 160 acres, but like most, only a fraction of it was actually planted with crops. The Dunham place had no more than fifteen acres planted, a smallish field of corn and a slightly larger field of spring wheat.

Near the house, there was a quarter-acre garden with neat rows of onions, potatoes, carrots, tomatoes, string beans, and such. I figured much of what they ate came from that garden. The wheat and corn, if it wasn't destroyed, would be their only source of cash.

I looked again to the Texas herd. More and more cattle were being pushed northward along Lone Tree. It looked like the Dunham farm was the only one directly threatened. The farm I had passed earlier was on the opposite side of the creek.

For the Dunhams, tragedy seemed so certain that it felt as if it had already happened. What could I do to prevent it? Why did I even care? These Texans wouldn't stop. They saw the Dunham farm, and they were heading straight for it.

I tried to tell myself it didn't matter. The summer heat would kill most of these crops within a month. Why should I care if a bunch of longhorns trampled them first?

I tried to accept this, but I couldn't make it stick. If the weather killed the Dunham crops, that was hard luck; if the Texans ruined them, that was wrong.

I gave General a kick, and we sped forward. Mr. Dunham heard the sound of hooves and looked up from his plow. For a moment, he appeared puzzled, but then he recognized me.

"Ho, if it isn't young Merritt come to call. What in the world are you doing out here?"

I pulled General up sharply and swung down from the saddle. Seeing my urgency, Mr. Dunham's grin disappeared.

"Something wrong at home, son?"

"No, sir, something's wrong here." Raising my hand, I pointed southward. "Look!"

Mr. Dunham swung around. Seeing the endless Texas herd crowding its way up Lone Tree, he let out a long, slow breath. For a few seconds he was still, then he turned and looked back toward his house. A few of his younger children were playing by the front door. Anna was nowhere in sight.

Turning back to the herd, Mr. Dunham took off his straw hat and blotted sweat from his forehead with a rolled-up sleeve. His grimy blue work shirt was soaked from the labor of plowing, and dirt caked the creases around his suspenders. I couldn't help recalling how many times I'd heard town folk claim settlers were lazy.

"I should've seen 'em," he said regretfully.

I stood silently beside him, one hand holding General's reins. He glanced once more to his house and then back again to the herd. "They aren't bringing those cattle through my place. I won't allow it."

Just then, a cowboy approached, riding alone a short distance down the creek. I guessed he was scouting for the herd.

"You there!" Dunham roared, loud enough to make me and General jump. The cowboy looked toward us, and Dunham bellowed out another order. "You! Come here!" The heavy muscles in his arms and neck came up with his anger.

Mr. Dunham had become so fearsome that I half expected the cowboy to turn and run. Instead, surprisingly, he wheeled his horse toward us and spurred it into a run. In a moment, he was before us, looking down from the saddle.

Now I knew why he hadn't run. This was no ordinary cowboy; this was Print Olive, the leader of the Olive cattle outfit. I'd seen him around Abilene. He was sort of famous, known to be as much gunman as cattleman. There were stories that he'd once hung a Nebraska settler for standing in his way.

Olive leaned forward in his saddle and fixed Mr. Dunham with a look that was calm and cold. One hand rested on his hip near his revolver.

"Stubble jumper, you had better be callin' your dog, 'cause if you're callin' me, I won't take it well."

Mr. Dunham was not intimidated. He took a step toward Olive and pointed up at him with a massive arm. "Take it as you like. I won't have my crops cut to pieces by that herd you're bringing up."

"We ain't turnin' aside," Olive answered. He glanced at Dunham's plow and at the long furrows ripped through the sod. He shook his head, disgusted. "Crazy fool, plowin' up good range."

"Texan opinions carry no weight here. This is our land, and you'll turn aside."

Olive gave him a menacing smile. "I'm in a charitable mood, but if you keep pushin', this'll be your shortest day."

Four more riders were galloping up from the herd. Olive turned to look, and instantly Mr. Dunham stepped past me and jerked Father's Winchester from my saddle. When Olive turned back to us, he found the rifle trained on his chest. I thought I saw his confidence sag just a bit.

As the horsemen pounded toward us, a voice called out from behind us.

"Father!"

Mr. Dunham didn't turn, not daring to take his eyes off Olive. "Anna, go back in the house."

Holding a pitcher of water, Anna was standing at the edge of the wheat field about a hundred feet away. Beyond Anna, I saw her frightened mother standing in the doorway of their soddy. A wide-eyed little boy was peeking around her skirts.

"Trouble, boss?" one of the Texans asked as he and the other men pulled their horses up around Olive. They were all armed.

"Yeah, I got a dirt man that wants me to trot my herd all over the countryside to avoid his weed patch."

"Is that a fact?"

"I s'pose we'd run our cattle down to skin and bones if I was the sort who could be ordered about by witless farmers." Olive locked eyes with Mr. Dunham. "But I ain't that sort."

Mr. Dunham leaned toward me. "Will, get away from here."

I shot a look over my shoulder. Anna had not retreated.

"Is she there?" Mr. Dunham asked.

"Yes, sir."

"Anna," he called without turning, "I told you to get to the house. Move!"

Anna took a few steps back but then refused to go farther.

It all reminded me of Hickok's face-off with the Texastown cowboys. Hickok had told my friends and me to get away, and he'd been right. But this was different.

I wanted to go. No one would have blamed me if I had. I was a kid. I had no business standing between a stubborn farmer and a bunch of hair-trigger Texans. I should've run to the house and taken Anna with me. Dragged her if I had to.

But I couldn't go. Something told me that having a kid standing among them would hold these men back. If I left, they'd feel freer to use their guns. So I stayed, praying that neither Dunham nor the Texans would be willing to shoot a man in front of me. I didn't want Anna to see her Father gunned down.

Just as I made my decision, Mr. Dunham spoke to me again. This time the quiet voice was gone. Sharp and fast, his words blasted over me. *"Will, go, now!"* It was the severest possible adult command. It forbade even the thought of saying no. Every impulse within me said to obey instantly. I braced myself, leaning into its force.

"No, sir!"

Mr. Dunham seemed astonished. He even took his eyes off the Texans for a moment to glare at me.

I glared right back, and then I glared at the Texans, who looked just as frustrated as Mr. Dunham. They too wanted me gone. Now they were uncertain. It was an opportunity, but I didn't know how to take advantage of it.

Olive broke the silence. "Farmer, you and your boy here

stand back. We're comin' through, and that's that. Don't die for this scratch farm."

In one action, Mr. Dunham cocked the rifle, an unmistakably threatening metallic click, and jabbed it toward Olive. "You'll go around, or I'll take you with me!"

Every cowboy's hand snapped to his gun. In a flash, revolvers were out at arm's length. Eyes stared hard, unblinking. Fingers twitched. A jumble of anger, panic, and fear balanced like a glass ball on the tip of a fence post. The slightest breeze or vibration and it would fall and explode into violence.

Everything was spinning out of control, and it seemed nothing could stop it. My staying wasn't going to stop the onrushing disaster after all. Maybe I was going to end up dead.

The tension was making General skittish. His ears were twitching about and he began to jerk his head up, almost yanking the reins from my hand.

And that's when an idea came to me. It was so obvious I marveled I hadn't thought of it before.

"Where's Mike Williams?" I said.

As tense as things were, they all turned to me.

"What's that, boy?" said Olive.

"You're Print Olive, aren't you?"

Olive looked surprised. "Yeah."

"Isn't Mike one of your men? Tall fellow, missing a pinky finger."

"Yeah, he's back with the herd. How would you know Mike?"

I pointed to Mr. Dunham. "I'm not this man's son. I live in Abilene."

"Uh-huh."

"Mike's a friend of mine. Maybe you heard him talk about pulling a kid's tooth with his horse."

Olive smiled, barely. "I heard."

"That was me, and my friend Jasper. Actually, Jasper was the owner of the tooth."

Some of Olive's men chuckled. Guns began to lower. I glanced over at Mr. Dunham. He was staring at me like I'd just dropped down from the heavens.

"Mr. Olive," I went on, "if you're looking for new grass, there's a real nice crossing just down the way."

Olive's smile disappeared.

"No, please, sir, hear me out. That crossing is wide and shallow. Good gravel bottom, no mud. All you've gotta do is put your herd on the other side of the creek. That's all. No need to run them all over the countryside. Just an easy crossing to open grass."

"That so?" Olive thought for a moment, and then his eyes narrowed. "Boy, if you live in Abilene, what're you doin' out here?"

Ah, that was a tough one. I couldn't say I was delivering a message from J. T. Merritt, the man who wanted to kick Olive and every other Texan out of the county.

"Me? Oh, I'm, uh . . ." Whirling about, I pointed at Anna. "I'm paying a call on Miss Anna Dunham."

It wasn't far from the truth. And Anna did look awfully pretty standing there by herself next to the wheat. Not one of those cowboys doubted me for an instant. They all grinned from ear to ear.

"Mr. Olive, can I show you that crossing now?"

Print Olive hesitated, studying me. "I think we can find it ourselves."

TWENTY-FIVE

Anna and I stood beside Lone Tree Creek. Downstream, the Olive outfit was pushing their herd over the crossing. Behind us, Caleb Dunham was back at his plowing, as if nothing had happened.

"Why'd he do it, Anna?"

"Do what?"

"Risk his life."

Anna's brow wrinkled. "Those people can't just run over us! What'd you expect?"

"Well, it's just that . . . Anna, I'm sorry to say this, but in a month the heat's likely to wreck your crops."

"Maybe it will, maybe it won't."

"Anna, your father knows the odds. He risked his life to keep cattle out of fields that're probably good as dead."

"What those men were going to do wasn't right."

"Yes, but—" I cut myself off. Anna's sullen look told me

she'd get angry if I pushed further. We were quiet for a while; both of us watching the distant cattle splash through the creek.

I'd delivered Father's message to Mr. Dunham, and I'd upset Anna with my questions. It seemed like a good time to leave.

"I've got to get going."

"Oh, no," Anna said quickly, "no, Mama's expecting you to eat with us."

"Thanks, but I've got food."

Anna became impatient. "Will, I think you saved Papa's life today. You can't just go. You have to stay and eat."

I nodded. "All right." I didn't really want to go.

Anna smiled triumphantly. "Do you see your cowboy friend out there?"

"Mike? Nah, too far off."

"Will, thank you." She was talking about her father now.

"Your father's got a lot of grit, Anna." I began looking for a way to change the subject. "Is that big yellow stone building down there a church?"

"Yep, that's what it is. All the folks hereabouts are helping to build it."

"Got to be expensive, a big stone building like that."

"Hasn't cost much of anything so far. There's a limestone outcrop south of the Smoky, near Enterprise. The men take wagons down there and cut the stone."

"That's five or six miles away!"

"More than that. To cross the Smoky, they have to go upstream a ways to catch the ferry. It's taken dozens of trips."

I shook my head in amazement. "Why do you want a church?"

Anna laughed, and my face reddened.

"Anna, I *know* what churches are for. What I mean is, why not go to town?"

"We want our own church. One near our homes."

I stared at Anna in amazement, and then I closed my eyes and grinned to myself. The joke was on me.

Near our homes—when Anna spoke those words, the truth finally hit me. I'd done my best to avoid the truth, but here it was staring me in the face—everything I'd ever heard or believed about these people was wrong. They weren't going to quit. They weren't here to make a quick buck. Or because they were lazy. Or because they were fools.

They were here to stay.

Just as Father had said.

Until that moment, I'd believed that the courthouse meeting was the turning point of my life. But I was wrong. In time, I would realize that this quiet conversation with Anna was where everything changed.

"What are you grinning at?" Anna asked.

"Nothing. Sorry. I've got one more question. Why do you have spring wheat?"

Anna sighed. "I thought you'd ask that. Papa had to decide what to plant last fall. Back then, he wasn't sure the winter wheat would succeed, so, like everyone else, he chose spring wheat."

"Ahh, he didn't trust my father's crazy ideas."

"Well, to tell you the truth, back then, he thought your father was a crazy townie with more money than sense." She eyed me to see if I was insulted.

"I'll tell you the truth, Anna. I've thought that myself."

"Of course, Papa doesn't think that anymore. He believes your father is a great man."

Hearing my father called a great man was strange. Even stranger, I wondered if it might be true.

"Papa will plant winter wheat for next year," Anna went on.

"He wants to break as many new acres as possible before then. He never stops. It worries Mama."

We both turned to watch Caleb Dunham work the plow across his land. Before this day, back to the beginning of time, nothing more serious than a grazing buffalo had disturbed this prairie grass. But today, just before dawn, the shining, steel wedge of the plowshare had knifed deep into it. And as the sun peeked over the horizon, Mr. Dunham had called to the oxen, "Get along, you lazy devils, get along!" The bulls had set themselves and then bent to the yokes. The leather harness went taut, creaking, and the blade began to run forward, ripping and slashing through the ancient sod.

The land did not yield easily. The surface sod was a dense, tangled armor of roots and fiber. Beneath it lay loose, fertile black loam, but to get at it, the sod had to be cut away. Four oxen, a heavy steel plowshare, and a man as powerful as Caleb Dunham were barely sufficient for the task.

"Anna, where are the horses that tried to run over me the first time I saw you in town?" I chuckled, thinking I was pretty funny, but Anna was not impressed.

"Ohhh, you must mean the two huge workhorses you walked right in front of without seeing."

"I saw them . . . sort of. They weren't that huge."

"They weren't ours either," said Anna, ignoring my snappy comeback. "We borrowed them from a neighbor. Oxen are so slow a trip to town takes forever. Out here, no one has everything that's needed, so people help each other."

Anna pointed to her father's toiling oxen.

"The two lead oxen are ours, but the rear oxen are Mr. Tolufson's. In a few days, he'll need help getting up the roof of his new barn, and Papa will return the favor."

Mr. Dunham halted his team and motioned us to join him.

As Anna and I trotted across the broken sod, it occurred to me that he had been working this field for more than five hours, and it was still morning. Townspeople were forever saying that settlers spent their days lying in the shade. I'd heard it a thousand times.

Mr. Dunham grinned as we came up. "All right, the lollygagging is over. I want the both of you to drive the team so I can attend to the plow."

"Papa, Will is going to stay and eat."

"Good!" roared Mr. Dunham, clapping me on the back. "That means we've got time to turn him into a farmer. Will, you and Anna get up there and do the thinking for these poor brutes." With that, he handed me a thin, flexible stick about five feet long.

I wasn't sure what was expected of me, but Anna led the way up to the lead oxen. They were heavy, muscular beasts, a little frightening up close, even if they were docile.

"Hello, Grant. Hello, Sherman," Anna said, patting each on the muzzle. She unwound two ropes from the wood yoke and tied them to the bulls' head harnesses.

"Will, I'm going to lead them so Papa gets a straight furrow, and you're going to keep their attention from wandering. If they start to slow up, take that goad and tap them on the shoulder. No need to whack them. Just let them know you're onto their game. Understand?"

"Yes, ma'am."

"Don't be smart."

"Yes, ma'am."

We kept the plow moving with hardly a pause for another hour. For me it was fun, something new and interesting. But I had the easy job, and I saw how hard it was for Mr. Dunham. Even with the oxen providing the pulling power, steering the plow and keeping the plowshare deep in the ground demanded all his strength. And he gave it, willingly, even happily.

"Anna," called Mr. Dunham, "what do you say? Shall I beat Tolufson's breaking record, an acre and a half in one day?"

Anna smiled devilishly. "Oh, I don't know, Papa. Mr. Tolufson is awww-fully strong."

"What! You try me, girl. I can do the work of two Tolufsons! You believe that, Will?"

I looked back and grinned. "Yes sir, two Tolufsons."

"That's right! Two Tolufsons—or ten townsmen! Take your pick."

Back and forth we went, an eighth of a mile before turning. In perfectly straight furrows, the gristly, matted sod was carved from the earth, curling heavily off the plowshare and falling aside. Dust filled the air. The work would have quickly exhausted an ordinary man, but it seemed to have no effect on Caleb Dunham.

His face and the granite muscles of his arms gleamed with muddy sweat, his drenched woolen shirt hung heavily on him, but his breathing came evenly and the plow remained rock solid in his grip. His strength was a marvel to me. Suddenly, the cowboys seemed like toothpick men.

Around noon, one of Anna's little brothers scampered out to tell us it was time to eat. I was ready, but Mr. Dunham was reluctant to quit. Grumpily, he unhooked the oxen, and we led them down to the creek for a drink.

The Olive herd was now fully across Lone Tree, spreading over the open grass on the far side. I supposed that if Olive had taken them farther north he would've found land even less occupied than here. At this point, though, crowding was hardly the issue. Print Olive had given as much as he was going to give.

He wouldn't move on, even if he wanted to, for the simple reason that Mr. Dunham had demanded he move on.

As our oxen drank deeply from the lazy water, Mr. Dunham stared at the vast blanket of longhorns so threateningly close. At the nearest edge of the herd, cowboys slouching in their saddles stared back.

"We're not through with them yet," he declared.

TWENTY-SIX

O h my, oranges!"

Mrs. Dunham's voice rose with delight as she pulled three fat oranges from the sack of food Mother had given me. Anna, her younger sister, and her two brothers crowded around, jostling each other to look.

In honor of my visit, Mrs. Dunham had put on a clean yellow dress, most likely her best, and pulled her hair back into a knot. The kids had freshly scrubbed faces and hands.

Reaching into the sack again, Mrs. Dunham produced a big chunk of store-bought ham and then a loaf of fresh wheat bread. She was thin and frail with hollow eyes. At first, she'd been shy around me. I think she knew how ragged she looked.

I had given her my sack without much thought. It seemed a small matter; the Dunhams were feeding me, so I didn't need it. But as I saw their joy, I realized what a treat it was for them.

"Will," said Mrs. Dunham, "this is just wonderful. I can't

remember the last time I had an orange. And fresh wheat bread! I'm so tired of making everything with cornmeal, but wheat flour is terrible expensive."

The children were all laughing as if it were Christmas morning. One of the little boys reached out and touched an orange with such curiosity that I wondered if he'd ever seen one before.

Mother had played a trick on me. My sack held far too much food for me alone, and it was full of items that were luxuries to the Dunhams. I realized she'd never intended them for me.

As Anna and her mother prepared our meal, I began looking around the soddy's interior. The first thing that struck me was how small it was. It would have been a cramped home for one person, much less six. There were no inner walls or rooms; privacy was just one more lost luxury.

With only two tiny windows, and with the door closed to keep the heat and flies out, it was dim inside. The trapped air, which I had to admit was comfortably cool, had a damp, musty smell.

On one wall, an old shotgun rested in a rack below a picture of President Ulysses S. Grant. To keep the dust down, most of the packed-earth floor was covered with tatty-looking rag carpets. In the far corner, a big family Bible lay open on a handsome carved mahogany stand.

Two lumpy, sagging, straw-filled beds were wedged at angles into another corner. They weren't roomy enough for the whole family, so some of the kids had to be sleeping on the floor, and maybe the supper table.

The soddy door banged open, and Mr. Dunham swept into the room, suspenders dangling at his waist. "What's this?" he called out heartily, wiping his hands still wet from washing on his dusty shirt.

"Oh, Caleb, look what Will brought us—oranges!"

Mr. Dunham's smile faded.

"Mother packed me a lunch," I said.

"Humph," he responded, trying to decide if my sack was charity, something I figured he wouldn't like.

"I hope it'll repay your hospitality," I said, trying to make it easy for him to accept.

"Mama," said Anna, "maybe we should all have some orange with our meal." She turned hopefully to her father. "Doesn't that sound good, Papa?"

Everyone looked to Mr. Dunham. He hesitated, but then his smile returned. "Sounds good."

The kids cheered, and Mrs. Dunham beamed.

As Anna and her mother set to work, Mr. Dunham turned his attention to me.

"Ever been in a sod house, Will?"

"No, sir."

"Well, what do you think?" He grinned, enjoying putting me on the spot.

"Oh, well, it's . . . um . . ."

"*Cramped* is the word you're hunting for, but that's all right. Someday, I'll build us a big stone house, like that church we're puttin' up. But for now this'll have to do, and it's not as bad as it seems. Not by half."

"I thought it'd have dirt walls inside," I said cautiously, "but you've covered them."

"Yep, ground up some of that yellow limestone and mixed it with ashes and river clay. Made a good plaster. Helps keep the bedbugs out. Lord, they're a torment."

I shivered at the thought and changed the subject. "It's cool in here."

"Sure it is. Walls are two feet thick. Cooler than that nice little wood frame box you live in. And in the winter it's warmer."

Mr. Dunham noticed his wife's neat yellow dress, then glanced down at his own grimy clothes.

"Looks like we're spiffin' up for your visit, Will," he said gruffly, loud enough for Mrs. Dunham to hear. "Come on outside. I want to show you something."

Walking rapidly with his hands on his hips, Mr. Dunham led me a short distance from the house. Suddenly, he turned to me, shaking his head irritably.

"You can't live out here and be troubled about clothes and what people think. It's no crime to work hard and get mussed up, now, is it?"

"No, sir, I don't s'pose it is."

And then I giggled. I tried not to, but I couldn't stop myself. Mr. Dunham was covered—covered—with brownish dust and dirt from head to foot.

He heard me, and for a moment, he didn't like it, but then his face softened.

"Ah, for cryin' out loud, you city people are a finicky lot." He began to brush and whack at his shirt and pants. Clouds of dust billowed off him.

"Best get upwind, boy!" he declared, and then he let loose a booming laugh.

I began to laugh too, and that made Mr. Dunham laugh even harder. We laughed until tears streamed down our faces and we couldn't catch a breath. We laughed so loudly the oxen stopped grazing to stare at us. Finally, with aching stomach muscles, we both settled down.

"Ho, boy, well, how do I look?" asked Mr. Dunham.

"Um . . . less dirty."

"Humph. Well, I'm not throwin' myself in the creek."

"I don't think there's enough time for that."

"No, there's not enough time. You're right about that. And

I'm sorry if I'm impatient, but there's so much to do—and never time enough to do it. We'll have a new life here, a good life, but I have to make the most of every day to get it. Sometimes I'm impatient."

"What do you want?"

"I always wanted my own land, and now I have it. Level land, rich soil, water. It's more than I ever dreamed, a quarter square mile. But Mrs. Dunham doesn't much like it here. She can't see the future I see. So I have to build that future. I have to put it in front of her as fast as I can, before she gives up. Anna keeps going. She sees our future."

Mr. Dunham stared across the creek at the big Texas herd. His face hardened and he muttered, "Nothing's going to stop me."

"Mr. Dunham, you were going to show me something."

"Oh yes, you bet!" He turned toward the soddy. "See how our soddy is dug into the slope? The roof extends straight out from the top of the slope. Look at it from the other side, and all you see is my stovepipe sticking up. That makes it nice in winter. We're protected from the frigid winds that come blowing down from the north."

"You've got grass on your roof."

"Sure we do. The roof is sod, just like the walls. Works like a charm, except when it rains."

"What then?"

"It leaks, that's what! You know what they say about sod roofs—if it rains one day outside, it rains two days inside. The sod loads up with water and never stops dripping. My missus doesn't like that, no sir, not one little bit."

"I guess not."

"Can't afford real shingles. I considered making some out of the cottonwoods down to the river, but I'm told they'd warp so bad they'd leak too. I did use cottonwood poles to lay the sod across, but they're pretty bad. You can see how they sag under the weight."

Mr. Dunham sighed, a little subdued now. I figured he was wondering if he'd ever find the money for a proper roof.

Anna poked her head out of the house and called us to eat. Mr. Dunham slapped me on the back. "Come on, city kid, you must've worked up quite an appetite watching me plow."

TWENTY-SEVEN

As we seated ourselves around the table, I noticed that each of us had a little white bowl of orange slices. And in the middle of the table sat my plump loaf of wheat bread. Everyone was laughing and talking; there was an air of holiday in the room.

"Will," said Mrs. Dunham, "pitch right in, help yourself to anything you see." She passed me a steaming bowl of ham and potatoes.

"Thank you, ma'am." I served myself and passed the bowl to Anna beside me. She winked as she took it.

"How is the plowing, Caleb?" asked Mrs. Dunham.

"Fine, fine, a little dry maybe."

A look of alarm came over Mrs. Dunham. "Dry, oh dear."

"Ah, now, Sarah, don't start that, we'll have rain soon enough."

"Caleb, what if—"

"What if, what if, there's no point in all this what-ifin'. Everything's going to be fine."

"But how do you know?"

"I just do. Anna, hurry up and pass them taters! We need more eatin' and less talkin' around here."

"Will," said Mrs. Dunham, "you've lived here longer than us. What will happen to our crops? Could they fail?"

"Oh . . . well, ma'am, I'm not a farmer. I couldn't—"

"Enough!" yelled Mr. Dunham. "I won't have this talk. We'll talk ourselves into fits."

Anna quickly changed the subject. "Will, how's that friend of yours?"

This only increased my uneasiness.

"You mean Jasper?"

"I suppose. The one with red hair."

"I'm not sure if he's my friend or not. Hard to say."

"Oh, Will, what happened?"

I hesitated and then decided to tell it straight.

"Like a lot of folks, he didn't appreciate my parents standing up for the settlers."

The room became silent. Mr. Dunham's fork hung halfway up from his plate. "You say a lot of folks?"

"Yes, sir."

There was another pause while Mr. Dunham considered this.

"Tell me, Will, since your parents spoke at the courthouse, has the town made it hard on your family?"

"Yes."

"Your father never mentioned this."

"No, sir, I don't suppose he would."

Mr. Dunham tossed his fork down. "Damnation, if that ain't a mean piece of business. I should've known."

As he spoke, I noticed a thin stream of dust sifting down from the rafters onto one of the beds over in the corner. With all the discussion, no one else seemed to notice.

"We never should have come here!" said Mrs. Dunham. "This is our fault, all this trouble."

"Our fault!" cried Mr. Dunham, coming up from his chair. "It is no such thing. This trouble, all of it, comes from those worthless Confederate Texans. I swear, we should've marched right down there after the war and thrown 'em all into prison. Our fault, ha!"

As Mr. Dunham raged, more and more dust streamed down from above. This time it was closer, sifting onto the floor between us and the beds. I wondered if that was the way it was in sod houses after the weather got drier.

"Will," Mr. Dunham continued, "your father has done the right thing, yes sir. Soon enough that'll be plain to all."

"Caleb, calm yourself!"

"No! I won't be shushed. The truth's got to be said. These damnable Texans are—"

Dust and clods of dirt began falling from above in a volume that couldn't be ignored. Suddenly, a brilliant narrow lance of sunlight shot down from a small opening in the roof and impaled the loaf of bread. In the murky room, the bread glowed like a fallen star.

We all looked up, and something that looked like a big heavy stick jammed straight down through the rafters, raining dirt and sod chunks onto the table. With a sharp crunch, a second object stabbed through, bringing another dazzling beam of light flashing down.

Mrs. Dunham shrieked, "Caleb!" and the children began to cry out. Still looking up, I took hold of Anna's arm, pushing my chair away from the table.

An enraged blaring bawl came from above. The objects that had penetrated the roof flailed wildly, and then, through the falling dust, I saw one of the rafter poles slide sideways.

A heavy slab of sod, and something else, something enormous, plunged down upon us. The table was instantly crushed flat to the floor, and an explosion of dense, blinding dust filled the room. Fearsome violent sounds and wild thrashing movement mixed with terrified cries and screams.

Anna was torn from my grip, and when I looked, she was gone, vanished into the swirling gritty fog. Very near, there was quick, heavy snorting and then a thunderous bellow. Something slammed my side and sent me sprawling to the floor. A chair flew over me, splintering against the wall and coming down on top of me.

Elbowing the wrecked chair aside, I sat up, staring hard into the thick dust for Anna and screaming her name. Before me, the faint outline of a longhorn appeared from the haze.

Now I understood. A stray from the Olive herd had wandered down the slope behind the Dunham soddy and right out onto their grassy roof.

The crazed steer lunged forward, whirling and kicking, its long curving horns sweeping through the clouded air. Frantically scrambling back, I struck something solid. Immediately, a massive hand grabbed my arm so powerfully that I yelped in pain. Mr. Dunham, eyes glittering, jerked me up and flung me toward the soddy's door. I hit hard, ripping the door from its leather hinges, and then found myself rolling over the ground in blinding sunlight.

Jumping to my feet, I turned to the soddy. The dark, yawning doorway, like a howling mouth, spoke with screams and cries and the sounds of things being torn and smashed. I could not make myself move.

The horror seemed to go on forever, but then a muffled blast shook the air, followed by a second. Except for soft sobbing and whimpering, the soddy went quiet. Dust rolled lazily out the doorway and was carried off on the hot summer breeze. My muscles went slack. Somehow, in that blind, violent room, Mr. Dunham had found his shotgun.

I began slowly moving toward the doorway, dreading what I might find. But before I could enter, Mr. Dunham appeared, wild-eyed and stricken.

"Will, saddle your horse. I have to ride for the doctor. Go!"

I ran, wondering who was hurt and how badly.

General was close by in a small cottonwood corral. He sensed my distress as I threw on his saddle, and by the time I led him to the soddy, he was tense and jumpy. There was nothing to tie him to, so, with my mind on Anna, I looped the reins around the saddle horn and left him just out front. Then, aching with fear, I stepped inside.

The dust had mostly cleared, and sunlight poured into the room through the fractured roof. The longhorn lay dead against the back wall, a twisted heap, one curving horn reaching menacingly into the air. The rest of the room was a shambles, everything in it upended and destroyed.

The younger sister stood just inside the doorway, holding her little brothers, one in each arm. Miraculously, they were unhurt. No one was hurt.

No one except Anna.

Anna lay on the floor near the center of the room. Her eyes were closed, and she would have looked drowsily peaceful if it hadn't been for the dark blood seeping across the left side of her dress.

My stomach rebelled at the sight, and I fell back, leaning heavily into the door frame.

Mrs. Dunham kneeled beside her daughter, softly speaking her name. Anna did not move or answer. I straightened and edged closer. With wonderful relief, I saw that she was breathing.

Mr. Dunham stood just behind his wife, staring down, one hand pressed against his bearded chin. Only moments before, he had been rabid to ride for the doctor, but now he seemed fixed in place.

"Mr. Dunham," I said in a church voice, "General's out front."

He didn't answer.

Mrs. Dunham glanced at me and then spoke to her husband. "Caleb, go for the doctor."

He didn't seem to hear, continuing to stare down at Anna.

"Caleb!"

As if awakened from a dream, Mr. Dunham looked at his wife in bewilderment.

"Caleb!"

"Sarah, what if . . . what if she . . . ?"

"Caleb, she won't die. She'll be here when you get back. Now go. It's a long way to town."

"No, I'm not going to town. I'm going for Doc Sully."

"Caleb, no! He's not a real doctor. I want the town doctor."

"Sarah, Abilene is ten miles from here. Sully is only four."

"No! Anna needs a real doctor."

"There's no time. Sully worked in a field hospital during the war. He knows injuries like this."

Suddenly, Anna coughed. It was a wet, gurgling cough, and it must have hurt because her eyes squeezed tight and her body curled to one side.

The sight snapped her father into action. He spun about and dashed for the doorway.

"Caleb, please—"

"*No!*"

Rushing toward General, he ran heavily over the thin wooden door lying just outside. It split at once, cracking with a loud pop under his weight.

For General, it was all too much. A big, noisy stranger hurtling at him, the sharp split of the wood; he bolted—and there was nothing to hold him.

For a few hundred feet, Mr. Dunham chased the panicked horse, but that only made matters worse. Soon it was clear that General was gone. Mr. Dunham slowed and then sank to his knees. He screamed at the fleeing horse, then bent forward, slamming his fists repeatedly into the earth.

There would be no doctor, not for a long time anyway. The thought of Jasper's parents, alone in their remote cabin, sick and dying, flashed through my head. Anna was going to die.

Abruptly, Mr. Dunham stood and began to run, heading north into the prairie. He was going for Doc Sully on foot. It was all he could do, but with the heat and knee-high grass his progress would be slow.

I sank onto the flat, yellow door stone that provided a step into the soddy. This was my fault. I hadn't tied General or kept hold of his reins. If I'd done either, General wouldn't have run off. It was a stupid, stupid thing, and now Anna would pay for my carelessness.

As I sat in the doorway, tearing into myself, the silence was almost, but not quite, complete. Behind me, I could hear Mrs. Dunham whispering softly to Anna. And from the far side of Lone Tree, the wind brought the faint lowing of the vast Olive herd.

As I listened to the longhorns, I hated them. I hated the Texans too. If they hadn't come here, there'd be no need for a doctor. Burning with anger, I turned and glared at the Olive cowboys sitting hunched in their saddles—

My eyes flew open, and I sprang to my feet, feverish hope surging through my veins. I turned into the house, and in my excitement, I tripped on the door stone and almost fell into the room. Mrs. Dunham looked up from Anna.

"Ma'am," I said urgently, "tell me the way to Doc Sully's."

TWENTY-EIGHT

I was running now, as hard and fast as I could. Across the fields, through the tall grass, along the side of Lone Tree, splashing down into creek, up the opposite bank, racing toward the huge Olive herd.

The Texans had horses.

I couldn't imagine why they would help me save a settler girl. Only hours before, they'd wanted to kill her father. I didn't know what I would say to them. I did know one thing—Print Olive would give me a horse, or shoot me; that's the choice I'd give him.

The Olive camp was set back from Lone Tree, and as I came up from the creek bed, I saw that I would have to pass near the grazing longhorns to reach it.

I kept running. But as I came closer to the herd, every head came up, every eye focused on me. My skin tingled under their gaze. The nearest longhorns began shifting around, snorting sullenly. Then the bawling began, starting with a few and then spreading to the others. Suddenly, the cattle were all moving. A few retreated, but most milled about nervously. Others started toward me, blowing, grunting, sweeping their horns.

I sensed the charge before I saw it. A surge of excitement swept through the herd, and then I heard the rapid thudding beat of hard hooves. I turned to see a mottle-faced monster hurtling at me, head down, horns reaching.

I tried to run faster, but I didn't have a chance. There was no place to hide, no tree to climb, nothing but flat open ground. All my hopes vanished. Everything would come to a terrible finish, and I wouldn't be able to help Anna after all.

Louder and louder, closing fast, heavy hooves hammering in time with rhythmic blowing snorts. I clenched my teeth, waiting for the bone-shattering blow. My mind popped with odd flickering thoughts: Mother in the garden, Anna's smile, my old green bedspread, the scent of Father's hair tonic—

The hooves were so close, so close.

Something came up beside me. I turned my head and found the large, brown eye of a horse fixed on me.

"Swing up, boy, swing up!"

A hand was thrust into my face.

"Swing up!"

It was Mike.

The instant I had his hand, Mike jerked upward and his horse cut hard to the right, leaping forward. My body seemed to snap up onto the horse's back. Clutching at Mike's shirt as the horse accelerated, I caught a blurring glimpse of a mottled head and a curved horn whistling by the horse's flank.

As we sprinted away, the charging longhorn let out a deep frustrated bawl.

"Kid, I had you wrong," said Mike, pulling up his horse.

"Betwixt you and that Jasper, I thought you were the careful one. Now, come to find out, you're a lunatic. What in the—"

"Mike, I need a horse!"

"I should say! Anyone wanderin' amongst wild cattle needs to get up off the ground."

"Mike—"

"These longhorns are mean! They'd just as soon hook your liver as—"

"Mike! A girl is hurt, hurt bad. I need a horse to fetch the doctor."

He turned in the saddle and studied my face, then said, "Hang on."

When we came flying into camp, Print Olive was sitting up against a mess wagon wheel oiling his boots with bacon grease. He jumped to his feet with a boot in one hand and a rag in the other. As I slid down from behind Mike, the whole outfit began gathering around. They were lean, agile men with shoulders slightly stooped from long hours hunched in the saddle.

"Print," said Mike, "the boy needs a horse to fetch a doctor."

Print Olive stared at me with unfriendly eyes.

"What happened, boy?"

"The girl you saw, Anna, she's been hurt, she's bleeding bad. My horse ran off, and if she doesn't get a doctor—"

"Mike," said Olive, "ride out and tell Billy to bring in the horses." Mike wheeled his mount and dashed from camp.

"Town doctor?" said Print, turning back to me.

"No, sir, he lives out here."

"How far?"

"Four miles."

"Eight miles around?"

"Yes, sir."

"You know how to get there?"

"I can find the way, yes."

Olive's men were already stringing out a big V-shaped rope corral, running a rope from the wagon out to a couple chest-high stakes rapidly pounded into the ground. Two other cowboys took up positions beside the corral, uncoiling more ropes, shaking out and sizing their loops.

I was so rattled that at first I didn't understand what was happening—they were going to help.

"Mr. Olive, thanks."

Olive had his boots on now and was kneeling, strapping on his spurs. He looked up.

"Well, I don't s'pose that crazy sodbuster would do the same for us, but nobody with an ounce of honor turns his back to folks that need help."

"Sir, I think Mr. Dunham would help you just like you're helping him."

Olive frowned. "Why'd he send you? Why didn't he come himself?"

"He set out for the doctor on foot. Probably never thought of coming to you."

Olive rubbed his stubbly chin and frowned again.

"What happened to the girl? How's a person get hurt standin' around a big ol' empty piece of land?"

That made me mad.

"Anna wasn't standing around. She was sitting at her own supper table when one of your steers fell through the roof and put a horn in her."

Olive's eyes widened. He took a deep breath and let it out slowly.

"Son, you ever rode a Texas bronc before?"

"You want me to go?"

"Yep. Sodbusters hereabouts won't believe anything we tell 'em. You'll have to speak for us."

"All right."

Someone sang out, "Horses, horses, horses!"

Olive stood up, spurs on, and looked out over the plain.

A tight mass of about fifty horses was coming fast. The air began to groan with the pounding of hooves. Riding beside the bunch, Mike and the wrangler guided them in with a steady flow of curses and piercing whistles.

"Here's what we're gonna do," said Olive. "Me and your ol' pal Mike are goin' with you. That way, if you get thrown, we'll be on hand to scrape you off the ground. We'll take an extra horse for the doc and pray he can ride it. Got that?"

"Yes, sir."

Olive must have seen the concern on my face.

"Listen, son, this'll be a killin' ride. We'll pick mounts that'll run every mile flat out, hopefully without droppin' dead under us. That's what you want, right?"

"Yes."

"Then understand, I'll put you on a horse that'll scare the hell out of you."

My heart sank.

The horses were rushing headlong toward the flimsy rope corral. It didn't seem possible that a single rope strung on wobbly stakes would stop them, but at the last possible moment, every horse threw itself back, sliding to a halt in a flurry of dust. Not one touched the rope.

Olive laughed. "Those jugheads are wild as cougars, son, but they fear the rope."

The two ropers stepped up to the makeshift corral, looking back to Olive, giving their loops a final adjustment. One of them was Jake Waring, the cowboy Hickok had manhandled for threatening the settlers who'd gotten their wagon stuck on the rails.

Olive called out, "Benito, rope out my top, Hammerhead. Jake, Straight Edge for the boy and Gold Dollar for the doc."

"Benito," Mike yelled, "get me Twist."

Knowing what was coming, the horses broke to the far side of the corral. But one after another, the four we needed were caught and pulled from the shifting, dodging mob. Quickly, the men descended on them with bridles and saddles.

I paced back and forth, restless to get going. The Texans worked fast, but nothing could be fast enough.

It took both Mike and Jake to saddle my horse. Straight Edge was a brown with white stockings and nervous, rolling eyes. The animal did its best to kick Mike and almost bit a hunk out of Jake's leg. With the saddle in place, Jake shortened the stirrups and then turned to me.

"There you go, kid. Gentle as a lamb."

Straight Edge was the most ferocious lamb I ever saw. Ears laid flat, legs splayed, muscles clenched, he eyed me evilly, hoping for a chance to kick me into the hereafter.

Jake grabbed the cheek piece of the bridle with one hand and Straight Edge's ear with the other, then pulled the horse's head down and around. "Get on!" he said. But as I went to put my foot in the stirrup, Straight Edge jerked his head up so violently that Jake's feet left the ground.

"He don't trust you, kid, but I'm gonna get you into the saddle anyway."

Jake tightened his grip on the ear, twisting hard until Straight Edge stopped fighting. Pulling the head down again, he took the tip of the horse's ear in his teeth and bit down. Straight Edge froze, and Jake gave me an urgent look that said climb aboard now.

I grabbed the horn, slipped my foot into the stirrup, and pulled myself up into the saddle.

Taking his teeth off the ear slowly, Jake held his breath for a moment, and when the fiery horse remained reasonably still, he sighed and looked up at me.

"Listen, when it's time, I'm gonna pass you the reins. To this horse, that says go. He's gonna move like nuthin' you ever felt before. Keep your weight forward. I don't want you tumblin' off the backside. Understand?"

I nodded.

"What's your name?"

"Will."

"Will, this horse is mean as a snake, but he's got power to burn, and he's hot-blooded. You know what hot-blooded means?"

"No, sir."

"He won't quit. He'll run himself to death if you ask him."

TWENTY-NINE

Olive rode up with the extra horse trailing at the end of a rope. Then Mike joined him on his black. Both men were pulling up on the reins, struggling to hold back their impatient, dancing mounts.

Something new came over Straight Edge. He seemed to realize suddenly that this would be no ordinary ride. Maybe he picked it up from us, or from the other horses, I couldn't say, but in that moment, he became . . . interested. His ears came up, and his heart began to hammer against my legs.

Jake gathered up the reins, which had hung from the bridle to the ground. The horse trembled, his breath coming quick.

"Ready?" Olive asked Jake.

"Ready."

Olive and Mike were off. Jake swung the reins up and I caught them. Instantly, Straight Edge's muscles slammed violently, hurling him forward. In a single jump, we were halfway across camp. Despite Jake's warning, it was all I could do to stay in the saddle.

Ahead, Olive and Mike were riding hard, but by the edge of the camp, Straight Edge had closed the distance with savage effort. At a tearing gallop, we shot like a wedge into the surrounding herd, scattering surprised longhorns like quail as we thundered through.

At Lone Tree, Olive never slowed, jumping his mount head-long into the creek bed. Mike and I followed, and the quiet stream stormed with spraying water as the hooves of one horse after another plunged through.

Now Olive waved me ahead. Without urging, Straight Edge pushed to the front. Only open prairie lay before us now, and I lay low into the horse's swirling mane and yelled, *"Go!"*

Straight Edge threw himself forward. His body began to drop down as he reached out with longer and longer strides, faster and faster, speed building. With every leap, Straight Edge seized twenty feet of prairie and slung it away.

Hot summer air blasted against my face as we hurtled over the plain. Beneath me, the grass flashed in a blur. Behind, a cyclone of swirling dust and flying chunks of sod filled the air.

"Hey!" I heard Olive call. I turned my head to him and he pointed. "There!"

Far away, I could make out the tiny figure of Mr. Dunham jogging heavily through the grass. Even at this distance, I could see he was tired. For a moment, I considered going to him but decided that would take too much time. It was coldhearted, but my job was to get the doctor as quickly as possible, nothing else.

We streaked northward, never slowing, devouring the long miles. The roaring drumbeat of the horses' hooves smashed the silence of the prairie. Straight Edge's nostrils flared wide, sucking in the blazing Kansas air. He gave all he had, straining with every jump to give even more, muscles compressing and exploding, his power seemingly bottomless. As Jake had said, I'd never experienced anything like it. My wonderment, though, was cut by a single thought—no horse, not even this one, could hold such a pace. And I couldn't let him rest.

Three miles out, we barreled up to a tiny creek and crashed through it, wheeling eastward along its banks. Somewhere along this creek lay the home of Doc Sully.

Ahead, I saw the dark, uneven walls of a soddy crouching atop a shallow rise. As we approached, no one could be seen, and it occurred me that Sully might not be home.

Nearing the soddy, I began tightening the reins, trying to drag Straight Edge's speed down. He resisted, and Olive yelled, "Pull up hard, boy, hard!"

Setting my feet in the stirrups, I pulled back brutally on the reins, leaning into them. Straight Edge's head came up, and he threw himself back on his haunches, sliding to a noisy stop. Olive and Mike came up on my left.

Quickly, I studied the horses. At best, we were only halfway through our journey. How much strength did they have left? At first glance, ribs heaving, mouths hanging open, foamy sweat lathering their flanks, they looked done in. But their heads were high, their ears swiveling, their eyes alive, and I decided they were still willing.

"Hello in the house!" Olive called out.

There was no answer.

"Hello!" I shouted. "Is this the doctor's house?"

The only sound was the breathing and bit champing of the horses. Then slowly the door creaked open narrowly, and a shotgun barrel poked out.

"Off my land, Texans!" a man yelled. He sounded afraid.

Olive's hand slid slowly back to his revolver. "We're lookin' for a doctor. Is that you?"

"Clear out! This is my land." The barrel of the shotgun shook in the man's trembling grip.

"Sir," said Mike, in his most persuasive tone, "if you'd just listen, we only want to—"

"You listen! I ain't tellin' you again. Clear out before I fill you up with buckshot."

"Mister, please," I said, "Caleb Dunham's daughter is hurt. She'll die if we don't fetch Doc Sully."

"I won't be tricked! Why would Texans come—"

"It's not a trick!" I yelled.

"Git! The pack of you."

There was only one thing left to do. I didn't want to do it because I wasn't sure how Olive and Mike would react, but there was no choice.

"Mister, my name is Will Merritt. My father is J. T. Merritt, and I need your help."

At once, the door opened fully, and a thin-faced man with long, stringy hair stepped cautiously into the sunlight. Slowly he lowered the shotgun.

"J. T. Merritt's son?"

"Yes, sir."

"Why're you with them?"

"Mister, are you Doc Sully?"

The man stared at me for a few seconds and then seemed to decide.

"No. Sully's place is up about a mile. You'll pass one place, the next is his."

"Thanks."

Olive was giving me a hard look, his brow creased in a frown. Here he was, riding down his horses to help the son of a man who opposed the cattle trade. I held my breath, wondering if he'd quit me.

"Well," said Olive coldly, "this is turnin' out to be quite a day, isn't it, Mr. Merritt?"

I nodded, looking him in the eye.

Abruptly, he wheeled his horse and spurred it into a run. Without a word, Mike followed.

They headed upstream. Toward Doc Sully's.

I turned back to the settler. "Thanks again, mister."

The man smiled. "Sorry I didn't help you sooner. Your father's given hope to people out here."

I felt a powerful surge of emotion when he said this. Love for my father. Fear for Anna. Feelings of responsibility.

Without answering, I relaxed the reins and let Straight Edge go. He had been straining against me, eager to chase the other riders. Now, as I released him, he vaulted forward.

Once more, he stretched out with long, reaching strides, accelerating hard. Tail flying, snorting with satisfaction at every bound, he dug into his pursuit. Soon, I was again alongside Olive and Mike.

We spotted Sully's place from a half mile off and swept toward it in a line. When we reached the doctor's door, I called out straightaway who I was and why we were there. This time there was no trouble. Doc Sully was home, and he grabbed his bag and climbed onto the extra horse without hesitation. He was a heavyset fellow, but he seemed to know how to ride.

We turned south, back to Anna.

Four miles to go. Again, we raced over the open land. Scorching heat and sun beat against us. The grass beneath seemed brittle now, hissing dryly under the rushing hooves.

The horses continued to give all they had, but there was a difference now. I could sense it. Their confidence was fading. The miles and the heat were hurting them.

Another mile, and it happened. Straight Edge stumbled. He

didn't fall, but I felt a buckling misstep. He caught himself, hardly slowing, but then, a short time later, it happened again. I knew what it meant. He was breaking down, his well of strength beginning to fail.

I glanced over at Olive's horse, Hammerhead. The beast's tongue lolled out the side of its mouth, its eyes bloodshot and bulging.

Another mile. The sun was terrible. My parched throat felt like it was closing up, and I blinked constantly against the searing wind.

Straight Edge's breathing was coming hard now, struggling to draw in enough air to feed his exhausted body. Then, slowly, steadily, his stride began to shorten. Around me, the pace of all the horses was dropping off.

I recalled what Jake had told me about my horse—"He won't quit. He'll run himself to death if you ask him."

I hadn't asked, not yet. But what if Anna died because we took ten minutes more to arrive? Or five? Or even one? I'd seen the blood seeping from her.

I shortened my hold on the reins and lashed Straight Edge's flank with the long ends. I hated to ask him to give more than he had, but I did it anyway.

Straight Edge jumped forward, not as strongly as before, but his speed began to build. Olive, Mike, and the doctor began spurring their horses to stay with me.

Ahead, through bleary eyes, I saw something, something upright in the waving carpet of tan grass.

Olive called out, "There's your settler!"

I rubbed my eyes and looked harder. Yes, there was Caleb Dunham, still fighting his way north.

I guided Straight Edge closer to Olive. "I'll stop for him. Go on without us!"

When we reached Mr. Dunham, I dragged Straight Edge to a halt while the others blazed past. Doc Sully gave us a wave and called out something that was lost in the din of hoofbeats.

Mr. Dunham looked stunned when I suddenly appeared before him on a Texas cow horse.

He was in an awful state, dead tired, shoulders sagging, his legs shaking from his long battle through the grass. What unsettled me, though, was his fear. Until this moment, he must have known he would never get the doctor to Anna in time.

"What is . . . what are they . . . ?" he said, struggling to find the right question.

"Mr. Dunham, it's all right. The Texans helped get the doc. He'll be with Anna soon. It's all right."

He smiled weakly, not completely convinced. "But why would they—"

I dismounted. "Mr. Dunham, take my horse and get home."

"Home, yes. I need to . . ."

I put the reins in his hands and lined up Straight Edge so he could climb on. I wondered if my horse would resist being given over to another stranger, but the long run had taken the fight out of him.

Mr. Dunham was so tired he needed a couple tries to pull himself up into the saddle. I winced as I watched the big man drop heavily onto Straight Edge's weary back. He was already used up and now he'd have to carry a rider twice my size.

Soon, I was standing alone on the endless plain. Except for the slight whisper of grass rippling in the wind, the silence was total. But for the first time, the size of it all didn't scare me. I looked all around. Nothing but grass. It was as if I had fallen off a ship in the middle of the sea.

Finding my way back to the Dunham place wasn't difficult; I simply followed the path the horses had trampled into the grass. I moved slowly though. It was much hotter down in the dusty grass than it had been high in the saddle of a running horse. And I was terribly thirsty. The last water I'd had was on the ride out from Abilene.

But a far greater torment than thirst was slowing my progress—dread over Anna's fate. I was returning to her, but I might also be returning to something I couldn't bear.

After trudging along for some time, I thought I heard something. I was so tired and so deep in my worries that I wasn't certain I'd really heard it. Suddenly, I was so completely drained that I sank down into the grass.

Sitting cross-legged, staring vacantly, I again heard the sound. It came from behind. Or maybe not. I had no energy to look. Noises didn't seem very interesting.

Then the noise, a snuffling snort, came once more, louder now. Suddenly the thought that it might be another longhorn burst into my head, and I jerked around in a panic.

General was plodding toward me through the grass. I won't say he was smiling, but he was obviously happy to see me. His reins were still looped around the saddle horn, just as I'd left them. With some effort, I stood and went to him. After I'd stroked his muzzle and given him a few "Good boys," I dragged myself up into the saddle.

We moved along quickly. General had none of Straight Edge's stunning speed, but he settled into a brisk lope and held it. That was fine. The doctor was already with Anna; speed no longer mattered.

We soon came upon a tiny creek where General and I both took a long, cool, glorious drink. Refreshed, we moved on.

Before long, I spotted the Olive herd and then the Dunhams' black stovepipe sticking up from the grass. Dread began to rise within me. In a few minutes, I would be back at the soddy.

What would I hear? Or see? Instead of heading for the soddy, I found myself veering west, toward Lone Tree Creek.

As I came nearer, I made out the Texan horses gathered in front of the Dunham soddy. One of them was down, lying on its side. It was too far to be certain, but I decided it must be Straight Edge. Carrying big Mr. Dunham must have broken him.

As I came up to Lone Tree, I brought General to a stop, dismounted, and stood beside him. Soon, I found myself again sitting in the grass. I would go no farther.

For half an hour I didn't move. General stood over me, occasionally nibbling at the grass, and I just sat, watching the soddy. I could see the caved-in roof, and the Texans standing around. Once, Mr. Dunham came out and seemed to speak to them. The horse that was down never moved, and I knew it was dead. I shook my head, staring into the tangled grass beneath me. What a cruel place this was.

When I looked up, a rider was loping toward me. As he neared, I recognized Mike. Presently, he pulled up his horse in front of me. I didn't stand, and Mike didn't get down.

"What're ya doin out here, Mr. Merritt?"

"I don't know."

"You don't know?"

"Is Anna . . . is she . . . ?"

Mike wiped some sweat from his neck and glanced back to the soddy. "She's alive, but I can't tell you she'll stay that way."

"How come? Why can't you?"

"Just can't. She could be dead in two minutes, or she could live to a hundred." Mike shrugged.

Tears began to run down my cheeks, and I dipped my head again.

"I can say this. She needed a doc for certain. It's like you said; she got gored by that steer. Doc Sully did a bit of operating and stopped her from bleeding out. He worked fast, had a sure hand. I think he's a man who knows his business."

"Is she awake?"

"Nope. She must've knocked her head on something. It seems to trouble the doc that she don't come to."

I nodded a few times, unable to say anything worth saying.

"Sully doesn't think the horn hit anything vital, and he did his best to clean out the wound, so if the corruption don't set in, she's got a good chance. On the other hand, fetching the doc killed Print's top horse."

I looked up. "Straight Edge is all right?"

Mike laughed. "Sure, go say hello. If he don't try to bite a chunk out of you, I'll give you my saddle."

For the first time since the noon meal, I smiled. Just a little.

THIRTY

Anna had been unconscious since the attack and showed no sign of waking. As the afternoon passed, I sat outside with her sister and brothers, waiting and hoping.

Back in Abilene, my parents would be watching for me, their fears growing with each hour that I failed to return. I should have gone home, but I couldn't. Soon, the sun lay on the horizon, and it was too late to make the long ride back to town.

I spent the night on a blanket just outside the ruined Dunham soddy. The kids lay all around me, but we spoke little. Perhaps I drowsed at times, but mostly I gazed up into the starry blackness.

The air hung warm and motionless, and the grass no longer stirred. The stillness was so complete that I could hear the hushed whispers between the doctor and the Dunhams as they sat beside Anna in the soddy. Sometimes Anna would groan or utter a delirious word, and I would sit up with a start, but she remained unconscious.

Earlier, Mr. Dunham and the Texans had used the oxen to drag away first the dead longhorn and then Print Olive's horse. Now the Texans were back with their herd in the dark distance. I wondered how Straight Edge was doing.

The night seemed never to end, but finally a sliver of the sun appeared on the horizon, and the day began as all days begin. I propped myself on my elbows and looked around. None of the Dunham kids were awake. Sleep had come late to them, and now they slept deeply.

I had been sitting on my blanket for maybe fifteen minutes when Mr. Dunham stepped from the soddy and came toward me. He was smiling. I held my breath, but his smile had already filled me with joy.

"Anna's awake."

"She's all right?"

"I guess you know she took a blow to the head as well as bein' gored. That's why she's been out. The doc says that if she hadn't come to by this morning, it would've been a bad sign."

"So, she's all right, then?"

Mr. Dunham's smile weakened. "No, the wound in her side is deep. Sully's cleaned it as best he could, but it's likely to fester, and . . . well, we just have to wait and see."

I stared at him, not knowing what to say. I'd wanted to hear that the ordeal was over, that Anna was okay.

"Listen, Will, I want you to go on home and tell the town doctor to come out here. No need to rush, Doc Sully's doin' fine, but havin' the Abilene doc take a look will be a comfort to Mrs. Dunham. Understand?"

"Yes, sir. Can I see Anna before I go?"

"Sure, if you can get past the doc."

Doc Sully only gave me about half a minute with Anna, but that was enough. She smiled and spoke in a voice that seemed strong, and she was happy to see me. I left feeling good, too good considering the danger she was in.

Twenty minutes later, General and I were riding south alongside Lone Tree Creek. We'd gone about two miles when I spotted a distant rider coming up the creek toward me.

This struck me as odd. It was very early. Who was this? Why would he be coming up Lone Tree at this hour? Settlers usually went to town for a big load of supplies, but this was just a man on horseback. Texans went to town to celebrate, and hangovers usually kept them from rising early. So who was it?

I started to get uneasy. This was a lawless country, and it was wise to be cautious about strangers.

It might be an Indian, and the idea of meeting an Indian in this deserted area made me even more anxious. Only ten years ago, this had been their land. In less time than that, we'd evicted them. The few I'd seen in town hadn't appeared threatening, but it was only natural that they'd be bitter, and maybe vengeful.

Whoever this was, it seemed smart to avoid him. I turned General, wading through the creek, and rode straight west. But as soon as I turned, the mysterious rider did the same. There was no question now—he was pursuing me.

Briefly, it occurred to me that the rider might be my father. But I could see that it wasn't. This man wasn't big enough and his horse was dark, not a gray like Rambler.

As the rider came nearer, I decided he wasn't an Indian either, but that didn't set my mind at ease. I'd made it obvious I wanted to avoid this person, and he was still coming—out here that meant trouble.

I doubted I could outrun him on fat, old General, so I dismounted and drew the Winchester from its scabbard. Then I pulled General around in front of me and stood peering over the saddle at the oncoming stranger.

Long minutes passed as the rider approached. I leaned against General, the rifle getting slippery in my sweaty grip. With the sun behind him, the rider's face was masked by shadow. He wasn't hurrying, and I wondered if he too was afraid. Finally, when he was within two hundred yards, he pulled up his horse.

"Is that you, Will?"

"Who's that?"

"It's Johnny."

"Who?"

"Johnny Hodge."

It was, it really was! I knew the voice. Greatly relieved, I stepped out from behind General.

"What're you doing out here?"

"I'm looking for you, ya dumb ninny, wha'd'ya think I'm doin' out here?" Johnny gave his horse a little kick and jogged over to me.

"Just you?"

"Geez, Will, your father's got all kinds of folks huntin' you."

Oh boy, I'd been so focused on Anna that I hadn't considered what Father would do when I didn't come home.

"Who's out here?" I asked uneasily.

"Ahh, let's see, your father is off to the west of here, Marshal Hickok is searchin' the creeks to the east, my father's followin' the railroad tracks, I'm right here, and you're in a world of trouble. I've never seen your father so upset."

"Ohhhh," I groaned.

Johnny got down from his horse and pointed at my rifle. "Were you figurin' to shoot me?"

"Huh . . . oh, no! I just didn't know who you were."

"Well, fire off a couple rounds. Maybe it'll bring your father to us."

I stepped away from the horses and fired the Winchester three times into the air.

"I'm glad you weren't swallowed up out here," said Johnny. He smiled. "I thought maybe you'd fallen down a well."

"Naw, I'm fine." I slid the Winchester back into the saddle scabbard.

"All right, if you didn't fall down a well, what *have* you been doin' out here?"

I didn't want to talk about it, but Johnny had come a long way to find me, so I told him everything, everything except that Anna's fate was still uncertain. I couldn't make those words come out.

Johnny didn't ask me anything more after that. We just stood there, holding our horses, waiting to see if anyone had heard my shots. After about five minutes, Johnny spotted a rider.

"There's your father, Will."

When he saw us, Father spurred Rambler into a run. I took a deep breath. He and Mother must have suffered through a terrible night when I didn't come home. I had good reasons, but I was still more than a little scared as I watched Father rush at us.

I looked to Johnny, and he gave me a genuinely sympathetic look. "Will, don't worry. He'll understand when he knows what happened."

"I don't know, Johnny. I don't know."

"Will, it'll be all right."

"Johnny."

"Uh-huh."

"Thanks for coming out looking for me. I guess I didn't think you'd do that."

Johnny patted me on the shoulder. "I only minded when my pa woke me at four."

I gave him a weak smile, but it vanished as I watched Father bear down upon us. Suddenly, the air around me seemed to fill with dread. Instinctively, Johnny began to back away.

Rambler charged up, and Father hauled back roughly on the reins, swinging down from the saddle even before the horse had fully stopped. When his feet hit the ground, he paused for an instant, taking me in, and then he came at me with long, relentless strides. His dark eyes never left mine, rooting me to the ground, cutting away everything but his own presence.

I thought I knew him. He and Mother were the two people I believed I knew better than any other. But now Father's face was unknown to me, rigid, distorted, almost wild. I was afraid of him.

"Father, I—"

I never finished. I held out my hands to stop him. Father grabbed my wrist and then my shoulders. His arms swept around, drawing me in, holding me, and after a bewildered moment, my arms tightened around him.

THIRTY-ONE

Mrs. Dunham believed Anna needed to be in town, where she would have a doctor nearby. And so, the day after my return, Mr. Dunham appeared at our door with his head down and his hat in his hand. After a few stumbling pleasantries, he blurted out his purpose—would we be willing to take in his daughter until she was well?

"Oh, you poor man!" Mother cried. "Of course Anna can stay with us, of course! Now, you come right in. I'll get you something to eat, and we'll get this all arranged."

Getting Anna out of the soddy seemed like a good idea, but when she arrived at our house, I was shocked at her condition. The long, dusty, jolting ride in a rough farm wagon had plainly been too much for her.

She had again fallen into unconsciousness. Her face, which had been so tan, was drained white, and most frightening of all, her wound was bleeding again. Mother sent me running for the doctor even before Anna had been lifted from the wagon bed.

We set up a bed for her in the parlor because it was a little cooler than upstairs. Dr. Jessup came and looked at her, but told us there wasn't much he could do beyond putting a new dressing on her wound.

The Dunhams, Mother, and I sat up all that night. Sometime after midnight, Anna awakened, and I was able to remind her that she was at our place and tell her everything would be fine. After a few minutes, though, her eyes slowly closed. I wondered if she'd understood anything that had been said.

The next morning, Anna was awake again and seemed much better. She napped on and off during the day, but was otherwise pretty much her old self.

Jenny was fascinated by Anna. To her, it seemed that she had suddenly and miraculously inherited a big sister. Jenny sat with Anna for hours, even when Anna slept. When Anna was awake, and sometimes even when she wasn't, Jenny would chatter away endlessly. And by the end of the first day, she had brought everything she owned—clothes, shoes, toys, knickknacks—down from her bedroom to show Anna.

The Dunhams remained with us two days but then had to return to their other children, who had been left with neighbors. It was sad beyond words to watch them go and leave Anna behind.

As their wagon rolled away that morning, I felt the wind come up, a little warmer and dryer than usual. It's always windy here, and someone new to Abilene might not have noticed the change. But it was almost August now, and the air gusting past me had a particular smell and feel. I knew what was coming.

This wind was different. It came from far to the south, born in the vast desert wastelands of Texas and New Mexico. And as it swept northward toward us, the air swirling and bumping across the baking landscape, it gathered up heat and left behind its moisture. It was not a powerful wind. It would not uproot trees or carry away buildings, but by the time it reached Abilene, it would be like fire without flame.

As the first breath of the terrible winds arrived, farmers all across the prairie would be looking up from their work. Anxiously, they would turn their faces into the burning air and wonder—was this the wind that would destroy them?

A wind like this did its work in only a few days. The green of the fields would quickly fade away. Supple leaves of corn would soon shatter in your hands, and the flowing waves of spring wheat would harden into brittle stalks. Instead of thriving life, only neat rows of woody skeletons would remain.

As soon as the Dunham wagon disappeared, I went inside and pulled a chair up beside Anna. Already, the temperature inside the house was climbing rapidly.

"How are you feeling, Anna?"

"I feel . . . warm."

"I know, it'll be hot today. Do you want some water?"

She answered so faintly that I found myself leaning forward to hear. "I'm okay."

Okay—that's what she said, that's what she always said, but Anna did not look okay. She looked frighteningly delicate, as if she could be broken by even the slightest setback.

"Can I get you anything?"

"Too warm . . . sleep, just for a . . ." Her eyelids fell.

Mother came in and stood beside me.

"How is she?"

"It's too hot in here!" I said irritably. "Why does it have to be so hot? Especially now."

Mother shook her head. "Will, I'm going to wash Anna's

hair and clean her up a bit. Why don't you go to the Red Front and pick up the mail and a few groceries. No need to hurry."

When I stepped out the front door, the wind was so hot and dry it felt like sandpaper on my skin. On the way through town, I stopped to look at the thermometer in the window of the newspaper office. It read ninety-two degrees, but I knew that an hour from now it would be even hotter. And in two hours . . . well, I didn't want to think about it.

I was distracted as I approached the Red Front, thinking about Anna and my new life. But when I stepped up onto its board sidewalk, a familiar voice jolted me from my thoughts.

"Hot enough for you?"

I turned and found Jasper standing in the awning's shade, leaning against the wall beside the chicken coup.

"I guess we're in for it," I said, forcing a wary smile.

Jasper came toward me. "I'll betcha half these chickens'll be dead of heatstroke by noon."

"Yeah, I suppose so."

"Maybe if we're lucky this heat will kill off a few of your father's farmer friends too. Wha'd'ya think?" Jasper looked steadily into my eyes.

"Yeah, could be." I felt ashamed as I said it.

"That'd be okay with you, then?"

"Sure. Who cares?"

Jasper relaxed slightly. "Ain't seen you in a while. What've you been doin'?"

My whole experience of the past week flashed through my head—my trip to the Dunhams', the longhorn coming through the roof, Straight Edge, Johnny Hodge, Anna staying at our place—it all spun past in an instant.

"Nuthin'."

"Me neither." Jasper sighed. "Kinda miss havin' you around."

"Same with me, Jasper."

And it was. I missed him. He was my best friend.

"Say, Will, come on with me. I'm meetin' the guys down to my place."

"Really?"

"Sure, and they ain't mad at you. I told 'em you got your head on straight about this whole farmer mess."

"Thanks." I felt genuinely grateful and frustrated at the same time. I was enormously happy not to be an outcast, but I also had a powerful urge to tell Jasper the truth. I wanted to scream at him that my head wasn't on straight, that a settler girl was staying in my house, and that the Texans could all disappear tomorrow and I wouldn't care. But I didn't.

"Come on," said Jasper, "it'll be like before."

I had an uneasy feeling that I shouldn't go, although I wasn't sure why. After all, Mother had told me to stay away from the house while she took care of Anna. So where was the harm? I'd drop by the Red Front later to get the things she wanted. Like Jasper said, it would be like before, and I wanted that. I wanted that very much.

"Sure, let's go."

A big grin burst across Jasper's face and then he laughed. "Yeah, right, let's go!"

Jasper and I crossed the tracks, heading for the Elkhorn. About a block down Texas Street, we spotted Gordon loitering in front of his father's store.

"Ho, look what we have here," Gordon called. "It's the farmers' friend." He didn't smile when he said it.

"Shut up, Gordon," Jasper said sharply. "I told ya it ain't that way."

Usually, Gordon fell in line when Jasper spoke, but this time he wasn't so easily cowed. "Where you been, Merritt? Makin' yourself scarce? Maybe you got a guilty conscience."

"I don't have a guilty conscience."

"That's right," said Jasper, "he don't have need of a guilty conscience."

"Hold up your hands," said Gordon. "Lemme see if you got dirt under your fingernails like your farmer pals."

I held up my hands. "Clean as yours, Gordon."

"I doubt that."

"Listen," I said, "don't lay this thing on me. I don't have any more control over my folks than you do over yours. This winter wheat is the worst thing that ever happened to me, and you're just makin' it worse."

Gordon stared at me for a moment, weighing my words. "Let's get moving," he said finally. "If my father sees me with you, he'll take the strap to me."

It wasn't an apology, but it was a sort of grudging acceptance. I knew I was on probation though. One wrong move and Gordon would go back on the attack.

When we got to the Elkhorn, we found Billy and Booth tossing playing cards at Billy's hat, which lay upside down against the wall on the shady side of the building. When they saw me, Billy didn't look at all happy, but Booth smiled, and then frowned, not quite sure how to react. Booth naturally didn't like my family taking up with farmers, but on the other hand, I had saved him from being run over by a train.

"Why's he here?" said Billy.

"Damn! I ain't goin' through this again," Jasper exploded. "Will's here 'cause I say so, Billy, and if you don't like it, take off!"

"Whatever you say, Jasper," said Billy scornfully. He turned and flipped another card at Booth's hat, missing by a yard.

"Billy," I said, "why're you mad at me? Other than being my parents' son, tell me what I've done." Then I raised my voice. "Booth, you've got no call to be mad either."

"Maybe we do, maybe we don't," said Billy. "I think we all got used to not havin' you around."

"'Tain't like that with me," said Jasper. "Like Will says, he ain't his parents. He'd just as soon load all these settlers on a train and send 'em on their way with a wave and a good riddance. Ain't that so, Will?"

"Sure that's so," I said without hesitation. A couple months ago, I would've said it with conviction, but now it was just a bald-faced lie.

"All right, then," said Jasper. "Will's gotten the wind knocked out of him by his folks, and you all want to kick him while he's down. I'm not gonna be part of that. So decide where you stand, ya hear, right now!"

Everyone was quiet. My eyes darted from one boy to another, but no one spoke. The hot breeze gusted, and a stray playing card came hopping and spinning over the ground and plastered itself against my pant leg. I reached down and grabbed it, and with a flip of my wrist, sailed it toward Billy's hat. The hat was maybe twenty feet away, but the card dropped in perfectly and disappeared.

At first, everyone just stared, but then Booth let out a whoop, and that got all of us laughing. Booth took a step forward with his hand out, looking down shyly, and we shook. I turned to Billy and then to Gordon. "Are we okay, then?" Billy shrugged and said, "Sure," and Gordon nodded coolly. For now, the worst was over, but it was a shaky peace.

After that, there was an unspoken agreement that no one would talk about my parents. We talked about cowboys, cattle, Texastown, and even settlers; we just didn't talk about my parents.

It wasn't long, though, before I realized that things wouldn't be like before. I was walking a thin line, measuring my words before I spoke, fearful that some telltale bit of my new feelings would slip out if I dropped my guard.

And I knew they were watching me. Maybe they could sense my doubts, smell my fear. Or, perhaps, it was what I didn't say that made them wonder. No, it wasn't like before.

"Hey," said Billy, "did any of you ever hear what happened to that settler that was on the platform atop the Pearl?"

We were all sitting in a circle in the shade of the building now. The heat was growing all the time, and the shade wasn't much relief, but it was all there was.

"Fell off, I hope," said Booth.

"Right onto the horns of a passin' steer," said Billy with a laugh. He glanced at me, and I immediately forced a laugh.

"Naw," said Jasper, "he quit, after sixty-three hours. Never made it to seventy-two."

"Coward," said Billy.

"Did they pay him?" I asked. Everyone turned to me with uncertain expressions, and I quickly added, "I hope not."

"The Pearl didn't pay him nuthin'," said Jasper. "A deal's a deal says the Pearl, so git!"

"So git!" said Billy, and we all laughed.

Still chuckling, Billy got up and strolled over to the outhouse at the rear of the Elkhorn. We all kept talking, but after a moment, Billy called out, "Hey, come on back here, you all gotta see this."

"Hate to tell you, Billy," Jasper called back, "but we've all seen that before. You just go on without us."

"I'm not jokin'," Billy insisted. "Come over here."

So we stirred ourselves, stepping out of the shade into the

almost painful heat of the blazing sun. As we approached, Billy was standing before the outhouse, holding the door open and staring at something inside. The door blocked the view of the interior, but I could see the tip of a man's boot poking out from beneath it.

THIRTY-TWO

When we came around behind Billy and looked in, there was a dirty, disheveled man curled up on the outhouse's narrow floor.

"Dead?" asked Booth anxiously.

"He's breathin'," said Billy. "I can see it."

"Naw, he's dead," said Gordon. "Dead drunk."

Suddenly Jasper laughed. "A dead drunk settler."

"Don't look that different from a sober settler," Billy added.

Jasper was grinning wickedly. "Let's get him out and take a look at him," he said.

"Ah, leave him there," I said. "He's a mess."

"I don't care," said Jasper impatiently. "Get him out."

"Yeah, but he's out cold," I said.

"So what!" snapped Gordon. "Anybody that passes out in a privy deserves what he gets."

"Will, if you're takin' up for this sodbust, just say so," said Billy.

"I'm not taking up for him. He'll just be hard to move, that's all."

"Yeah, sure," said Gordon scornfully.

They were right; I was taking up for him. I was worried about what they might do to him. But I was right about how hard it would be to move him. A full-grown man wedged into a cramped space and unable to lift even a finger to help is heavier than you'd think.

Jasper stepped over the fellow and up onto the outhouse seat. He tried to lift the top part of the man's body while the rest of us pulled and tugged on arms and legs. The man's shirt ripped when Jasper pulled on it, so after experimenting a bit, he discovered that the best handhold was the man's long bushy beard.

One way and another we hauled the poor settler into the sunlight and then stood over him, breathing hard, a wolf pack around a fresh kill.

He wasn't much to look at. Aside from the full beard, he had stringy sandy hair that looked like it had been cut with a dull knife. His rough woolen shirt, now torn at the shoulder thanks to Jasper, was so grimy I figured no amount of washing could ever get it clean. The seat of his pants had been patched with cloth from a Chapman Grist Mill grain sack. On his feet were worn out, Civil War–style boots that came most of the way up the calf, the kind of footwear our townsmen had stopped wearing years back.

We propped him up in a slumped sitting position.

"Uh-oh," said Billy, "we don't have all of him yet." He reached into the outhouse and produced a frayed straw hat. "Fit for a king," he declared and then jammed the hat so far down on the man's head that his ears folded over.

"Fit for a king," Booth crowed.

That got us all laughing, even me. What was the harm? He

did look ridiculous. And it was his own drunkenness that had stolen whatever dignity he might have had, so why not laugh?

I laughed, but I was also disgusted. This was the kind of useless fool that gave settlers a bad name. It was easy to believe, as Gordon had said, that he deserved whatever he got.

"He stinks," said Booth, scrunching his nose.

"Wha'd'ya expect?" said Jasper. "He just spent the night in an outhouse."

"Yeah, but he stinks kinda peculiar," said Gordon, "even considerin' the outhouse."

"His sleeves look like they're burnt in places," I said. "And look how red his hands are. I think they're burnt too."

"That's why he smells funny," said Billy. "He's smoky."

Jasper was getting impatient again. "Who cares? He probably crawled out of someone's smokehouse before bedding down in my outhouse."

After that, we just stood there. We had him, but we weren't sure what to do with him.

Suddenly, Jasper jumped, as if an idea had hit the top of his head so hard it jerked his feet off the ground.

"I got it! You're gonna love this." He wheeled and ran into the storage shed that hung off the backside of the Elkhorn. We heard him rummaging, and then he reappeared pulling a small flatbed wagon by its long handle.

"What's that for?" asked Gordon.

"I know this looks like a scruffy old wagon," said Jasper, "but it's not. It's a royal carriage for our potentate of the prairie."

"Hey, that's right," exclaimed Billy, "a man of his nobility doesn't just lay about in the dirt. He wants to get up and see the sights."

"And we are but his humble subjects," said Jasper.

We grabbed the fellow and dropped him onto the wagon

like a sack of potatoes. For the moment, he sat there, hunched forward, but then he slowly began to tilt and would have fallen off if I hadn't grabbed him.

"We ain't done yet," said Jasper. "He can't go out in public looking like this. We need to fix him up a bit."

Again, Jasper ran to the shed. There were more rummaging sounds and then he was back, this time with an open can of paint and a big house-painting brush.

"Folks need to understand he's a blue blood," Jasper said gleefully. He dipped the brush deep into the can, and it came out dripping with blue-gray paint.

Jasper pushed the settler's hat up, gave us a devilish grin, and then slapped the big brush onto the man's face, slathering the bluish paint over his forehead and working down to the beard. He stuck the brush back into the can and then finished the job, painting man's neck. For the first time, the fellow let out a sputtering groan as the paint ran over his nose and filled the crevice between his lips.

"Ain't that a sight?" Jasper said, admiring his work.

"If it ain't, I don't know what is," said Gordon.

"Whoa, watch out, Will. He's fallin' again," said Jasper.

I pulled the man upright and then held on to his collar to keep him in place. The man's hand lay on the wagon, and I again studied his red, blistered skin.

"His hands are burnt pretty bad," I said. "Maybe he should go to the doc's."

"Maybe he should go to the devil," said Jasper irritably. "His hands ain't so bad that it kept him from totin' a barrelful of whiskey up to his mouth."

"He don't feel nuthin' anyway," said Billy. "And who cares if he does?"

"He does need somethin' though," said Jasper. "He needs an

announcement. Somethin' to tell folks what he's about. Like how the newspaper announces when someone important comes to town."

This time Jasper dashed into the saloon and returned after a moment holding a small sign with a long loop of string running through two holes at the top corners. The sign read, ASK FOR CREDIT THEN DROP DEAD.

"My uncle won't miss this for a while," Jasper said.

He jerked a piece of straw from the settler's hat. Then, dipping the end of the straw into the paint, he began writing on the back of the sign. When he was done, he slipped the sign's loop over the man's hat and blue head, allowing it to hang from his neck. The sign read, PRAIRIE POTENTAIT.

"Looks purty," said Booth with a giggle.

"Cain't nobody say we didn't treat him with the respect he deserves," said Jasper.

"Yes, sir, this is the royal treatment," said Billy, and we all laughed. We were having so much fun we'd almost forgotten how hot it was.

And so we set off, Booth and Gordon out front towing the wagon by the handle, me bringing up the rear, still grasping the man's collar to hold him in place, and Jasper and Billy strolling along our flanks calling out things like, "Make way, make way, royalty coming through!" and, "Bow and scrape for the potentate!"

Pretty soon, all of us were hollering and causing quite a stir. As we moved up Texas Street, people came to their doorways and poked their heads out of windows to see what was going on. We were a welcome distraction from the maddening misery of the relentless heat. A bunch of crazy kids towing a drunken blue-faced settler with a pathetic straw hat and a scrawled sign hanging from his neck. The onlookers began calling to others to come see and yelling out their own humorous insults. By now, I'd forgotten my misgivings and laughed freely along with the others. It *was* like before. I felt good.

But Jasper wasn't done. He had a settler in his grip, and enough wasn't enough, especially when people were cheering him on.

"Stop!" cried Jasper.

"What?" said Billy.

"I said stop. Boys, this is wrong, and we ought to be ashamed."

"Ashamed?" said Billy, clearly astonished.

"I said ashamed and I meant it. Here we are takin' his nibs out for the grand tour, and we ain't paid no attention a'tall to settin' him up with some proper head gear." Jasper was trying to act serious, but a grin swelled up in his face until finally it burst into a laugh. "Ho boy," he exclaimed, "this is my best idea yet!"

Still grinning, Jasper produced a bone-handled pocketknife from his pants pocket and snatched off the settler's miserable straw hat. He plunged the knife through the crown of the hat and sawed all the way around until the uppermost part came loose and fell to the ground. He then jammed it back on the man's head and looked at me.

"Will," he said, "I'll let you do the honors." He pointed to a rather large, and fresh, pile of horse droppings. "Gather up some of them horse apples and fill up the gent's hat. I hear it's all the rage in Europe these days." He pushed my hand away from the man's collar and took hold of it himself.

I hadn't seen this coming, and I just stood there, kind of befuddled.

"Go on, Will," said Billy. "Fill him up."

I took a step toward the horse droppings but then stopped. "Why do I have to do it?"

"Someone's got to," said Gordon. "Why not you?"

"Yeah, you ain't special," said Billy, "so go ahead."

"Do it, Will," said Booth.

"Aw, geez, I don't know, I just . . ."

"Will," said Jasper, "you can wash your hands right off in the horse trough. Go on!"

"No one's ever seen the beat of this," Billy enthused. "Folks'll talk about it for years."

They were all staring at me now. Waiting to see what I'd do. Naturally, I didn't want to grab up a big pile of horse plops, but that wasn't the real problem. I'd just reached my limit on what I could do to this poor man. But I knew—I could see it in their faces—that if I refused, I would be cast out, and I wouldn't be allowed back in.

"It's hot out here, Will," said Jasper. "We ain't got all day."

"Gawd," said Billy, "this fool settler's just an old tosspot. What do you care?"

"I just don't want to pick up a bunch of crap," I said. "It's no big deal."

"You're right, it ain't," said Gordon. "Like Jasper said, you can wash off in the trough right after."

"Yeah, Will," said Booth, grinning, "it's funny."

I stepped around Jasper and over to the pile of droppings, looking down at it. I stopped again. Behind me, I heard the settler groan quietly.

"Will!" shouted Gordon. "For cryin' out loud, get on with it!"

So I leaned over and stuck my hands under the pile and scooped up as much as I could. It must've been fresh, because despite the heat, it was damp, and some of it fell on my shoes. As I came back to the settler, the man's hand came up and clawed drunkenly at the wet paint slathered on his face. He coughed and paint drops blew from his lips.

"Go on, Will," said Jasper with a laugh, "dump it in there."

And I would have, I hate to say it, I would have.

But as I reached over the settler, I felt a hand close firmly on my upper arm and pull me back.

THIRTY-THREE

"Will," said Hickok with an unnerving steely calm, "put that back on the ground where it belongs and go wash your hands."

My face flushed red with sudden shame, and I turned away, emptying my hands as if I were holding hot coals. Quickly, I scuttled to the nearest horse trough and plunged my arms in to the elbow, furiously scrubbing my submerged hands. I would have given anything for some soap.

When I returned, Hickok was leaning over the settler, wiping paint from his eyes and mouth with a handkerchief. My friends were standing around the wagon, hands in their pockets, looking uncomfortable. Hickok straightened and held out the paint-stained handkerchief to me. "Take it," he said. I took it and began carefully folding in the paint splotches. It was a task that allowed me to avoid the marshal's stare. I lay it in the wagon when I was done folding.

"All right, here's what we're gonna to do," said Hickok. "You four"—Hickok pointed to Jasper, Booth, Billy, and Gordon—"go home and don't let me see you again today. Understand?"

Everyone nodded, including me, until I realized that Hickok hadn't included me in his orders.

"What about my wagon?" said Jasper with just a hint of defiance.

"You can pick it up later at the jail," said Hickok.

Jasper brightened. "So you're arresting him?"

"No," said Hickok, "I'll tote him to the jail and lay him out until he sobers."

Jasper scowled at this. "I want my sign. You don't need that."

"No, I don't." Hickok produced a large, vicious-looking knife, and in one quick movement, he cut the string around the settler's neck and then tossed the sign into the dirt at Jasper's feet. "Now, get moving."

I started to leave with them, praying I might be allowed to slink away, but that was not to be.

"Will!" Hickok said sharply. "Grab that wagon handle and head for the jail."

With Hickok behind, holding the man upright, I gripped the wagon handle with both hands and leaned forward, straining, until the wheels began to move. When we arrived at the little jail two blocks away, I was red-faced and sweating.

Hickok unlocked the heavy, sheet-iron jail door and swung it open. When he returned, he removed the man's ruined straw hat and tossed it behind him. Lofted by a sudden gust, it sailed far down the street.

"Get ahold of his legs, Will. We'll take him in and drop him on one of the cots."

I wrapped my arms around the man's legs at the knees while Hickok lifted his upper body. Staggering with the weight, I sidestepped away from the wagon and up onto the sidewalk, then backed through the doorway, almost falling when my heel caught on the sill.

Inside the jail, it was hot but slightly cooler than most buildings. The walls were a foot thick and built of our local yellowish limestone. Against the opposite wall was a row of four iron cages, seven-by-seven-foot and rising almost but not quite to the timbered ceiling. Each cage was built of crosshatched, flattened iron bars and had a fat, dark gray padlock hanging from its door. The floors were made from sheets of iron jail plate to stop unrepentant cowboys from trying to tunnel out. Today, only the far left cage held a prisoner, a bleary-eyed cowboy with a big white bandage wrapped around his head.

"Got yourself another victim, Marshal?" the cowboy called out as we entered.

"How's your head, Nate?" said Hickok.

"Not so good."

"Then shut up if you don't want it to get worse."

"Yesss, sir."

"Will, keep going, all the way down."

Unsteadily, I shambled around until my backside was aimed in the right direction and then continued on. We headed for the cage at the opposite end of the row from the cowboy. Sweat had soaked my shirt and was beginning to run steadily down my cheeks.

"That fellow looks dead," said the cowboy. "Say, Marshal, do y'all paint your departed folks blue up here in Kansas?" He chuckled.

"Where's Conkie?" Hickok asked, ignoring the cowboy's jest.

John Conkie was the jailer. He was missing a leg from the war, but was still considered good enough with a gun and strong enough of nerve to fill the needs of the job.

"He limped off a while back," said the cowboy, "and I ain't seen him since. Marshal, could ya leave that front door open to let some air in? It's hellish hot."

"Your comfort's not my concern, but I may leave it open for this poor fellow."

We laid the settler on the cot in the last cage, and I backed away, mopping sweat from my face. Hickok stood over the settler, studying him. He reached down and took hold of the man's nearest arm at the elbow, lifting it up to get a better look at his burned hands and singed shirtsleeves. He turned and looked hard at me.

"We didn't do that!" I said quickly. "He was like that when we found him, honest."

The marshal turned back to the settler. He reached down and shook him vigorously by the shoulder. "Hey, wake up there." The man's eyes fluttered, and he mumbled something we couldn't understand, but he was clearly still unconscious.

Hickok snorted in frustration. Motioning me to stay put, he left the cage. When he returned, he tossed me a grimy hand towel.

"Clean him up."

I nodded silently and sat down on the edge of the cot. The paint was still wet, so most of it came off, but not all. This fellow was going to have a bluish tint for a while no matter how well I scrubbed him.

From the other end of the cages, the cowboy called out, "Hey, kid, let this be a lesson—don't paint 'em up till you're sure they're dead."

Hickok didn't bother to protect me from the cowboy's taunts. He sat slumped at a small desk out in the walkway, watching me intently, a pained expression set in his face.

Uncomfortably aware that Hickok's eyes were on me, I

continued working at the paint. Swabbing the man behind his ears, trying to get at the backside of his neck, rubbing at the sun-etched crevices around his eyes and mouth and forehead. Even unconscious, it seemed to me the saddest face I'd ever seen.

Again the settler seemed to come to and speak. This time I made out the word Katie, or maybe it was Cady.

"I better get the doc for those hands of his," Hickok said abruptly. He stood, grabbing his chair and bringing it with him. Stepping into the cage, he thrust the chair up against the wall roughly.

"You sit right there until I get back with the doc."

"Yes, sir," I said, moving from the cot to the chair.

Hickok turned to leave but then came back to me.

"Why'd you do this?" he said, pointing to the settler.

"I don't know."

Hickok stepped closer, looking down on me in my chair.

"Why?"

Standing over me like that, his face grim and hard, I might have felt threatened, but what I sensed most clearly was his disappointment. What I'd taken part in, what he'd seen me do, had shaken his faith in me. He had believed there was something worthwhile in me, and now he wasn't sure. He deserved an answer.

"I wanted to keep my friends," I said, looking down, shamed and heartbroken.

There was a long moment of silence. Sweat dripped from my chin onto the cage's iron floor and quickly evaporated. I looked up again and met Hickok's gaze.

"Will," he said, nodding toward the settler, "I don't know what this fellow's been up to. I don't know if he's in any trouble. You stay here with him until I find the doc. *You* keep him safe."

And then Hickok did something extraordinary, something that sent a cold shock racing out from my chest and spreading through my entire body. He drew one of his two shining revolvers from its holster and held it out to me.

"Take it," he commanded.

I wanted to jump up and bolt from the cage, but I held out both hands, and he laid the gun in them. Slowly I closed my fingers around the barrel and handle and lowered the gun into my lap.

And then he left, without a word of advice, or encouragement, or even caution. I was on my own.

I lifted the revolver slightly, still holding it with two hands, not daring to touch the trigger. It was astonishingly heavy. I knew exactly what it was. I'd read the books and magazines. It was an ivory-handled .36-caliber Colt Navy revolver. This gun, along with its mate, was perhaps the most famous weapon in the world. It was a gun for killing, a gun that had killed.

Any red-blooded man or boy in America would have given anything to hold that revolver—but just then, I would have given anything to be in my mother's kitchen helping her peel potatoes.

As I sat there, holding that fearsome chrome burden, I wondered what I would do if Jasper and the guys, or anyone, came in to harm the settler. I stared at the front door, which Hickok had left open, filled with dread that anyone but the marshal or the jailer would try to enter. Through the opening, I could see the hot wind sending streams of fine dust skimming over the surface of the heat-whitened street.

"Katie!" the settler called out sharply, and I jumped at the suddenness of the sound. This time I had no trouble understanding him. "Katie. Ohhh, my little Katie," he said more quietly, and then a moment later, yelling, hands flailing in the air, "Stop! No! Don't run, no, stop, oh please . . ." His voice trailed off; his eyes had never opened.

I don't know how long Hickok was gone. I suppose it was only about fifteen minutes, but it passed with unbearable slowness. In time, though, he did return. The doctor would be along in a few minutes was about all he said. He held out his hand, and I gave up his revolver, feeling the weight transfer from me to him. "Go on home, Will."

Nothing had happened while he was gone. No one had threatened my settler. No one had forced me to put my finger on the trigger, or pull back the hammer, or raise the gun. I had not had to tell anyone that I would shoot if he did not stand back. I had not had to send a lead ball hurtling across the room at another human being. All I'd done was hold that gun in my sweaty hands and pray that I would not be called upon to even consider any of those terrible acts.

I'd held guns before, of course. There was nothing new in that. I'd been hunting with Father. And on my way back from the Dunhams' place, I had even pulled Father's Winchester from its scabbard to protect myself.

And that was the difference. Here in the jail, it wasn't myself I was protecting; it was someone else, a complete stranger. For fifteen minutes his life had been in my hands. For that time, I stood between him and whatever might have threatened him. And to my great surprise, I took it very seriously, which was what frightened me. I knew that if I'd been called on to protect him, I would have done so. Odd, considering that only a short time before I had treated this man worse than a dog.

During those minutes, sitting in my chair, holding Hickok's revolver in my lap, something changed inside me. After that, no one would ever again persuade me to place so little value on another human being.

"He called out some more stuff," I said to Hickok, "something about Katie."

Hickok didn't respond. He walked over to the cot and looked down at the man.

"He never really woke up, though. More like he was dreaming or something."

Hickok nodded, still staring down at the settler.

I was reluctant to leave. It was hard to shake off the responsibility I'd been given. I was this man's protector now, and I wanted to stay with him. And to tell the truth, I also wanted Hickok to tell me that everything was all right, that I was forgiven, that I had done well, but he was silent.

Reluctantly, I got up from my chair. I wiped my sweaty hands on my shirtfront. Hesitantly, I went over and stood beside the marshal, and after a moment, I leaned over, feeling awkward, and patted the man on the shoulder. "Bye," I said, and then I turned away, stepping from the cage and heading as quickly as I could for the street.

At the other end of the row of cages, the cowboy prisoner dozed, snoring faintly. He'd slept right through my small, short-lived drama, never realizing that for a while I had been his jailer.

THIRTY-FOUR

Downhearted, I made my way to the Red Front to get the items Mother had originally sent me to pick up. Thoughts of Hickok, the settler, my friends, and my own actions swirled about in my head like the wind-tossed playing cards that cartwheeled down Texas Street.

I'd only been gone two hours, but with every passing minute of those hours the air had become dryer and hotter. Clouds of fine, flinty dust were lifted from the baking street and spun about with each sharp breath of the southern wind. My skin prickled in the ever-growing arid heat, and I rubbed endlessly at my eyes to keep them clear of airborne grit.

I got in and out of the Red Front as quickly as I could, and carrying a small box of purchased items and the day's mail, I set off for home at a brisk pace. Mother hadn't told me to return home at any particular time, but I knew I'd been gone longer than expected.

All along the way, glum shopkeepers and clerks stood in doorways or propped themselves uncomfortably in open windows, trying to escape the unbearable heat of their stores' interiors. At the newspaper office, the thermometer now read 104 degrees, and it was not yet even noon.

When I stepped through my front door, I let out a quiet groan. The house was an oven. At once, I set down my box and went into the parlor where Anna lay. All the windows were open, and dust wafted in with each burning gust, settling on every surface, settling on Anna.

Mother was wiping Anna's forehead with a damp towel. When she turned to me, I was stunned to see that she was crying.

"Oh, Will, she's so hot. I don't know what to do."

I misunderstood what she meant, just as I'd misunderstood Anna earlier. "The thermometer at the newspaper office says it's 104 already."

"No, Will, it's fever, terrible fever. I changed the bandage and her wound has corrupted."

I heard soft crying behind me and turned to see Jenny standing in the farthest corner of the room with tears running down her cheeks.

I tried to control my panic, but terror was careening down every nerve in my body.

"I know where the doctor is," I said.

Mother responded immediately.

"Run."

I did run, back to Texastown and the jail. Most of the way I ran straight into the fiery face of the southern wind, cursing it with every step. I sped along brilliant, withering streets, normally bustling but now nearly deserted. In all of Abilene, nothing moved if it didn't need to.

When I burst through the jail door, Hickok was standing

just outside the settler's cage. He spun as I rushed in, reaching for his gun, and then seeing me, was about to take me to task. But I had no time for that, not even from him.

"I need the doctor," I gasped. "Anna's real sick."

Dr. Jessup stepped into the walkway. He had his sleeves rolled up, and sweat had soaked through his shirt around the edges of his suspenders.

"What's wrong, Will?"

"She's boiling with fever, Doctor. Mother's scared to death."

"All right. I'm done here. Just let me get my bag together."

Dr. Jessup was older than most men in town, maybe a few years shy of fifty. A little overweight with graying brown hair and wire-rimmed glasses, he was not impressive at first glance. But he had what people wanted in a doctor, an air of confidence and a way of talking that made you believe things weren't as dire as you'd thought.

"Marshal, I've taken care of Mr. Krause's burns. I'm sure he'll be fine. Keep him here till tomorrow though. I want to take another look before he goes home."

Hickok nodded. "Thanks, Doctor."

"One more thing, if he asks, tell him no charge for my services. He's got enough troubles."

"I'll tell him."

"Doctor, please," I said, "can we go?"

"Hold on, Will, I'm coming."

Out on the street, the doctor and I set off at a brisk pace in his buggy.

"Doctor, is Anna going to be all right?"

"I'm sure she's developed a pretty straightforward corruption of her wound."

"But what if she—"

"Will, I hear you all had some fun with Mr. Krause."

"The marshal told you?"

"Nope, I just guessed. I asked him about the paint I found here and there on Mr. Krause's face. He didn't name names, but he said some boys got ahold of poor Mr. Krause and put him through the mill. You've got blue paint on your fingers."

I was scared and angry and not as charitable as I'd been earlier.

"Yes, and I'm sorry I had a part in that, but he sort of asked for trouble, getting dead drunk and all. Besides, we didn't hurt him."

"No, you didn't hurt him," said the doctor with a sharp edge in his voice. "I suppose it was a fluke of good fortune to fall into the hands of such fine, caring gents as yourself and those other young fools."

"I told you I'm sorry."

"Look at it this way," said the doctor, "if it wasn't for that settler, you wouldn't have found me so easily."

"I suppose so. Is he going to be all right?"

"Ah, thank you for asking. If you mean his burns, yes, but no he's not going to be all right."

"I guess not, anybody that drinks like that."

"He's not a drinker."

"Well, he's no teetotaler."

The doctor didn't respond, and we went a ways in silence. Finally, I had to ask.

"So, why isn't he going to be all right?"

"Again, I'm glad you asked, Mr. Merritt, because I'll enjoy telling you. Mr. Krause has a wife and five children, two boys and three girls. The Krauses arrived here late this spring, and Mr. Krause immediately set to work plowing the fields and getting in his first crop. He spent so much time in his fields that he never finished his soddy's fireplace or bought a proper stove. So his wife did the cooking outside over an open fire.

"Yesterday, Mrs. Krause was cooking supper, and the littlest of their girls—Mr. Krause calls her Katie, but Mrs. Krause usually calls her Katrina—got too close to the fire, and it caught the bottom edge of her dress. Of course she ran, and that made it worse, much worse. Her mother had stepped into their soddy, but her father saw it happen and he ran after her from the field, caught her and rolled her and beat the flames out with his hands."

"Is she going to be okay?"

"No, not ever. Katie died last night. She was six."

I filled up with shame. Once again, all my assumptions had been wrong.

"I'm sorry, Doctor. I didn't know." As the words came from my mouth, I was immediately aware of how poor and feeble they were. More so considering the role I'd played in making the tragedy even worse.

The doctor didn't answer. Abruptly, he snapped his whip over the horses and the buggy's pace quickened sharply. After a moment, talking more to himself than me, he said in a low voice, "Lord, this country is hard on children."

I knew it was true. Only a month ago, Jimmy Lester, a ten-year-old boy from my school, had drowned in the Smoky while swimming with friends. Mary Cotton, only three, had died of diphtheria in April. Lizzy Johnston, eight, had had her ankle crushed by a freight wagon on Cedar Street.

And now there was Anna. How hard would this country be on her?

When we arrived at my house, Dr. Jessup went straight to Anna without a word. Mother backed away from Anna's bed and stood perfectly still, her head tilted down, a cheek resting in the palm of her hand, waiting. When the doctor straightened and turned to us, the look on his face told us that Anna was in terrible trouble.

Mother didn't wait for him to speak. She looked instantly to

"All right, here's what we're gonna to do," said Hickok. "You four"—Hickok pointed to Jasper, Booth, Billy, and Gordon—"go home and don't let me see you again today. Understand?"

Everyone nodded, including me, until I realized that Hickok hadn't included me in his orders.

"What about my wagon?" said Jasper with just a hint of defiance.

"You can pick it up later at the jail," said Hickok.

Jasper brightened. "So you're arresting him?"

"No," said Hickok, "I'll tote him to the jail and lay him out until he sobers."

Jasper scowled at this. "I want my sign. You don't need that."

"No, I don't." Hickok produced a large, vicious-looking knife, and in one quick movement, he cut the string around the settler's neck and then tossed the sign into the dirt at Jasper's feet. "Now, get moving."

I started to leave with them, praying I might be allowed to slink away, but that was not to be.

"Will!" Hickok said sharply. "Grab that wagon handle and head for the jail."

With Hickok behind, holding the man upright, I gripped the wagon handle with both hands and leaned forward, straining, until the wheels began to move. When we arrived at the little jail two blocks away, I was red-faced and sweating.

Hickok unlocked the heavy, sheet-iron jail door and swung it open. When he returned, he removed the man's ruined straw hat and tossed it behind him. Lofted by a sudden gust, it sailed far down the street.

"Get ahold of his legs, Will. We'll take him in and drop him on one of the cots."

I wrapped my arms around the man's legs at the knees while Hickok lifted his upper body. Staggering with the weight, I sidestepped away from the wagon and up onto the sidewalk, then backed through the doorway, almost falling when my heel caught on the sill.

Inside the jail, it was hot but slightly cooler than most buildings. The walls were a foot thick and built of our local yellowish limestone. Against the opposite wall was a row of four iron cages, seven-by-seven-foot and rising almost but not quite to the timbered ceiling. Each cage was built of crosshatched, flattened iron bars and had a fat, dark gray padlock hanging from its door. The floors were made from sheets of iron jail plate to stop unrepentant cowboys from trying to tunnel out. Today, only the far left cage held a prisoner, a bleary-eyed cowboy with a big white bandage wrapped around his head.

"Got yourself another victim, Marshal?" the cowboy called out as we entered.

"How's your head, Nate?" said Hickok.

"Not so good."

"Then shut up if you don't want it to get worse."

"Yesss, sir."

"Will, keep going, all the way down."

Unsteadily, I shambled around until my backside was aimed in the right direction and then continued on. We headed for the cage at the opposite end of the row from the cowboy. Sweat had soaked my shirt and was beginning to run steadily down my cheeks.

"That fellow looks dead," said the cowboy. "Say, Marshal, do y'all paint your departed folks blue up here in Kansas?" He chuckled.

"Where's Conkie?" Hickok asked, ignoring the cowboy's jest.

John Conkie was the jailer. He was missing a leg from the war, but was still considered good enough with a gun and strong enough of nerve to fill the needs of the job.

me and said, "Will, get over to your father's office and tell him to go for the Dunhams."

"Yes, ma'am."

"Then come home."

"Yes."

As I rushed again down the burning streets, I suddenly recalled Mr. Dunham saying that his soddy, with its two-foot-thick walls, was much cooler than the fancy wood houses of Abilene. And now, here was Anna, on fire with fever, lying in our sweltering house. It was a cruel joke.

I found Father sitting in his desk swivel chair under the awning out front of his office. Like most everyone else, he'd given up on work and was just trying to find some relief from the heat. At first, he was delighted to see me, but as soon as he understood what was happening, he saddled General and left for the Dunhams'.

Having seen Father off, I hurried home. Once more, I considered Mr. Dunham's claim that soddies stayed cool even in the worst heat. Of course, Anna's fever and infection couldn't be cured by a cool room. Still, it seemed reasonable that she'd have more strength to fight her fever if she wasn't lying in our broiling parlor.

I snorted in frustration. We'd never get Anna back to the Dunham soddy. The ride would kill her. But what else could we do? The town did have an icehouse, but that would be too cold.

Dr. Jessup was standing beside Anna's bed talking quietly with Mother when I returned.

"Doctor," I said, "I have an idea."

"Will, please," Mother snapped, "not now."

"Mother—"

"Will, not now!"

"*No!* I've got something to say. It might help."

Mother was taken aback, but she let me speak.

"Doctor, over at Hodge's equipment yard there's an old soddy, one of the last in town. It would be a lot cooler than our house, and maybe less dusty because you could keep the windows shut. Anna might be better off there."

"Nonsense," Mother harrumphed, "that old dirt thing. Go on now, let me speak to the doctor."

"He's right," said the doctor.

"What?"

"I'm sorry, Mrs. Merritt, but he's right. A soddy would be much cooler than here, and because we can keep the windows shut, cleaner. Will, get on over to the Hodge place and tell them I'm bringing Anna over. They won't say no."

An hour later, Anna was in the Hodges' old soddy. And indeed, inside that dim, thick-walled little room, it was remarkably cool and still. But this was only the beginning of the battle. Dr. Jessup had blocks of ice delivered by Mr. Edwards, and then the doctor, Mother, Mrs. Dunham, and Mrs. Hodge worked in shifts pouring cool water over Anna's body in a desperate attempt to prevent the fever from consuming her.

And all the while, as the fires of infection raged within Anna, the superheated southern winds fell like swirling hellfire upon Abilene.

Although I wasn't often allowed inside the soddy, I spent most of my time nearby. Johnny and I were given the job of shuttling water from the well when it was needed, but mostly we just waited. The nights were too miserably hot to sleep, and I was frequently there until sunrise.

Jenny would often come to me, take my hand gently, and then ask, "Is Anna going to get better?" I always answered yes. Jenny would then sit quietly, saying little, but rarely taking her eyes from me. Before long, I realized she was searching my face for signs of doubt.

Sometimes I would keep Mr. Dunham company. Mostly, though, I passed the time talking with Johnny, both of us lounging on the shiny new farm equipment arranged in rows across the Hodges' big lot. During those times, I decided I liked Johnny, and I think he decided the same about me.

"Strange, isn't it?" Johnny said one evening.

"What's that?"

"You and me, sitting here, talking. Not long ago, we wouldn't have had one good word for each other. And the both of us keeping watch on a settler girl, a girl who lives in your house. It all would've seemed crazy even a month ago."

I smiled. "Things hardly ever work out like you think, huh?"

Just then, Mr. Dunham appeared from the darkness. He sat down with us and leaned forward, staring at the ground. For a while no one spoke. Our moonlit shirts fluttered in the never-ending wind. Suddenly, he came up straight, pushed his longish hair from his face, and turned to me.

"My crops are gone."

I glanced at Johnny, but neither of us spoke.

"I won't even be able to pay the doctor."

I had to say something. "Mr. Dunham, you can't be sure about your crops. Maybe they aren't as bad as you think."

It was a lie. His crops were gone. Nothing could survive the heat we'd seen in the last few days.

Mr. Dunham stood up, shaking his head. "What a fool I've been, bringing my family here . . . look what I've done to my Anna." The wind blew his hair down over his face again. He pushed it back, and shaking his head, he wandered back into the darkness.

I turned away from his agony, gazing into the wind, south toward Texastown. Despite all that had happened, Texastown was still there. But now I saw no glow of torches above the rooflines, nor heard any sounds carried on the wind.

THIRTY-FIVE

I don't know what's gonna happen," said Jasper. "My uncle's saloon is pretty slow most of the time. Just like the rest of Texastown."

It was around noon, and Jasper and I were walking alongside the tracks, going nowhere in particular. He was doing the talking, and I was trying to seem interested.

Several weeks had passed. The fearsome southern winds were gone, and while that was a relief, terrible damage had been done to settler crops.

"Yep," Jasper went on, "cattle prices are so low the big drovers are still holdin' off sellin' their herds, still prayin' prices'll go up. It's killin' my uncle."

"Why's that so bad for your uncle?" I asked a question now and then so Jasper would rattle on and I could think my own thoughts.

"Geez, Will, don't you know nuthin'? Most cowboys have

been waitin' here for months, and lots of drovers won't pay them until their herds sell."

Apparently, Jasper expected me to make some kind of comment here.

"Hey, Will, are you listenin'? What the heck's wrong with you?"

"I'm listening. The cowboys are broke."

"Uh-huh. Not as broke as those fool settlers though. When the winds fried their crops, it felt like Christmas on a warm day, didn't it?"

"Yeah, sure, I—"

Down the street, I'd caught sight of a familiar horseman coming into town. I gave him a big wave, and after moment, he recognized me and waved back.

"Who's that?" Jasper asked.

"Mike Williams, the fellow that almost got you strangled by Phil Coe."

Jasper's face brightened. "Oh, yeah. Sure it is." He let loose his own big wave, which Mike returned.

"I hear he's quit with the Olive outfit and is workin' at the Novelty Theatre now."

"Is that the horse that pulled my busted tooth?" Jasper asked.

"No, that's another horse." The horse was Straight Edge. Apparently Williams had bought him from Olive.

"Oh, too bad, I woulda liked to seen that horse again. He was somethin'."

"Yeah."

Of course, in my opinion that other horse wasn't but a shadow next to Straight Edge. I longed to tell Jasper who Straight Edge was and what he'd done, but I couldn't.

Resuming my friendship with Jasper and the others had never gotten easier. I had too many secrets now, too many lies to tell. The fear that something would slip out was always with me. So far, I'd been lucky.

There was, though, more to my situation than just keeping secrets. I was weighed down with guilt. Many of the things Jasper said about settlers were intolerable to me now. And yet, outwardly, I chose to go along.

As these thoughts ran through my head, I saw something that made me forget my troubles. About a block up the street, I spotted Anna.

This was the first time she'd ventured so far from our house. She was thinner than before, hollow cheeked and a little unsteady on her feet, but she was getting stronger every day. She was carrying our shopping basket, and I assumed she'd talked Mother into letting her go to the Red Front. I smiled.

"Whatcha thinkin', Will?"

I'd been so pleased to see Anna out in the world that for a moment I'd forgotten Jasper. That was a mistake.

While she was recovering, Anna's injuries had kept her inside our house and out of sight. Still, it was a small town, and word gets around. Before long my friends got wind of an ailing girl staying with my family. When asked, I was vague but sidled up to the truth as close as I dared.

My parents were already guilty of association with settlers, so revealing that they had invited one into our home didn't make things much worse for me. What fretted me was that Jasper might discover that our visitor was the very settler girl who had busted his tooth. I simply couldn't predict how he'd react.

Anna was actually improving rapidly. Her own basic strength combined with the efforts of the doctor and the ladies had seen her through. Soon she would return to her own home, and I would get out of the pickle I was in, hopefully unscathed.

At the same time, though, it pained me terribly even to think of her leaving.

But now Anna was just up the street, coming toward us. At any moment she would see me and wave or call my name.

"Jasper, come on, let's go to the Alamo." I turned south, veering toward Texastown. "Come on, let's go."

"Huh? Well, sure, if you want. I thought we'd go to Billy's."

"We can see him later. Come on."

"Geez, what's the big rush?"

"Come on!"

"All right! What's the—"

Jasper had stopped dead. He was looking up the street, staring intently. I held my breath, but I knew it was too late.

"Hey, Will, lookit there. Isn't that the stupid farm girl that busted my tooth?" He raised his arm and pointed. "See . . . isn't that her?"

I didn't answer. Jasper turned to me, and when he saw the expression on my face, he seemed to realize that something wasn't right.

"What?"

"Come on, let's go."

"No, not yet." Jasper whipped around toward Anna, then he looked again at me. "That *is* her!"

"Let's go, Jasper."

"No." He shook his head, studying me, trying to figure out what was going on. "I'm not going anywhere. That clodhopping girl owes me a tooth."

"Forget it. That was months ago."

"Months ago! So what? I'm still missin' a tooth, ain't I?" Jasper set off, marching rapidly toward Anna. He laughed viciously. "An eye for an eye, a tooth for a tooth."

"Jasper—"

He glanced back, but never slowed. "What's it to you, Will? Why're you takin' up for her?"

"I'm not, it's just that . . . this'll only stir up trouble."

"Trouble don't mean nuthin' to me."

By now, Anna had seen us. She stood at the edge of the boardwalk, perfectly still, watching as Jasper barreled toward her.

"Jasper, stop!" I shouted.

"No!"

"Leave her alone. She's been sick, she's—"

He whirled to face me. "She's been sick?" He jabbed a pointing forefinger into my chest. "And how—would—you—know—that?"

"Because . . ."

"Beee-cawse what?"

"Because she's the one that lives at my house."

There it was. I suppose it was right to stop lying, but, oh, it cut Jasper deep. A plain, simple look of pure hurt came into his eyes. It only lasted an instant before the anger pushed it aside, but it was a hard thing to see.

"I'm sorry, Jasper. She's my friend, but so are you."

"Ohhh no! Not anymore I'm not." He gave me a rough shove and turned again toward Anna.

Jumping forward, I threw myself in front of him, blocking his way with hands outstretched. "Stop! Just stop!"

Jasper froze. For a moment, I thought he'd see reason. I started to explain. But with my first word, Jasper's face began to contort, and I knew I was wrong. He screamed and flung himself at me, catching me hard on the cheek with a big roundhouse that knocked me back. I heard Anna cry out my name, and then Jasper slammed his body into mine, throwing windmills of fists as we fell to the ground.

He crashed down on top of me, swinging wildly, bellowing

with every punch. His face glowed red, eyes bugging out crazily. Flecks of spit flew from his mouth.

Then, unexpectedly, there was a pause in the flurry of blows. He was leaning out, reaching for something. I jerked my head in the direction of his arm. A few feet away, a length of rusty iron chain lay partly buried in the dirt.

He wanted to use that chain on me. I might be in a fight for my life, and so far, I wasn't doing very well.

I couldn't defend myself lying on my back with Jasper pummeling me from above. I had to get free, and I had to keep him from getting that chain. I grabbed him hard by the shirt and tried to roll him off, but he immediately threw a leg out to brace himself.

A punch came down hard, catching me above the eye. Again, Jasper lunged for the chain. I caught his sleeve, dragging his arm back, and he reacted with another punch to my face and another grab at the chain. This time he got it.

I watched his fingers close around the end of the chain, and then one by one the crusted links began popping from the packed earth as he jerked his arm upward. In the next instant, the entire length would sling high into the air, and he would bring it slamming back down. I braced myself for the blow.

It never came. To my amazement, Jasper suddenly seemed to lift away from me, rising rapidly, straight up, as if he were weightless. I saw the soles of his shoes flash by, and then he was gone.

"Are you all right, Will?"

Hickok stood over me, seeming to tower into the clouds. I sat up, looking around, and found Jasper sprawled ten feet away, right where Hickok had thrown him. The chain now lay in the dirt between us.

I felt a hand on my arm, and Anna's face appeared. "Your

eye's cut, Will." She leaned closer, studying me, and smiled. "Not bad though."

I turned again to Jasper. He was on his feet now, legs apart, fists clenched at his sides. I saw the look in his eyes. His anger wasn't used up. If Hickok hadn't been there, he would have come for me again.

"Jasper," said Hickok, "get out of here."

Jasper's eyes never left me. He didn't move.

Hickok took a step toward him. "Go."

Jasper glared at the marshal, still not moving. He coolly slapped the dust from his pants, and after one more threatening look at Anna and me, he turned and walked unhurriedly up the street.

THIRTY-SIX

What was that about?" Hickok asked.

Just then, I was distracted by the fierce pounding of my heart against the wall of my chest. I turned to Anna and then to Hickok with a puzzled look.

Hickok gently put his hand on my shoulder. "Will, what was that about?"

I tried to speak but my mouth was so dry that the words couldn't escape. I swallowed and made another attempt. "Nuthin'," I rasped.

I felt foolish, but if I explained, I would have to admit that I'd kept Anna a secret. She had probably figured that out anyway, and now I was sure she believed I was ashamed of her.

"Nuthin'," said Hickok with a sigh. He leaned close to inspect the cut above my eye. "I can see that."

I dabbed at my eye with a grimy finger. It was still wet with smeared blood but no longer bleeding. Anna was watching me with concern, and I smiled, trying to reassure her, but the smile came out as a crooked, unnatural thing that betrayed how shaken I really was. Self-conscious, I looked away, combing the fight-tangled hair from my face with my fingers. As I did, I felt my hands trembling and quickly crossed my arms to hide them.

Anna pretended not to have seen. "Jasper doesn't like me," she said to Hickok.

Hickok's eyes went wide. "What! How could anyone dislike a girl as beautiful as you?"

Anna's pale face blushed slightly. "Jasper doesn't like settlers, hates us actually . . . but he's Will's best friend."

"I don't think so," I said, almost whispering. I spit some blood into the dirt.

"Jasper is Will's best friend," Anna repeated. She gave me a smile, a wonderful smile, a smile that made the whole world shrink down until only she remained.

"So, you see, Marshal, knowing me puts Will in a difficult spot. And Jasper too."

Standing next to small and frail Anna, Hickok looked a full two feet taller. Hands on his hips, big polished boots planted solidly on the ground, his silver Colt pistols gleaming, he was about as impressive as a human can get. You got the feeling that if a cyclone came along, Anna would be the first thing to blow away and Hickok the last. Anna, however, noticed none of this, and as Hickok gazed down at her, he was, well, respectful.

"I have to admit," Anna went on, "it didn't help that I busted Jasper's tooth."

Hickok let out a hearty laugh. "Busted Jasper's tooth! And you seemed like such a polite young lady. I wouldn't have taken you for a brawler."

Anna giggled. "Sir, I am no brawler. It was an accident."

As the talk between Anna and Hickok flowed around me,

I began to calm down. "She's a little bit of a brawler," I put in. "She just doesn't want to brag."

"Well," said Anna, "I guess I won't sit still for being treated like a dog."

"Marshal," I said, "this's how we got into that fix in Texas-town. We were getting what was left of Jasper's tooth pulled when Phil Coe lit into us."

Hickok turned to Anna. "What's your name, girl?"

"Anna Dunham."

"Anna's staying at our house," I said. "She's the one that had the run-in with the longhorn."

"Well, Miss Dunham, if you don't mind my saying, you look a little wobbly."

"Oh, no, I'm all right."

Anna wouldn't admit it, but she wasn't fully recovered, and her strength gave out quickly. And, to tell the truth, my fight with Jasper had left me a little wobbly too.

"Since we're talking," I said, "maybe we should get off the street and sit down."

We stepped over to a bench on the front wall of a nearby store. Anna and I took a seat, and Hickok leaned against an awning post. As we talked, he couldn't seem to relax. Every few seconds, he would turn his head, first one way and then the other, scanning the street. I realized that when Anna and I seated ourselves against the store wall, we'd forced Hickok to stand in front of us with his back to the street. Now he felt vulnerable. I knew then that he was still getting threats.

"Marshal," I said, "take my seat and get out of the sun."

"Yes, Marshal, if you're looking for someone, you could see better," said Anna.

Embarrassment flashed over Hickok's face, followed by irritation that he wasn't quick enough to hide.

"Don't worry about me."

Now that he knew his watchfulness was obvious, he checked about himself less often, but that only increased his uneasiness.

"Anna," I said, changing the subject, "I've told you about me and my friends sneaking down to Texastown and—"

"And nearly starting a riot," Hickok interrupted.

"No . . . well, yes . . . anyway things kinda went sour, and you should've seen the marshal. This big Texan saloonkeeper, Phil Coe, was strangling poor Jasper, and the marshal came along and flattened him. Just like that. And, Anna, no fooling, Phil Coe is big as a house." I made a motion with my arm like a falling tree. "Boom! That's when we almost had a riot."

"Lot of good it did," said Hickok. "Coe's ornery as ever." Despite himself, he glanced left and then right. His eyes came back to me, and I saw the embarrassment again.

"You still have trouble with Mr. Coe?" Anna said.

"Every day. Business is slow, Phil is usually angry and always drunk. When I enforce the city rules, he says I've got it in for him because he's a Texan."

"But that's not so?" asked Anna.

"All the saloon owners think I'm hard on them. Meanwhile, the council thinks I'm too easy on them." Hickok smiled. "Fact is, all I want to do is play poker." Then with forced casualness, he turned to look behind himself.

Anna didn't understand his watchfulness. She scooted over on the bench, and said, "Marshal, sit here, you can see better."

I decided I had to say something. "Anna, the marshal gets notes from people threatening to kill him. They're nothing but back-shooting trash, but it's still a worry."

"Oh, I see," said Anna slowly.

"It's a painful truth," said Hickok. "The world has more back-shooters than it deserves."

"I'm so sorry," said Anna.

"Don't you worry," said Hickok. "It's easier to make a threat than deliver on it."

"Your job must be lonely," said Anna.

For a few moments no one spoke. Anna's observation surprised me. I knew Hickok's job was frightening and nerve-racking, but Anna had looked deeper. Hickok was so famous I'd never considered that he might be lonely, but as soon as Anna said it, I knew it must be true.

"Anyway," said Hickok, "that night in Texastown, it was actually Mike Williams who quieted those cowboys. He's a tad too sure of himself, but at that moment, he was the right man in the right place."

"He can sure talk," I said.

Hickok looked doubtful. "He'd jump into a hornet's nest certain that he could talk his way out of being stung. But he knows the Texans, and so far, he's tamped 'em down without getting their backs up."

"At the Novelty?" I said.

"Yeah."

"Hey, look behind you," I said abruptly.

It was a poor choice of words. Hickok snapped around so quickly that Anna jumped. But when he saw who it was, he relaxed. "Speak of the devil," he said. Mike was coming across the street and grinning in a way that said he was about to hatch one of his ideas.

"Uh-oh," said Hickok.

"Afternoon, y'all," Mike called out cheerfully.

"Mike," said Hickok, "before I even hear it—no!"

"Marshal, I don't have any notion what you're talking about. It's a nice sunny day, and I'm feeling good about the world." He swept off his hat. "Good afternoon, Miss Dunham."

"Anna," I said, "this is Mike Williams."

"Good afternoon, Mr. Williams."

"You look quite well. I don't believe I've seen you since that terrible day at your home."

"I'm sorry not to recall your visit, but I'm very much better, thanks in part to you."

"No, ma'am. I didn't do a thing worth mention. It was Will here that—Good Lord, Will, what stampeded over you?"

"I've already questioned him about it," said Hickok, "and according to him, nuthin' was what happened. But to me it looked a lot like a fight."

"Ahh," said Mike. "How's the other guy look?"

"You two leave Will alone," said Anna. "He's had enough trouble for one day."

Mike reached out and tilted my head back for a better look. "So, Marshal," he said casually as he studied my eye, "how's the collections going?"

"Ho boy, here it is," said Hickok.

"Just idle conversation," said Mike innocently.

"Collections are going fine, Mike, just fine."

"Hmm, is that a fact?" Mike patted me on the top of the head like a puppy and stood back. "Because, you know, there's usually at least one hard case that holds back."

"Coe."

"Yes! It does seem there's a rumor that Mr. Coe is in arrears with his saloon license fee. Naturally, I don't put no stock in it, a fine gentleman like that."

"He's put me off twice," said Hickok. "I'm speaking to him once more, today, and if I don't leave with money in hand, I'll bring his house down around his ears."

"You don't say!" said Mike. "Why, I heard that too."

"I'm also gonna wring Conkie's neck for his big mouth."

"Your jailer? No, sir. Actually, I can't recall where I heard it."

"All right, get on with it. What's your big thought?"

"Now, Marshal, I haven't had a single thought all day."

I stifled a laugh, but Anna giggled noticeably.

"Tell me," said Hickok, "or I swear I'll lock you in a cell with Conkie for a week."

"All right, here's the deal," said Mike, throwing off all pretense. "I'll bet you a steak dinner I can get Coe to part with his fee money."

"Remember when I said I was inclined to say no. Well, this is it—no!"

"Don't be so quick. If I fail, you get a free steak dinner, and you can still bring the seven plagues down on Coe."

Hickok softened slightly. "What makes you think you can get blood from that Texas turnip?"

"I'm a magician, Marshal, and magicians don't reveal how they do their tricks."

"Magician, huh? How'll I feel if Coe shoots you?"

"Hungry, 'cause you'll never collect on that steak. So, is it a deal?"

"Well, it's true, I'd rather have Coe shoot you than me. This is on your own hook though. Don't come crying to me if the magic blows up in your face."

"You know, Mike," I said, "Coe knows you played a part in that tooth-pulling mess. He's not one of your biggest admirers."

"All in the past, young Will, all in the past. Once he heard I signed on with Olive, I was back in good standing." Mike smiled at Hickok. "Coe likes Print."

"Mr. Williams," said Anna, "aren't you taking a risk on something that's not your business?"

"She's right," said Hickok.

Mike was getting huffy now. "No risk, none a'tall if you handle things proper, and I will."

"Can we watch?" I asked a bit too eagerly.

Hickok was still, thinking. I glanced at Anna. For the first time in weeks the color was back in her face. After the long inactivity and boredom of her recovery, all this man-eating talk about Coe was getting her blood up.

"Not a word of this to Mrs. Merritt," Hickok said, glancing first at me and then Anna.

Anna and I let out a whoop. Then, realizing our enthusiasm might seem heartless to Mike, I said, "Coe won't know what hit him, Mike. You could probably talk him into turning Yankee if you wanted."

Mike's sly smile said he agreed.

So we set off, first dropping by Hickok's austere little office on the second floor of the courthouse to pick up the license fee paperwork. Leaving the courthouse, we headed south, crossing the tracks, and then went a block west on Texas Street to the Bull's Head.

After the Alamo, the Bull's Head was the most popular saloon in town, but you wouldn't have known to look at it. It was a rough, two-story, clapboard building with a big red Texas star painted on one side and 5¢ CIGARS painted in five-foot letters on the other side.

To the front, a large sign that read BULL'S HEAD TAVERN stuck out over the sidewalk awning. On it, the image of a longhorn bull looked down with rascally insolence. Earlier in the season, the sign's larger-than-life portrayal of the bull's male anatomy had offended the morals of the city fathers. The cowboys thought the sign hilarious, but the council had had Hickok order Coe and his business partner to alter or replace it. They had irritably chosen to alter the sign, but the affair hadn't improved relations between Coe and the marshal.

We all paused a little east of the infamous saloon on the opposite side of the street. It seemed peaceful enough. Its doors and windows were open to the street, and all was quiet. A slouching cowboy strolled out, wiped his mustache with a shirt-sleeve, and then shambled on up the street scratching an armpit.

"Looks safe enough to me," said Mike.

"Trouble always starts out looking safe enough," said Hickok.

"Mike," I said, "I think my mother would cook you a steak for doing nuthin' more than showing up. And she's a lot nicer than Mr. Coe."

"I don't doubt it, Will. But I enjoy a challenge. Besides, this is good practice."

Mike let his words hang until someone took the bait.

"All right, I'll ask," said Anna. "Practice for what?"

"Congress," said Mike. "I believe I can talk folks into electing me to Congress."

"Here?" I said incredulously.

"Naw, not here. Even I can't smooth talk a bunch of North-erners into electing a son of Missouri. No, sir, I'm goin' home in a few weeks. I'll smooth talk my brother Missourians, tell 'em I've met the devil himself in Yankee Abilene and learned his tricks. I'll tell 'em that since I'm knowin' Satan's capers and schemes, I can sure make Congress cry uncle."

Hickok rolled his eyes. "Poor, unsuspecting Missouri. It's like the whole state is asleep on the railroad tracks and a train's coming."

"Mr. Williams, when you're elected," said Anna, "will you invite us to Washington?"

"Sure I will," said Mike cheerily. "We'll have lunch with President Grant, and I'll make *him* pay for it too, that damn Yankee hyena."

"I'd sure like to see that," I said.

"And so you shall, God willin', but first I've got to talk Mr. Coe out of some ill-gotten gains."

After checking his shirt pocket for the license papers, Mike started for the Bull's Head, but then turned back to us. Undoing his gun belt, he handed it to Hickok. "I don't need this. The more peaceable I look, the better." Then, more somber than before, he strode across Texas Street and through the saloon's open doorway, disappearing into the interior shadows.

We all stared transfixed at the doorway, as if at any moment it might pucker up and spit poor Mike violently back into the street. But there was nothing—no sounds, no commotion, no nothing—for about sixty seconds.

Suddenly, there was an outcry, almost an explosion of men yelling and shouting at once. A deck of cards flew out an open window, separating in the air and blowing about the street.

"Damn!" Hickok hissed. He tossed Mike's gun belt to me and, jerking out one of his own revolvers, lunged toward the Bull's Head. Again, a shout erupted from inside the saloon.

"Marshal, wait!" I said. "That's a cheer. Those men are happy, not angry."

Hickok halted and listened. It was true; men could now be heard laughing and talking merrily. After a moment, Hickok slid his revolvers back into their holsters and came back to us. He shook his head in amazement, looking very relieved. "Maybe that boy is a magician."

It was ten minutes before Mike reappeared at the saloon's doorway. We stared, itching to hear his tale, but Mike paused at an awning post and leaned against it. He looked our way, favoring us with a self-satisfied grin, and then pulled a wad of bills from his pocket.

"He did it!" I said.

"That rascal," said Hickok.

Mike fanned out the bills and ran a finger over the tops, counting each one, grinning to himself.

Anna couldn't wait any longer. "Mr. Williams, you get over here right now."

Mike shrugged cheerfully, hopped off the sidewalk, and jogged across to us.

"There you go, Marshal." With a twirling flourish of his wrist, he handed the bills to Hickok.

Hickok shook his head in amazement. "When and where do you want your steak?"

"Monday night, Drover's Cottage. And I want one of their Eastern corn-fed steaks, not any of this tough-as-saddle-leather longhorn."

"Done," said Hickok.

"But, Mike," I said, "how'd you do it? I figured Coe wouldn't pay even if you stuck a gun to his head."

"Magic, son. I got the magic. Nuthin' else to tell."

"Mr. Williams," said Anna in her sternest voice, "if you don't tell what happened in there, I think we're all just going to die of curiosity. So please, sir, do not trifle with us."

Mike laughed. "All right, no trifling. I figured it was like Will said, Coe wouldn't pay if I marched in and demanded money. So instead, I marched in and announced I was there as a representative of the city, and that the city was buying drinks for the house."

"That's when they cheered?" I said.

"Yep. This time of day there was only six or seven barflies in there so it didn't cost me much, but it got things off on a friendly note. Then I slapped the license down on the bar in front of Coe, and I says, 'Mr. Coe, I know you've got your reasons for holding up on paying this money, but the town has kids who'll go without schoolbooks unless everyone that owes pays up.'"

"Pretty good," I said, nodding appreciatively. "Not true, but still good."

"Ah, Coe wouldn't know that. Anyway, he's listening, but I can see his heartstrings haven't been sufficiently plucked. So I fired my next volley. I leaned forward and says in a low voice, 'You know, Mr. Coe, there's Yankee saloon men all over this town rubbing their hands together, hopin' and prayin' you won't pay. They figure the city'll shut you down, and they'll steal your customers and line their pockets with money that should've been yours.'"

"Oh yeah, now that's a good one," I said.

"Well, Coe reached into the cash drawer right then and came out with the fee money. 'Mr. Williams,' he says, 'I was willin' to pay all along if only someone had treated me with some respect.' Then he says, 'I cannot say no to a gentleman,' meaning me, and hands over the money."

Hickok snorted at this, but he was clearly pleased. "You'll get your steak, *Mr. Williams*. As for me, I've got to get along and handle a few chores." Hickok paused and studied Anna. Then he turned to me. "Will, I think you should take Miss Dunham by the arm and see her home. She looks a bit done in to me."

I grinned like the Cheshire cat. Hickok had cleared the way for me to do the very thing I wanted most to do. He'd been friendly to me since breaking up my fight with Jasper, but it was only now that I was sure he'd forgiven me for my part in tormenting poor Mr. Krause.

"Anna," Hickok added, "you were right. My job can be lonely, and it's not a good thing. After today, I think Will here is quit with Jasper and his other friends, so you stick by him, see that he doesn't get too lonely himself."

"I will, Mr. Hickok," said Anna, taking my arm.

Hickok departed, and when he was far enough off not to hear, I asked the question that had been puzzling me.

"Mike, why'd you offer to get that money from Coe? Everything turned out fine, but it could've gone bad, and no one expected it of you."

Mike frowned, his eyes following Hickok down the street. "He needed help."

"Marshal Hickok? Why would he need help?"

"Yes, Marshal Hickok. There's not a minute of the day or night that he doesn't wonder if someone's going to put a bullet in his back. It's wearing on him. He's on a hair trigger, and so is Coe. I figured that if they came together right now, someone wouldn't walk away. So I stepped in. And besides, I'm good at this sort of thing."

THIRTY-SEVEN

The weeks rolled past, but my break with Jasper didn't heal. Now and then I'd catch sight of him in town, but he always ignored me.

From Billy and Gordon, I got threatening stares and name calling. Apparently, Jasper had told them I was an outcast again. Only Booth resisted being hostile, but even he didn't dare to be friendly.

Mostly I managed to avoid trouble. I did have a horseshoe thrown at me once. It missed, and I never saw who'd thrown it. Another time, as I looked into a store window, my eye caught the reflection of Jasper standing just behind me. I turned, but he was already walking away, never having said a word. The hate I'd seen on his face left me shaken.

Now it was Anna and Johnny Hodge who were my closest friends. And that was fine. I missed the old times with Jasper and the others, but Anna and Johnny made my life good.

Anna was still living with us, even though she was well enough to go home. I assumed the Dunhams were so penniless after the loss of their crop that my parents had offered to let her stay. That was my guess. I never asked. As long as Anna was there when I came down to breakfast, I was happy.

One morning as Anna and I stepped outside to go to the store, we halted almost at once and inhaled deeply through our noses. I turned to her, and we laughed as soon as our eyes met. We both smelled it—the first whiff of fall. It's not that it was cold—it wasn't—but something in the air said summer was over.

We weren't the only ones to notice. The next day, dozens of Texas herds came in near to the stockyard. For most of the summer, the drovers had held these cattle out on the prairie, hoping prices would rise. Instead, prices had fallen even lower. Now the drovers had given up. Cold weather was coming, and they were all rushing to get out, taking whatever they could get.

Suddenly, the Great Western Stockyards, nearly deserted for months, was working around the clock. Big stock trains stacked up back-to-back from the pens deep into town. Dust and noise and the odor of longhorn fanned out over the city.

It seemed like the rousing days of early summer, but it wasn't. Glum Texans stood along the fences, shoulders slumped, silently thinking their own thoughts. Most would not make anywhere near the money they'd expected.

Texan troubles were opening eyes around Abilene. Even in good times, the Texans had never really been liked, but now, as they became increasingly bad-tempered and short on spending money, the town's attitude toward them hardened.

Most folks still believed that next year would be better, a return to the good old days. But when Father preached that farming and winter wheat were Abilene's future, people were starting to pay more attention.

And Father was once again up to some secret business out on the prairie. Day after day, without explanation, he rode out of town and disappeared into the grasslands. Often, the sun was setting before he returned, tired and dusty. Whenever I asked what he was up to, he would only say, "Looking around, just looking around."

Then, without the slightest warning, Father again changed my life and the life of Abilene forever.

It was a late September morning, and I was in our barn raking out the horse stalls. Feeling thirsty, I turned to get my water jug and was startled to find Father standing quietly at the stall door, staring at me.

"Father, don't do that! I almost jumped out of my skin."

A smile flickered on his face and then disappeared.

"Sorry, didn't mean to scare you. Come on out here. I need to talk to you."

I couldn't tell what was coming, good or bad, but from the look on his face, I knew it was something big.

"Will, I realize you've been wondering about some things I've been doing lately."

"I figured you'd tell me when the time was right."

"Thank you, Will, I appreciate that. And I guess this is the time—I've been buying land."

"Land! But why?"

"To farm."

"But government land is free. Why buy it?"

"I bought land enough for a hundred farms. Far more than I could get from the government. I've acquired ten thousand acres from the railroad and from private individuals."

"Ten thousand acres!"

"It's all located alongside or near the tracks from Abilene almost to Chapman."

I whistled. "That's ten miles."

"Yes."

"But what'll you do with so much land?"

"I'll plant every inch in winter wheat. It'll be the best advertisement in the world for Abilene and Dickinson County. When the trains bring new settlers, they'll look out and see exactly what winter wheat can do for them."

As he spoke of his plans, Father's voice rose and his words came on faster and faster. I knew he was excited. A big project like this was just the thing that got his blood up.

"But, Father, you're not a farmer. And besides, no one could farm that much land."

"No, I'm no farmer, but I know someone who is. Mr. Dunham is going to be my general manager. It'll be his job to hire and look after all the men and families who'll work this land."

Wow! Now I was excited. At the very least, this meant the Dunhams wouldn't move away, something I'd worried about considerably. This was a great day, but then Father made it perfect.

"The Dunhams will live here in Abilene."

"The whole family is coming here? No kidding?"

"No kidding. Caleb has rented a place over on Buckeye. He and I will need to work too closely for him to be out on Lone Tree."

"But what about their farm?"

"Caleb didn't want to leave it, that's true. But I'm paying him well, and he knows this is his chance to make it big. Besides, the Dunhams will still own the Lone Tree farm."

"Buying so much land must've cost a lot of money."

"Most of what we have, and more, if you count what I borrowed."

"Oh. What does Mother think?"

"Will, she has supported this craziness all the way. If she'd been opposed, I would've dropped it. But she's set her sights on what this country can be, and she's willing to take a risk to make it happen. Abilene has turned your mother into a bigger plunger than any gambler that ever worked the Texastown tables."

"Strange, huh?"

"Mighty strange." Father grinned. He was happy, but I saw the weariness behind his exhilaration. For months, as he assembled this vast purchase, he had worked in secrecy, living with the risk and fear of putting everything we had on the line for an idea. I imagined him awake in the dark of night, staring at the ceiling, wondering if he was doing the right thing, wondering if his idea might become another "setback" that would hurl us all back into poverty and a life of wandering.

"Father, the land and everything, it's a good idea, right?"

"I'm sure of it."

"Does it scare you?"

"Oh sure, a little. But I'm doing it anyway."

Father grinned again, and this time, the weariness had vanished.

THIRTY-EIGHT

It was now early October, a time when the weather skipped about like a top spinning across the warped boards of a foot-worn sidewalk. In the space of a few hours, it might dip back into the warmth of summer and then lurch forward into the crisp chill of fall.

Father's big move into farming was now common knowledge in town and out in the settlements. Even his opponents gave him credit for putting his money where his mouth was. Western people admired a man who was willing to take a risk, and Father's risk was so substantial that more than a few held him in a certain degree of awe. Everyone knew that this was what it took to build a new land, and in the end, even the humblest among them would gain some measure of well-being from the efforts of those who thought big.

School had begun again, and Anna was now one of the students. So far there had been no trouble with Jasper or the others.

I avoided him and stayed close to Johnny Hodge and his friends. Still, Jasper's hard feelings toward me were obviously as raw as ever, and I knew he was only biding his time. It was not his nature to forgive and forget.

I had no doubts about Anna, but for a time, I just couldn't fully accept Johnny as a close friend. In only a few months, my world had been turned upside down, and now, as my friendship with Johnny grew, I couldn't shake the feeling that I was betraying . . . something.

But time passed and worked its magic, and one day I realized that I had stopped thinking of Johnny as the son of a farm implement dealer. He was indeed my good friend, and I was his. Not long after, the last molecules of what I had once been evaporated off into the Kansas wind and bothered me no more.

One late afternoon, Hickok appeared at our door and asked my mother if he could take me to the Novelty Theatre on the following evening to see Shakespeare's *King Lear*. He told her that Mike Williams, who still worked at the Novelty, was returning to Missouri in a few days, and this might be my last chance to see him. "And besides, Mrs. Merritt," he said, "it won't hurt Will to take on a little culture."

Mother liked that, but the Novelty was south of the tracks, and she hesitated, saying that she would have to speak with Father. Hickok nodded and prepared to leave, but then Mother held up her hand and said, "Mr. Hickok, I've changed my mind. Certainly Will may go. With you watching over him, I'm sure Mr. Merritt will find no fault."

Of course, I never believed that Hickok's goal was to give me a dose of high culture. I assumed he was being kind, figuring I'd lost all my old friends and might be lonely. That's what I thought at the time anyway.

And so, after supper on Thursday, October 5, 1871, I said

good-bye to Mother, Father, and Anna and set out to meet the marshal at his office in the courthouse. The play started at eight, but I was to meet him at six thirty.

It was chilly that evening, noticeably colder than the night before, and Mother had insisted I wear my heavy winter coat. I'd objected, worrying that the bulky coat would make me look like a mollycoddle to the great plainsman. Mother, however, would not be put off, and I grudgingly worked myself into that scratchy woolen monster.

The sun was only just below the horizon, but the twilight was dimmed further by a looming bank of clouds spreading across the land to the northwest.

When I reached the courthouse, I went up the echoing oak stairwell to the second floor and then down to the end of a dim hallway. There I stopped at a plain windowless door with the word MARSHAL painted on a plaque at adult eye level. I raised my hand, hesitating a few inches from the lacquered wood, and then knocked tentatively.

"Come in, Will."

I opened the door. Hickok was tilting back in a swivel chair with his calf-leather boots up on a scuffed and scarred desk. A bottle of bourbon about three-quarters full stood beside his boots. To my dismay, he was in his shirtsleeves despite the chill of the unheated room.

"Pull up a seat." He gestured to a chair against the wall to my right. His hand held a small glass with just a swig of brown liquor coloring the bottom.

I towed the chair over to the desk and then quickly took off my coat, hanging it over the seat back before sitting. I glanced around the room, but there wasn't much to see. Hickok's gun belt lay within easy reach on the edge of the desk. Otherwise, except for a few papers and a freestanding coatrack that held his hat and coat, it would have been easy to assume the office was unoccupied. I smiled, not sure what to say.

Hickok stared at me for a moment, and then tossed down the remaining bourbon in his glass.

"Ever see a buffalo, Will?"

"Yes, sir."

Hickok nodded slowly, continuing to stare at me. "Ever see ten, all at once?"

"Um . . . no, I don't think so."

"Hmm, not even ten."

"No, sir. Why?"

Hickok looked at his empty glass. He set it on the table and began to rotate it slowly between his thumb and forefinger.

"When I first came here after the war, there was no end to them, millions, beyond believing unless you witnessed it."

"That must have been—"

"And you've never seen even ten."

"No, sir. I wish—"

"The hunters have split the main herd. It's now two herds, northern and southern. As we sit here, the southern herd is being destroyed. A thousand hunters, using guns that can cut a man in two, have it surrounded on the plains two hundred miles to the southwest of us. Before long, it will be gone. Then they'll turn on the northern herd, and it too will be gone."

"I sure would've like to have seen—"

"The Indians tried to stop it. Have you ever seen an Indian?"

"Yes, sir."

"Ten at once?"

"No, sir."

"And yet, they were here, on these plains for thousands of years."

"Yes."

Hickok grabbed the bottle of bourbon and poured about an inch into his glass.

"Will, do you know who it is that actually defeated the buffalo, and the Indians? Do you know who will sweep away the cowboys . . . and me?"

I was confused, not sure what all this was about.

"As I recall," said Hickok, "you didn't think Mr. Krause, that miserable drunken farmer you and your friends tormented, was all that impressive."

"Not then, sir."

Hickok sipped his bourbon, then set the glass back on the desk.

"Odd as it may seem, Will, it is Mr. Krause, that poor little tormented man, who will prevail over every obstacle. There is nothing that can stand against him. In the end, the buffalo, the hunters, the Indians, the cattlemen, the gunmen, and even the prairie grass itself will all be pushed aside by the Krauses and Dunhams of the world. The line of settled land will push across the prairie like a river out of its banks."

"Yes, sir." About then I realized that this was the reason Hickok had brought me here. He didn't care a fig about the play. He had something to tell me.

"All this talk about the Texans, should they go or should they stay, it's all claptrap. They're going. It's only a matter of when."

"Do you think that's a good thing?" I asked.

"I have no idea."

"But you must think something."

"Is a train a good thing?"

"What?"

"A train. Is it a good thing?"

"Sure."

"What about a train with no engineer? Is that a good thing?"

"No."

"Same train—so why's a train with no engineer not good?"

"It could crash. People would get hurt."

"Will, I think you'll grow up to be a good engineer. Not for a train, but for this land. Someone who can keep people from being hurt."

"Me? How can I—"

"Between your father and mother, Will, you take most after your mother. J.T.'s a good man, but he's in love with the chase, the gamble. He loves feeling the angry breath of risk on the back of his neck, something I know about myself. But he might chase the wrong things for the sport of it. Fly off the tracks. It's your mother who's the engineer. She keeps him pointed in the right direction. You can do the same thing."

"For who?"

"For Kansas."

"But how?"

"People listen to you, Will. That's the kind of person you are."

Again I wasn't sure what to say. Hickok didn't seem to expect me to say anything. He stood abruptly, took his hat from the coatrack, and, with some care to get the angle just right, placed it on his head.

"Ever seen Shakespeare's *King Lear*?" he asked as he buckled on his gun belt.

"No, sir."

"It takes place in a strange world of castles and kings and dark lands. But it's about the struggle for control of a kingdom. Maybe not so different from Kansas."

Hickok slipped on his coat. I was glad to see that it was a winter coat, not the thinner broadcloth coat he usually wore.

He adjusted the set of the coat on his shoulders and then grinned at me. "Long ago, back in England, my ancestors worked farmland owned by Shakespeare himself."

"Really?" I laughed as I pulled on my own coat.

"That's the family legend."

"So your great-great-great-grandfather probably saw Shakespeare and talked to him and—"

"And paid him rent."

"Yes! Paid him rent. That's something. Makes seeing this *King Lear* even more interesting."

"Have you seen any Shakespeare plays?"

"No, sir."

"Well, I guess we'll fix that tonight, won't we?"

"Yes, sir."

That seemed like a sure bet at the time, but we were both wrong. It would be three more years before I saw my first Shakespeare play. And I've never seen *King Lear*.

THIRTY-NINE

Around seven o'clock, Hickok and I stepped over the last rail of the tracks that divided Abilene from Texastown.

It was fully dark now, dark enough that it was difficult to see where we were putting our feet. The clouds that rested on the horizon earlier had now spread over the town, adding to the gloom. It was no longer chilly though—it was cold. I had my hands deep in my pockets, sheepishly glad that Mother had made me wear my coat.

Fifty yards off, I could see the dancing glow of windblown street torches blazing over Texastown, just as they had back in the spring. And between the buildings on Texas Street, a sight I hadn't seen in a while—throngs of cowboys flowing along the sidewalks.

I glanced up at Hickok. "Look at that!"

"Busy, isn't it?"

"But why?"

"Quite a few herds have been shipped out. Now the men that minded them are spending their last pay before they go home."

The tone of Hickok's voice told me he didn't much like this, and I wondered if he was about to tell me to go home.

"Marshal, if you don't think I should—"

"It's fine. Follow me."

We headed west along the tracks, moving carefully in the darkness.

"Where are we going?" I asked.

"We'll enter Texas Street farther up and then walk the length back to the theater. I want to see how things look before we get settled at the play."

We turned south on Mulberry when it crossed our path, and a few moments later, Hickok and I stood in the middle of Texas Street looking east. Behind us, the life of the infamous street had dwindled to mostly quiet homes and day shops and was dark and deserted. But before us, looking down three blocks into the heart of Texastown, the street seemed to pitch and sway with currents of humanity surging about beneath the shuddering circles of orange torchlight.

Hickok and I stood there in the still darkness and watched the swarming crowds. I felt as if we were just outside the reach of a cyclone, peering studiously into its roaring, gyrating funnel.

"Coats," Hickok said rather severely to himself.

He wasn't talking about the cold. I knew instantly what he meant. All those Texans, and every one of them wearing a coat, or a duster, or a long jacket—coats that might conceal guns.

"Well, at least the cold has chased the flies away," I said.

Hickok laughed, and I was pleased to have lightened his load just a bit.

"Take a good look, boy. Texastown in all its glory. Chances are you'll never see it like this again."

I looked, and at first it did seem like the good old days of spring, but then I realized there was a difference. The carnival atmosphere was gone. The peddlers and barkers, the fortune-tellers, the Armless Wonder, Professor Xerxes and his Ancient Egyptian Worm Destroyer, the six-fingered three-card monte dealer, all were gone. And from what I'd read in the *Chronicle*, even many of the gamblers and dance hall girls had left, return-ing to Kansas City or Chicago or St. Louis.

Tonight Texas Street belonged to the Texans. Bored men with their final month's pay in their pockets and little to do but drink and look for trouble. Angry men who might feel that tonight was their last chance to settle grudges against Hickok and Abilene.

Without a word, Hickok moved forward and I followed, out of the darkness and into the torchlight. I felt the air leave my lungs as we stepped into the cyclone.

At once I could feel their eyes on us. Eyes that followed us from all sides, even from above, staring down from balconies and upper-level windows. Hickok returned every look, his head constantly moving, taking it all in, missing nothing.

"You scared, Will?" he asked.

"No, sir."

"Liar."

"Yes, sir."

"Want to go home?"

"No."

"Sure?"

"I guess I can take it if you can."

"Good for you."

Hickok made no effort to move to a sidewalk. He walked right down the center of Texas Street. I supposed he wanted everyone to know he was there. The cowboys parted like the

Red Sea as we came through. I trailed just behind and to the side, following in his wake.

As we moved through them, the laughter and loud talk fell away, rising again only after we'd passed. A few spoke, usually something like, "Hey, Marshal, that the best you can get for a deputy?"

Hickok came right back at them. "He'll do for keeping the likes of you in line."

Suddenly Hickok veered off his course. He had seen something. As the crowd opened up, I saw about fifteen cowboys rushing our way in a tight pack. At first I feared they were coming for us, but it was quickly clear that they were intent on something else.

High above them, a dozen hands held aloft a frightened man dressed only in faded red long johns.

Hickok put himself directly in their path and yelled, "Stop!"

The men lurched to a halt so rapidly that they lost their grip on Mr. Long Johns, who yelped and then tumbled to the ground at our feet with a heavy *thump*. He was a middle-aged fellow with a round, clean-shaven face and wire-rimmed eyeglasses that had somehow kept their hold on his ears.

Pointing to the prostrate man, Hickok addressed the cowboys. "What's this?"

A lanky, angular-faced cowboy with a flowing mustache stepped forward. "Now, Marshal, we didn't mean to drop him like that, but you sort of surprised us."

With a groan, Mr. Long Johns sat up. "They tried to kill me!" he declared in a high-pitched voice. "If you hadn't come along, I don't know—"

"Now, that ain't true," said the angular cowboy. "We were just—"

Hickok held up his hand and looked down at Mr. Long

Johns. "Sir, I've half a mind to arrest you." He pulled back his coat to reveal his badge.

"Wha—arrest me! What about them?" the man wailed.

"Yes, you. Even in Texastown we don't allow folks to run around in their underwear."

I began to relax. Even though Hickok's expression was grave, I understood that he wasn't taking any of this seriously.

"Wait just a minute, Marshal. This is not as it seems, not a'tall. I was kidnapped by these ruffians."

"Kidnapped. And how is it, sir, that you came to be in your underwear? Is it your custom to set out for the evening dressed in this fashion?"

"No! No, sir! I am a respectable man on business from Chicago, Illinois. The representative of Hoisington and Company ladies' fine underpinnings."

"Under-what?"

"Underpinnings." The man lowered his voice. "Corsets and suchlike."

"Ah. And tell me, sir, what are you doing here in Texastown? Are you in search of customers for ladies' fine underpinnings?"

The cowboys were now chuckling quietly and sometimes snorting as they tried to control their laughter.

"Um, no . . . I'd heard about the place and thought I'd look around and see— But hold on now! The important thing is that these ruffians attacked me. *They* took my clothes, and I demand justice."

"Yes, a reasonable request," said Hickok, "but it's been a long season, and our stock of justice is very low at the moment."

"What? I've never heard such impertinence. What is your name, sir? I shall report you to your superiors this very night."

"I am Wild Bill Hickok, sir, the man-eating scourge of the West, and I warn you that only a liberal display of cringing civility will allow you to escape with your good health. Do I make myself clear?"

"Oh dear."

"That's more like it . . . and get up out of the dirt, man. Have a little self-respect."

Feeling sorry for the fellow, I took a step forward and offered him a hand. He accepted and rose painfully to his feet.

"You all right?" I asked.

"Yes. I think so. Who are you?"

"I'm Wild Bill's deputy." I couldn't resist. The cowboys exploded in unrestrained guffaws.

"Enough of that!" Hickok boomed, turning to the cowboys. "Now, why has this gentleman been abducted?"

The cowboys grew quiet, looking at each other uncertainly. I figured no one wanted to fess up, but there was another problem.

"Well?" said Hickok.

More silence. Finally the angular cowboy said, "Abducted?"

Hickok rolled his eyes. "Yes, abducted. Why have you stolen this person? Kidnapped him."

"Ohhh!" said the angular cowboy. "Well, we caught him wearin' a plug hat. On our street!"

Hickok turned to Mr. Long Johns, who by now was visibly shivering. "Sir, were you in fact wearing a plug hat on Texas Street?"

"Plug? I had on my stovepipe . . . What's that got to do with—"

"Mister," I interrupted, "I can explain. Up in Chicago, or even north of the tracks here in Abilene, your stovepipe is a respectable gentleman's hat. But down here on Texas Street, you're in a little piece of the South, and a stovepipe is called a plug hat. It's the hat Abe Lincoln wore, and to these Southern men, a plug is an insult."

The cowboys all nodded, and someone called out, "You tell him, boy!"

"See there, Will," said Hickok with a grin, "I told you people would listen if you spoke up."

"You got no complaint, Chicago man," the angular cowboy said firmly. "Some folks down here might've shot that hat off'n your head. Maybe took your head with it." He gave Hickok a sly look. "Not that any of us boys is carryin' a firearm, Marshal."

Hickok's voice hardened. "That's good, Texas. We're all getting along here. I'd hate to have a sudden falling-out."

I decided that this was a good time to speak up again. "Marshal, this fellow's getting awful chilly."

Hickok nodded. "All right, gentlemen, Honest Abe has suffered enough for his choice of headgear. I want someone to see he gets his clothes back and doesn't freeze to death."

"Now hold on, Marshal," said the angular cowboy, "we was havin' a lot of fun with this fellow. Now if'n you take away our fun, I think it's only fair that you stand treat for the mess of us."

I figured that wasn't going to fly, but Hickok surprised me.

"I guess I can bear the cost of a round. You boys do deserve credit for not killing this poor fool. But get him back into his duds."

The angular cowboy, who appeared to be in charge, spun around and called out, "Duff, where are you, son?"

From the back of the group, a youthful voice whined, "Ah, come on, why me? It's always me."

"That's right, Duff, it's always you. Get on up here and take this Chicago fella to find his clothes."

Duff turned out to be a kid about my age with ears he'd have to grow into and a rash of pimples on his cheeks. He shot me a mean look, probably because I was staying and he was going.

Still grumbling, he set off with Mr. Long Johns in tow, the pair of them quickly disappearing into the crowded street.

"Are we still going to the play?" I asked Hickok tentatively.

"Sure, we've plenty of time," he answered heartily. "Besides, if we're late, I'll tell 'em to start it up again."

I grinned at this. There were some advantages to being Wild Bill.

FORTY

I always figured that if you started slicing Texans open, you'd find a quiet, hidden fillet of admiration for Hickok in every one of them. The marshal had all the qualities—courage, skill, intelligence, determination, physical presence—that Texans valued in each other. It was just that they were so certain he'd been hired to use those qualities against them. So even as they admired him, they wanted to bring him down.

The manner of the angular cowboy, whose name was Burdett, only fed my unease. He came across as friendly, but there was something calculating about him, something that made me eager to get away from him. But that was not to be.

"Now, Marshal," said Burdett, "we all hear of this feud betwixt you and Mr. Coe. And seein' as how you're standin' treat, wha'd'ya say we kill two birds and go on over to the Bull's Head and give Mr. Coe our business. Can't hurt, and it might help y'all get past this bad blood."

I thought this was a perfectly awful idea. Better to keep Hickok and Coe apart rather than throw them together. But almost at once, Hickok answered, "I'm game."

Burdett had trapped him. The marshal had to say yes. Refusing would be seen as a sign of fear, and the mob milling around us was always sniffing the wind for even a whiff of weakness.

I don't know why Burdett did this. He didn't seem like a genuine hard case. Perhaps he and his friends thought bringing Hickok and Coe—Texastown's two big bulls—together would be exciting. Of course, down here, excitement was liable to get someone killed.

Somehow word of what was happening passed through the crowd like a diphtheria epidemic. By the time we got to the Bull's Head, the whole street seemed to be coming with us. At the door, Hickok paused and leaned down to me. "You stay out here," he said in a low voice, "and if anything goes bad, you run. Got it?" I nodded unhappily. Like the cowboys, I too wanted to see what would happen.

Hickok pushed through the door, followed by Burdett's crew and a throng of other cowboys. Almost at once, I heard Coe yell out, "Well, lookit here, if it isn't Abilene's mighty dog assassinator come to call. What the hell can we do for ya, Wild William?"

"I'm standing treat for some of these Texas boys," said Hickok. "So start lining up your watered-down drinks."

Oh boy, I thought, here we go. Even as my anxiety grew, I just had to see what was happening. Looking around, I noticed that despite the cold, the top sash of the window to the left of the door was open a few inches. I climbed up onto the windowsill and pulled the sash down another half foot. A steady waft of warm, body-heated air smelling strongly of stale tobacco pushed through the opening. But from that higher position, clinging to the top edge of the window sash, I was able to see over the heads of the men filling the barroom.

The Bull's Head wasn't a fancy place, but it wasn't a dump like Joe Hardeman's Elkhorn either. The barroom was relatively plain except for a massive black-walnut bar, intricately carved and inlaid, that ran thirty feet down the right wall. This extravagant bar, backed by a polished ten-foot mirror that reflected rank upon rank of sparkling glassware and bottles, gave the place an air of class that would have vanished without it.

Out on the raw plank floor, half a dozen worn and battered gaming tables covered with faded green baize were crowded with Texans determined to gamble away their final wages. Overhead, big kerosene ceiling lamps lit the room with a marvelous brightness, far exceeding the dim lighting of most homes.

Coe, wearing a starched white shirt with the sleeves rolled up, stood behind his thronelike bar flanked by two of his bartenders. His coal-black hair, oiled and combed straight back, gleamed under the kerosene lights. As Hickok approached, Coe's mouth curled up into something that would have been a grin on anyone else but seemed another thing entirely on him. Leaning forward, arms spread wide, his outsize hands gripping the edge of the bar counter, he looked huge.

Even though I'd seen Hickok do it before, it seemed that no one could face down such a formidable man. Fear for the marshal flashed through me, and then, oddly, fear for our town. Texan resentment and bitterness had been bottled up all summer, and Hickok was the cork. Who would stand between us and a vengeful Texastown mob if our champion were to fall?

Coe had been drinking right along with his patrons, and it showed. He was loud and challenging in his manner as Hickok came up to the bar.

"Ordinarily, Wild William, I'd have to throw you out," he

boomed, "but seein' as how you're buying for these Texas gents, I'll make an exception."

Smug and confident, Coe glanced left and right for the approval of the Texans gathered around, approval they gave instantly with a jeering laugh. I saw Burdett turn and grin at his outfit, obviously pleased with the trouble he'd stirred up.

Men standing at the bar cleared to the sides so that Hickok and Burdett's men could step up. Coe's bartenders quickly spread glasses in front of them and began pouring whiskey. Coe insisted on pouring Hickok's glass himself, which he filled noticeably short.

Hickok made no complaint, downing the drink in one quick toss.

"I hope that wasn't too strong for you," Coe said as Hickok set the glass back on the counter.

"No danger of that," Hickok came back. "The Smoky Hill runs shallow downstream for all the water diverted off into your whiskey barrels."

Despite themselves, some of the cowboys laughed at this, and that wiped the smile off Coe's face at once.

"Say, Mr. Coe," said Burdett, "you gonna swallow that kind of talk?"

"No, I ain't!" Coe almost yelled. "I run a square place, Marshal. This is just the kind of talk you Northerners like to lay about to keep us Texans down. Well, it ain't gonna play in here."

"Make him take it back," called out Burdett, loud enough for all to hear. "Make him back water."

Hickok spun about and grabbed Burdett by the throat, yanking him up close. "Are you stirring the pot here, Burdett? Maybe it's you that needs to back water." Hickok's grip tightened until Burdett's eyes bulged.

Coe's hand disappeared under the counter and came out

with a gray-barreled revolver. Men backed away immediately, and a few bolted out the door beside me. Even as I braced for the explosion, I didn't leave my window, although that would've been the sane thing to do.

"You been talkin' big, Coe," someone called from the crowd. "Now's your chance. Take him down."

So far Coe hadn't actually pointed the revolver at Hickok. He was hesitating, unwilling for the moment to cross that line.

With a backward shove, Hickok released Burdett, who immediately gasped in air and then went into a fit of coughing.

"Well, Coe, thanks for the drink," said Hickok, "but I've got to get going." He raised his voice, speaking to the room now. "Got to get over to the Novelty. They're doing Shakespeare tonight. Should be a great show. If you boys get tired of losing your money, head over and get yourself a dose of culture."

As Hickok spoke, Coe's revolver slowly drifted lower until his hand rested on the bar counter. He looked defeated. The room hummed with whispers and low grumbling.

Hickok slapped a gold piece down in front of Coe and then leaned toward him. "Put that gun away, Coe. Put it away and keep it away. The season's over, you made good money. Don't spoil it by going home to Texas in a pine box."

The barroom was silent now. Hickok turned to Burdett and patted him on the shoulder. "You all right, son?" he asked. His cockiness gone, Burdett nodded, rubbing his neck.

"Good," said Hickok. He turned and strode toward the door. Men moved aside sullenly as he came.

When Hickok stepped outside, I jumped down from the window and came up alongside him, grinning like a lunatic.

"Oh, man, that was something!" I gushed. "I guess you showed them a thing or—"

Hickok's hand shot up and caught me by the ear, pinching

until I yelped. He kept right on walking, keeping such a quick pace that I had to break into a trot to keep from being hauled along by my ear.

"You are no longer my deputy, Mr. Merritt," Hickok declared in an exasperated voice. "You are demoted back to fool kid." He pinched my ear a bit harder.

"Owww, but I—"

Hickok gave my ear another good twisting pinch.

"What were you doing up in that window?"

"I just wanted to see what—"

"Ahh, you just wanted to see. That explains why you put yourself high in that window where you'd be most likely to get hit if there was gunfire."

"Well, I—"

"Did you see anything that was worth trading your life for? Anything worth the price your parents would pay in heartache?"

"No, sir."

Hickok snorted in disgust.

"But," I said, "it was still a hell of a thing to see."

Hickok laughed so loud that some cowboys walking ahead of us jumped like surprised cats. He gave my ear one last stinging twist and let loose.

FORTY-ONE

S ome colder now, isn't it?" said Mike.

"Summer's over for a fact," I replied. "I hear you're going home to Missouri."

Mike and I were standing at the top of a short stairway that led up from the floor of the Novelty's big open hall to the side of the elevated stage. Mike's job as special deputy was to turn away anyone trying to get backstage who didn't belong there. Usually that meant curious, or lovesick, cowboys. The heavy velvet stage curtain was drawn back a few feet at our side so that Mike could stand in the opening and keep an eye on both the public hall and the backstage areas.

"Yep, goin' home tomorrow. My first train ride." Mike hesitated, then leaned close and whispered, "Will, d'ya think them monsters are safe?"

I had to grin. "If something's gonna do you in, it's not likely to be a train."

"Oh, sure . . . but . . . it's just that I've never been on any-thing so big. Or so fast. Somethin' that uses fire to move itself. Seems chancy, leastways to me it does."

"Mike, remember swimming the Smoky while it was flood-ing? *That* was chancy."

He laughed. "I'm glad to be goin' home though. I've been gone almost four years, and I miss it. I know my ma's worrying, and that frets me not a little. Funny, I couldn't wait to get away, and now I can't wait to get back."

"You'll be home before you know it. Folks will likely throw you a big party."

"Yeah, and I *do* have some stories to tell, don't I? Dang, I'll bet the girls gather 'round three deep to hear my adventures."

I nodded as I peered behind the curtain. In the middle of the stage, surrounded by the interior of an ancient castle, Hickok was chatting with one of the actresses. She wore the costume of a queen, or a princess, a richly embroidered crimson dress flowing to the floor. Her long dark hair came down from a bejeweled silver crown in two carefully woven thick plaits that lay along her chest. Something in her hair sparkled when she moved. I thought she was beautiful.

As I watched, Hickok leaned close and said something to her. She threw back her head and laughed, louder and more freely than respectable Abilene women would allow themselves. But it was a fun laugh, and Hickok was grinning. I found myself wishing it was me talking to her.

"Pretty, isn't she?" said Mike.

My face flushed instantly. "I guess so," I said, making a big effort to sound bored.

"You guess so. For a minute there, I thought she'd cast a spell on you." He arched an eyebrow, obviously amused at my discomfort.

I squirmed, embarrassed that my thoughts were so easily read. I needed to change the subject.

"Mike, I don't s'pose you heard about the marshal taking on Phil Coe. It was something!"

Mike's amusement faded into a frown. "When was this?"

"Ah, Mike, don't be so fretful. He made a whole saloonful of Texans back water. Fifty or sixty of 'em!"

"When was this?" Mike said more forcefully, glancing over at Hickok as he spoke.

"Just now. Just before we got here. Don't worry, nobody got hurt, not serious anyway. But you shoulda seen it. He went right into the Bull's Head and faced 'em all down. Coe even pulled a gun, but he didn't have the guts to use it." I laughed, but Mike wasn't sharing my enthusiasm.

"I don't understand. Why'd he go into the Bull's Head?"

"Aw, some cowboy named Burdett kinda dared him. He had to go. But he made Burdett sorry. Wrung his neck like a chicken." I laughed again.

"Damn."

"Stop worrying! Coe's over at his place, and the marshal's here taking in a play. It's done."

"Was Coe drinking?"

"Sure, but so what? From what I hear, he's always drinking."

"Tonight's different. Coe's been shamed in front of his own people. Whiskey'll only make it worse. You say it's over, I say it ain't."

"Aw, Mike, geez, the marshal didn't go into Coe's place looking for trouble. They're the ones started it. You can't sweet-talk your way out of everything. Sometimes talk isn't enough."

"Is that so? Look, most of us aren't Wild Bill. Most of us have to talk our way through life."

"Sure, I know."

"You know, do ya? All right, then, see this Texan coming down the aisle, the one with the gray hat?"

"Uh-huh."

"He's gonna come up these stairs and try to get backstage. I know the look."

Sure enough the fellow marching down the aisle wasn't looking for a seat, and he wasn't slowing as he neared the front.

"He's comin', Will. Mr. Hickok would throw him out, but you aren't big enough, so think quick, talk him out of his idea."

"No!"

"Here he is, Will. What're you gonna say? Start thinking." Before I could protest again, Mike stepped behind the curtain.

Sure enough, the Texan came to the end of the aisle and marched straight up the stairway toward me. When he was about halfway up, I started talking.

"Sir, you don't want to go back there." I moved to the landing at the top of the stairs, holding my hands up palms out. "It'll spoil the magic if you see how it's done."

"I don't care nuthin' for that! I want to see one of them actress girls, up close."

"Oh, well . . . maybe I can help. Is this your first theatrical extravaganza?"

"Uh-huh . . . but listen, I want to see them actresses. Step aside." With that, he put a hand on my chest and pushed me back as he came forward. In a few steps, we were past the curtain and backstage. And there was Mike, back to the curtain, grinning at me.

"I understand," I continued, "and I'm sure they'd like to see you too, but—"

I saw Mike's eyes flick across the stage toward Hickok, and that made me look. Hickok had stopped talking to the princess and was now staring angrily at the Texan. He would be coming for him any moment. Mike was motioning anxiously to Hickok to stay put, but I figured I had about ten seconds to save this poor stupid Texan.

"Good Lord, sir," I said, raising my voice, "don't come back here *before* the show! Don't you know? Bad luck. That's what theater people think about seeing the public before a show. Why, you'll jinx 'em if you come back here. All these actresses are terrible superstitious. They'll blame *you* for every trifling mistake. You won't be able to crowbar a polite word out of 'em after that."

"Oh," said the cowboy. At last I'd made an impression. He stopped pressing me back, and although he couldn't resist using his opportunity to glance around the stage, it was plain that he was pondering what I'd said. And then he took a step back.

"Ya think maybe I could see 'em after the show?"

"Maybe so, maybe, unless they see you standing here behind the curtain. If you jinx 'em, you're dead."

The cowboy retreated at once, stepping hurriedly back through the curtain opening.

"I don't like a jinx neither," he said. "Saw a fella kilt by lightnin' oncet 'cause he'd been jinxed. Anyway, thanks."

"Think nothing of it, sir. You just didn't know the ways of the theater, simple as that. Now, if you don't mind me saying, go on and get yourself a good seat and enjoy the show."

The cowboy couldn't resist one last peek over my shoulder at the backstage area. But after that, he shrugged and headed back down the stairs.

"Pretty good there, young Will," said Mike, coming forward again. "I could only have done a little better myself."

Hickok came up beside us. He still looked angry, and I suddenly realized that the Coe incident had had more effect on him than I'd thought. Mike, however, was too wrapped up with my success to notice the signs.

"Marshal, did you see our boy Will in action?"

"Yeah, I saw."

"Did pretty good, I'd say."

"Maybe so, but that dim-witted rube got more consideration than he deserved. I'm sick of the whole lot of 'em."

"Now, Marshal, the season's almost over. If we can just take it easy for—"

"Don't tell me to take it easy! I've had my fill."

"I know, but—"

"No, you don't. These Texans better walk a big circle around me."

Mike opened his mouth to say something, but Hickok rolled right over him.

"I'll tell you something else. A Texan that gives me a fair shake is rare as angels' visits. For five months I've been cussed and back talked and threatened. I've been shot at half a dozen times. So, Mike, if you ever live even one day watching your back every second, you talk to me then."

"I was only trying to—"

"Just tonight, this very night, Phil Coe pulled a gun on me. I might've killed him if *our boy Will* here hadn't been in the way."

"Sorry, Marshal," I said meekly.

A look of intense frustration came over Hickok's face. "Don't be, you probably did me a favor. The point is, I'm not in the mood for advice or going easy. I'm in the mood for giving as good as I get."

Now it was Mike's turn to be meek.

"I didn't mean to tell you your business, Marshal. You've been nothing but good to me."

"I know you didn't. Hell, you're probably right. But I'm not going to . . . Never mind. I've had my say. Will, let's go watch the play and forget all this."

"Sounds fine."

"Good. Our seats are right up front on the far end. There's cards on them saying 'Reserved.' Go on down. I'll be along in a minute."

"All right. You coming, Mike?"

"No, I stay near the stage. There's always at least one of these country-boy Texans that thinks the play is real and tries to rush up and save the damsel."

"Fools," said Hickok under his breath.

I headed down the stairs into the hall, which by now was pretty much full of laughing and chatting playgoers. The Novelty was one of the few places where Texans and locals mixed together. Generally, everyone was on good behavior, and unpleasant incidents had been rare.

The Novelty had about thirty rows of seats, the first three being regular oak chairs with seat backs. Behind them, all the other seats were bare plank benches. For the tony folks there was a row of private boxes, each about the size of a big packing crate, running along both sides of the hall. These were raised a few feet from the floor so the occupants could better see and be seen.

Already the room was hazy with smoke from the cigars sold at a stand near the entrance. It being wintry, the body odor one would've expected in the summer was fairly tame, barely detectable under the smoke, the fragrance of ladies' perfume, and the acrid anquitum some of the cowboys used to keep lice under control.

Up on the forward edge of the stage, a man was moving along the row of kerosene footlights, trimming and lighting each one in turn. On the walls around the stage were crudely painted panels advertising local businesses. And stitched onto the big crimson stage curtain, a six-foot-square cloth sign read:

ABILENE, KANSAS
RESPECTABLE
HEALTHFUL
PROFITABLE

As I passed along the front row of seats, I saw the town's leading lights sitting side by side with some of the more substantial Texas drovers.

The town ladies were turned out in their best beaded and embroidered silk dresses, sitting a bit uncomfortably forward in the small chairs to accommodate the huge bustles that were all the rage.

The local men, most in dark suits and vests with gleaming silver watch chains and highly polished black shoes, occasionally tugged at their rigid neck-biting collars and squirmed in their stiffly starched white shirts.

The Texans, of course, wore their best boots rather than shoes, and often had highly colorful silk vests, items that our men regarded disapprovingly as "showy," or worse yet, "flashy."

People I knew waved and said hello. Mr. Tower, who ran the train depot, called out asking where my parents were. I paused and called back, a little louder than necessary: "They're to home. I'm here with Marshal Hickok." And just as I'd hoped, folks were both surprised and impressed.

I admit I was pretty excited. I was about to see a play that would bring to life a distant place and long-ago time. It all seemed very exotic. I felt grown-up and about as sophisticated as a small-town Kansas boy had a right to feel.

As Hickok had said, at the far end of the front row, I could see the white "Reserved" cards lying on the seat bottoms of the last two chairs. But just before I reached our seats, two young cowboys came around the other side and flopped into them. They immediately slouched back and extended their legs. One of them snatched the card from under himself and flicked it into the aisle. They grinned at each other and seemed quite pleased with themselves.

"Hey, those are my seats!" I said.

The cowboy closest to me, sporting a thin immature mustache, looked surprised and then gave me a look of disdain.

"Kid, if these seats were yours, you'd be sittin' in 'em, but you ain't."

"No, these seats are reserved."

The cowboy stared blankly at me, then turned to his friend, a skinny fellow with a drooping right eyelid and an impressive scar just above on his forehead. The friend looked up at me and quickly seemed to decide that I wasn't to be trusted. He frowned and shook his head. That was good enough for the mustached cowboy.

"Get lost."

"No! Those are my seats." I pointed to the remaining white card that was peeking out from beneath the mustached cowboy's rear. "Look, you're sitting on the card that says so."

The mustached cowboy looked where I was pointing and then pulled the card from under himself. He stared hard at it, then held it up for his friend to see. Again the friend shook his head side to side.

"Look here, city boy," said the mustached cowboy, "we paid for these chairs. We paid more than we could afford just to sit up front, and no Yankee trickster is gonna swindle us out of 'em. So, for the last time, git."

"But you saw the card!" I said, almost yelling. I glanced

from one cowboy to the other, but oddly they seemed genuinely confused by what was happening. I just didn't get the feeling they were trying to steal my seats. And then I figured it out— they didn't know how to read.

Too late. Hickok had come up the row behind, and quick as a blink, he grabbed both of them by their coat collars and yanked them up out of their seats. The mustached cowboy's chair fell backward, and Hickok gave it a kick that sent it flying into the stage's support wall.

"Hey, what the—" cried the mustached cowboy. But Hickok was in no mood for talk. He came through the opening where the chair had been, hauling the two unfortunate cowboys with him.

"Marshal," I said, "I don't think they know—"

Hickok wasn't listening to me either. Still clenching their collars, he spun the cowboys around and hustled them up the aisle, almost at a run, toward the exit. Some of the Texans in the audience rose from their seats, trying to decide if they should interfere. But Hickok and the two cowboys and I quickly disappeared through the doors at the back of the hall, and none of the Texans chose to follow.

Close behind Hickok, I was still trying to make him stop and listen. It was like reasoning with a wind-driven prairie fire. Slowing for nothing, he rushed through the lobby with the two cowboys straight-armed in front of him.

Unlike his friend, the mustached cowboy wasn't going quietly. He howled all the way. "We paid for them seats, we paid, you can't treat us like this, you damn crooked thief, you hear that, thief, there's gonna be a judgment for this, a judgment for certain!"

He kept it up even as Hickok slammed them through the Novelty's big front doors and onto the veranda. The droop-eyed cowboy suddenly lost his feet and started to fall, but Hickok jerked him up and shoved him hard off the veranda into the street.

Seeing a chance, the mustached cowboy tried to quickly twist out of the marshal's grip. But Hickok kept his hold and with his free hand grabbed the cowboy from behind by his belt. A few rapid steps and a solid kick in the behind sent the still hollering cowboy flying off the veranda and tumbling into the dirt and horse manure. As soon as he'd stopped rolling, he was back on his feet and yelling.

"You ain't so powerful much! Bossin' folks like they's dogs. You'll get a takin' down soon enough. Hell's own trouble. Don't think you ain't."

"Ah, shut up," said Hickok. "Get on out of here before I throw the both of you in the calaboose." His rage appeared to be used up. He looked tired.

"No! I'll have my say. This town ain't so much. Not so much a'tall. Back in Texas, I dreamed of seein' Abilene, but I been treated raw since I got here. Texas boys can't get a breath of air or a polite word without havin' their pockets picked by the double shufflers runnin' this hole. And, ohhh, if you want a good thrashin', just try complainin'. Ain't that so, Mr. Wild Bill?"

Hickok didn't answer. But he took a slow step closer to the cowboy, moving to the very edge of the veranda. As always, it was like watching a snake coil.

"Look, cowboy," I said, "you got cause to be some mad, but fact is, you took our seats. That's what those cards said. If you'd known how to read, none of this would've happened. Maybe that isn't your fault, but it isn't ours either. So just go."

"Ya know, kid," said the cowboy, "all your blatherin' is like water off'n a duck's back to me. They start liars out young up here. I wouldn't b'lieve a Yankee preacher's newborn babe."

"You don't have to believe a thing," said Hickok. "You need to get going."

"Oh, we're goin'. Sure we are. But maybe us and all the others you've high-handed will just up and burn this burg as a fare-thee-well. What d'ya think a that?"

Hickok stepped down from the veranda. "I think you're the youngest windbag I ever met."

"You're another!"

The marshal lunged forward, and even though the mustached cowboy retreated fast, Hickok would've caught him, but it didn't happen.

Somewhere down Texas Street, a gunshot hammered sharp and clear in the frigid air. Hickok halted, turning to look down the crowded street. The mustached cowboy and his friend skipped away, forgotten. The piercing crack of a second shot came to us. And then another.

Hickok gave me a dead serious look and said, "Don't follow me!" Then he rushed off toward the gunfire.

FORTY-TWO

The shots had come from the west, and as soon as I heard them, I figured it was Coe. I suppose Hickok thought the same. But the shots didn't sound like they came from the Bull's Head. They were closer, nearer the whereabouts of the Alamo around the next corner. On a night like this, though, it was hard to tell.

For a time, after the marshal had gone, I just stood there on the Novelty's veranda. What should I do? Should I do anything?

And then I remembered what Mike had said—Hickok had shamed Coe in front of his fellow Texans, and that meant more trouble was coming. I hadn't believed him, but I did now. I whirled and ran back into the Novelty. Mike had also said that most people had to talk their way through life, and no one talked better than him. Maybe he could stop this before it spun out of control.

As I rushed down the aisle toward the stage, the house lights were being turned down, and the big curtain was rising. The audience had gone quiet, and my rapid footfalls on the board floor seemed very loud. Someone called out an irritable "Quiet there!" as I sped past. Mike had moved down from the stage and was now standing against the wall at the bottom of the short stairway.

"Mike, the marshal needs you!" I called. Several people seated nearby hissed, "Shhhh!" but I paid no mind. "Mike! Please, we need to go."

The curtain continued to lift, and the stage lights revealed the stone-walled castle interior I'd seen earlier. Three men in the rich costume of an ancient time stood in the center of the stage.

"Will, quiet!" said Mike. "The play's starting."

"Mike, there's been gunfire. Marshal Hickok left. I think it's Coe."

Before Mike could answer, the baritone voice of one of the actors filled the hall:

I thought the king had more affected the Duke of Albany than Cornwall.

My eyes never left Mike. He understood now. I knew because he looked afraid.

"Where?"

"Maybe over around by the Alamo. I can't be sure."

Mike's hand flicked down and touched his revolver, as if to assure himself that it was there.

"Don't worry, Will, it'll be all right." He grabbed his hat and coat from behind the stair railing. "Go have a seat and enjoy the show. Understand?"

"Yes."

"I'll help him, Will. We'll both be back in a few minutes."

As he spoke, he pressed his hand against the revolver through the thickness of his coat. I don't think he knew he was doing it. He was scared, but he was going anyway.

I watched him hurry up the aisle, and just as he disappeared through the doors, the truth settled on me. And I turned and ran.

Mike's usual confident cockiness had vanished. This time even he didn't believe talk would be enough. Tonight, men were determined to kill each other.

As I sped up the aisle, past blurring rows of carefree playgoers, I heard the deep resonant words of King Lear, like the voice of God himself, speak to me from his ancient fortress of stone:

Meantime we shall express our darker purpose.

Out in the street, I tore into the restless shifting throng of Texans, searching ahead for Mike even as I dodged and weaved and bumped through the crisscross of humanity.

I didn't know what I would do when I found Mike, or the marshal. Neither would be glad to see me. Still, I couldn't sit safe and warm in a theater while my friends were in harm's way.

As I came flying up to Cedar Street, the press of milling cowboys thinned, and I caught sight of Mike about fifty feet away. I didn't want him to spot me yet, so I slowed, keeping a distance. A moment later, he turned down Cedar, disappearing from view as he ran along the sidewalk toward the Alamo.

When I swung around the corner, I saw why the crowd had thinned behind me. Texans from all around were moving toward the area in front of the Alamo. I jumped onto the sidewalk and rushed forward until I was only fifteen feet behind Mike.

Even though I hadn't yet seen Hickok, I knew he was somewhere ahead. Many cowboys were gathering in the street, leaving the sidewalk clear enough for me to hold my position behind Mike. But Mike was advancing more cautiously now, walking briskly but not running.

Suddenly, a roar of voices, catcalling and laughing, erupted from men I couldn't yet see. And then Coe's voice, insolent and smart-alecky, rose up from the din: "I was only shootin' at a stray dog, Marshal. No need gettin' all het up." Another shout of crowing, jeering Texans burst into the chill air.

Now I saw Hickok. Looking past Mike and others on the sidewalk, I could see him standing up on the Alamo's low veranda, feet apart, holding both big silver Colts out before him. A little closer and I spotted Coe. There he was, stinking for trouble, at the front of a tight knot of about seventy Texans. A big rectangle of light pouring out of the Alamo's central glass doors cast Hickok's shadow, like a demon spirit, over Coe and the men behind him.

As Mike moved forward, I went with him. When another roar went up from Coe's Texans, Mike pushed his coat back and grasped the butt of his revolver.

As we came closer, Coe too reached under his coat, coming out with a big gray-barreled revolver, the same one he'd pulled earlier. Jabbering drunkenly, the mob howling behind him, he began waving the revolver in the air.

Hickok was inching closer to Coe, and I started to relax. A few more seconds, and Coe wouldn't know what hit him.

And then, in an eyeblink, it all blew up. And even though I was right there, I couldn't say if it was an accident or done on purpose.

Coe raised his gun into the air, swinging it around, calling out something to his Texans, and when he brought the revolver back down—*bang*—it fired. A big plume of smoke filled the air between him and Hickok. They were only ten feet apart, but the slug missed Hickok, plowing into the boards between his boots. Instantly, the marshal fired back, both revolvers, and Phil was hit square in the body and slammed back into the crowd.

At the first shot, Mike leaped forward, yanking his revolver from its holster as he jumped onto the Alamo veranda. The air was full of smoke now, drifting about in a crazy quilt of harsh light and black shadow. I saw Hickok turn toward the sound of Mike's clattering footfalls, his arm shot out, and he fired again. At once, the life within Mike was gone, and he went down hard onto the planks of the veranda. He didn't yell or cry out, he just went down. I never saw him move again.

Hickok whirled back to the Texan mob. For a moment, he stared at them, waiting to see if there would be more trouble. But the fight was out of them. Hickok raised a revolver, pointing to one of the men standing over Coe's prostrate body and said, "You and your men pick up Mr. Coe and get him to the doctor." The man was Burdett. He looked stricken, his mouth slightly open, his eyes glazed with horror and disbelief.

"The rest of you clear the street," Hickok commanded. "Now!" With hardly a sound, they did as they were told.

Although I was still standing, it was as if what I'd seen had knocked me insensible. I suppose I went for a spell without breathing, because suddenly my body jerked, and I took a gasping gulp of air as if I'd just broken the surface of deep water. An instant later I was shaking all over.

Mike was lying mostly on the veranda, excepting one foot that hung over the outside edge, the toe of his boot not quite touching the dirt. Hickok, farther down, was still facing the Texans in the street.

I gathered myself and took a step to go to Mike, but my legs buckled at once, and I fell to my hands and knees. Taking hold of an awning post, I pulled myself back to my feet and took a few tottering steps over to Mike. I kneeled down beside the veranda and lay my hand on his back, not knowing what else to do. Just then I heard Hickok call to a few more cowboys: "You three pick up that back-shooter over there and get him to the doc too."

When I heard that, I looked up to Hickok, and I saw the surprise on his face when he recognized me.

Tears spilled down my face. "Marshal," I said, "this is Mike."

FORTY-THREE

A man shoots his good friend, and in the odd little universe of Abilene, it all made perfect sense. Perfect senseless sense.

When I arrived home, Father was waiting up for me in the parlor. He was in a cheery mood, expecting to hear all about my evening of high culture. But when I came into the lamplight, and he saw my face, he set aside his questions. I claimed not to be feeling well, and as quickly as I could, I left him and went up to my room. I closed the door quietly, not wanting to wake Mother, and as the door clicked shut, I saw that my hands were still trembling.

The following day was Friday, but when Mother came to wake me for school, I again said I wasn't well. She came into the room and put her hand on my forehead, checking for fever. "You're cold," she said. I nodded, expecting her to ask if I was trying to play hooky. But like Father the night before, she studied my face and knew that I was not right. "Try to get some sleep" was all she said.

I don't know if I slept or not. Around midmorning there was a light knock on my door that I didn't answer. After a short pause, Father opened the door slowly and stepped in. I rolled over to face him, and as soon as I saw his face, I knew that he knew. Then, despite all I could do to stop them, the tears came again.

Father got my oak chair from the corner of the room and pulled it up to my bed. In the quiet of my room, it creaked loudly as he settled his weight onto it. He took a deep breath as if preparing to lift something heavy.

"When I got to work this morning, all anyone wanted to talk about was what happened last night."

I sat up and leaned against the wall.

"Is Mike gone, for certain?" I asked.

"I'm sorry, Will, but yes. The word is that he"—Father hesitated, searching for the gentlest word, then gave up—"died instantly. He didn't suffer, Will. This Coe fellow is still hanging on, but the doctor doesn't think he'll live much longer."

I nodded, staring down at my hands, unable to look up.

"Will, did you see this happen?"

I nodded again. The tears flowed once more.

"I understand that Coe was leading a group of Texans, and they were out looking for trouble. The town seems to believe that the marshal was not to blame. It was a tragic accident."

"Is Mr. Hickok all right?"

"The mayor told me he wasn't injured."

I shook my head. "He went sort of crazy after he saw Mike."

"Crazy?"

"He was quiet at first, crouching beside Mike, perfectly still. But when he stood up, he had this look."

"I see."

"He went raging up and down Texas Street, driving every-one out. I sat there with Mike, and after a time, there was no one left in Texastown. No one. It was almost silent. Finally, the doctor came, but there was nothing for him to do."

"It was a terrible accident, Will."

I shook my head. "No, it was my fault."

"What?"

"Mike would be alive if I'd stayed out of it. I knew there was going to be trouble, and I pushed him into it. He didn't want to go, Father, but I pushed him and he went. If I'd done nothing, Coe might still be dead, but Mike would be alive."

Saying those words brought out a sharp sob from deep within me. Father's head sank. He just didn't know what to say. But after a moment, he looked up.

"Will, if you'd known Mike was going to be shot, wouldn't you have tried to keep him away?"

"Yes."

"But you didn't know, did you? All you knew right then was that Mike might be able to stop the violence. He'd done it before; you did know that. What happened next was more than you, or anyone, could figure. Only God knew what would hap-pen. You were just one of the players in a terrible tragedy. You aren't to blame."

My emotions must have overwhelmed me, because the next thing I knew, Mother was standing beside Father.

She stood there with her right hand pressed against her chest just below her neck, as if she were holding herself back. I knew she wanted to come forward and hold me, but she didn't. Not too long ago she would have.

I was more man than a boy now, and she was no longer sure

how to behave toward me. It would be up to me to ask for her help.

I didn't ask. I didn't think anyone could help. No words or hugs or tender looks could ease my sorrow. I believed I had to find my own way. I was wrong though. No one copes with something like this alone. Mother and Father were there for me, and that was always a floor to stand on. But it wouldn't be my parents that would get me through. It would be Anna.

"Are you all right, Will?" Mother asked.

"Yes."

"Are you sure?"

"Yes."

FORTY-FOUR

Real Cheyenne probably would've known they were being followed.

It all began with a spell of warmer Indian summer weather and an idea of Johnny's—we would go night fishing. And to make it interesting, we would do it as the Indians had, with a homemade torch and spear.

Anna and I thought that sounded magnificently adventurous, and the preparations kept us occupied much of the day. I doubt the Cheyenne would've admired our efforts, but in the end, we had a fairly respectable kerosene-soaked corncob torch and a sharpened two-prong wooden spear.

Around dusk, feeling like mighty hunters, we made our way south, passing through Texastown and then out onto the road that led down to the Smoky Hill.

Somewhere along the darkening streets of Texastown, we were joined by unseen companions.

———

It was now late October and Texastown was much changed. With most of the cattle sold and cowboys gone, it was oddly quiet. Unlike the past, though, no new herds would arrive next year.

It was surprising the way our town's fate had been decided. All summer Father had used logic and salesmanship to convince Abilene that farming, not cattle, was our future. He'd had some success, but in the end, it was embarrassment that turned the tide.

Newspapers all over America had picked up the story of Hickok's gunfight with Phil Coe. They portrayed Abilene as a lawless nest of evil, a place where Texas desperados ran wild in the streets and the marshal was crazed with bloodlust. That was bad enough, but there was worse: They made fun of us. We were, they snickered, a bunch of weak, silly fools who couldn't run a proper, civilized town.

It wasn't true, of course. Our people were tough and smart. That's what it took to come here and build a new life. We could stand a lot, but we couldn't stand being laughed at. It cut us where we were most vulnerable: our pride.

It also shook our faith in the future. What would happen to us if our reputation for violence kept new people and businesses from coming here? Abilene would wither like the leaves at the end of a broken branch.

The town's reputation had already been a problem. In the rest of the country, many believed that life here was just one endless gun battle.

And now a tragic gunfight was again confirming the belief that Abilene was too dangerous for honest, God-fearing folks. Suddenly, more and more townspeople were heard speaking out publicly against the cattle trade, and arguments raged among us. Many still supported the Texans, but their numbers were falling.

The final blow came when Father, as president of the new Farmers' Protective Association, wrote a notice, which he sent to newspapers throughout the cattle-raising areas of Texas. The notice read:

> *We, the residents of Dickinson County, Kansas, most respect-fully request all who have contemplated driving Texas cattle to Abilene the coming Season to seek some other point of ship-ment, as the inhabitants of Dickinson will no longer submit to the evils of the trade.*

It was a bold move, and some said it was wrong of Father to speak for the town, but most seemed to realize that the battle for our future was over. From this time on, the farmer would be king.

Many of Texastown's saloons and dance halls had already closed. A few, including the Alamo, had been taken apart board by board and shipped out on railroad flatcars. These houses of sin would be reassembled in either Wichita or Ellsworth, towns that were gearing up to take on the cattle trade Abilene had rejected.

Perhaps the most visible sign that our cattle days were over was the dismantling of the sprawling Drover's Cottage. Already, workmen had removed the third floor, and the rest was disap-pearing fast. Huge stacks of boards that had once been an Abilene landmark now sat forlorn beside the tracks.

Rumor said that Jasper's uncle would soon break down the Elkhorn and move it to Wichita.

As for Hickok, well, I hadn't talked to him since Mike's

death. It wasn't that I hated him; it was just that I didn't want to relive what I'd seen. I'm sure Hickok felt the same, because he never tried to speak to me either. Although he was still marshal, he kept himself closed off from almost everyone. He could still be found playing cards in the remaining saloons, but he rarely spoke beyond the requirements of the game. He drank more than before and lost more often than not.

As it turned out, the words I spoke to him as I kneeled beside Mike's body were the last I ever said to him.

Single file, Anna and I followed Johnny along a narrow path that wound through the dense growth of trees and underbrush that flourished along the river. A three-quarter moon gave just enough light for us to see our way.

By our standards, Johnny was the expert, having night fished twice before. As for me, I knew as much about night fishing as I did about piloting a steamboat. For some reason, though, Anna seemed to believe I'd practically invented the sport. Enjoying her approval, I hadn't quite told her the truth.

Several times as we moved along, I thought I heard something behind us, never very loud or close. Once, I turned and looked, but in the thick jumble of moonlit foliage, I couldn't make out anything specific.

Soon we emerged from the trees at the water's edge. Before us, shimmering in the moonlight, was a quiet inlet protected from the sweeping current of the main river channel. The place hummed softly with the sound of countless leaves fluttering in the night breeze. Teetering on a low bank, a gnarled old cottonwood thrust a twisting branch far out over the inlet.

"Perfect," said Johnny with satisfaction.

"Yep, perfect," I echoed, although I had no idea why it was

perfect. I looked out beyond our little inlet. The Smoky was on the rise and moving fast, swollen by recent rains to the west. For October, it was a fairly warm night, but I knew the water would be cold.

"Will, what kind of fish can we catch?" Anna asked eagerly.

"Oh, well, hard to say. We might catch, um . . . lots of stuff."

"Sure," said Johnny, "like Will says, there's catfish, bluegill, crappie, bass, walleye, you name it."

"Right," I said, "we'll eat for a week."

"Say, Will," said Johnny, enjoying my discomfort, "didn't you tell me this was your favorite night fishing spot?"

"You bet. Old family secret." I flashed him a threatening look, but Johnny was undaunted.

"Tell me again, what makes this spot so special?"

I glanced at Anna nervously. She smiled, waiting for my wisdom.

"It's good because . . . well, you can see for yourself, can't you?"

"Yessss, I do see, it's still and shallow here. That must be it, right?"

"Shallow, yes. And still, uh-huh."

"Will," said Anna, "I can't wait to tell your father that you took us to your family's favorite spot."

Sweat percolated on my forehead. Suddenly, I couldn't take it any longer.

"Ah, geez, Anna, I've never night fished in my life."

That's when I saw the smile on her face.

"Aw, you two!" I cried. "And you, Anna, you knew all along."

"All along," said Anna gleefully. "But I still like you, even if you wouldn't know a cat from a catfish."

"I'd know a cat . . . in good light."

More laughter.

"All right, geniuses, show me how to catch a fish."

Johnny handed me the torch. "Shinny out over the water on that big ol' cottonwood branch. At the fork, light it up and wedge it between the branches. Then come on back."

"I can do that."

"Hopefully the light will attract some fish."

After I'd put the torch in place, Johnny went first. "Whoa, cold!" he cried, as he waded barefoot into the knee-high water. About fifteen feet out, he paused, lowering the spear tip until it was just below the surface. Searching the murky water, he stood perfectly still. After a few minutes, he moved a little farther out, and waited again.

For a while there was nothing, but then he tensed and began to follow something with the tip of the spear. Abruptly, he jabbed down hard. "Ahhh, missed! Too fast!" He got a couple more chances, but missed them too. "It's not easy," he sighed, handing the spear to Anna to try her luck.

But Anna's luck was no better, and soon the spear was in my hands. I took off my shoes, rolled up my pants, and waded out until I was directly beneath the torch.

"Water's pretty cold, huh?" called Johnny.

"If it was any colder, I'd be standing on top of it."

"Hold the spear tip just under the water, and when a fish comes by, follow him a ways with the tip and then jab. Jab hard, pin it right to the bottom."

I nodded, barely listening. I'd heard it all when he told Anna. It seemed that none of this instruction mattered much; I wasn't going to catch anything. But soon a long dark shape, about a foot and a half long, glided into the circle of torchlight. When it came close, I moved the spear tip along with it, and then thrust down. I must've closed my eyes for an instant, because suddenly the tip was stuck deep into the mud, and the shaft was jerking around in my hand. I looked closer into the churning muddy water, and began to yell, "I got it, I got it! What do I do?"

Johnny and Anna leaped up from a toppled tree trunk they'd been sitting on. "Hold the spear down," Johnny hollered. "Put some weight on it. Don't let it come up. Okay, reach down and get your hand under the fish. Don't try to lift it out by the spear tips. Get your hand under it."

I did, and when I had a good grip, I lifted the wriggling fish out and ran splashing to shore.

"Slow down! You'll trip and lose him," Anna called excitedly.

"I've got him! I'm all right!"

I came out of the water and slid the fish into an old flour bag that Anna and Johnny were holding wide. Tossing the spear behind me, I peered down into the dim interior of the bag. Johnny was tilting the opening toward the torchlight, but it was hard to see.

"What kind is it?" I asked.

"I think you got yourself a catfish," said Johnny. "Pretty good size too."

"Look at that!" I crowed. "And you two didn't think I could do it. Come on, admit it."

Before they could answer, I sat and quickly slipped my shoes back onto my freezing feet. Glancing up, I found Anna grinning at me.

"What?"

"Pure luck," she said.

"Luck, ha! Pure skill's more like it."

"Luck," said Johnny. "You probably used up a whole month's supply."

Focused on our joshing and the bag with its flopping fish, at first we didn't notice the footsteps. Then there was a sharp crack, a dry stick splitting under pressure. I glanced up carelessly, and then froze.

A silent figure, backlit by the wavering flame of the torch, stood only ten feet away. All around, other dark shapes were stepping into the clearing from the blackness beneath the trees. Realizing that something was wrong, Anna and Johnny straightened up, turning toward the approaching shadowy strangers. At our feet, ignored now, the bag jerked slightly with the final efforts of the catfish.

I couldn't make out the face of the person nearest us, but the outline was unmistakable. He took a step forward and picked up our spear. In the same moment, the torch sputtered and went out.

"Hi there, ol' buddy," said Jasper. "Whatcha doin'? Killin' things?"

FORTY-FIVE

A in't this a treat?" said Jasper. He stepped close and tapped the prongs of the spear on my shoulder. "Seems like forever since we all got together."

I slapped the spear aside and stepped closer to Anna. "What do you want?" I said coldly.

"I swear, Will, I'm startin' to think you aren't glad to see me."

"Just tell us what you want."

"Ahhh, come on, I know you've got new friends now, but don't be snooty. Say, it's so dark maybe you don't recognize all the folks that've come to visit."

Including Jasper, there were nine of them, all around us now. There was no escape, and whatever was going to happen was good as done, but Johnny didn't seem to understand that yet.

"Jasper," said Johnny, "why don't you go back—"

"*You* shut up!" Jasper bellowed. "I might take sass from my old pal Will, but not you." He took a breath and then continued. "Like I was sayin', Billy, Gordon, and Booth is right over there. Say hello to Will, boys."

"I told 'em, Will," said Gordon. "I told 'em you didn't have your head on straight. And I was right, wasn't I?"

"Now hold on, Gordon," said Jasper. "Don't be ill-mannered." He turned to me. "You gotta excuse Gordon. Ya see, his father's boot business along with Booth's father's Texastown hotel have both gone bust. They're tearin' down the hotel, just like they'll be tearin' down my uncle's saloon. Oh, and Billy's father just lost his job at the stockyard. Seems there's not much future in stock."

"Jasper, I'm sorry about that, but we didn't—"

Johnny interrupted me, almost yelling. "That's got nuthin' to do with us!"

Jasper whirled on him, prodding his chest hard with the twin spear points. "Is that a fact? I say you've got plenty to do with it. You sell the machines that ruin the land for cattle."

"But we don't ruin anything," said Anna. "We make the land produce."

"*Produce!* You produce nuthin' but pain. Look there! You see him?" Jasper pointed to a blond, thickset boy coming up beside Johnny. "That's Case Johansen. His father was let go permanent from his blacksmithin' job at the Twin Livery. Why? 'Cause the Texans have left and took their horses with 'em. Horses that ain't comin' back. Ever."

"That's right," said Case. His arm shot out, catching Johnny hard on the shoulder and knocking him back. "We got to step aside, so the likes of you can get on with your *producin'.*"

Case was almost nineteen, and he was a mean one. Despite the age differences, though, they all gave way to Jasper, and he dominated for one reason—his hatred burned the hottest.

They gathered tightly around us in the darkness, and one by

one, Jasper told how the end of the cattle trade had hurt them. As he spoke, one story upon another, the tension rose.

I was afraid now. Here, in the night, in the woods, there were no rules. The growing menace settled upon us like a poisonous fog. We were in real danger.

So far, Jasper was only talking, but I knew him. He would drag this out, poking and prodding, waiting for someone to make a mistake. He didn't have to wait long.

"Give me our spear," Johnny demanded.

"Why? You want to get back to fishin'?"

"Yes, I want to get back to fishing."

"Course you do. But, Johnny boy, you ain't picked the right spot. That's the key to good night fishin'. Pickin' the right spot."

"Johnny," I said, "let it go."

"Yes," Anna said, "it's not important."

"It's our spear. I'm not leaving without it."

"Yep," Jasper continued, "this spot is pretty poor. Now, I know what you're thinkin'—Will caught a fish here—but like you said, Will is lucky. I hate to tell you, Johnny boy, you aren't lucky."

"I'm lucky enough."

"No, no you're not. But we're here to change all that. Here's the problem: There ain't no fish in here. They're out there." Jasper pointed to the frigid, rushing waters of the main river channel. "That's where you should be if you want to catch somethin'."

"Jasper—" I said.

"Shut up, Will," said Jasper, speaking in a low, calm voice. "You're startin' to make me mad."

"Yeah, shut up, Will," Gordon repeated.

Jasper turned and walked to the lapping water of the inlet. "You want your spear, Johnny? Go get it." With that, he hurled the spear over the inlet toward the river. It disappeared into the darkness, and a moment later, we heard a faint splash. Jasper raised his arms in triumph and spun around to face us. "One more thing, Johnny boy: I hope you can swim."

Case grabbed Johnny first, seizing him by the upper arm; then Billy and two others jumped him. They began to drag him up the downstream side of the inlet, toward a bank that fell off into the Smoky Hill's seething current. Johnny fought, but they easily overpowered him.

As soon as I moved, they were on me too. I heard Anna yelp, but I could do nothing. Hands seized me from all sides, and I was thrown to the wet, sandy soil, facedown, pinned by arms and knees, a hand gripping my neck.

"*Jasper* . . . stop!" I screamed. "Stop! What are you . . . Booth! Gordon! Make him . . . stop! Make—"

A knee dropped heavily onto the back of my neck, pressing my face down until watery mud closed around my nose and mouth. I heard Gordon's voice hiss in my ear: "We didn't come here to stop." Panicked to catch a breath, one arm flailing free, I sucked in only gritty muck. Coughing violently, I inhaled again with a frantic jerk that only sent more mire-thickened water down my throat. The world began to fade. I heard Anna let out a cry, and then another, but fainter this time, as if she were far away. Strength ebbing, my flailing arm slackened and then drifted down and lay still beside my head.

Suddenly the weight pressing on me eased. I was able to twist my head from the mud just enough to catch a breath of air. Gasping sharply, coughing, gasping again, spitting gooey mire, I felt strength begin to flow back into my muscles. Sounds that had seemed to be drifting farther and farther away began to return.

Gordon's voice whispered, "Someone's comin'!"

Hands still held me down, but the knee abruptly lifted from my neck.

Another urgent whisper. "What do we do?"

"I don't know. I don't—Who'd be out here anyway? Who—"

"He's singin'."

It was true. I heard it. Singing.

I was now free enough to turn my head and look for Anna. In the feeble light, I found her about twenty feet away. She was on her feet, but still being held.

"Anna!"

"Will—"

"Shut up!" said Jasper. "Say another word and you'll regret it."

I sat up and looked for Johnny. Out near the inlet's mouth, Case, Billy, and the others still held him. They stood bunched in a tight knot, dark against the sparkling backdrop of the surging river. They too were listening to the approaching singer.

A horse blew nervously. From the sound of his progress through the brush, the singer was not riding alongside the river but angling toward it. He was close enough now that I could make out the words of his song.

> On the banks of a lonely river,
> Ten thousand miles away.
> I have an aged mother
> Whose hair is turnin' gray.
> Then blame me not for weepin',
> Oh, blame me not, I pray—

"Cowboy," said Booth from the darkness. "Drunk."

Apparently, in the general quiet of the inlet, the cowboy's raucous little opera, more shouted than sung, could even be heard by Booth.

"What's he doing?" said Jasper, almost to himself. "There's nuthin' out here."

> For I must see my mother
> Ten thousand miles away.

"Jasper, he's heading for the river," I said.

"That's crazy," said Jasper.

"Drunk," Booth repeated.

As if to confirm Booth's opinion, the cowboy began a new song.

> Oh, pity the cowboy,
> So bloody and red.
> His pony fell on him,
> And mashed in his head.

Abruptly, the cowboy laughed uproariously, an unsettling sound in the eerie dimness of the woods. "And *mashed* in his *head*!" he yelled before falling into another wild bout of laughter.

"Drunk," said Booth again, quietly.

"Shut up, Booth!" ordered Jasper.

We could see the cowboy now. Riding a black horse, he had come out of the trees along the upstream shore of our inlet, still heading for the river.

"Jasper, he's going to cross," I said.

"That's crazy. The river'll kill him. Why—"

"Booth's right, he's drunk and got himself turned around. I'll bet he thinks this is only Mud Creek."

Jasper jerked around and cupping his hands to his mouth, called out to the cowboy, "Hey! Where are you goin'?"

"Hey to you too!" the cowboy yelled back, laughing and apparently untroubled to find he was not alone.

We were all gripped now by the drama unfolding before us. One by one, the hands holding me released, and when I stood up no one stopped me. I glanced again at Anna and then to Johnny. They too had been released. The boys that had held Anna now stood a couple feet in front of her. Johnny and his captors, a tight ball before, were now a line of five silhouettes. As the cowboy's peril had grown, we'd been forgotten.

The cowboy continued for the river, riding slowly, still singing foolishly to himself. Despite this, none of us had moved. I suppose we just didn't believe he would do what it seemed he was doing.

The cowboy reached the riverbank, and at the edge, without a pause, he spurred his mount and jumped over. In an instant, they were gone. And still, none of us moved.

After a long terrible moment, dark heads broke to the surface about a hundred feet downstream, first the horse and then the rider. I heard a choking gasp, then another, and finally a strangled call.

"Help! H-h-help—"

This, it seemed, was what we'd been waiting for. We exploded into frenzied action, everyone running toward the river.

And then Jasper took control.

"Stop! Don't run toward him. He'll drift past before you get there. We have to get in front of him." Jasper called to the boys that had been holding Johnny. "Case, he's comin' toward you. Try to grab him. If you miss, stay with him, don't lose sight of him."

Case yelled, "Right!" and he, Johnny, and the others turned toward the water.

Then, almost in front of them, the glistening black form of the cowboy's horse lunged from the water and onto the shore in a sparkling cloud of moonlit spray. I froze, watching to see if the cowboy would follow, but he did not.

"Mister!" Jasper screamed. "Call out. Don't stop or we'll lose you. Keep callin'."

At first there was no answer, but then, just downstream of the mouth of the inlet, the cowboy again surfaced, arms thrashing. "Help! I can't—can't swim." He seemed farther out now. The current was pulling him toward the center of the river.

Now it was Johnny who yelled. "Keep callin'. Don't stop. Keep callin'!" He and Case and the others ran along the bank above the water, trying to keep pace with the struggling cowboy, trying to hold him in sight.

Jasper turned to our group. "Come on. We'll cut through the woods and get ahead of him."

Without hesitation we followed him into the trees. The idea was to cut across the base of a looping bend in the river and come out below the cowboy. In the distance, muffled by the trees, I heard the others shouting, and less often, the cowboy crying back from the cold, roiling water.

With Jasper leading, we crashed through the thick tangle of bush and branch, heedless of the pain, torn and scratched, slowing for nothing.

"We'll get him," said Jasper. "You'll see. We'll get him."

Anna was right behind me, and I turned to check on her. In the near darkness, I couldn't see her face, but she knew what I wanted. "I'm okay," she said.

Even as we rushed headlong, I had to marvel at the oddity of our situation. Print Olive had said that nobody with an ounce of honor turns his back on someone who needs help. Somehow, that honor had risen up among a mob of boys bent on cruel revenge, and possibly murder.

Now we were together. If you fell, the others picked you up. If there was an obstacle, someone called a warning.

Through the brush ahead, I saw the glint of moving water,

and then we burst onto another moonlit shore. Upriver, the Smoky Hill curved around toward us, straightening itself after its long circling turn. Except for the sound of churning current, it was quiet, and I saw no one upstream. Not the cowboy, not Johnny or Case, not anyone.

Maybe, as Jasper hoped, we'd gotten in front of the cowboy. At any moment, we might see his bobbing head come around the river's bend.

"Look for a branch we can use to reach out with," Jasper ordered. While Jasper kept watch, we scoured the debris along the tree line. "Here!" Anna yelled as she dragged a long tree branch from a tangle of growth under a dying cottonwood. Quickly, we fell upon it, stripping away its smaller branches until we had a crooked pole about twelve feet long.

We rejoined Jasper beside the river, and we waited, everyone scanning the onrushing water and praying. Time after time, Jasper shouted to the river, "We're here! Call out. We're here!" He waded out, up to his knees, holding the tree limb upward.

"Jasper," I said, "don't go out so far."

"I'm okay," he answered, never taking his eyes from the river.

But the water was pulling hard at his legs, and I waded out behind him and took hold of his belt. He said nothing.

The minutes passed. And with each tick of time, our hopes fell. Jasper continued calling, but the rest of us began to look at each other and shake our heads.

Then, from upstream, there was an answer. Hearts leaped, and after a moment the voice came again. But it was only Case. Turning our eyes from the water to the shore, we made out the forms of Case, Johnny, and the others picking their way along the edge of the debris-cluttered riverbank. They were leading a riderless horse.

Still, we clung desperately to our hope. But as soon as Case was close enough, he shouted, "Did you get him?"

We knew it then. The cowboy lost. The river had taken him, and there was nothing we could do. Nothing.

For a long while, we all stood together, silently watching the water, hoping for the impossible. But there would be no miracle. One by one, without a word, the boys began to turn away, drifting back up the shore or disappearing into the woods.

At last, only Jasper continued to search the rolling waters of the Smoky Hill. Johnny had stepped back to the trees and slumped exhausted to the ground.

Still gripping Jasper's belt, I was now watching him, not the river. Motionless, he stared into the water as if mesmerized.

I felt Anna's hand take mine, and after a time, she leaned close and said, "Bring him in." I turned to her, and she looked past me to Jasper and said it again. "Bring him in."

I released Anna's hand and took two steps forward, putting myself at Jasper's side. It was only a few feet, but it was deeper, and the current pressed more powerfully at my legs. I hesitated, not sure if I should, and then I put my hand on his shoulder.

"It's over," he said.

"Yes," I answered, "it's over."

Jasper lowered his head, taking his eyes off the river for the first time, and wept.

EPILOGUE

I am ninety years old.

In the long span of my time, I have experienced events and inventions beyond imagining. I have owned an automobile. Flown in an airplane. I have read books deep into the night by the brightness of electric lights. I have talked with people on the other side of our planet by telephone. I have seen the life of one of my great-grandchildren saved by antibiotics. I have lived through the Great Depression and two world wars. I have seen the atomic bomb destroy whole cities in a single flash.

But because I was a part of it, the great experience of my life has been the transformation of the wilderness prairie into a place now called the Heartland. We became what my mother had hoped, a land of orderly farms dotted with homes and churches and populated by hardworking men and women. We became what my father had predicted, a land that produces wealth as nothing else in human history. A land that feeds our country and the world beyond.

Yes, I am old. Abilene and I have aged together. In our youth, though, there were no old folks like me in all of Abilene. It was a young person's town. And now, I've outlived them all, even my Anna.

As I write this, it is seventy-five years ago to the day that I accompanied my father to the depot to meet Mr. Hickok. And after all this time, I never again met anyone like him, and never expected I would. He was a man produced by a time and place that has vanished.

After the gunfight with Phil Coe, he stayed on as marshal for a few months. But with the Texans gone, we really didn't need a marshal like Mr. Hickok. So, twelve days before Christmas, he was let go.

His life never went quite right after that. A few years later, he got married and tried to settle down. But then news came of a gold strike in the Black Hills of South Dakota, and . . . well, I think he just couldn't resist one more adventure. He went to the mining town of Deadwood, and within a month he was murdered, shot from behind as he played cards.

Jasper and his uncle moved away from Abilene. For a long time I heard nothing. Then, some years later, I got a letter from him. It was the first of many. Down through the decades, we wrote back and forth regularly, but I never saw him again.

His youthful dream was to go to Texas and become a cowboy, but he spent most of his life in Arizona, where he worked for the railroad. Then, about fifteen years ago, his daughter wrote to tell me that he'd been killed in an automobile accident. One of my great disappointments is that I didn't find a way to see him once more. Now I never will.

Johnny Hodge took over his father's farm machinery business. He was a good businessman and became quite successful. He married early and had six kids. Around 1900, he bought a farm up in the Buckeye area of our county. He didn't personally run it, but he loved to go up there and do chores and watch over it. Often, he'd walk out into the middle of those big fields and just stand there, running his hands through the heads of winter wheat, enjoying the smells, the silence, and the vastness. That's how I like to remember him.

As for my father, well, he brimmed with restless energy all his days. He kept selling land, but he also ran for political office, and for a while he even tried the newspaper business. His real claim to fame, though, was his Abilene farming enterprise, which grew so large that he became widely known as the Wheat King of Kansas.

But, as I've said, he was restless, and in the early 1880s, he just up and quit farming. He and Mother moved to Colorado, where he threw himself into building irrigation canals that brought water to hundreds of thousands of farm acres. After a while, people were calling him the Irrigation King.

Father made fortunes, lost them, and made them back again. He always had an eye for opportunity and never drew back from risk. It was as if this new Western country had been made for J. T. Merritt.

Mother's short speech at the courthouse meeting changed her life. She was never content to stand in the shadows after that. In time, she found her voice in the women's suffrage movement, the struggle to win the right to vote for women. Mother traveled all over America supporting the cause. On one occasion, she even spent a night in jail after being arrested at a demonstration.

My little sister, Jenny, went to Colorado with my parents. Eventually, she married a Denver banker and became quite a society lady. It never went to her head, though, and I often called on her for advice, especially when I was in politics. Like me, she never forgot Wild Bill, and whenever she spoke of the day she climbed into his lap while Mother played the piano, people would stop whatever they were doing and gather around to listen.

Four years after the end of Abilene's cattle days, Anna and I were married. When my parents left for Colorado, we moved into their house, the one I'd grown up in. Those were wonderful days. I don't think you could've found two happier people.

The frontier times were mostly over by then, and people were settling down to the job of building our state. I started out working for Anna's father. Caleb was prospering. For some years he'd been buying farmland, and he needed help supervising his holdings as well as Father's. Anna and I would often hop in the buggy and ride all over the county looking at the crops. To tell the truth, she always had a better feel for farming than I did.

Before long, I needed to strike out in my own direction. I'd always involved myself in the affairs of the town, so one day I decided to run for city council. Despite my youth, and maybe because I had my father's name, I was elected. That was the start of my long career in government. In time, I was sent to the Kansas House of Representatives, where I served as a representative for twenty-two years.

In 1885, Caleb built a large Victorian home up on North Buckeye Street. Built of our own yellow limestone, it became known as Dunham House.

On the day the Dunhams moved into their new home, Anna's mother and I stood in the yard, watching as her furniture was carried up the broad front steps. "In all my life," she said, "my dreams were never larger than a new dress or a wood floor under my feet. Caleb was right to come here."

After her parents passed on, Anna and I made Dunham House our home. In time, one of our grandchildren was born there. I live in the grand old house to this day.

Anna and I were married sixty-eight years, a very long time, but not nearly long enough. She was my truest friend, my wisest advisor. She possessed all the good qualities I wasn't given. She made me laugh, and what's more, she made me laugh at myself whenever I got too self-important. She saved me from myself a thousand times, and I cannot imagine what would have become of me without her. Three years ago, she passed away, and I feel the loss of her in every moment.

I've led a good life, perhaps even a charmed life. Sometimes when I think about the good things that are behind me, it makes me sad. But not for long. Anna wouldn't like that.